Enjoy the book.

The Blacklock Mysteries
On the Right Track

Steven Clifford

authorHOUSE®

AuthorHouse™ UK Ltd.
500 Avebury Boulevard
Central Milton Keynes, MK9 2BE
www.authorhouse.co.uk
Phone: 08001974150

© 2008 Steven Clifford. All rights reserved.

No part of this book may be reproduced, stored in a retrieval system, or transmitted by any means without the written permission of the author.

First published by AuthorHouse 11/24/2008

ISBN: 978-1-4343-1769-8 (sc)

Printed in the United States of America
Bloomington, Indiana

This book is printed on acid-free paper.

For Mum, the first one always had to be for you….

For Grandad, the original writer in the family….

and

For Vanessa, a beautiful friend, always and forever.

Chapters

Prague 1

China against polystyrene 4

Talk on the terrace 9

Rush hour 12

Mediterranean mood 24

Deadlines and destinations 29

Scott's brief 33

Ships in the night 36

Conference of convenience 41

Grand Central 44

The Trans-Oceanic Express 59

Champagne reception 65

Observations carriage 79

Cocktail hour 91

Four courses of digestion 101

Poker faces	110
An invitation and a rendezvous	118
Sunday roasting	126
Happy Anniversary!	131
Thirteen at dinner	138
Anyone for brandy?	151
A good hand dealt by Clarissa	159
Things that go bump in the night	169
The morning after	178
Speculation	188
Departure announcements	203
A tale of unrequited love	220
Accusations and alibis	234
Avril Kennedy's story	247
A matter of cigarettes	254
Staff inquisition	268
Quiet drinks	279
The calm before	291
Background backup	303

Jessica Rae's scoop...310

The pieces of the puzzle...318

Unlocked 329

End of the line 346

Grand Terminal...356

Prague

The sun was shining with surprising intensity for February. On the west banks of the Vltava River, Walteau Lenoir sat drinking hot tea, served with honey and lemon. Lenoir liked this area of the Czech capital. Quite distinctly off the tourist track, he favoured the neighbourhoods of Mala Strana and Smichov.

He sat now on a street named Namesti Rijna enjoying the surroundings of the cafe Apostrof. Many were drawn to the cafe for its fine selection of art and while Lenoir admired it, his real reason for going was the people. He was not from Prague, but Paris, not that his apartment there was often frequented. His business took him around the globe more frequently than there were weeks in the year. London, New York, Tokyo, Hong Kong, Sydney, Los Angeles.

But it was not business that had brought Walteau Lenoir to Prague, he was there for no other reason than for the fact that he enjoyed the city. Lenoir was not a young man. He was nigh on sixty-three and despite this, still had a work schedule that would exhaust a thirty year old. A lucrative career had meant that Lenoir was always able to enjoy the pleasures of life. And he did.

By looking at him, his finely tailored suit, his groomed white moustache, his sizable paunch which had gotten considerably larger in recent years, he gave the air of someone who could definitely afford the finer things in life. Lenoir had decided when he turned sixty that he would invest in two foreign properties. He chose one in Venice and one in Prague. Venice was his retreat in the summer and Prague was for the colder, winter months. These two cities were Lenoir's favourites in the whole world. Lenoir had loved Venice since visiting in his late teens, but he had not visited Prague until later in life. Lenoir was one of the few westerners to actually see behind the Iron Curtain, and it was that Prague that Lenoir had fallen in love with. Lenoir had been in no way promoting communism. If anything, Lenoir was more of a capitalist than most.

But Lenoir was one of those people that liked to go places and be somewhere different. He despised tourists who went abroad to have a little slice of their own country, only hotter. People that would use a roll of camera film on a statue or building or landmark without bothering to find out anything about it, or more importantly, why it was there and what it stood for. And what Lenoir had not realised until after he had bought an apartment there, was that Prague was a very different city to the one he had fallen in love with back in 1977. It had never been a problem before as Lenoir preferred to visit in the winter months when the city was quieter. However, Lenoir never forgot the time just after he had found a perfect apartment close to Wenceslas Square, when he decided to spend a weekend there in early July. Lenoir was repelled to find Old Market Square, his favourite haunt for a Sunday afternoon drink, overrun with hordes of tourists. There were pensioners by the coach load, stag and hen nights running amok and school trips that couldn't be controlled by their teachers. After that, Lenoir stayed away from the tourist areas of the city and rarely left the west bank.

It was places like Smichov that he spent most of his trips. And he made his trips religiously, the last weekend of every month. Lenoir was wealthy and frivolous enough to be known to visit Prague for just an afternoon if his work schedule did not permit longer.

Lenoir refilled his cup and sat back, content. He looked around the cafe and watched the people happily. In the corner sat two elderly men, regular fixtures at the cafe. They always sat in the same spot and appeared to have been playing the same game of chess for two years now. It was lunchtime so that meant there were always at least half a dozen workers from the factory over the road present, eating their food noisily. Lenoir watched them and admired them. He admired their honesty and their lifestyle. Not glamorous, but decent and good. Maybe it was a lifestyle Lenoir wished that he had chosen. Then there was his love for the people that worked there. Lenoir had a good friendship with Sergei who owned the cafe and he knew all the waitress's names, even the new girl Rosa.

Time passed, the workers paid and left in their typical way that involved raucous laughter. Their departure left an obvious silence. The old man at the table in the corner made a checkmate. Lenoir was quietly observing the surroundings when he noticed his right hand, resting on his leg, had started to shake. That's odd, he thought. Lenoir was a man that liked his drink, and he had done a shot of absinthe the night before, but he never usually got the shakes from it. It was then that he saw a thin green rim around his cup. A pattern he hadn't noticed before?

Any thoughts going through Lenoir's head immediately vanished as his left arm began twitching, right before a jolt of pain swept through his entire body. He tried to stand but a convulsion made him spasm and lose his footing. With a strangled yell he fell to the floor, pulling the table cloth and tea pot with him. He writhed on the carpet, riddled with pain. Someone screamed, people rushed forward. Sergei scrambled to the phone. But it didn't matter. Before he had finished dialling the number, Walteau Lenoir was dead.

China against polystyrene

The door swung painfully on its hinges as Tim Anderson walked into the dusty ramshackle vestibule of his apartment building. Tim's baggy jeans, loose green t-shirt and scruffy, slightly long brown hair gave him the distinct impression of a student. His boyish good looks were betrayed by what had evidently been a heavy night before.

From somewhere down the hall on the right came the snores of his landlord. The vestibule was cluttered with rubbish from the apartments. An old bicycle leaned against the staircase, while a withered spider plant in a crocheted basket dangled next to part of an old kitchen fan. To the left were the tenant's pigeonholes, but most were only occupied by dust, the full ones containing junk mail or bills the owners would rather forget about. Tim started up the stairs, pulling out his keys as he went, all the way to the top floor. Tim avoided the elevator at the best of times, it being not one of the most reliable pieces of machinery. Tim lovingly referred to it as the "giant hunk of shit".

Tim gave a curt nod to his neighbour, Mrs Krakowski, as he passed her. She was thankfully struggling to close a bag of rubbish, which meant that he wouldn't be drawn into a tedious twenty minute conversation with her. As he got to his door he wedged his newspaper under his arm and tried to find the right key with one hand, while simultaneously trying to balance coffees and bagels in his other. After several infuriating moments he unlocked it and as he walked in, used his foot to slam the door behind him.

The apartment was a noticeable improvement from the hallway and general interior of the building. This had to do with the painstaking hours it had taken to make the apartment liveable, and the lack of those said hours on the rest of the building by Tim's landlord. As a result, despite being situated in New York's Greenwich Village, the rent was almost as affordable as it got in Manhattan. Tim and his flat mate had taken three and a half months to completely renovate it when they moved in four years ago. On entering, Tim walked straight to the kitchen and dumped the bagels on the breakfast bar. The main area of the apartment was one big room, the breakfast bar looking over the main lounge with doors to the bedrooms on the far side. To the left of the room was a big raised bay with a dining table in it and doors beyond which led out to a small balcony. It was from the balcony that Tim's flat mate, Scott Blacklock, appeared. Scott, even in a vest and pyjama bottoms looked a lot smarter than Tim. His short hair and perfectly kept stubble gave him an air of sophistication and crispness. His eyes, while not large, gave off a clear blue alertness.

Tim threw the bag of bagels in the air. "Breakfast's up!"

Scott walked past the dining table just in time to catch the bag. He caught them against his chest with one hand and gave a look of disgust as he saw the label.

As he walked over to pick up his coffee, he said, "Why you can't walk one block further and go to a decent bakery, rather than that crappy vendor on the corner is beyond me!"

Tim rolled his eyes as Scott headed to the kitchen. He retorted, "Well, Scott, you know I'll always support the underdog rather than a greedy corporation."

"Yeah, yeah! That and you're just too damn lazy!"

Tim smiled although Scott didn't see it. This was typical morning banter for them - especially when Scott could take advantage of Tim suffering from a hangover. Like this particular morning.

Scott proceeded to pour his takeaway coffee into a mug, a ritual for him as he thought it just wasn't right to drink anything from polystyrene. As Scott walked back outside, Tim heard a disembodied voice from the balcony.

"This coffee's shit as well!"

Scott and Tim had met when they were fourteen, when Scott had moved to New York and they ended up in the same class at school together. Scott was the newcomer with no friends and a funny accent. Their teacher had sat Scott next to Tim and told him to show him around and make him feel welcome. At first, Tim had been embarrassed to look after the new unpopular boy. However, first impressions of a fourteen year old can be deceptive. They soon realised they shared a similar sense of humour, and a similar love of Super Nintendo. It didn't take long for Tim to realise that Scott was smart beyond his years. And as their school years went on, Scott had shown Tim that drive and ambition could take you far in life.

"What do you want to do when you grow up?" Scott had asked Tim one afternoon a few years after they had first met, on their way home from a video night at a friend's house.

"I don't know. I'd quite like to be an explorer. You know, traipsing through the jungles of the unknown, finding mystical temples."

The film they had just seen was Indiana Jones and the Last Crusade.

Scott smiled, "You do understand Harrison Ford isn't going to live forever because he drank from the Holy Grail?!"

Tim rolled his eyes. "Yes, I know! But, you know, a job that meant I could see the world. That would be cool."

Scott leaned forward, as if he was telling a highly kept secret. "Well, now that you're thinking about what to do with your life, you have to look at it like this. What do I enjoy doing most in life? Think about what you can see yourself doing for the rest of it without getting bored. Then find a job that means you'd be able to do that. Focus the talents you've got towards that end point. And work on the talents that you don't have to achieve this goal."

Even at a young age, Scott had been very eloquent.

"But, like what?" asked Tim, looking confused.

"You really like writing your short stories."

"Mr Brown says that they're too factual for a creative writing class." said Tim glumly.

"Well I for one like facts." said Scott, trying to save the suggestion.

Sensing that this had not been the best example, Scott pointed to the small camera around Tim's neck.

"OK, another example. You haven't put that camera down since you got it for your birthday. You obviously enjoy taking photos."

"Yeah, but I'm not that good at it." Tim said honestly.

"Well then, that can be one of your talents that you should start working on."

"What about you then?" said Tim, turning the conversation back to Scott, "What do you enjoy doing most in life?"

Scott smiled, "Well I do like a good puzzle."

They walked on for several moments, Tim looking thoughtfully into the distance. He then stopped and said,

"Wait! I've changed my mind! I know something that I'd never get bored of! Head of wardrobe for Baywatch!"

This time it was Scott who rolled his eyes. Tim had recently begun noticing girls.

A lot.

Tim carried on, "No, something better! No, a job where I could have K.I.T.T. from Knightrider as my company car!"

"I'm started to get worried now." Scott said dryly, "Do you secretly want to be David Hasselhoff when you grow up?!"

Tim laughed, "There are worse people!"

Although he didn't say it often, Tim valued their friendship very highly, as looking back at his teenage years, he realised that he easily would have drifted through life had it not been for meeting Scott. It was one of the many reasons they were still loyal friends fourteen years on.

Tim walked out onto the balcony where Scott was sitting and once again felt the heat hit him. New York could be notoriously hot and sticky in the summer and this year had been no exception. They were into the third week of September and were still enduring temperatures in the high nineties.

Even though it was not yet ten in the morning, the balcony was blisteringly hot as Tim sat down.

"So," said Scott as he lit up a cigarette, "heavy night last night?"

Tim took his time answering as he had just put half a bagel in his mouth, "Just a few drinks with Miranda in Soho to celebrate"

"I take it Wharmby liked the article?"

"Looks like it could be the best selling copy of the year."

Tim was a travel reporter for the global magazine Travel Today and had not long returned from a trip in Cancun, Mexico. He had just completed an in depth study of the history surrounding the Chichen Itza ruins.

Scott was impressed by the news, "That's great! You see, sharing a tent with scorpions for a month was worth it in the end!"

"I said Wharmby told me it was selling well, he forgot to actually give me any credit for it" said Tim glumly.

Scott smiled, "Yeah but he's your boss. He's not supposed to make you feel good about yourself."

Tim smiled back, "Too true."

Scott turned and raised his mug. "Well, congratulations from me anyway. Cheers!"

Tim complied and raised his cup. However, there was no sophisticated clink as it was china against polystyrene.

They sat there then for quite a while in comfortable silence, Tim reading his paper, while Scott smoked and watched the people on the street below. It was a rare occasion to spend a Sunday morning with them both at home; as it wasn't often that their jobs would permit it.

As Scott had left his bagels untouched, he suggested a proper breakfast on him, at Tim's favourite cafe, Belingoes. Tim was about to respond when Scott's phone rang from the lounge.

"Hello?"

"Scott. It's Katherine. I need to see you."

"Katherine, it's Sunday morning!"

"New evidence. The Stoltzkin case is about to fall through."

Scott for the first time started listening properly. He asked, "Where are you?"

"At the office, how soon can you be here?"

"OK, give me thirty minutes"

"Make it twenty." Katherine's voice changed, "Scott. It's Golic. He's dead."

Scott took the information in. He replied, "I'll see you in fifteen."

And with that, Katherine hung up. Tim walked in from the balcony and asked, "Anything up?"

Scott was already rushing to his room to get dressed, "Sorry, breakfast's off, work calls!"

Tim groaned, flopped on the sofa and shouted through to Scott in his room,

"Hey, how come this always conveniently happens when the food's gonna be on you?!"

Talk on the terrace

Gerry Kennedy puffed on his cigar and sipped brandy as he stood on his penthouse terrace in the Upper West Side and admired the view. And it was a view worth admiring. From where he stood, he had a clear view of Central Park and the impressive skyscrapers of Midtown and the Garment District. Dusk had set in over the hazy skyline and Gerry stood and watched the city getting ready for the night. Gerry Kennedy had a distinguished face, complimented by a small moustache. It was a face that earlier in life, had been reminiscent of a fifties film star. The fact that he was wearing a dinner jacket and bow tie only highlighted the look. However, his face now showed how events in the recent past had aged him. Events that had also had no small impact on his health. His stature had become slighter, and now he resembled a tortoise that was very slowly retracting into its shell.

Gerry swirled the ice in his tumbler and smiled with irony. His doctor would be furious to know he was drinking. Or smoking, he thought, as he puffed on his Havana. But right now, Gerry couldn't give a damn what his doctor thought. Gerry looked out at the small cars making their way around Central Park and contemplated the predicaments that had plagued him in the last six months, and then moved onto the action he would have to take in the near future.

For once, Gerry wasn't happy that the weekend was over. The week ahead involved a trip to Los Angeles to meet with financiers and lawyers before returning to New York on Friday to then leave again on Saturday. Too much travelling and too many unpleasant meetings lay ahead.

The sound of heels clicking on the terrace roused him from his thoughts and he turned slightly to see his wife appear from their apartment. Avril Kennedy emerged wearing a long black cocktail dress, complimented with a sapphire choker, obviously the best that Fifth Avenue could offer. Avril Kennedy was anywhere between her late forties and late fifties, depending on how generous the estimate was. However, because of Gerry's recent health issues, she still looked at least fifteen years younger than her husband. Avril Kennedy looked like a woman who should have been in show business but was now past her prime. To be in the spotlight had definitely been an ambition for her, but by the time she had reached her late twenties, she had come to realise that she just didn't have the x factor. It had been around that time that she had met Gerry, an esteemed movie producer on his way up. She was instantly attracted to what he could offer her, so instead of being in show business, she married him and helped control the show business. And for over twenty years, they had been a force to be reckoned with. Until recently.

"Gerry, you know you shouldn't be smoking that." Avril said in her usual motherly tone.

"I know dear."

"Well you shouldn't pay that doctor three thousand dollars per appointment if you're just going to completely ignore his advice."

"Yes dear."

Avril started fussing with her hair, "You'd better be done soon as the car's already waiting downstairs. And I want to get there early, stay for as long as it's socially acceptable and then leave. You know how the Camber-Smiths bore me."

"Yes dear."

"Can you believe that they hired out two whole floors of the Waldorf? How pretentious! As if they have enough contacts to raise that big a charity event! And you just know it's going to be full of these twenty year old airheads that haven't a clue how to spend Daddy's fifty million that they've just inherited."

Gerry turned to her, "You didn't have to accept the invitation!"

Avril looked shocked. "What? And let the majority of New York society know that I don't support a charity?"

"You just said that the Camber-Smiths didn't have that many contacts. And I bet you can't even remember what the charity is!"

Avril looked flustered, "That's beside the point. Anyway, did you remember to pick up the tickets today?"

Gerry smiled, "Aah, you always know the perfect time to change the subject."

"Well, did you?"

"Yes, yes. It's all sorted. We depart at noon on Saturday."

Avril's expression turned serious. "You do realise that this could just be a big waste of time. And money."

Gerry turned to look out at the view and puffed on his cigar. "You and I both know that this is probably the last chance we're going to have. That we don't really have any options left."

"So what are we going to do if it doesn't work? What then?"

Gerry stared grimly at the ice in his glass, "We're just going to have to make it work."

"And if we can't?"

"Then we'll just have to come up with a new plan."

Gerry looked at his wife and knew from her expression that his words hadn't comforted her. He continued, "Avril, I'll make sure that we're OK. I always have, haven't I?"

Avril gave a small smile. "I know" she replied, the smile quickly fading, "But I just can't believe we have so much resting on this now."

This conversation was one that Gerry didn't want to have. He said, "Now come on, don't worry about this now. Get your coat, all you need to worry about tonight is how you're going to manage to be polite to Barbara Camber-Smith for a whole evening!"

Avril smiled again and placed her hand on Gerry's arm gently before heading inside.

Gerry stood there for a few moments longer, thinking about the promise he had just made his wife. His face turned to a grimace again before he drained the contents of his glass, and dropped the stub of his cigar. As he left the terrace, its embers briefly burned on before dying out.

Rush hour

Rush hour was still not in full swing on Monday morning when Scott Blacklock entered the foyer of the Zirconia building just off of Wall Street in the Financial District. Although Scott appeared the efficient businessman in his dark suit and crisp shirt, a closer look revealed eyes that were red and bleary from too little sleep. Scott had forgone his relaxing Sunday and had been here at work until gone midnight with Katherine. As he took out his security pass, the early morning security guard called Geoffrey said,

"In early this morning Mr Blacklock? Taking advantage of all that overtime!"

Scott gave a weary smile and replied, "No rest for the wicked."

Geoffrey had been a security guard there for about a thousand years and had a one-liner for everyday of the week and eventually Scott had grown accustomed to just smile and give a perfunctory one-liner back. A man of such routine, it had come as a great shock to Scott when Geoffrey had once said his Thursday line on a Tuesday.

Scott had worked at Zirconia for six years and had been partnered with Katherine Fowley for two. Born in England, Scott and his mother had moved to New York when his parents had divorced. However, after graduating, Scott returned to England to study a degree in criminal psychology and finished top of his class. He had come back to New York at the age of twenty one when his mother fell ill. It was not long after when Zirconia approached Scott to join their ranks as a D.R.I agent.

Zirconia was an insurance giant that dealt in insuring the assets of art galleries, media tycoons, global corporations and anyone else who might have multi-millions to keep safe. In terms of scale, Zirconia insured one third of the world's wealth.

An average policy was between twenty to thirty million dollars so in the event of a theft claim or any claims that had suspicious circumstances, Zirconia would pass the policy to the Department of Recovery and Investigation.

Most employees found its abbreviation amusingly ironic as it was the department you were most likely to become an alcoholic in, what with its stress and heavy workload.

D.R.I was a fairly small but very select group of people. Their main objective was to make sure that if it was at all humanly possible, Zirconia could be prevented from having to write a very expensive cheque to their client. While still maintaining the company's good name and reputation, of course.

In theft cases, members of the department would often liaise with the police and aid them in their investigations. Although the agents had no actual police authority, most police squads were appreciative of the extra help, especially because the D.R.I members were highly trained and their knowledge and insight was often invaluable.

This practice was also followed when it came to potential fraudulent claims or claims where foul play was suspected.

This latter type of case was what was pre-occupying Scott's thoughts as he pushed the elevator call button just as the clock in the foyer chimed eight 'o' clock.

He gave a curt hello to Lee Shipton, a fellow colleague of D.R.I as he entered the lift.

Lee was not a member of D.R.I that Scott particularly liked. He was always too smug and liked to take all the credit for every piece of work that he was involved in, no matter how small. Scott did not want Lee to distract him from his thoughts, so he pulled a week old fax out of his briefcase and pretended to read.

Scott rode the elevator up to his office on the 27th floor. He passed the two receptionists for the department, Colette and Carol and smiled at them both. In return, they both gave a flirty wave and then giggled to each other. As he pushed open the door, he heard a frustrated groan and turned to see Katherine trying to open a drawer on her desk that was notorious for sticking and breaking her nails. She gave up and buried her head on her desk in an impressive pile of scattered paperwork. She looked up when she heard Scott and removed her glasses, which were wonky from lying down. As Scott placed his briefcase down, Katherine stood up and smoothed her wavy brown hair, which Scott presumed she had probably been tearing out moments earlier.

Scott smiled, "No sleep either?"

Katherine leaned on his desk as he sat down. "I think I grabbed a couple of minutes somewhere between 4.07 and 4.09."

Katherine paused before saying, "Scott, Peterson is pissed. I got in an hour ago and he'd already left three messages. He said that Stoltzkin is furious at the search warrant. Especially as it turned up nothing. We have to give him our report at 8.30, before Stoltzkin and his lawyers arrive at 9.00."

When Scott had first started, he was a fresh-faced junior. He was often dismissed, and was not given any cases of his own, allowed to support others who would then treat him as a glorified coffee boy. It was not until the now famous Glengarry murder that people first took notice of Scott. Glengarry was a wealthy, but scrupulous millionaire from California who had a substantial life insurance policy with Zirconia. Members of the department were brought in, as with the body suffering from severe burns and decomposition, it was virtually impossible to identify, save for his wallet. Zirconia wanted to make sure that Glengarry hadn't faked his own death. It was Scott, while observing the case, who noticed the suspicious details of Glengarry's wife's alibi. At the time of the murder she had claimed to be across the country in Philadelphia, a fact that was backed up by credit card receipts of plane tickets.

Scott was the first to pick up on the fact that the time difference between the states made a hole in her alibi, and could have allowed her to kill her husband. Then, purchasing a second plane ticket, this time with cash and an alias, she was able to be in Philadelphia when she would receive the news. When a search came up with scraps of burnt ticket stubs in Mrs Glengarry's bedroom waste bin, she broke down and confessed. As it turned out that it wasn't a fraudulent claim, Zirconia still had to pay out. However the money went to the other more deserving family members, and the fact that a member of the

D.R.I had caught a scheming murderous wife had done wonders for the company's reputation and Scott had gotten his first break.

Now five years later, Scott and Katherine were the driving force of the department. Although Scott had garnered respect from his peers for his successes in the field, the voices above had varying attitudes to the way Scott worked. While many on the board of Directors were impressed by Scott's success ratio, others felt that his methods of work often didn't fall into their codes of conduct. It was ironic that one of those said people was Scott and Katherine's superior, Ralph Peterson.

"So, Scott," Katherine continued, "Please tell me that you've had some moment of genius in the night that might help in the report we have to give in half an hour. That somehow proves that Stoltzkin, a well respected businessman, a man who has friends in Congress, also has connections with the Mafia. And that he hired some of their best men to steal his own fine art collection so he could then reap the insurance rewards."

Katherine slumped in the chair opposite him, with a dejected look. Scott was disheartened at how beaten Katherine looked. He said,

"No, I didn't. But are you saying now that you don't believe it either? You don't think he's guilty?"

"No, that's the thing, I do. But with Golic's murder, I don't see how we can convict Stoltzkin."

Golic had been a policeman from Precinct 14 who had been working undercover in Mafia circles and was prepared to testify to witnessing Stoltzkin with several senior gang members, exchanging information. That was until he was found dead in his apartment the morning before. Scott had been sure that Stoltzkin was hiding the art collection somewhere in one of the outbuildings on his estate. With Golic's testimony, they had been able to obtain a search warrant. The majority of their Saturday had been spent arduously combing Stoltzkin's estate. But all they came up with was an even more outraged Stoltzkin who now not only wanted the insurance payout immediately, but was threatening legal action as well. So it had been a double blow when their star witness was found murdered. He had been shot by a sniper rifle through his apartment window. In front of his wife and child. When Katherine got the news, she was immediately on the phone to Scott and his intended relaxing Sunday had become a long stint in the office until the early hours. Scott and Katherine had spent hours poring over their notes on the case, re-examining the evidence and doing endless background checks on anyone who might possibly have a connection and implicate Stoltzkin.

But they had found nothing.

Scott looked up at the clock and saw that it was almost ten past eight. He rubbed his eyes and said, "There has to be something we've missed. Some clue.

Let's think about Stoltzkin. He's a man of style. He likes things done with flair. Right?"

Katherine said, "We know who Stoltzkin is. I think I read his file about a hundred times yesterday. Karl Stoltzkin, fifty seven. Emigrated from Russia in the fifties. Studied Philosophy and has written two books about the classic philosophers. He's a shrewd businessman. During the seventies he became a corporate shareholder in almost half of the firms in the financial district. In the eighties, he set up his own art foundation. In the nineties, he became a trustee to three major art galleries and two museums. And now, if you can believe it, he also owns a chain of high class restaurants named after his favourite philosophers that serve fine European cuisine. He lives the high life, has practically a palace at his estate as well as seven other houses around the world, in Japan, South America, Europe. I could go on..." Katherine said, and then caught her breath, before saying "And yet somehow in fifty minutes, he's going to make Zirconia write him a cheque for two hundred and forty nine million dollars!"

Scott chewed on his pencil, deep in thought. Katherine looked at him.

"Scott, did you hear any of what I just said?"

Scott looked up. "No I was listening very carefully. Why did you mention his restaurants?"

Katherine looked surprised for a second, and then said, "Well, I've eaten in two of them. Fantastic food."

"Which ones?"

"Socrates, in the Upper East Side. And Diogenes on Mercer St. in SoHo. Why?"

"Do you think he could have had his collection stashed there?"

Katherine got up and said, "Scott, everything Golic had found out pointed to Stoltzkin's estate as it was out of the city and secluded, while his penthouse or any of his properties in the city were considered too close to his art gallery."

"Maybe he was on to Golic and was diverting him? Just bear with me, do you think he could have stored them at one of his restaurants?"

"Well Socrates is a very small, intimate place, with the kitchen in view. Diogenes is a big place, but it's filled with huge beer barrels, and the kitchens are all out of view. They may have storage in the floors above, and I suppose either could have cellars?"

Scott's chewing became more frantic for a second, and then the pencil dropped.

"Barrels?"

Katherine looked perplexed: "Yeah."

"Doesn't it make sense that if Stoltzkin was going to pull a stunt like this, he'd want to put his own signature on it?"

"I suppose. Where are you going with this?"

"I don't claim to know a lot about philosophers but didn't Diogenes live in a barrel?"

"Yeah, that's kind of why the barrels are there. Barrels, Diogenes, it is a theme restaurant. Diogenes and his family fled to Athens when his father was accused of forgery. There he met the philosopher Antisthenes who eventually let him become his pupil. He had no house or possessions and lived in a barrel, but all who saw him were attracted by the beauty and majesty of him. The story's something like that."

Scott looked impressed. He said, "I didn't realise you were up on your philosophers?"

Katherine blushed and admitted, "It was written on the back of the menus in there. That's about all I could remember."

Scott chuckled, "So Diogenes lived in the barrel…."

"You said that."

"INSIDE the barrel."

"Oh." Katherine finally saw where Scott was going. "The art!"

Scott swirled in his chair and picked up the Stoltzkin file where Katherine had put it down. He said, "Wouldn't it be the perfect ploy to use Diogenes to slowly ship his collection out to Europe? He would love the audacity of it."

Katherine for the first time in the last twenty four hours looked alive as she realised that Scott's theory could be true. But something held her back. "Scott, we're still never going to be able to get a second warrant on one of Stoltzkin's properties."

Scott ignored her and kept on reading.

Katherine continued, "And besides, we have less than an hour."

Scott pored over the file and then ran over to Katherine's desk and searched through her paperwork. Katherine followed him, "What are you doing?"

Scott found what he was looking for, checked it again and looked up at Katherine.

"While you've been worrying about second warrants and the like, I've just checked that all of Stoltzkin's supplies for his restaurants come from the Newark docks, where it gets delivered on a cargo ship from Rotterdam, Holland."

He then handed Katherine what he had found on her desk. He continued, "And your background check tells us that one of Stoltzkin's properties is a house in Rotterdam. It would be the perfect place to use his contacts to get discreet buyers and then sell it out through Europe."

Katherine looked down at her background check, seeing the pieces falling into place.

She looked up, "Scott, we still can't....."

But Scott was already out the door and running for the elevator.

As Scott rushed out of the foyer onto the street, he was momentarily surprised to be struck by heavy rain. He allowed himself a brief smile that the glorious weather would choose to break today. On the morning that he now had to try and get a cab to a restaurant over thirteen blocks away, illegally break in, find a hidden art collection, and get back again. In rush hour traffic. And in thirty seven minutes.

As his second taxi cab ignored him, he heard a shout from the revolving doors of the building. Katherine ran out, and like Scott, was surprised by the rain. She immediately wished that she had thought to grab her jacket as her lightweight suit was instantly drenched.

"Scott, we don't have time. Or the authority."

Scott continued trying to hail a taxi cab. When a third went past, Scott swore and checked his watch. He turned to Katherine, "Look, you try and get a cab; I'm going to try and run it."

"Run it?!" Katherine exclaimed.

But Scott was already stepping out into the traffic and running across the road, darting past the cars and starting a cacophony of horns. As he dodged the people on the sidewalk, he felt the rain whip against his wet clothes and had to slow as water got in his eyes. He checked his watch, 8.31. He would have to run blind.

On a slower, but somewhat drier route, Katherine sat in the back seat of a yellow cab tapping numbers into her phone. Ironically, it had taken no time for Katherine to get a cab. But then, she was wearing a fitted skirt suit with a white shirt, and it was raining.

"Hello?"

"Dan, it's Katherine Fowley. Where are you?"

"East Village. Why? What's up?"

"Are you in your car?"

"Yeah. What's this about?"

"Get to Diogenes on Mercer St. in SoHo. You know where that is?"

"Yeah. You want me over there now?"

"Please. Hurry, use you siren."

"Gotcha."

Daniel Povey was a sergeant from Precinct 49 who Katherine and Scott had met a year ago when they worked on a case together. Although not a detective in charge of a case, Daniel was always ready to help out. For them, he was an emergency police backup if a situation ever needed authority or an arrest had to be made and the detectives in charge weren't around. Or, which was more often the case, when they were doing something they shouldn't. But Daniel would always help, even if it sometimes meant putting his neck on the line. Scott thought he helped because he had a crush on Katherine, while Katherine thought it was because he had a crush on Scott. On that part, they were unsure, but they were always grateful to have him as an ally.

In this case, Daniel was no extra authority at all when what they needed was a judge's order, but Katherine thought that they were going to need all the help they could get.

Scott bent over in pain. Running twelve blocks had given him a pain searing stitch. It was a momentary respite as he glanced at his watch and continued running. 8.39. Diogenes appeared on the right quicker than he realised and as he ran to the corner, he saw in amazement, Katherine emerging from a cab. Katherine had a knack for doing things like that.

As he ran across the street, she smiled and said, "I got him to run a few lights. Enjoy your run? You look like shit!"

He paused, catching his breath. Before he had time to respond, he practically had to throw himself to the curb as a squad car lurched around the corner with it's lights flashing, Daniel Povey at the wheel.

As Scott picked himself up, he turned to Katherine, "You called him?"

"Of course" she said with a smile as Daniel emerged from the car, and then added,

"I think we need all the help we can get!"

"So folks, what's up?" said Daniel as he swaggered up to them. Daniel took his police walk so seriously it always brought a smile to Katherine.

Daniel nodded, "Scott, always a pleasure." before turning to Katherine and saying, "So, Katherine my dear, are you eventually going to tell me why I'm here?"

Katherine pointed to the restaurant. "We need to get in there."

Daniel wavered, "Well shouldn't you have gotten a warrant?"

Scott interrupted, "Dan, we don't have time. Our whole case is depending on this. We need to get in there. Even if only for a few minutes."

"We've only got a few minutes!" added Katherine pointedly.

"OK, OK, I'll see what I can do." sighed Daniel.

"Good. Katherine, get on the phone and get Detective Manners down here to cordon off this building." said Scott quickly.

"But, what if we don't find anything?" asked Katherine.

"Then Detective Manners will be the least of our troubles." said Scott grimly.

As Katherine climbed into the squad car to make her calls out of the rain, Scott checked his watch as he followed Daniel to the side door of the restaurant. 8.42.

Daniel was just about to test the strength of the lock when the side door opened and they were confronted by a young cleaner who was carrying two bags of rubbish. He looked Spanish and could have been no more than twenty.

"Yes?"

Daniel was flustered for a moment before regaining his composure.

"Good day, my name is Sergeant Povey of the NYPD and this is my...associate, Mr Blacklock. Last night, there was a violent attack just outside this restaurant. We would like to talk to some of the staff to see if they saw anything."

The boy seemed quite daunted by the uniform. "No one is here. Just me, cleaning."

Daniel saw his intimidation and took his moment. "Then if you'll just let us come in for a few minutes and I can ask you a few questions."

"I wasn't here last night."

"Just a few moments of your time…" Daniel smiled and placed his hand on his belt, just close enough to his gun to make the boy quickly nod.

The boy dumped the bags and led them through the back passage and into the kitchen. The kitchen was clean and empty. The work surfaces were sparse and the utensils were all racked up. As Daniel led the boy to the corner of the kitchen to ask him some fabricated questions, Scott quietly disappeared through the swinging doors into the restaurant. The room had a higher ceiling than Scott had expected and the lights were off so the slanted light coming through the blinds gave the room a grand ghostly feeling. Scott moved quickly to the large barrels and examined them for any kind of opening. They were enormous and there were seven of them so it took Scott several moments to examine them. After pausing for a second, he ran back into the kitchen where the boy was now sweating profusely under Daniel's questioning. Scott approached them and said, "So Mr....?"

"Buente."

"Mr Buente, Sergeant Povey may have told you, but this attack last night was done with a heavy blunt object. Do you have anything like that here?"

Mr Buente now looked like he was about to cry. "We have an axe in the back courtyard. For the firewood to go in the restaurant."

"Thank you Mr Buente." said Scott as he rushed outside and came back in moments later wielding a sizable axe. Before rushing back into the restaurant, he paused to say, "Don't worry Mr Buente. Your blunt object isn't missing, which means you're not a suspect anymore."

There was no look of relief on Mr Buente's face as it was one of complete bewilderment, a look matched by Daniel.

Scott once again headed for the barrels and as he approached, swung the axe above his head. It hit the first barrel hard and left a gash in the wood. Scott felt a tinge of hope. Although these barrels seemed to be made of oak, they had actually been disguised and were made of cheap board wood. Scott pulled the axe out and ripped the fragmented wood apart, his heart in his mouth as he peered inside.

The rain was pouring so hard that Katherine didn't see the figures approach the car until the driver door and back passenger door were opened and Scott and Daniel climbed in.

"Drive Dan!" Scott yelled.

Daniel hit the ignition and started the sirens wailing. As they pulled away, the car clock lit up. 8.51.

As Daniel floored it, swerving cars that weren't getting out of the way fast enough, Katherine turned to the back seat. She asked, "What happened? I got Detective Manners to head down here."

Scott grinned and said, "Well, he's going to have something to cordon off!" as he revealed what he had been sheltering from under his damp suit jacket. A picture frame containing a painting by Renoir, "This was the only one small enough to take."

Daniel swerved another car and made a precarious turn at an intersection that meant crossing three lanes of traffic at breakneck speed. Scott added, "Oh you might also want to tell Detective Manners that he should expect to find a very scared Mr Buente locked in the meat storage. And send him my apologies. I expect he didn't know anything about it, but couldn't be too sure!"

Scott grinned as Katherine gave a look of disdain before being catapulted across the car as Daniel made another turn.

Scott's watch read 8.59 as they ran through the rain and into the foyer of Zirconia.

As the lift doors closed and Katherine pushed the button for the top floor, they all heard the foyer clock chime nine 'o'clock.

Katherine opened the door to the Director's boardroom to be confronted by a very red faced Peterson and the rest of the Committee, sitting across from Stoltzkin and four of his lawyers.

Peterson rose out of his chair and was about to shout a tirade before his expression completely changed when he saw what Scott was holding in his hands.

But this was nothing compared to the look that ran across Stoltzkin's face, as he turned in his chair and the colour drained from him.

Mediterranean mood

The clear blue waters lapped quietly on the hull of the yacht as Clarissa Jordan lay on the sun deck and sipped her martini. She adjusted her large sunglasses before positioning herself more into the sun.

The boat, called the Wonder, was moored in the stretch of water between the two peninsulas of Kassandra and Sithonia in the region of Greece known as Halkidiki. The yacht was quietly impressive, 80 ft long with a 30 ft main sail. It had a large open padded sun deck to the fore and a dining area to the stern, before leading down to a diving platform. The inside was just as plush, full living quarters and three cabins; all decked out in deep oak and maroon furnishings.

Clarissa sat up for a moment and watched the distant bustle of the small tourist village of Pefkahori. She thought about getting into the launch boat and heading into the village. But the thought was fleeting. It would be too much hassle, too much attention. She smiled at the lie to herself. She knew the problem was that there wouldn't be too much attention. It had been Clarissa's idea to hire the yacht as it meant keeping away from the public. But it was boring. When she had said to her husband that she wanted the yacht to look at beautiful places in the Mediterranean, she had secretly hoped that they would moor off of Monaco, or maybe Cannes.

The truth was that he had chosen somewhere that hid them from the public a little too well.

Clarissa Jordan had until fairly recently been known as Clarissa Lavelle, an international star of the show business world. Clarissa was the daughter of film director, Olivier Lavelle and Broadway actress Lydia Cline. When she was only nine, she got her first part in one of her father's films " Meadows" and by the age of sixteen was doing a stint on Broadway, playing the daughter in the "The Secret Diary" opposite her mother. She had been in five Broadway shows, made twenty films and garnered numerous awards all by her mid twenties. Clarissa then briefly flirted with a singing career but had limited success outside of the U.S. However, she still managed to release two albums that sold almost ten million between them. The sudden death of her father and then her mother three months later shook Clarissa's life. For the first time, she withdrew from public life but was only gone for nine months before returning with her most critically acclaimed Broadway play. It was a small one character piece that was described by critics as her "most intimate work ever". Clarissa always knew which buttons to push with the media, and her downscale, low profit return ensured that it would be a big one. A string of films followed and three years later, at the age of thirty-three, she won her first Oscar. Her brother, Christopher, following in their father's footsteps, had directed an adaptation of Macbeth, in which she picked up the award for her part as Lady Macbeth.

However, Clarissa soon left Hollywood, famously saying she was bored of it. She returned to New York and in the last five years, had intermittently performed at select theatres, given cameo roles in films by directors of high regard and written her autobiography. But now at forty-one, she still commanded the centre spotlight. She had a body that looked ten years younger and her face, while not as perfect as the air brushed publicity photos, was still hardly lined and had the glow of a healthy San Tropez tan.

It was not just her appearance or her work that kept her in the headlines though. Clarissa's love life had been a rollercoaster of a ride in the last twenty years and the press and public had eagerly been following every moment. Clarissa had once said in an interview that she had been proposed to thousands of times. The figure was probably accurate as in twenty years; Clarissa had been engaged seven times and was now on her fourth marriage.

She was first married when she was eighteen and the marriage lasted eighteen months. He had been a promising baseball star but the pressures of a very public marriage made him turn to cocaine. The media loved it.

After four short engagements, Clarissa married for the second time when she was twenty-nine, in the same year that her parents died. He was a fellow actor and at the time she had said,

"He's my Saviour. I don't know what I'd do without him."

That marriage lasted four years and they split amid rumours that he was too jealous of her success following her Oscar win.

The third marriage, six years later, was an unremarkable event that only lasted six months. The husband wasn't famous. The public wasn't interested. Until the separation a year and a half ago, when an ugly divorce had to be settled in court and Clarissa was the talk of the town again.

And now, Clarissa had been married again for ten months, and for the first time had taken her husband's surname, leaving her now famous Lavelle surname to become Clarissa Jordan. The gossip columns were full of speculation that this name change meant that this time, he must be the one. But the public were not interested in Clarissa living happily ever after, as this time there was an added twist. Her husband, Wall Street hotshot, Mark Jordan had a twenty-two year daughter, Amy. The media were fascinated as Clarissa had always said, "I will never have children. They piss me off!" and now here she was playing the role of step-mother. There were also rumours that they didn't get on, as Clarissa was jealous of her stepdaughter's youth and beauty, and that by association Amy had started attracting paparazzi herself.

Clarissa's rays of sunlight were blocked as Amy Jordan stepped onto the sun deck, putting her long dirty blond hair up with a clip. In a string vest and cropped shorts, Amy did look young and beautiful. And from Clarissa's reaction to her stepdaughter's arrival, there appeared to be a touch of truth in the media's rumours.

"What do you want?" scowled Clarissa as she topped up her drink.

Amy hardly acknowledged her and instead looked to the shore. She replied, "I was looking for Dad."

"Well," said Clarissa as she stopped her sarong blowing away, "It's quite obvious that he isn't here. So if you don't mind, you're blocking my sun."

Amy turned with a look of disgust at Clarissa lying in her bikini. "Don't worry. I'm heading into the village now." She added with a smirk, "Dad was right about this area being great for cheap leather!"

As Amy walked inside, she heard the words "Pissy little bitch."

A comment that was also heard by her father, Mark, as he exited the cabin from the other side of the boat. Mark Jordan was a tall, stocky man of forty-five, with greying dark hair. He had trained as a lawyer at Columbia and been an excellent litigator in Washington D.C. When he turned thirty, he turned to New York, to Wall Street. And that was where he had spent the last fifteen years, amassing a tidy fortune. It was in New York where he had met Clarissa, eleven months ago.

"Clarissa!" Mark said warningly.

Clarissa looked guilty for a second before replying, "Well she implied that I...."

"You what?"

Clarissa stood up and moved to the other side of the deck. She said bitterly, "What does it matter? We all know that in the end, you'll take her side. So let's just not waste time."

Mark hated it when Clarissa used that line. He was well aware of the fact that there was no love lost between his wife and daughter, but he was a hopeless optimist thinking that with enough trying, they would eventually get on. Amy and Clarissa had first met last Thanksgiving and the meal had not been a success. Clarissa was uncomfortable. Amy was awkward.

Christmas was just as frosty despite spending it in Dubai, and Amy didn't even come home from Boston for her Spring break. This holiday was only the third time they had met. They had boarded the boat on Sunday evening, and there had already been several snide comments. And it was only Tuesday.

An uncomfortable silence lasted for several moments. Clarissa turned around to face her husband. She said, "Look, let's just forget it. Did you sort things for Saturday?"

Mark hated confrontations and was glad at the change of subject. He said,

"Yes I've just had confirmation that our tickets are waiting for us back at home. We leave at noon on Saturday."

Clarissa asked impatiently, "So when do we get back to New York?"

"We'll dock the boat on Thursday evening then catch a plane later that night. There's a stopover at Heathrow and we should get to J.F.K at about seven." explained Mark.

Clarissa gave a look of disgust. "What? Seven, Friday evening?! And then have to leave again on Saturday morning?! I shall want to be rested! We'll dock the boat tomorrow and get back on Thursday."

Mark's face fell, "But I promised Amy we'd take a look around Thessaloniki tomorrow. See the sights."

Clarissa pouted, "But Mark…"

"I promised."

Clarissa's look changed to a seductive one. As she spoke she slowly moved across the deck and let her sarong fall, revealing her toned stomach. She spoke softly, "How about we just go for dinner there on the way to the airport?"

By this point, she had reached Mark and placed her hands on his belt.

"Well I don't know" he said hesitantly.

Clarissa started to kiss his neck. She said soothingly, "We'll see the city at night. It will be romantic."

Mark's resolve weakened. "That does sound nice."

Clarissa spoke between kisses. "Good. Then let's stop discussing this and take advantage of having the boat to ourselves."

As Clarissa began to unbuckle his belt, she looked over Mark's shoulder. Amy was speeding away in the launch boat and Clarissa allowed herself a small smile.

Deadlines and destinations

Across the street and up a little from Madison Square Gardens, Tim Anderson sat alone in a booth by the window. He was in the diner on the ground floor of the New Yorker hotel. Open to non residents, Tim came here when he fancied a breakfast that would keep him full until it was time to go to bed. It was ten thirty in the morning and Tim had already been into work and finished for the day. He had just waited forty five minutes for a five minute meeting with his editor, Raymond Wharmby. It had been a very good meeting and Tim sat contentedly, waiting for his Grand Slam Number Two.

Tim had a very on/off relationship with his boss, whose happiness seemed only to depend on the numbers of copies sold. But despite this, Raymond Wharmby had a certain fondness for Tim. He saw him as his protégé and had been the one who spotted Tim four years ago. Back then Tim had been doing freelance work and part timing as a wedding photographer. Wharmby was impressed by the quality of his work and Tim had immediately accepted the offer of a job as a travel reporter. His articles, right from the start, were well received and Tim was often the choice to do the main feature. He was also chosen often as he provided fantastic visuals to his pieces. But even then, he could still walk into Wharmby's office and catch him on a bad day and come out feeling like shit.

And, with Wharmby, it was always a gamble as to what kind of day it was.

Today though, despite him looking very red faced when Tim had entered his office, was obviously a good day for Wharmby. And he had in turn, made it a good day for Tim.

Tim had already enjoyed a momentary break before going back to work for his next assignment. While Scott had rushed off to long hours of painstaking work on Sunday, Tim had instead gone for a picnic in Central Park with some friends and worked off his hangover by drinking numerous bottles of beer and stayed there until the sun set over the city. Monday and Tuesday had been a chance for a flying visit up to his parent's place in Syracuse. Although Tim was twenty-eight, he had a seven year old sister, Holly. Tim's parents, Jack and Maggie, had been married for thirty five years and Tim had been an only child for twenty one years until Maggie mistook being pregnant for the menopause. When they found out, they were overjoyed. They had worked hard all their lives and were due to take early retirement that year. Tim was already living in New York by then so Holly was always desperately happy when her big brother would come to visit. She doted on him and Tim was lucky enough to be in the country for her seventh birthday. She didn't know he was coming and he arrived in time to bring the cake in for her.

Tim had left on Tuesday afternoon to be back in time for his meeting with Wharmby that morning.

He ruffled his tousled, light brown hair and looked up to see Miranda Green enter the diner with a thunderous expression on her face. She stomped over to the booth, and sat opposite Tim, her large bag knocking over most of the condiments on the table.

Miranda Green also worked for the magazine Travel Today. She was a consultant that dealt with historical sites and had a wealth of knowledge on Architecture. Miranda was a petite twenty five year old with short, cropped blonde hair. Miranda had only been with the magazine for little over a year, as she had spent her early twenties travelling around the world. Although her job sounded exotic, Miranda's work rarely allowed her to leave Manhattan. Instead, she liaised with the reporters in their offices and helped provide detailed information about the destinations they were travelling to. The fact was that through the luxuries of modern technology, the wonders of the Internet and e-mail, Miranda's job was largely confined to a desk. As a result, Miranda was always slightly jealous of Tim's traveller lifestyle.

"Good Morning Sunshine." Tim said chirpily.

Miranda's face did not show the same chirpiness. "It is for some." she retorted.

Tim put the condiments upright. "Now come on, it can't be that bad." he said, still smiling.

Miranda glare continued for a second before she allowed herself a smile. A smile which widened when Tim's breakfast arrived. After ordering a coffee, she said, "Well, that's true. I could be sat in a diner about to kill myself with enough fat intake to put down a small elephant."

Tim grinned as he started to tuck in. "Yes, but only a small one. No, seriously, what's the matter?"

Miranda's smile dropped as she began to explain, "There I am thinking, at the end of today, I've got a long weekend out in the Hamptons. Kate on the 2nd floor managed to get us keys to this swanky beach house. But at nine thirty this morning, Wharmby tells me that that dick Carter in your department has forgotten to mail me that he's doing a three week round trip of Italy and that it's in the next issue. It is, in fact, the main frigging article! Wharmby says that I have to help him prepare which means that it's good-bye to the Hamptons."

Miranda exhaled and then gave a large sigh. Her coffee arrived and she immediately perked up. She took her first sip and allowed herself to savour the coffee. She smiled and indicated to the mug, saying, "Sorry, I'm only crabby because I didn't even have time for one of these this morning. So, Mr Anderson, why is it that you seem to be a man of leisure lately?"

Tim took his time answering as he finished off a hash brown. He chuckled "You must have been Wharmby's meeting before me. Now I know why he was so red faced!"

Miranda smiled, "I did kind of express my anger. Why did he want to see you?"

Tim continued "He told me that he's going to nominate my recent Mexico piece for the Franklin Award."

"Wow. Congratulations!"

"He's only nominating it. It might not even get in."

"Still, that's pretty good."

"And it gets better. I've got a week off. I leave for California next Tuesday to attend a journalism conference. That'll be really boring, but then he's given me an assignment I've been wanting for ages. Camping in Yosemite. It'll be beautiful out there at this time of year."

Tim realised that that was the last thing Miranda wanted to hear now. He said, "Shit, sorry. I'm hardly cheering you up here, am I?"

Miranda had already finished her coffee. She replied, "Don't be silly. I'm happy for you. And besides, you're here for another week, which means that you can take me out on Saturday night to celebrate. A double celebration! For you, and for me, as by that point, I should have hopefully finished this shitty Italy piece and be able to enjoy a one day weekend."

"OK, but what if you haven't finished it?"

Miranda smiled as she stole one of his sausages, "Well, I'll still get drunk as I'll be in the shit anyway!" She took a bite and added,

"The deadline is at noon on Saturday."

Scott's brief

Although Stoltzkin's arrest on Monday had solved their case, it was still far from closed. Scott and Katherine had spent the last couple of days collating their evidence in order to hand it over to the NYPD to complete their full investigation. A preliminary hearing was being set and in several months, the case would be taken to court. Scott and Katherine would have to make statements and appear in court. It would not have been the first time for either of them. Scott and Katherine were pleased with their work, so it was a surprise when, at Thursday lunchtime, Peterson called their office and asked to see Scott, and only Scott.

Katherine said, "Uh oh, that only usually happens when he's pissed at you."

Katherine's words echoed in Scott's head as he rode the elevator up to Peterson's office on the 46th floor. He walked down the hallway and gave the office door a quick rap.

"Come in."

Scott entered into Ralph Peterson's plush office and saw Peterson sat at his large oak desk talking to Greg Vanderman, one of the other directors. Vanderman finished his conversation with Peterson and said, "Don't mind me Scott, I was just leaving."

As he walked past Scott, he patted him on the shoulder. "Good work with Stoltzkin."

Scott gave him a smile of gratitude, which quickly dropped when he turned back to Peterson.

As the door closed behind Scott, Peterson said in a gruff voice. "While Mr Vanderman may be applauding your efforts, there are some of us that cannot overlook that your actions on Monday morning, while ending in a good result, were completely unlawful."

"Sir......"

"All I can say is that you're damn lucky that Officer Povey had a plausible enough story about witnessing suspicious activity. But I don't believe a word of it. I know you bent the rules. Even before I heard you didn't have a warrant."

Scott shifted uncertainly, not knowing if it was appropriate to sit. He asked, "Excuse me for asking Sir, why would you think that?"

Peterson gave a look that made Scott uncertain if it was pride, bemusement or anger. "I could tell by the damn glint in your eye when you walked in with that painting."

Scott suppressed a grin. "Is that why you called me in Sir?"

"No, it isn't" Peterson said, looking grave, as he shifted in his chair and held out a file for Scott. "This has just come in."

Scott took the file, sat down opposite him and opened the folder. The client name at the top had an impact that made Scott take a second look. It couldn't be.

Peterson continued, "As you can see, this client is obviously top priority to Zirconia, especially with the associated media angle. I will be requiring your full efforts on this."

Scott looked down through the file and couldn't find what he was looking for. He said, "But, I don't understand. There's nothing here to say what claim's been made."

"That's because there hasn't been a claim yet. I'm assigning you with a very unusual task. I know this isn't in the D.R.I's job description, but I want you to carry out surveillance on this client."

"But why?" said Scott bewildered. D.R.I dealt with things after the fact, not before.

"Several threats have recently been placed to this client, concerning items that are insured with us."

"Well then surely this file should be for the police then?"

Peterson removed his glasses and placed his hands on the table. He said, "The police are conducting their own investigation. After the most recent threat last Saturday, the Directors feel that we should also conduct our own, private one." He said, stressing the word private by leaning forward.

"If it becomes known that Zirconia prevented a theft from a client of this magnitude, then the good publicity for the company would be endless. However, you must obviously understand the sensitivity in the nature of this course of action."

Scott looked back down at the file; amazed at the job he'd been given.

He asked, "What about Katherine?"

Peterson replied, "I need Katherine to tie up the Stoltzkin case. If she can help in any support function, use her. But I would imagine with you gone, she'll be quite busy."

Peterson made it clear that the meeting was over. As he put his glasses back on, he said, "I think you'll find everything in the file. Daylight's burning Mr Blacklock. I suggest you make a start. I'm not sure if our client is even in the country. Your usual expenses will be doubled for this investigation."

Scott stood up and walked to the door. He turned and asked, "Sir, why did you give this case to me?"

"It's an unusual case. You work unusually."

Scott smiled as he opened the office door. He thought he might just have had a compliment from Peterson. As if noticing the smile, Peterson added,

"Scott. When I said unusual, I did not mean illegal. My patience is wearing thin. Remember, PRIVATE investigation."

Scott headed for the elevator. He had known that Peterson would not have let him leave on a good note, but forgot that in an instant as the brief in his hand reminded him that he had just been given a very different assignment.

Ships in the night

The sun was just breaking the picture perfect blue sky on Friday morning as Passenger Flight 228 was climbing away from Logan International Airport in Boston, Massachusetts. Clarissa Jordan sat in First Class trying very hard to calm her anger.

It had been one thing after another. In the end, they had missed their flight from Thessaloniki on Wednesday evening, instead having to settle for Thursday afternoon. They had arrived at Heathrow in the early evening only to be told that there was a problem with their onward flight. They had to wait for six hours before being told that they would also have to get a connecting flight at Logan International. Clarissa wouldn't have time to do anything by the time they got back to New York. A point she made clear several times to Mark and Amy on their journey home. Neither Mark nor Amy had pointed out that they had missed their flight on Wednesday night because Clarissa hadn't gotten ready in time, having already made them forgo their trip to Thessaloniki.

She sat there annoyed. Annoyed that Mark was able to fall asleep anywhere at the drop of a hat, and annoyed at the sound of Amy's chirpy chatter from the seat behind her. She was talking to the passenger next to her, an equally chatty red haired woman. A Doctor or psychiatrist or something. Clarissa had lost interest in eavesdropping at that point. She knew she should have booked the tickets herself and stuck Amy in economy. Or "World Traveller", as they seemed to be calling it these days. Making the cheap people feel less cheap thought Clarissa, her nose flaring. She sat there, unable to sleep, unable to talk to the slumbering Mark next to her. She gave a loud sigh and ordered her second martini of the day.

Another person who had reason for annoyance that morning was Henry Broadside as he rushed into the departure lounge at Logan International to see his plane, Flight 228 taking off. He slumped into a seat, and then cursed as he shoved his shoes back onto his feet, having carried them on his run from the metal detector checkpoint. His curse was aimed at the cab driver, who had broken down on the Freeway.

Henry Broadside, Harry to all who knew him, was an intense looking man in his late thirties. While he was good looking, he was good looking in a dense sort of way. He was a barman at Fandangos in Boston, a pleasant unassuming bar and grill. It wasn't the flashiest place, but Harry liked it for that. He had led a life of varied jobs in varied cities, drifting from one place to the next, moving on when he felt the time was right. He considered himself a free spirit. As such, Harry had never really had a career but a variety of careers. He had worked in countless hotels, restaurants and bars, in some working up to an assistant manager. However he never took anything seriously enough to want the full responsibility of it. He had been a plumber, electrician and labourer. At the age of twenty, he had even done a stint with a touring circus.

A short time ago, on a chance meeting, Harry had fallen in love and had left all that behind for six months, living a life in New York that he never dreamed he could. However, the relationship ended as suddenly as it began and Harry had arrived in Boston, unsure where his life had left him. He got himself sorted with somewhere to work and live, but was unhappy with both of them. His job and flat were expendable and he didn't care about leaving them behind now he had decided to return to New York.

Or for him trying to return, he thought, as he stood up and strode toward the ticket counter.

Harry Broadside's obviously disgruntled actions were observed by a couple sat at a table close to him. The man, a fit athletic type, found his swearing amusing, while the woman, a smaller, frailer creature, looked at the man in disdain for grinning. The man had an attractive, masculine chin with dark black hair and a dazzling smile. The woman had a petite frame and a pretty, but wooden face, resembling that of a doll. With both it was difficult to guess what age they were, looking like they could be anywhere in their early to late thirties. The woman sipped her iced tea while the man watched Harry Broadside walk back into the lounge, looking even more furious. As he slumped back in the same chair, the man exchanged a glance with the woman, stood up and walked over to him.

He approached and said, "You know what they say, worse things happen at sea."

Harry looked up angrily, "Excuse me?"

The man offered his hand. "Anthony Stuart."

Harry didn't take his hand, instead standing up. "What do you want?"

Anthony gave a big smile. "I couldn't help but guess that you missed your flight."

Harry became very red-faced, "Yes, I did. And I'm glad that my antics have caused you amusement."

Anthony's smile didn't falter. "You misunderstand me. I was only offering to help."

Harry retorted, "And how are you going to do that? Are you going to somehow get me to New York by tomorrow morning? Because no one else in this airport can seem to! It's still the holiday season and the next flight available gets in tomorrow night."

Anthony ignored his irate manner and continued, "It just so happens, that we have a spare ticket. A friend of ours couldn't make it. We're on a plane that leaves at 8.45 this morning."

Harry's face completely dropped for a second before saying, "Really? You would?"

Anthony said, "I'd be happy to."

Harry immediately offered his hand. "Henry Broadside, but please, call me Harry. Thank you very much. I'll be happy to offer you the full price of the tickets plus something extra."

"No need. There will be a charge to change the name on the ticket, but it should be minimal. Anyway, let me introduce you to my wife." Anthony said as he led Harry back to their table.

"Caroline, this is Harry Broadside."

Caroline Stuart stood up and shook hands timidly with Harry. Anthony indicated a chair, "Please, have a seat."

As they all sat down, Harry said, "Thank you both. This really is very kind."

Anthony replied, "Don't be silly, Caroline and I will pleased of the company down to New York. It's Caroline's first time to the Big Apple. Isn't it?"

Caroline gave a smile.

Anthony continued, "It's nice to be getting away for a break! I'm a lecturer here in Boston and Caroline is a child minder. Are you from Boston?"

Harry hesitated before saying, "Not originally. I'm a barman here now." He took another look at Caroline, recognition on his face. "It's a place called Fandangos. You look familiar. Did you work there when I started?"

Caroline blushed and replied, "Yes. I thought I recognised your face from somewhere as well. I did some part time hours there, but I left shortly after you started."

Harry grinned, "Wow! Small world!"

Caroline responded with a small smile.

Anthony asked "Why are you headed to New York?"

Harry hesitated again, "I used to live there."

"A native New Yorker? That's settled then. You can take me and Caroline out for a drink this evening. That'll be repayment. I expect you know some cracking places to go."

For the first time in the conversation, Caroline seemed to come to life. She said in a harsh whisper. "Anthony, you know we were meant to visit my sister."

Anthony looked at her for a second before turning back to Harry. He said "Oh well, she'll be up to Boston again soon."

"Anthony!"

Anthony turned and glared furiously at her, a glare which she met defiantly.

Harry already felt awkward at being questioned on his reasons for going to New York, so now being caught in the middle of a marital squabble, he decided to take his opportunity.

He rose and said, "I think I'll go and sort this name change on my ticket. Thank you again."

As he walked away, heaving a sigh of relief, he heard Anthony and Caroline continue the argument. He could still hear that she had also wanted to go up the Empire State Building on their one night in New

York. He was out of earshot to hear Anthony's reply and was quite glad to be. As he walked to the ticket counter, he wondered if it just might be easier to walk to New York.

Conference of convenience

Scott sat pensively on the balcony of his apartment as the heat was cooling into a warm Friday evening. Scott had his feet up on the railings with a cigarette in one hand and a glass of red wine in the other. Since Peterson had seen him yesterday, Scott had spent most of the last thirty hours studying over his new assignment. The client that Scott had been assigned to was not an easy person to track down. His research had told him a lot about the client's background and life history but was scant on their recent activities. Scott had become resigned to scrutinizing thousands of travel records and plane passenger lists and an hour ago had found out that his client had flown into New York today.

He sipped on his wine, his mini celebration for locating the client. He then took a drag on his cigarette, his way to distract him while he waited for an important call about what his client's next move was.

Scott was roused from his thoughts as he heard the apartment door and turned to see Tim walk in, obviously having just come from the gym. He chucked his bag down and shouted "Hey" as he grabbed a bottle of water from the fridge.

Scott returned the greeting just as Tim came out and leant against the doorframe.

Tim gulped most of the water in one breath and said, "Long time, no see. Where have you been all week?"

Scott took a sip of wine. "Working."

Scott proceeded to tell Tim about the antics of Monday morning and the prominent arrest of Stoltzkin. However his story ended there when Tim excitedly remembered that he hadn't told Scott about Wharmby nominating his Mexico piece.

Tim said, "We should celebrate, on our double success."

As he said this he headed into the kitchen. He continued, "Have you eaten? Maybe I could make my famous celebration fajitas? Then a night on the town?"

Tim's good mood stopped Scott from pointing out that he still had just as much work to do now. Instead he asked, "So how much more time have you got off?"

"Well" Tim said as he opened a bottle of beer, "Wharmby's given me a camping trip in....."

It was then that the phone rang. Scott jumped up and ran in to grab it. Tim looked over from the kitchen.

"Important call?" He asked.

"Work stuff. I'm waiting for a call from Dan Povey." Scott replied as he picked up the phone.

A voice on the other end of the line said, "Hi Scott. It's Dan. I got it! Just remember, you didn't hear this from me."

Tim tried to make out what the conversation might be, but soon gave up and took his beer out to the balcony.

Scott listened to Daniel, thanked him and said goodbye.

Daniel had told him that although his client had only arrived in New York today, they were leaving again tomorrow morning. They were departing at midday from Grand Central Station on the Trans-Oceanic Express, a very expensive and prestigious express train with only a select number of suites on board. Its destination was Los Angeles, where it would arrive on Tuesday.

Scott put down the phone and headed back out to the balcony. Tim looked up and said, "Anything urgent?"

Scott rested against the bars of the balcony. He replied, "Fairly. I'll tell you in a minute. You said something about a camping trip?"

"Oh yeah. Wharmby gave me a camping assignment in Yosemite! Can you believe it? I've always said I'd love to see it, haven't I?"

Scott's mind had gone back to thoughts of his client. Tim took a swig of his beer and carried on; unaware that Scott was now only half listening. "It'll just be me and a ranger. The full experience of the wilderness. Oh, and I have to do a crappy conference in L.A. before that. I fly out next Tuesday."

Scott's mind vaguely tracked some of what Tim had just said. He stirred from his thoughts. He asked, "L.A? Next Tuesday?"

"Yeah" answered Tim as he twirled the bottle top on his finger.

Scott grinned. "Perfect!"

"What?" said Tim, dropping the bottle top through the grill of the balcony.

Even though Scott told Tim practically everything, the plan for his next assignment meant that it was probably best keeping a few things to himself for a while.

"Oh nothing." He turned to Tim as he sat down and said. "Seeing as how you've got some time off and I've just solved this case, why don't we have a proper celebration?"

Tim look confused. "Yeah, I just suggested that."

"I was thinking not so much fajitas as taking a train across America? Arriving in Los Angeles next week in time for your conference?"

Tim's look of confusion didn't go away. "OK, where did that come from?"

"Come on Tim, I never get the chance for a holiday and how often do you get the chance to travel without writing?"

"No, I completely agree with you. But what made you think of that? And what would you do when we got to L. A?"

"See the sights; take a picture of the Hollywood sign. The usual stuff. Anyway, what do you say?"

"Sounds like a great idea. You paying?" Tim joked.

Scott stood up and said as he ran inside, "You just leave the finer details to me."

As Tim remained outside, Scott picked up his phone. If there was one benefit to being a member of D.R.I, it was that Zirconia's wealth and influence meant access to contacts in high places.

Scott dialled the number and when Katherine answered the phone he said,

"Katherine, my sweetest, dearest, favourite partner, I need to ask you a really big favour."

Grand Central

The gilded clock above the information stand showed ten past eleven when Scott walked down the steps into the impressive atrium of Grand Central Station on Saturday morning.

While trains heading across the country usually all departed from Penn. Station several blocks away, the Trans-Oceanic Express left from Grand Central. Scott had reckoned that this was to give the passengers a grand send off. Waiting in Grand Central Station was a lot more pleasant than the underground maze that was Penn. Station, itself an impressive building until it was torn down several decades ago. Scott remembered watching Miranda and Tim debating over that argument. Tim ended up saying "I don't get what all that fuss was about over that! We got Madison Square Garden instead! Much better!"

Miranda hadn't agreed.

As Scott stood at the top of the main stairs, the sunlight glared through the upper windows, making an impressive display on the floor below. Just like the classic black and white photos you see on stands along Central Park, thought Scott as he scanned the vaulted room for two people.

He had left Tim packing at the apartment an hour ago to head into work. He had arrived at their office to find Katherine still trying any means possible to obtain tickets on the Trans-Oceanic Express. And they were very hard to come by. Most people had to book months in advance to get tickets.

Katherine had promised to have them at the station before the train left and Scott had arranged to meet Tim at eleven. But as Scott hauled his travelling case to the counter, ten minutes late himself, it came as no surprise to see that Tim wasn't there. More worryingly,

On the Right Track

neither was Katherine. Realising that without tickets, Scott couldn't check in anyway, he decided to store his case at the luggage counter in one of the corridors off of the main atrium. As he took his ticket from the attendant, he heard a shout from across the foyer. He turned to see Tim walking towards him. Scott was surprised at Tim's appearance as, while he was dressed casually, yet looking fairly smart in trousers and a lightweight jacket, Tim was quite the opposite. Tim was wearing trainers that had been with him around the world at least six times. These were accompanied by his comfy "travelling" jeans that stood up by themselves, along with his favourite hoody. Tim placed his oversized rucksack down and checked that his hiking boots were still attached to it by their long shoelaces.

Tim said, "Sorry I'm late. Traffic's a bitch."

Scott said in an exasperated voice, "Tim, did you not look at the stuff I printed off the website about this train? It's very exclusive, the type where you have to be smart for dinner. Not in your hiking boots!"

Tim moved past Scott and handed his bag over the counter. "Chill out! Remember, this is a vacation. I did look at the website. I've got a couple of smart shirts and trousers. And I figured I could just borrow one of your suits. I know you always take at least three!"

"You thought you'd just borrow mine?!"

Tim picked up his ticket and thanked the attendant before answering.

"Come on Scott, I'm going to Yosemite after this. What need do I have for a load of smart clothes in the middle of a forest?"

Scott saw that Tim had a point. He also realised that it was his desire to blend in on the train that was making him snappy. The fact that he was actually at work was one that he still had to tell Tim.

He said, "I'm sorry, just a bit tense that our tickets arrive on time."

Tim turned, "What? We don't have tickets yet?"

"Don't worry, Katherine will be here in time. How about a quick drink? We've got half an hour."

Tim's face immediately brightened. "Now you're talking, I could murder a beer."

"It's just gone eleven in the morning. I was thinking more of a coffee."

As they headed for Cipriani Dolci, an Italian bar on one of the balconies of the central atrium, Tim said "Well, that's fine. You have your coffee. And I'll have my beer. And all will be right with the world. You didn't really expect me to wait until the champagne reception to have a drink. We are on vacation."

Scott turned, impressed, "You really did look at the website!"

Tim smiled for a second before his face dropped. "Shit! Drinks tonight. I was supposed to be taking Miranda out. I'd better get my phone from my bag and apologise."

Scott watched him run off towards the lockers. Before Tim got lost in the throng of people he shouted, "Grab me a beer!"

Scott proceeded up the steps and across to the bar at Cipriani Dolci where he ordered a beer and a double espresso. As he turned from the counter in search of a table, he walked into a woman who promptly dropped her bag on the floor.

"Oh, I am sorry," said Scott as they both bent to pick up her bag. It had snapped open and alongside her purse, which had slipped out, was a ticket for the Trans-Oceanic Express.

Scott looked up to take a look at the lady. She was an attractive woman with red hair tied up in an elegant twirl. She could have been in her early forties but looked good for it and was dressed in a smart black trouser suit. Scott repeated his apology as they both stood up again.

He said, "Sorry I couldn't help noticing. Are you taking the Express?"

The woman looked cautious for a second before saying, "Yes. Why?"

"I'm also travelling on the Express. Perhaps I should introduce myself; I hear there are only a few of us on the train. My name's Scott Blacklock."

The woman's face immediately broke into a smile as if she had been dying to speak to someone. She took Scott's hand and said,

"Nice to meet you. I'm Dr Pennington. Please, call me Daphne. Are you vacationing by yourself also?"

"No, I'm travelling with a friend. He should be here in a moment. Would you like to join us at a table?"

Daphne had already picked up her coffee. As they walked to a table, Scott wondered if he had had a choice asking that question. They found a table in the corner at the edge of the balcony, giving them a good view of the main hall.

"So," Daphne said as she sat down, "Is this your first time on the Express?"

"Yes, have you done the trip before?"

Daphne looked pleased at the chance to tell a story. She settled in her chair and started, "Oh, yes. A few years ago, my husband and I took the Express. I thought it was fantastic. They take such good care of you. And the changing scenery of America is fantastic to watch. Mind you, we had to save hard to go. It's not cheap. Is it?"

Scott was about to reply but had the feeling that when Daphne Pennington was speaking, questions were usually rhetorical.

She continued, "In fact, the only thing that tainted the holiday was the fact that my husband was there."

Scott choked on his espresso at Daphne's bluntness.

"Yes, George and I never did get on very well. We spent most of the trip at either end of the train. We both found it quite annoying that they made us sit together at dinner!"

Daphne paused long enough for Scott to presume she had finished.

He asked, "So George is.....?"

Daphne took a gulp of coffee. "Dead."

She paused before saying. "It happened a year ago now. I think it was quite a relief for both of us."

Scott for the second time almost choked on his espresso.

Tim wrenched the bursting top zip on his rucksack open and extracted his phone. As he balanced his bag, he speed dialled Miranda.

"Hello?"

"Miranda, it's Tim."

The voice suddenly sounded brighter. "Hey, guess what? I managed to finish the piece by ten this morning. Already handed it in."

"That's great. You're free!"

"I know, so I was thinking, let's not wait until tonight to go out. How do you fancy getting a bit tipsy having a liquid lunch? My treat!"

Tim hesitated. "Aah, well Miranda, that's kind of why I called. I can't make lunch, or this evening either."

"What! Why?"

"Well, because I'm kind of leaving New York in just over half an hour."

"Going where?"

"Los Angeles."

"But you don't have to be there until next week?"

"I know. I'm going by train. Scott organised it, as a vacation. It was all last minute and I said yes forgetting about tonight. I'm sorry."

".........."

"Miranda? Are you pissed?"

"All I can say is you owe me big time when you get back Tim Anderson."

Tim smiled. "Oh I know. Anything you want."

"It's dangerous making promises like that. I have at least two weeks to write a list of things I want."

"Well you'd better get writing then! Although I'm not streaking at anymore baseball games!"

"I'll bear that in mind. Go catch your train."

"Ok, I'm sorry again."

"Yeah, yeah. I'm fine; it's romantic comedy night on the movie channel anyway."

"My god, I am sorry!"

Miranda laughed. "You take care Tim."

"I will. Bye."

Tim placed his phone back in his bag and handed it back over the counter. It was then that he heard a voice say, "Well, well, if it isn't Tim Anderson."

Tim turned around. Who he saw did not particularly fill him with joy.

He replied, "And if it isn't Jessie Rae."

Jessica Rae was a woman of about Tim's age. She had short dark hair and a pretty face that was spoiled by too much make up. Her rather shapeless grey suit masked an attractive figure. Jessica and Tim had met six years ago, after meeting in a bar and discovering mutual interests. They were both young eager wannabe reporters, dreaming of the big time. They had even dated for a while, until Tim realised that he didn't matter in Jessica's life. In fact, nothing mattered in Jessica's life except her career. They split up when they had both gone for the same job, and Jessica had got it, after using some of Tim's writing pieces as her own.

Tim had found that their ideas of journalism differed greatly, but Tim was still amazed at how Jessica would step on anybody to get further ahead. She had even seduced her sister's husband, a lawyer, just to get a story on his firm's dealings with a Hollywood starlet. After they had parted ways, Tim occasionally heard of Jessica's exploits, from the unethical ways she had been promoted, to breaking the law in order to get an exclusive. Jessica had become very successful in her career and was now the number one celebrity expose reporter in New York.

"Don't call me Jessie, you know I hate that." Jessica said as she walked over to him.

Tim folded his arms. He said pointedly, "So Jessie, How's it been?"

"Oh, you know. Very good. But I'm sure you've heard how good."

Tim pulled a blank face. "No, actually I haven't."

Jessica knew what Tim was doing. Whenever they had crossed each other's paths in the last six years, the conversation would always go the same way. Tim subtly trying to antagonize her. She knew he had grown to hate her. But what did he know? He just wrote for a travel magazine. Not in the big money like her.

She changed the subject and asked, "So, going anywhere special? Writing a mundane report for your little magazine?"

"Los Angeles, actually."

"Well, what do you know? So am I." Jessica gave a false sweet smile. "We'll have to do lunch out there."

Tim returned the false smile and replied, "What a great idea. But I don't get there until next week, and I'm really going to be too busy to listen to even five minutes of your bullshit."

Jessica's face dropped. "Next week? What train are you going on?"

Tim replied, "The Trans-Oceanic Express. You?"

"The same."

They both moved slightly closer to each other and said at the same time, "Why are you on that train?"

Tim replied first. "Vacation. You?"

Jessica looked cagey. She questioned, "Vacation?"

Tim said, "Yes. Why? Are you working?"

Jessica paused before saying, "Yes. I'm getting an exclusive."

Tim asked, "On whom? One of the passengers?"

"Yes." Jessica said, gloating now. "Do you not know who you're travelling with? Clarissa Jordan and her new family. I'm getting the exclusive of my career! For a second I thought that you might have been competition. But the shocked look on your face clearly shows me you had no idea."

Tim said, "Really? As in used to be Clarissa Lavelle?! Wow!"

As Jessica pulled her ticket out of her jacket pocket, she said, "Silly me. What was I thinking? How could I possibly have suspected that travel reporter Tim Anderson could comprehend a big assignment like this?"

She continued, "Well it looks like we'll be able to do lunch on the train now. I'm so glad you'll be able to listen to all of my "Bullshit"."

Jessica pulled her sweet smile again before she turned and walked away towards the platforms.

Meanwhile, not that far away, Scott was having a much more pleasant conversation with Daphne Pennington. Well, conversation in so much as Daphne was talking and Scott was listening.

Scott had learnt a lot about Daphne over their coffee. Daphne was originally from Chicago but now lived in both Oxford and Boston. Daphne was a psychiatrist, and ran practices in both countries. She blamed the fact that she was so talkative on her job being one where she had to listen all day.

Scott personally thought on first impressions though, that Daphne would be quite terrifying to get counselling from.

She said, as if reading his thoughts, "You're quite right. People are often surprised to hear I'm a shrink. They find me far too blunt. But that's my approach. You'd be surprised the number of patients that appreciate it when you cut through the crap. My first husband, Bill, couldn't stand the way I always say what I think, regardless of the situation. I told him he should have realised that before he married me. George, the second one, was a lot more like me in that respect. I think that's why we didn't get on. Too similar, you see."

Scott gave a polite nod. He had finished his espresso about five minutes ago and was now in need of a cigarette, nervous that Katherine had still not shown. The laws of New York State prevented him from smoking inside, and while Scott did actually find Daphne's attitude refreshing, the words of her conversation were slowly becoming lost to him. His mind drifted and he found himself scanning the atrium again.

It took Scott several moments to realise Daphne had stopped talking and had actually asked him a question.

He said; "I'm sorry, what?"

Daphne asked again, "I said, so what made you decide to take this vacation?"

Scott recited his cover story. "Well I have quite a hectic job, so I rarely get time off and just thought it would be a nice little trip to do."

"Ooh, what do you do?" asked Daphne with interest.

"I work in Insurance." replied Scott. The interest on Daphne's face fell, as Scott knew it would. It was always very convenient for him as that line was a sure way to end a conversation.

Daphne politely tried to divert the topic. She said, "And you said you're travelling with your friend?"

Scott was about to reply when he saw Tim heading back over to them. He said; "Yes, he's just on his way over now."

As Tim approached the table, Scott said, "Hey Tim, I'd like you to meet Daphne Pennington. She's also taking the train with us. Daphne, Tim Anderson."

Daphne smiled and held out her hand, "It's very nice to meet you."

Tim shook it as he sat down. He said excitedly, "Scott, do you know who's on this train? Clarissa Lavelle! Can you believe it?!"

Daphne said, "I think you'll find her name is Clarissa Jordan now."

Scott looked over Tim's shoulder. He added, "You'll also find that she's walking through the station behind you."

Clarissa Jordan walked through Grand Central Station with a presence that was noticed by many. While wearing dark sunglasses to look inconspicuous, her tight fitting red designer skirt suit with matching heels did little to avert attention from her. It was a typical statement for Clarissa. It was "Look at me, but don't look at me."

She strode purposefully through the station carrying her purse, while her husband Mark and stepdaughter Amy seemed to have been left with the rest of the baggage, wheeling two large trolleys.

Scott, Tim and Daphne sat at their rather secluded table and watched them as they arrived at the entrance down to the track. They observed as Clarissa started complaining to the ticket attendant that there was no one available to pick up their luggage from their car outside. This went on for a matter of minutes before being resolved by Mark who calmed Clarissa down and then sorted out the tickets. The whole time that this was happening, Amy had sat on one of the trolleys, looking extremely bored.

As they watched, Tim said, "She's still in amazing shape isn't she? I remember having a poster of her on my wall when I was fourteen. She'd just been in "Nights of Arabia". I used to have such a thing for her."

Daphne seemed un-impressed; "I expect that amazing body came at an amazing price."

Scott grinned at Daphne's comment. He said "I hear there's a remarkable amount of interest in this new family of hers with the media. The whole thing about her being a stepmother now."

Tim turned back around in his seat to face the other two and said; "Isn't that the truth? Scott, I just bumped into Jessie Rae."

"That piece of work? What did she want?"

"She's only travelling on the Express, to get an exclusive on Clarissa."

Scott gave a look of interest at this before Daphne said; "Well I doubt they're all enjoying it."

Scott looked at her quizzically, "What makes you say that?"

Daphne leaned forward as if the information she had was top secret. She said,

"I travelled down to New York on the same plane as them. I actually sat next to the daughter. Her name's Amy. Nice girl."

"Yes, she seems very nice." said Tim. He did not hide the fact that he was staring at her low cut jumper and snug jeans.

Scott ignored Tim's letching and turned to Daphne, "So, is there any truth to the rumours that they don't get on?"

Daphne shrugged, "They didn't talk to each other the whole time I was in their company, but I'm sure it true."

"What makes you say that?" asked Scott.

"Well" Daphne took another sip of coffee and spoke as if she were in the know. "It's obvious, isn't it? You only have to look at Clarissa to see she's a bitch."

This was not just the opinion of Daphne Pennington that morning. Sat in dark sunglasses herself, not six tables away from Scott and the others, Avril Kennedy spied Clarissa and her family as they made their way towards the Express, waiting at Platform 13.

Avril peered over the top of her sunglasses at Clarissa and said, "Look, there she goes. The poisonous bitch!"

When she received no response, she nudged her husband sat next to her who was showing no interest, reading the paper.

Avril repeated, "I said the bitch has arrived!"

Gerry did not even look up from his paper. He said, "I heard you the first time, my dear. We did know she was travelling on this train, so I fail to see the excitement of her walking through the train station."

Avril looked over angrily, "How can you be this calm?"

Still, Gerry read. He answered, "I can be this calm because there is no need to get angry. Yet."

"Yet! How far does it have to go for you?" Avril said incredulously.

Gerry said, more sternly this time. "I will take it as far as it needs to go."

He checked his watch and added, "And now, we need to go. It's twenty to twelve. We're supposed to board at quarter to."

Avril and Gerry slowly rose from their table and headed towards the train, Avril keeping one eye on Clarissa.

Back at Scott's table, Tim finally turned around as the Jordan family disappeared from sight. He said, "Thank you Scott! This is definitely going to be an interesting vacation now."

Daphne spoke up and said, "Well Gentlemen, I think it's probably time I went and checked in. Will you join me?"

As she rose from the table, Scott replied, "We'll meet you on board. We've just got to go pick up our luggage."

She nodded, "Ok, I'll see you at the reception. It was very nice to meet you both."

Daphne picked up her bag and made her way out of the bar.

Tim leaned over and said, "Just got to pick our luggage up or just got to actually get tickets for the damn thing. Where is Katherine?"

"I know," said Scott anxiously, looking at his watch. "I hadn't planned for her to cut things this finely. Tell you what, you go get the luggage and I'll check at the counter, just in case she left them there and we missed her."

They split up, but as Scott arrived at the information counter he had to wait as a couple had just arrived before him.

The man said, "Anthony Stuart. I'm here to collect tickets for the Trans-Oceanic Express."

The attendant handed him his tickets, and arranged for a porter to collect his luggage. He also reminded the couple that there would be a champagne reception at twelve fifteen in the Lounge Car.

Anthony thanked the attendant and said, "Thank you very much, that sounds great.

Champagne for lunch eh, Caroline?"

Scott looked on as his wife snapped back, "Anthony, I already told you I've got a headache."

As they set off for the train, Scott could still hear Caroline Stuart chastising her husband for not just wanting to settle in their room and unpack, while he continued to say in his jolly mood that he just wanted to meet the other passengers.

Scott was so distracted that he forgot to move forward to the counter. However, while he was watching the Stuarts leave, he saw Katherine running down the steps into the foyer, looking very red faced.

As she jogged up to him, she waved two tickets in the air and said breathlessly, "I've already rung ahead so they should have changed the passenger manifest to your names by now. You have no idea what it took to get these."

As she spoke, Tim arrived from the other direction carrying their cases. He shouted over, "Hey Katherine, you made it. We were starting to get worried."

Katherine handed the tickets to Scott. She said, "I had to persuade an Italian couple to cancel. And it was their honeymoon, and they had saved for two years to go."

Scott was impressed. He asked, "Wow, what did you have to do?"

"I managed to get them tickets on a cruise. And gave them compensation."

Tim looked confused. "What? I don't understand. Why have you gone to all this trouble?"

Katherine looked at Scott to see what answer he would give. Instead he gave one of the tickets to Tim and said, "I just really wanted to take the Express. Tim, can you go on and I'll meet you on the train?"

Tim took the ticket and eyed them both warily. He said, "Ok. See you soon Katherine."

Katherine smiled. "You too Tim."

Once he was out of earshot, Katherine asked, "You're not even telling Tim why you're going?"

Scott said matter of factly, "I knew I'd have to tell him at some point. He's not stupid. He'll already suspect something now. But I thought that to begin with, it would help my cover if he didn't know."

Katherine said apologetically, "Sorry, I shouldn't have opened my big mouth."

"It's OK." Scott smiled, "But please don't tell me this means we have a honeymoon suite?!"

She grinned, "No, don't worry. You won't have to put up with Tim's incessant snoring. It seems Mr Vivaldi had the same problem. Mrs Vivaldi had booked adjoining cabins."

"On their honeymoon? That's not very romantic."

"Lucky for you. Anyway, I'm double parked so I'd better go and it's quarter to twelve so you'd better go too."

Scott looked at his watch and saw she was right. He said, "I'll try and contact you if I can, let you know what's going on. Good luck with Stoltzkin."

"Thanks, good luck to you too. I'll speak soon."

Katherine smiled again quickly before turning and running back up the steps to the entrance. Scott watched her go, feeling slightly uneasy that for the first time since they had started working together, they would not have direct support from the other while both on very important assignments.

Scott walked down the incline to the platform and approached the train, taking a moment to appreciate its grandeur. While most trains in America had the look of large metallic toasters, the Express had a much more traditional wooden design, painted a deep crimson. The train stretched for twelve carriages, connected to a shiny, state of the art locomotive, looking a little out of place at the front of the train. As his eyes followed the train down, he saw a short, quite rounded man in a smart suit waiting by the carriage doors. As he approached, the man gave a large smile and said,

"Welcome onboard the Trans-Oceanic Express. My name is Patrick Lambert and I am here to see that you have the perfect trip with us on board the Express."

"Thank you, my name is Scott Blacklock." replied Scott as he presented his ticket.

Patrick Lambert stepped aside and allowed Scott to step onto the train. He said, "But of course, if you just wait one moment, someone will see you to your cabin."

Scott was about to thank him again when there was the sound of running down the platform and a voice shouting.

"Hey! Hey! Not leaving yet I hope!" shouted Harry Broadside as he dashed down the sloped platform.

Patrick Lambert again gave his large smile and began to give his welcome aboard speech to Harry Broadside, while he, in return, was searching through all his pockets to find his ticket.

Seeing as how no one had materialised to show him to his suite, and Mr Lambert was busy with Harry Broadside, Scott had a look at the map of the train on the wall to his right.

Locomotive (Staff Only)
{
Staff Quarters (Staff Only)
{
Storage Carriage (Staff Only)
{
Kitchen (Staff Only)
{
Dining Carriage
{
Lounge
{
Reception (You are here)
{
Sleeping Carriage 1 (Suites 1, 2)
{
Sleeping Carriage 2 (Suites 3, 4, 5)
{
Sleeping Carriage 3 (Suites 6, 7-8)
{
Sleeping Carriage 4 (The Thistlewood Suites)
{
Observation Carriage
{
Cocktail Bar + Rear Balcony

After studying it with interest, Scott sneaked a look at the passenger manifest that Mr Lambert had left on a small table at the entrance to the carriage.

As he looked down the list of names, Scott was reminded of something Tim had said only twenty minutes earlier; this was going to be a very interesting "vacation".

The Trans-Oceanic Express

New York – Los Angeles
Passenger Manifest

Suite 1 - Dr Daphne Pennington

Suite 2 - Mr Anthony Stuart
           Mrs Caroline Stuart

Suite 3 - Ms Jessica Rae

Suite 4 - Mr Henry Broadside

Suite 5 - Ms Amy Jordan

Suite 6 - Mr Gerry Kennedy
           Mrs Avril Kennedy

Suite 7-8 - Mr Tim Anderson
             Mr Scott Blacklock

Suite 9-10 (Thistlewood Suites) - Mr Mark Jordan
                                    Mrs Clarissa Jordan

The Trans-Oceanic Express

"Good Morning Sir, Welcome aboard the Express. Would you like me to show you to your suite?"

The sound of the soft feminine voice made Scott jump as he quickly put the manifest he had been studying closely back on the table. He turned and looked slightly sheepish as the woman approached.

She was a petite lady in her late twenties, although her uniform white blouse and black knee length skirt did nothing to complement her figure. She had jet black hair and had distinctly Italian features.

"Hello Sir, my name's Rosalie." Hearing her speak a second time, the accent was clearer and confirmed Scott's thoughts.

Scott smiled and said, "Hi, Scott Blacklock."

Rosalie returned the smile and leant past Scott to pick up the manifest. She said,

"Suite 7-8. The adjoining suite to Mr Anderson."

Scott averted embarrassment by going to pick up his bag.

Rosalie stopped him and said, "Oh, don't worry about those. Bradley will bring them to your room. Please, follow me."

As Rosalie headed off to the right to go through to the next carriage, Scott for the first time noticed the decadence of the interior. The entrance carriage might well have been the reception of a plush hotel. A corridor headed off to the left and the foyer was complete with leather armchairs and a reception desk. It was from there that Rosalie picked up a card key and they took a right turn on the way to the next carriage.

Rosalie led him through two carriages, each with a single corridor on the right of the carriage with the suites on the left. Suites 1 and 2 were in the first carriage, 3, 4, and 5 in the next. The panelling of the corridors was burled wood grain in deep cherry and the decor was reminiscent of a style that was fashionable over half a century ago. Scott commented to Rosalie as they walked through at how impressive the train was.

Rosalie said, "Yes, it is lovely. This is the first trip since its last refurbishment."

They arrived in the third carriage and Rosalie led him to the third and last door of the corridor and used the keycard to unlock it. She held the door open and Scott entered to a surprisingly large bedroom with a small double bed in the corner. The fact that the carriages were not that wide was made up for by the length of the suites to still give a spacious atmosphere. There was even a small bathroom in the corner. There was also a wardrobe and a small armchair with a reading desk by the window. In the left wall there was a sliding door which led into Tim's cabin.

Rosalie placed the key card on the table and said, "I hope everything is to your satisfaction. Bradley will be along in just a few moments with your bag. We depart in ten minutes and the champagne reception is at a quarter past twelve. If you need anything, just press the red button on the phone next to your bed."

She smiled and left, closing the door behind her. Scott sat on the bed for a moment. He was just about to inspect the room when the sliding door slid open and Tim appeared, leaning in the doorway with his arms folded. He nodded behind him and said,

"Scott I am very impressed. This is very swanky."

He added with a grin, "However, I can't help but notice that your room is slightly bigger than mine."

Scott got up and looked into Tim's room. Having the central cabin had meant that Tim's room did look slightly squashed. Tim walked over to his bedside table and picked up a brochure. He said, "While I was waiting for you I had a little read. It's quite interesting."

He sat on the bed and began to read in the voice of a cheesy tour rep,

"The Trans-Oceanic Express - See the beautiful country of America from the luxury of the finest travelling experience in the world!

The Trans-Oceanic Express takes you from coast to coast in fantastic style. As the beautiful scenery of America rolls past; you can enjoy the best selection of Manhattan cocktails in the cocktail bar. That is if you're not enjoying the delight of the observation carriage. The observation carriage has panelled glass throughout the walls and ceiling to give a more complete 360 degree view of the wonders of America. With our luxurious seating, it becomes very easy to wile away an afternoon enjoying a drink and maybe watching the sunset. The carriage is even more spectacular at night when, weather permitting, you can star gaze to your hearts content. That is of course if you're not mingling with the other guests in our lounge. The lounge's fine furnishings let you relax and take morning tea or make your pre-dinner drinks a pleasure. We are even licensed for gambling so you can enjoy a friendly game of Poker or Blackjack at our card table. And all this between sampling the finest gourmet fancies, freshly made and prepared by our world class chef, Andreas Russelli. The dining carriage is a place where you can enjoy cuisines from all over the world while absorbing the sumptuous surroundings.

All of your experience is added to by the service of our dedicated staff, who will be happy to help at any hour of the day or night. We have 24 hour room service on board. Please dial 1 on the phone next to your bed."

Scott was about to speak when Tim stopped him. He said,

"Oh no, and there's more!

The Trans-Oceanic Express: A History

The Trans-Oceanic Express is run by Trans-Continent Inc. which was founded in 1988.

Trans-Continent Inc. is a global company that has the reputation for the best luxury travel in the world.

(For information on our other holidays, like the wonder of the Trans-Carribia Dream, "The world's most exclusive yacht", or the equalled pleasure of the Trans-Europia Bullet, please press 3 on your phone.)

The Trans-Oceanic Express was actually the idea of a Scotsman, a man named Angus Thistlewood. Angus Thistlewood was a very skilled designer in the forties. He wanted to make a train that was so luxurious, the passengers were not even aware they were travelling. He meticulously planned and designed the train, but sadly, in 1949, he died shortly after completing the design for his perfect Express. The plans went unnoticed until his grandson, Jake Thistlewood discovered them. Jake Thistlewood, who now lived in America, founded Trans-Continent Inc. with the Trans-Oceanic Express after he had industriously created his Grandfather's dream. To honour him, the most luxurious suites on board, (Sleeping Carriage 4) are named The Angus Thistlewood Suites."

Tim stopped reading and looked up, "Wonder who's staying in those? I bet its Clarissa."

Scott smiled at Tim's perception, recalling what he had seen on the manifest. He had actually started to lose interest in the brochure and was about to say so when Tim continued.

"This year marks the twentieth anniversary of the Express and to celebrate the occasion, the train has undergone its third and most extravagant refurbishment to date. This is so the Express can still exude the charms of the forties, while still secluding the height of modern technology.

The Trans-Oceanic Express only shares its tracks with other trains in the stations of New York and Los Angeles. Jake Thistlewood bought an old disused goods train track that stretched the United States. The only railroads that exceed it in length are the Trans-Siberian railway and the Indian Pacific railway in Australia. He spent time restoring it before the Express's first trip in the summer of 1988. The Express used to take six days to cross America but now does it in four, the train…"

Tim was interrupted by a knock at Scott's door. Scott gladly turned into his room and answered it.

A young man in his early twenties stood at the door. He had dark floppy hair and a big American smile. He said as he picked up Scott's bag.

"Hello. Your luggage Sir."

Scott thanked the porter and tipped him as he placed his bag on the bed. As he closed the door, he heard Tim start from the brochure again and quickly looked in his pockets for his cigarettes.

Further down the train, in the carriage adjacent to the dining carriage, Patrick Lambert stood in the kitchen having a final staff meeting before the train departed.

There was seven staff on board, including Lambert.

As Lambert stood speaking before them, many had to avoid the slightly comical fact that they all dwarfed Lambert's small slightly rotund frame. Stood towards the door of the staff carriage, the two drivers, Henry Stephenson and Robert Dunn lurked behind the others. They didn't much care for Lambert. Their part of the job had nothing to do with the fancy facade that Lambert performed day and night, playing the inviting host. And this prep talk of his was falling on deaf ears as far as they were concerned. However Lambert never confronted either of them. Their jobs were too pivotal to the smooth running of his train. Stephenson was also the Signalman, while Dunn was the Chief Maintenance Engineer on board.

Stood in front of them, listening more intently were Rosalie Gobetti and Thomas Seymour. Due to the amount of staff on board, all of them had several jobs.

Rosalie was a waitress but also had chambermaid duties. While Rosalie stood next to Thomas, her dark skin highlighted the fact that Thomas Seymour was a very pale young man. He had a slight frame and his shirt looked too big for him. Thomas Seymour was a waiter, but was also a kitchen porter who assisted Andreas Russelli.

The head chef stood away from the others, behind his work counter. He had decided that he was not going to stand to attention, and so was putting the finishing touches to his canapés for the reception. As Lambert was about to begin, he realised someone was missing.

Bradley Hawkins entered the kitchen and gave his trademark grin. Bradley was the head barman and had an established career working in the top cocktail bars around the world. His talents did not end there, as he was also a classically trained pianist. However this did not mean that he escaped from porter duties.

As well as all their jobs, apart from the drivers, the others all worked shifts on room service. This was a job that Lambert didn't escape either, much to the amusement of the drivers. It was always a pain to have the graveyard shift on room service. And it was always the way that the guests who spent the most on their travel, wanted the most ludicrous things at the most ridiculous time in the morning.

Lambert turned and said, "Ah Bradley, hurry up."

He continued as Bradley leaned against the counter next to Rosalie.

"Now as I was saying, as this is the company's Anniversary trip, these guests are expecting the very best treatment. And with the profiles of some of our guests, I want them to have the best service possible. Now you all know what you have to do. Bradley, is the bar in the lounge ready?"

Bradley grinned, "Champagne at the ready Boss."

Lambert preferred being called Sir and Bradley knew it. He chose to ignore it and turned to Andreas. He asked, "Everything ready Andreas?"

Andreas didn't look up and grunted, "Of course it is."

Lambert looked to Thomas Seymour, someone who wouldn't question his authority.

"Right Thomas, help Andreas here with lunch. Rosalie, you can help Bradley in the lounge." He tapped his watch and said, "And Drivers, noon is approaching. I think it's time. Meeting dismissed."

Henry Stephenson and Robert Dunn headed to the engine. As they walked, Dunn mimicked Lambert's tap watching and "Meeting Dismissed". Stephenson laughed loudly, and then added several expletives for him.

Meanwhile, Lambert had left Bradley and Rosalie waiting in the lounge and had headed to the reception to show his guests through. As he arrived at the desk, he waited for "Curtain up" as he liked to call it. His stomach flipped in excitement as he felt the initial screech of the wheels and a jolt of movement as the Trans-Oceanic Express pulled slowly out of Grand Central Station.

Champagne reception

Scott stood in the corridor of his carriage and looked out the window as the train headed through the northern suburbs of New York. The motion of the train had only just got going when they had stopped and realigned the Express onto the Trans-Oceanic track. While he stood waiting for Tim, he envied how his friend was here merely to enjoy himself. Scott on the other hand, was just about to go to work.

The sound of a door opening made him turn. As Tim came out of his cabin, Scott tried to hide the look on his face when he saw that Tim had still not changed his clothes. They walked through the carriages and didn't come across anyone until they encountered Patrick Lambert for the second time. Stood with his podgy hands in the pockets of his finely tailored waistcoat and his small pince-nez perched on his nose, he certainly did look the part.

To the point of excess, Scott thought as he approached and offered his hand.

"Welcome Mr Blacklock. Mr Anderson. I take it your suites are to your liking?"

As he shook hands with both of them, Scott replied, "Superb, thank you. Surprisingly spacious."

Lambert smiled as though this was the first thing every guest said to him. He replied,

"You've certainly picked the perfect time to travel with the Express. She's never looked better. But please, let me show you to the lounge."

He showed them past the reception counter and gestured to the carriage beyond.

The lounge was long and elegant and the fine mahogany furniture was complemented by brown leather chairs and dark green walls. There were two armchairs to the right of the entrance and a low settee with a coffee table to the left. Beyond that was a card table and beyond that, more settees. At the other end of the carriage to the right, was a rather grand bar, with several stools around it.

Tim and Scott were the first guests to arrive as the carriage was empty, save for Bradley and Rosalie standing at the bar, ready with a tray of champagne flutes. Lambert gestured to them and said, "Rosalie and Bradley will look after you. If you'll excuse me."

They watched Lambert return to the reception, and were slightly startled to turn back around to see Rosalie standing next to them, having effortlessly crossed the carriage with her tray, both quickly and silently.

"Champagne?" she offered with a smile.

They took a flute each and headed to the settee opposite the card table. As they sat down, Tim took a long swig of his champagne and asked,

"Is this the plan until L.A then? Sit down and drink all day?"

Scott replied sardonically. "Pretty much. That's why I thought it would be perfect for you!"

Tim finished his drink and said, "There's another thing I wanted to ask you. What was that whole deal with Katherine at the station? My love of a good drink surely can't be the reason you tried so hard to get on this train. And the fact that Katherine got them for you makes me think you're on a job."

Scott tried to act like he had not just been caught, but wasn't sure if his face gave him away or not. He was able to avert Tim's eyes by the distraction of Lambert entering with a couple. As they followed Lambert, the man's dark grey suit seemed incredibly dull next to the lady's red and black patterned trouser suit.

Scott and Tim stood up as Lambert brought them over.

"Mr Blacklock, Mr Anderson, allow me to introduce you to Mr and Mrs Kennedy."

Scott and Tim shook hands with them both. Avril Kennedy smiled and said in her heavy New York accent, "Well if it isn't nice to have some fresh blood at one of these affairs!"

Scott and Tim glanced at each other, uncertain of quite what exactly Mrs Kennedy was implying. This didn't go unnoticed by Avril.

She continued, "Oh no, what I meant was that Gerry and I find that we always end up travelling in the same social circles. So what do you two do?"

Tim answered first. "I'm a travel reporter. I write for Travel Today. I'm also a photographer."

Avril replied, eyeing Tim's garments. "Ah well that would explain the.....attire."

Gerry tried to overshadow his wife's bluntness by interjecting, "And you, Mr Blacklock?"

Scott gave his standard response, "I work in Insurance, in the Financial District."

Avril gave a smile and didn't try to hide the sympathy in it, "That's nice. I'm sure it must be very interesting for you."

"Yes, it is." Scott replied, aware of the irony that his "interesting" job meant that he already knew a fair bit about Avril and Gerry Kennedy. A fact that made him keen to start asking them some questions.

This wasn't the opportunity though as the arrival of Daphne Pennington stopped him. She walked over, still dressed in her black suit, but her red hair that had been tied up before, was now down in an elegant bob.

Introductions were done again with the Kennedys and Daphne.

Daphne and Avril struck up a conversation about their outfits. Rosalie offered them all champagne, and the ladies sat down together, quickly in deep conversation. Rosalie turned to Gerry who stiffened and paled in the face before shaking his head at the offered champagne. As she walked away, Gerry leaned over to Scott and said, "Fancy getting something better than this bubbly crap at the bar?"

Scott obliged and turned to see if Tim was going to join them, but he had headed to the end of the carriage, where Amy Jordan had just walked in. She had changed into a small summer dress, and as she stood there, looking around the lounge, her pose did nothing to disguise her youthful toned body.

Scott knowing all too well what Tim was like, decided to keep one eye on him as he took a bar stool next to Gerry Kennedy.

Bradley stepped forward and gave his big smile.

"Welcome Gentlemen. Bradley Hawkins at your service. What can I get you?"

Scott recognised him as the man who had brought him his luggage. He said, "A man of all trades. Impressive service on this train."

Bradley smiled and said, "Ah, but my true talent lies behind the bar. Any drink in the world, just ask."

Gerry grunted and said, "Scotch on the rocks for me."

Bradley maintained his smile and looked to Scott. "Some kind of fruit juice, surprise me!"

Amy stood hesitantly at the entrance, realising her father was not there yet. Tim approached with a wide smile and said,

"Hi, my name's Tim. Tim Anderson. Thank God! Someone else in their twenties! For a minute, I thought this was going to be a very boring trip!"

Amy returned the smile and said, "Are you implying that I'm going to make this journey interesting for you?"

Tim grinned. "Maybe."

"And what makes you think that?"

"Well you don't strike me as the type of person who only talks about who the latest "Nouveau Riche" is, or want to have an endless debate about the justice system or foreign policies of this country over cigars and brandy!"

Amy folded her arms and said, "I happen to be studying Law at the moment."

Tim's face reddened. Amy smirked and said, "And I have been known to puff on the odd Cuban!"

Tim smiled when he realised she was joking.

He decided to play back, "You are talking about a cigar?!"

Amy mouth opened in shock and then she giggled. She said, "You're very rude Mr Anderson!"

He replied, "I prefer the word cheeky."

He then pointed a finger in the direction of the Kennedys, "But don't you think that I'd be better company than them?"

Amy's smile widened and she said, "Maybe."

She finally offered her hand, "My name's Amy."

"Nice to meet you Amy. It's Amy Jordan isn't it?"

Amy's grin dropped slightly, "How did you know that?"

"I saw you at the station with Clarissa Jordan. Are you her step daughter?"

Amy's smile now completely vanished. She said, "Oh please, don't tell me you're another Clarissa fanatic? Do you know how many of them I've had to put up with since my father married her?"

Tim asked flirtatiously, "Well they can't outnumber the Amy fanatics surely?"

Amy's smile returned.

"My God! What kind of a line is that?!"

Jessica Rae spoke rather loudly as she walked into the lounge. She was still wearing her ill fitting grey suit, but had changed her shirt for a low cut top. Her short dark hair looked sleeker than in the station, but her make up was just as heavy. As she moved over to them, she asked, "Timmy, aren't you going to introduce us?"

Tim didn't hide the look he gave Jessica before saying, "Amy, this is Jessie Rae. Jessie, Amy Jordan."

As she shook hands with Amy, she smiled and corrected Tim. "It's Jessica. Very nice to meet you Amy."

Jessica removed a packet of cigarettes from her purse. She lit up and said to Tim, "Now Tim, why don't you go and get us girls some drinks while we get acquainted?"

As she spoke, she moved to link arms with Amy and head to the armchairs.

Tim started to object but stopped at the arrival of Lambert.

He came jogging from Reception with a pained, embarrassed look on his face.

Lambert gently tapped Jessica on the arm and explained to her that smoking was only permitted on the balcony at the back of the train. As Jessica entered into a conversation with Lambert about the laws of smoking, Tim took his opportune moment to show Amy to the two armchairs, taking two glasses of champagne from Rosalie's tray as they slid behind Lambert.

Scott who had been watching out of the corner of his eye, now smiled in amusement as he watched Lambert ushering Jessica out, grumbling loudly about her rights.

Bradley placed his and Gerry's drinks down and moved to a discreet distance at the end of the bar. Another aspect of the Express's service was the discretion of the staff. Too often, sensitive information of the high profile guests could be overheard, and it was always expected to fall on deaf ears. Trans-Continent made all of their staff sign confidentiality agreements before working for them. In any event of a scandal where an employee was the source, it would mean that not only would they be fired, and most likely sued by the said guest, they would also be sued by Trans-Continent. It was the company's way of protecting themselves from any previous employees.

Gerry nodded to the women talking and finally spoke, "My wife has the incessant ability to talk to anyone she meets about fashion. Personally, it's all a bit lost on me."

Scott looked over and saw that Daphne Pennington had actually been stopped from speaking by Avril Kennedy. Although he already knew the answer, he asked, "Does your wife work in fashion?"

"No, she's just obsessed with it. Like most women in New York who can afford it."

"Or husbands that can afford it." Scott observed from Gerry's tone.

Gerry grunted, "Too true. We run a business together. But you wouldn't believe some of the items I find on our business account receipts!"

Gerry Kennedy's attitude may have seemed like that of a grouch, but Scott felt that he had a deep affection for his wife as he looked at her.

Scott sipped his juice and then asked, "So what avenue of business are you in Mr Kennedy, if I may ask?"

Gerry took his time in answering, "My wife and I own Moonshine and Starlight productions. I'm sure you may have heard of it?"

Scott had, and not just from reading Peterson's dossier. Moonshine and Starlight productions had been one of the biggest companies of the last thirty years, originally producing Broadway shows. They had also been big in Hollywood for the last twenty years, where the Kennedys had branched into film. Their movie career had started promisingly with the well received thrillers Wishing Well and Hopeless, followed by the hugely successful historical romance Winter of Passion. However, reviews of recent flops such as "the ill conceived" horror Crying Mirror and the "poorly plotted" drama No Return had left their reputation in Hollywood in the balance. The newspapers had read: "It seems there really could be "No Return" for Moonshine and Starlight". In the last few years, they had shifted their focus back to Broadway, where their success seemed to have been returning, until recently.

Scott replied with an impressed tone, "Really? I've seen a couple of your films. And I took my mother to see "When the morning comes" on Broadway two years ago."

Gerry showed a small amount of pride, "I'm glad you enjoyed some of our work."

Scott added, "I remember my mother was so excited to see it. She couldn't wait to see Clarissa Lavelle perform."

Gerry tried to hide his discomfort at Scott's mention of that name by shifting on his stool, but not enough that Scott missed it.

He continued, "I hear she's on this train. Is she travelling with you then?"

Gerry replied, "If she is on this train, its news to me."

Abruptly he stood up. "I expect I will say hello to her then if that is the case. If you'll excuse me, there's only so long a man can leave his wife unattended without being reprimanded."

Scott watched him return to his wife and murmured to himself, "I don't imagine your leash is always that tight."

Scott observed him for a second more before draining the contents of his glass and asking Bradley for another.

"Not on the champagne then Mr Blacklock?" said a woman's voice.

Scott turned on his stool to see Daphne Pennington take the seat that Gerry had just vacated.

He replied, "I try not to drink before lunchtime as a general rule."

Daphne smiled as she smoothed her auburn hair and adjusted her jacket. She giggled, "Oh I know. I finished that champagne a little too quickly. And the bubbles always go straight to my head!" She pointed to his glass. "I see you're on juice. Good Idea! Bradley dear, serve me up one of those!"

Bradley nodded obligingly. Daphne paused for a second. "Oh, chuck vodka on top then!"

She turned to Scott and laughed. "Well, I am on vacation!"

Scott returned the smile. While Daphne seemed like she could be a lot to deal with for long periods, Scott couldn't help but find her happy enthusiasm pleasant after talking to Gerry.

They sat facing each other which meant that they could see the others further down the carriage. Tim was talking animatedly to Amy in the armchairs in the corner, while the Kennedys were talking at a much lower level on the settee.

Daphne indicated to the Kennedys and said, "They seem like a nice couple. She's such a darling. Mind you, he wasn't overly friendly. Did you find that?"

Scott answered. "Just a tad."

Their attention was averted by new arrivals at the door to the lounge, Lambert showing in Anthony and Caroline Stuart. Anthony had changed into a suit, but wore his shirt open, without a tie, as if to show off his pectoral muscles. His relaxed appearance looked at odds next to his wife's prim brown dress.

They smiled as they passed Tim and Amy and then Avril introduced herself to them, speaking very much to Anthony and his attractive face. Anthony greeted her enthusiastically while Caroline stood behind him and smiled meekly.

Daphne and Scott watched them as they talked. Daphne noted, "The poor love seems a bit intimidated by all this."

Anthony excused themselves from the Kennedys when Rosalie appeared and offered champagne. Anthony thanked her while Caroline asked for a lime and soda water.

Anthony moved over to Scott and Daphne and extended his hand,

"Anthony Stuart. Nice to meet you." He said as he shook both their hands.

"Scott Blacklock. Nice to meet you too."

"And my name's Daphne Pennington. A pleasure to meet you." Daphne said smiling, as she held onto Anthony's hand for a moment too long.

Anthony turned slightly and said, "And this is my wife Caroline."

Caroline stepped forward and smiled. "Hello."

After a moment of silence, Anthony said, "I must say this is a mighty fine train, isn't it? We've been looking forward to this trip for ages. Caroline's been so excited, haven't you?"

Caroline nodded by way of response.

Anthony continued, "This is the first time Caroline's been anywhere further than Massachusetts. We live near Boston. I think she found New York a bit awe inspiring, didn't you?"

Caroline answered, "It is a lovely city."

Daphne agreed. "I couldn't agree more. I love New York. And you're from Boston! Such a nice surprise! Me too!"

Anthony raised an eyebrow. "Oh?"

"Yes. I have a practice there. I also have one near Oxford in England. So I split my time between the two. I go through phases. Sometimes I like living over here, and sometimes you just need to get away to England's countryside."

Anthony said, "Sounds lovely to have the choice. I'd like to go to England, but poor Caroline here doesn't much like flying. She says the flights are too long. She gets these terrible migraines and then you never hear the end of it!"

"Anthony!" Caroline whispered in a harsh manner.

There was an awkward silence and neither Daphne nor Scott knew where to look. The moment was broken by Rosalie walking over with Caroline's drink.

Anthony said, "It was nice to meet you both. We look forward to talking more on this fine journey. If you'll excuse us."

They both smiled politely as he led Caroline to the settees at the far end of the lounge.

Daphne leant over to Scott and said, "She reminds me of my first husband. Can't take the smallest of jokes!"

As her eyes followed Anthony briefly, she took a sip from her drink and added, "He, on the other hand, could be fun!"

Scott didn't pay attention to Daphne's last comment as he was watching the new arrival. Jessica Rae returned to the lounge, her hair now slightly windswept from standing on the outside balcony. She chose to ignore Tim who was still deep in conversation with Amy, having cleverly chosen a position in the room that meant no one could sit and join them. Instead, she turned and headed for Scott. As she approached, she said in her usual sarcastic voice, "Scott Blacklock, It's been far too long. How are you?"

Scott had as much reason to dislike Jessica as Tim did. Aside from how she had treated Tim, he was also all too aware of what type of person Jessica Rae was. Katherine Fowley's cousin James Garland had worked at the same magazine as Jessica. He was caught with drugs in his office and subsequently lost his job, despite denying all knowledge. Katherine firmly believed that her cousin had been set up as he never touched drugs. This was an opinion that Scott agreed with. Although they couldn't prove it, they were sure Jessica had been behind it, especially as she had been promoted into his position soon after.

Scott replied with forced politeness. "I'm fine thanks, Jessica. This is Daphne Pennington."

Jessica gave an insincere smile. "Hello."

Scott asked, "Jessica, what a funny place to bump into you! What on earth are you doing here?"

Jessica retorted, "Vacationing for all you care." She gestured behind her. "But I'm sure your friend told you why I'm here. Excuse me."

She moved around the bar and said, "Oi Bartender! A nicely chilled sauvignon blanc."

Scott didn't see Bradley hide a look of annoyance at Jessica's rudeness as he saw Lambert showing Harry Broadside through to the lounge. Harry stood there, dressed casually, wearing the same pleasant yet slightly blank look on his face. His stance mimicked that of Amy Jordan when she had entered. He was obviously looking for somebody he knew.

Daphne looked up from her drink to eye up the new arrival. She said to Scott,

"Any idea who that is?"

Jessica, stood on the other side of Scott, turned around to look and exclaimed,

"My, My! Look what the cat's dragged in! Why on earth is he here? This is fantastic! My story just got a whole lot better!"

Harry Broadside finally eyed the Stuarts in the far corner of the carriage and decided to head over to them. As he approached the three sat at the bar, Jessica made to intercept him.

She said to Scott. "I feel I must introduce myself."

Scott put a hand on her arm and said, "You know Jessica, not everyone is here to be a part of your story. Maybe you should just let him enjoy his holiday."

Jessica pulled her arm away, by which time Harry had passed them and was now talking to the Stuarts.

She turned to Scott and said, "You're not going to stop me from talking to people Scott. You can't keep an eye on me for the entire journey."

She picked up her glass and strode down to the top end of the carriage and took a seat by herself at the door leading to the Reception.

Daphne's face showed a look of confusion. She asked, "What was all that about? Who is that Jessica? And who is that man?"

Scott paused before saying, "I think you'll probably be finding out in a moment."

It was then that Lambert showed the final guests through. Clarissa Jordan walked through in a figure hugging red dress and heels, evidently wanting to be the last to arrive and to make the biggest impression. Mark Jordan followed dutifully behind.

Scott and Daphne watched from the bar as Lambert fussed around Clarissa, talking about the luxury of the train and what a privilege it was to have her on board.

Daphne whispered. "Lambert's such an ass licker, isn't he?"

Scott chuckled in response.

As Clarissa made her way down the carriage, Amy and Tim stood up. Amy introduced Tim to her father. Clarissa, however, showed no interest and continued through the carriage.

"Clarissa darling, what a wonderful surprise! How are you?"

This sudden and rather loud exclamation had come from Avril Kennedy, who stood up and gave Clarissa an air kiss on both cheeks. Clarissa's immediate look of shock was quickly hidden behind a face very used to acting.

She looked Avril up and down before saying, "Avril sweetheart, this is a surprise! And don't you look.....nice. I did see that suit somewhere on Fifth Avenue. Last Season. I thought it was a bit too garish for me to pull it off. But you do it perfectly."

Avril gave a forced smile in return. Gerry rose from his seat and spoke,

"Clarissa, it's lovely to see you. You're looking divine, as always."

Clarissa smiled sweetly, "Thank you Gerry. How are you both doing? I haven't seen any of your films out recently? And how's the show going now?"

Avril and Gerry both showed obvious signs of awkwardness at the questions. Gerry coughed and said, "It's good. But, actually Clarissa, it's a stroke of luck that we bumped into you. Do you think that I could steal five minutes of your time at some point?"

Clarissa rolled her eyes. "Look Gerry, I can see where this is going. I left for a reason.

I am on vacation with my husband. Anything you want to say can be said to my manager."

As she said this, Mark walked over to meet them. She briefly hugged her husband's arm. "Avril. Gerry. This is my husband, Mark Jordan."

Mark shook hands with them. As brief pleasantries were exchanged, Clarissa turned and looked around the carriage. Her eyes fell on the group at the end of the lounge. Her gaze stopped on Anthony Stuart who was sat facing her. She watched him as a small curl came to the side of her mouth. He looked up and their eyes met. It was then that Harry Broadside, who had been facing Anthony, turned around.

Clarissa's mouth dropped for a second, and then gave a look of indignation. If Harry saw her expression, he chose to ignore it as he stood and walked over to her, smiling.

He said, "Clarissa, what a surprise! Wow! You look fantastic."

Clarissa put a hand on her hip and shot Avril and Gerry a look before saying, "Well, it seems to be my day for these "surprises"! What are you doing here Harry?"

Harry smiled and said, "I'm on vacation. You look more gorgeous than ever Clarissa!"

Mark Jordan stepped forward sternly and extended his hand. "Mark Jordan. Clarissa's husband. Mr.....?"

Harry shook his hand. "Broadside. Excuse me, Mr Jordan."

Harry linked his arm with Clarissa's and started to move her away. He said in a quieter voice. "Clarissa, I know this might not be an appropriate time but I think we should have a talk."

Clarissa pulled her arm away and stepped back next to Mark. "You're right Harry. It isn't an appropriate time so forget it. I'm here with my family. So leave me alone."

She turned away from Harry and took Mark's arm, drawing him away from the Kennedys.

She paused and looked around before saying in a louder voice, "And what does it take to get a fucking drink around here?!"

The silence that followed Clarissa's outburst highlighted painfully how everybody in the carriage had been listening to their conversation. Scott and Daphne rather obviously tried to invent a talking point, as did Amy and Tim. Gerry and Avril sat back down quietly on the settee. While Rosalie rushed over to serve Mark and Clarissa with drinks, Harry turned and marched to the end of the bar.

Clarissa and Mark sat on the central settee and the carriage remained in silence. Lambert decided now was the moment to give his welcome speech and moved forward, making a little cough before speaking.

"Ladies and Gentlemen. It is my great pleasure to welcome you aboard the Trans-Oceanic Express. I hope that you have all settled into your luxurious suites."

Lambert's enthusiasm fell short of breaking the atmosphere in the room. Undeterred, he continued,

"This is a very special trip for the Trans-Oceanic Express as it marks the twentieth anniversary of this train. And for this landmark, the Express has had its most fantastic refurbishment to date. To mark the occasion, we have prepared a special anniversary dinner tomorrow evening. And now, I will tell you a little about our route. We are now heading towards upstate New York, before we turn west and head through Pennsylvania. By this evening, we'll be passing through Ohio. Through the night, we will pass Indiana and into Illinois. After that it's the flat plains of Iowa as we have a superb Sunday lunch. All of our exquisite cuisine is prepared and cooked by our award winning chef, Andreas Russelli. Then it's on through Nebraska into the beautiful ruggedness of Colorado and the Rockies. We then travel through Utah and the stunning deserts of Nevada, before passing the bright lights of Las Vegas and entering into California where we should roll into Los Angeles at about lunchtime on Tuesday. All of the country's wonderful scenery can be best seen from the observation carriage, which is found towards the rear of the train, just beyond your suites. It is virtually all glass panelled and the views are always second to none, as I'm sure you'll all soon agree with me."

Lambert chuckled in spite of the fact that most of the passengers seemed quite obviously bored. He continued,

"If you require any information about any of the places we will be travelling through, there are information brochures situated around the train, or just press 50 on your room phone. Or you can always seek me out, as I am more than happy to tell you all you need to know."

Tim whispered to Amy, "Sounds like a barrel of laughs!" and she giggled, rather too loudly. Lambert adjusted his pince-nez at the interruption. He clapped his hands.

" Right well I'm sure you're all fancying a little nibble, so if you'd like to head through to the dining carriage, Andreas has put on a fine luncheon for you all."

Nearly all the passengers stood up immediately, pleased at the thought of food and Lambert not talking anymore.

The other guests filed through to the dining carriage as Daphne said discreetly, "So, come on, who is this Harry Broadside?"

Scott checked to see that Harry had left the bar before saying, "Clarissa's last ex-husband."

Daphne and Scott got down off of their stools as she said, "Well, since my first trip, Lambert certainly hasn't become any less of an ass!"

As she buttoned her jacket, she finished, "But the level of gossip this time is off the scale in terms of my expectations!"

Scott followed Daphne through to the dining carriage, and couldn't help thinking how right she was.

Observations carriage

The clear blue sky over the green countryside of Pennsylvania was pleasing to the eye as Scott looked out the floor to ceiling window of the observation carriage. The gentle valleys and sloping trees reminded him of the countryside of England. Lambert's boast about the observation carriage had not been untrue, as it did feel as though you were sat in a travelling greenhouse. The tinted windows gave the carriage a warm, relaxed feeling. The time was approaching three in the afternoon and Scott sat with a cup of tea, feeling amply fed from lunch.

Moving to the dining carriage had eased the uncomfortable atmosphere of the champagne reception somewhat. Scott had sat with Daphne and had been regaled of the story of her first visit to New York when she was seventeen, and how she had been arrested for her participation in a rally that had gotten out of hand. After everyone had suitably had their fill from the "Smorgasbord of culinary delights" (Lambert's words), the passengers had dispersed throughout the train.

Clarissa and Mark had returned to their suite, as had Caroline Stuart. Anthony Stuart had stayed in the lounge, having a drink at the bar with Harry Broadside. Jessica Rae was nowhere to be seen. Probably in her room writing up her notes, thought Scott.

Scott sat back in the comfortable armchair in the corner of the carriage. From his position he could see the Kennedys at the opposite end, on one of the settees that looked out at the view. Gerry was leant back and looked like he could have been sleeping. Avril was leant forward, looking at a magazine on the coffee table in front of her.

Sat opposite Scott, drinking a long island ice tea and reading the newspaper was Tim, who had chosen to sit with Amy Jordan during lunch. Scott stared out at the passing trees, and was roused from his thoughts by the feeling of someone watching him. He turned to see that Tim had put down his paper and was looking at him expectantly.

Scott asked, "What?"

Tim said, "I think it's time you and me had a little chat."

"About what?"

"About why we're on this train."

Scott returned to looking out of the window. He said, "I don't know what you're talking about."

"Scott, I hate to say it, but when it comes to me, you're a shit liar! I wasn't born yesterday. Katherine getting us the tickets. The phone call from Dan Povey last night. The atmosphere on this train, and that was just at the reception!"

Scott turned to face him, sighed and said, "I knew I would have to tell you at some point."

He moved to sit closer to Tim. He started,

"On Thursday I got a call from Peterson with a new assignment. It was an assignment to carry out surveillance on Clarissa Jordan. Clarissa has her estate and assets insured through Zirconia, including the famous Warwick black diamond, which she had embedded into a choker. The diamond alone is insured at thirty five million."

"Thirty five million?!!" exclaimed Tim loudly.

Scott said quietly, "It's a very big diamond, and rare. It could make very expensive jewellery with even the smallest fragment from it."

"Ok, but why the need for surveillance?" Tim asked.

"Just over a month ago, Clarissa received a threatening letter. It came by post to her New York residence. It came on a Saturday. She's received one every Saturday for the last four weeks."

"What kind of threats?"

"The notes were made from letters cut from magazines. They claimed in no specific terms that Clarissa had wronged them. That what was most precious to her would be taken away from her. It was only in the last note that the Black Diamond was mentioned specifically. The writer claimed they wanted to rip the diamond from her neck."

"Letters cut from a magazine?! Not very original!" said Tim, to which Scott nodded in agreement.

Scott replied, "I know. That part has been bugging me. It's almost like the perpetrator is making a joke with the obvious cliché. Or has no imagination!"

Tim asked, "So, are you saying we're here because you think the person who sent these notes is on this train?"

Scott paused. "I don't know. I was only trying to stay close to her. But the arrival of so many unexpected guests connected with Clarissa speaks volumes. But now I've told you this, I want you to...."

They were interrupted by the arrival of Amy Jordan. Tim looked up and smiled, "Hey Amy. Amy, I don't think you've met my friend Scott yet."

Scott smiled and shook her hand. "Hi."

Amy asked, "Can I join you? I'm not interrupting anything?"

Tim looked at Scott and then back to Amy, "Take a seat. Scott was just telling me about his week at work. Boring stuff! Scott works in Insurance. Really, you're rescuing me!"

Scott moved back to his seat to allow Amy to sit down. He said, "Thank you Tim. What a great first impression you give of me!"

The tone was sarcastic, but the thank you was genuine. Tim was usually reliable when it came to matters of discretion, but Scott knew that he would still use this information to make inside jokes.

As Amy sat down, she said, "Don't worry, Scott. I'm sure the work you do is very interesting."

Tim said, grinning, "Sometimes you'd be surprised how interesting!"

Scott threw Tim a look and changed the subject, asking Amy, "How are you enjoying the Express so far?"

As she got comfortable in her seat, she pushed her hair behind her ear and said rather quickly, "Oh my God! You have no idea what it's like to have other company! We only got back to New York yesterday after a week in Greece. Which would have been nice, except Clarissa hired a yacht for privacy, so I had to spend a week with my father and her! Fawning all over each other most of the time! So while I usually find train journeys tedious, this one is a welcome relief!"

Scott asked, "What do you do? You seem to have a good deal of time off!"

Amy smiled. "I'm a student. I'm studying at Harvard. It's funny, I know that Anthony Stuart guy. He's a lecturer there. He doesn't seem to have recognised me, but then there are a lot of students! I've seen him around campus, my roommate used to have such a crush on him. Not my type though!"

She finished the sentence with a little flash of the eyes towards Tim.

"What are you studying there?" asked Scott, noticing the subtle hint, even if Tim didn't.

"Family Law. I'm going into my final year the week after next. I'm really not looking forward to it!" she said with a little laugh.

Tim said, "At least you're having one hell of a summer trip! You seem to travel more than I do, and I'm a travel reporter!"

Amy replied, "It would seem that way, but my idea of a fun summer is not spending it with Clarissa. Greece was me acting the dutiful daughter, pretending that I like her. Plus it is nice to spend time with my dad. Not that I get much when she's around."

Scott asked, "Why are you taking this trip with them then?"

"I was going to be staying with a friend in L.A for the end of summer break anyway. I was going to fly over, but Dad wanted me to come with them. And this is the only two weeks I'll probably see him before Thanksgiving."

Scott sat back and probed cautiously, "So you and Clarissa don't see eye to eye?"

Amy spoke with surprising contempt, "Clarissa and everything about her detests me. I can deal with the way she speaks to me, because I can see that she's jealous of me. She wishes she could be my age again. Or at least look this young without surgery!"

She spoke, not as though she thought a lot of herself, but as if she had just stated a proven fact. She continued, "But the way she treats my father sometimes. And he just takes it."

Scott noticed Amy clench her fist slightly. "Because he, like so many other men, is wrapped up in the wonder that is Clarissa."

Scott had been taken aback by her volatile response, and hoped that Jessica Rae wasn't lurking around any corners, taking notes. He observed the young woman in front of him and wondered who out of Clarissa or Amy felt more jealous and threatened.

Amy seemed to suddenly shake her anger off and said, "Listen to me, I must sound like just as big a bitch!"

Tim smiled and put his arm along the back of the settee, "I don't know. You seem like a pretty nice bitch to me!"

Amy smiled back, and said, "Well seeing as how I thought you were a dick when we first met, you're actually quite an amusing dick!"

As they were laughing, Thomas Seymour entered the carriage, looking his usual pasty colour. He said, "Excuse me, can I get you any refreshments?"

Amy sat up excitedly, "Ooh, yes please. Tim's cocktail is looking really good. I'll have one of those."

Tim added, "I'll have another one too please."

Scott raised an eyebrow at Tim, who still had over half his current drink left.

Tim added, "What? This way the kind gentleman won't have to make two trips!"

Thomas gave a nervous laugh, people skills were not his greatest asset. He asked Scott, "And for you Sir?"

Tim answered for him, "Yes he'll have a drink. One for him too."

Scott interjected, "If you're determined for me to drink something alcoholic, I'd prefer a vodka and grapefruit juice."

"Certainly Sir." Thomas said.

"Make it a double!" shouted Tim to Thomas as he left the carriage.

Amy said, "So anyway, happier topics than Clarissa. You two are fellow New Yorkers. Born and bred?"

Scott answered, "No, I was born in England, I moved to New York when I was a teenager. I then went back to England for a few years to study but have now lived in New York since I graduated."

"Wow, quite a trans-Atlantic traveller." She turned to Tim, "What about you?"

"I come from Syracuse. My family moved to the Big Apple when I was ten. They moved back up there after ten years, but I was addicted to the city by then!"

Amy said, "Syracuse? Really? My mother's family is from there. My mom was born there."

Scott asked, "Does she still live there?"

"No. My mother died when I was nine. My mom had moved to New York and married my dad by the time I was born. She's buried there now though. I always visit on her birthday. It's in the spring, and it always looks so beautiful there."

Tim said, "I'm sorry to hear about your mother. I'd just assumed your parents were divorced."

Amy replied, "Its ok. It's been a long time without her. And I'd say I've coped better with it than my father did. He just threw himself into his work. Until Clarissa came along. She's been the first proper relationship since my mother died. I suppose she must bring him some happiness, so for that I'm grateful. But I'm also grateful that I live in Boston at the moment."

"Do you prefer Boston to New York in general then, or is it the distance from Clarissa you like?" Tim asked.

"Oh, I do like Boston, and the Harvard campus is wonderful, but my heart is in New York."

Amy's mention of the Harvard campus again triggered an old news story in Scott's head. He asked, "Wasn't there a murder at the Harvard campus a couple of years ago?"

Amy said excitedly, "Yes, it happened in the November of my first year. Emma Jones, I think her name was. I didn't know the girl. She was a senior, but my friend lived in the same building as her. It was all a very strange affair, She was quite pretty, but wasn't an overly popular girl and kept herself to herself. There were rumours that she had a secret fling going on. There were all sorts of guesses as to who it could be. Some reckoned it might even have been a lecturer. Anyway, the girl came from a wealthy family, and the day before her body was found, she withdrew the total amount of her savings account, close to a million dollars. The money was never found."

Tim said, "Maybe she went on a massive shopping spree? Did they check her wardrobe for shoes?!"

Scott chuckled and Amy elbowed Tim in the ribs. She chided him, "It's not funny. It was creepy at the time. She was found dead in her room. There was no sign of a break in. She must have let her killer in. It turned out it was a janitor who was obsessed with her."

Tim said, "Ok, ok, you're right. That must have been very creepy. You must all have been very scared." He then added with a smirk,

"Did you and your girlfriends have lots of sleepovers to make you feel safe?!"

Amy rolled her eyes. "Typical male. Can you turn any story into a lesbian fantasy? If you must know, my six foot five boyfriend who was an American footballer made me feel quite safe."

Scott grinned at Tim's hesitation over a comeback. Amy seemed like someone who gave as good as she got.

Tim nodded. "Oh I'm sure he did. What with all that padding!"

Their banter was halted by the arrival of Thomas with their drinks. He laid them down on the table in front of them and left, passing Daphne Pennington on the way.

Amy noticed her and said, "Daphne, would you like to join us?"

Daphne smiled at the offer, but said, "Thank you Amy, but I've said I'd have a sit with the Kennedys. I'll come back over in a bit."

Scott took his opportunity to avoid feeling more like a gooseberry than he already did. He stood and said to Daphne, "I might join you, if that's ok?"

Daphne said, "Certainly. Don't forget your drink."

Scott turned to pick it up and said to Tim and Amy, "Play nicely, Children." and then just to Amy as he walked past. "Don't let him have another cocktail."

He followed Daphne down the carriage and Tim and Amy vaguely heard Daphne say hello to the Kennedys.

Amy asked Tim, "I wasn't boring him, was I?"

"No, no. That's just Scott. He likes to network."

Amy nodded as though she understood. "Ah, he works in Insurance. They're always on the lookout to try and sell you anything!"

Tim said with a grin, "Close enough, so this six foot five, American football playing boyfriend, does he have a good sense of humour? I can't imagine he has."

"Ex-boyfriend."

Tim said with more interest, "Ah, now that makes for a much more pleasant conversation. So what went wrong?"

Amy turned to Tim and smiled. "No sense of humour."

Avril sat back in her high armchair as she told the others a story. It was of her brother's last visit to the Hamptons (simply wonderful) as a guest at the house of a certain Hollywood star (surprisingly obnoxious).

With her coiffured ash blonde hair and her amount of expensive jewellery, she sat with a regal air.

On the settee that faced the windows, Gerry sat at one end, looking as though this was the hundredth time he had heard this story. Daphne, at the other end, was positively giddy at the juicy celebrity gossip. Scott sat in the chair opposite Avril, listening but not really hearing the words. He was too busy observing Avril and Gerry, wondering where the power lay in their relationship. On the surface, to others, she was very much the spokesperson and would appear to wear the trousers. But Scott suspected that behind closed doors, Gerry was the one in charge. He was the brains, she was the P.R.

As the story reached its climax, where Avril's brother walked in on said Hollywood star in a compromising situation with the pool boy, Scott heard movement in the carriage behind him. He looked around to see Caroline Stuart enter alone, and then watched her sit down in a big armchair in the middle of the carriage. She quickly pulled out a book and began to read, her small face puckering up in concentration.

Scott turned around to hear Avril say, "And so, he let my brother Walt have the use of his yacht in the Hamptons for the summer if he didn't mention anything! Can you believe it?"

Gerry interjected, "I'm sure he said borrow it for a long weekend."

Avril said harshly, "Who's Walt's sister, Gerry?!"

Daphne said in delight, "What a fantastic story! Oh, you must hear stories like this all the time through your line of business."

Avril sat up even straighter in her chair as she said, "Well, yes. But if their friends of ours, then we would never betray a confidence."

Daphne leaned closer and asked, "Have you got anything juicy on Clarissa Jordan then?"

Scott watched both the Kennedys bristle at the mention of her name.

Avril paused before saying, "We have worked with her in the past, yes."

Daphne said, "Yes, I saw you say hello to her at the reception."

And then she gave a look as if Avril was being crafty. "But you didn't answer my question! So is she a celebrity friend that you wouldn't say anything about? Or is it that she's not, but there isn't any gossip about her? Because I don't believe that!"

Gerry and Avril both looked uncomfortably at each other. Scott gave a small smile, as he realised that Daphne was doing all his work for him.

After a second or two of silence, Gerry suddenly rose and said, "I think what my wife is trying to say is that it's probably not too polite to talk about someone when they're in a close vicinity. Now if you'll excuse me, I'm rather tired, I'm going to retire to my room."

As Gerry walked down the carriage, Daphne and Scott watched him go, before quickly exchanging glances with each other. Avril leaned forward and said, "I'm sorry if Gerry seems abrupt. He's been travelling quite a lot and hasn't been getting much sleep."

Daphne said, "Don't worry about it. It's fine. We understand."

She then noticed Avril's necklace fall out from her jacket and said, "Oh my God! That's stunning!"

She moved to look closer at the diamond encrusted pendant. "It's beautiful!"

Avril showed her proudly, "A little treat from Gerry. It's from Tiffany and Co. The place where I had this suit tailored is only two blocks away from there."

"Is that near Gucci?"

Scott watched Daphne and Avril descend into a conversation of where to make the best purchases on Fifth Avenue and decided that he was probably not going to discover anything further, except maybe the average price of a pair of Jimmy Choo shoes.

He finished his drink and made his polite excuses. As he walked back down towards the front of the train, he saw Caroline still sat reading, her small frame engulfed in the oversize chair. He decided to seize a moment where she was not half hidden behind her husband.

He said, "Hi, it's Caroline, isn't it?"

Caroline looked up, apparently rather startled that someone had spoken to her. She replied, "Oh yes. And it was Mr Blacklock, wasn't it?"

"Please, call me Scott. How are you enjoying the journey so far?"

She carefully slotted her bookmark into the page of her book and placed it primly in her lap. She said, "It's lovely. So fancy. I'm a bit in awe of it all really. Especially with some of the people on this train. I must have seemed terribly shy earlier. I'm just not that good with big crowds."

Scott smiled, "I can understand, and so many introductions all at once!"

Caroline asked, "Are you and Miss Pennington travelling together?"

"No, I'm travelling with my friend Tim." He pointed to behind her, where he was still sat with Amy. He asked, "Have you and your husband left any kids at home for this getaway?"

Caroline replied quickly, "No, we haven't got any children, maybe someday."

Scott asked, "Have you and Anthony been married long?"

"Seven years now, we've been together for ten though."

"And you're both from Boston, aren't you?"

"Well I moved to Boston to study. I met Anthony when I was working part time in a bar."

Scott found it hard to imagine the very prim woman in front of him working in a bar. Maybe she wasn't so uptight when she was younger, thought Scott. He asked, "What were you studying for?"

"To be a nursery school teacher, which I now am. I work at the Georgina Stanier School in Boston. I look after twenty children. All under five!"

Scott replied, "Wow! That must be quite a job. You must have to have eyes everywhere!"

Caroline said proudly, "I do run a tight ship, so to speak. You could say I'm very efficient at my job."

Scott said, "But the kids must be a handful?"

Caroline smiled, "Yes, and especially on trips out, like to the park. Even with helpers, you'd be surprised how much mischief a toddler can get into when your back is turned for a second."

Scott said, "I bet they come back with all kinds of cuts and bruises!"

Caroline looked at him seriously, "Oh no! Not when I'm looking after them. And I always have my first aid kit at hand!" She gave a little laugh and said, "Anthony always chides me about it, saying how I take it everywhere!"

Scott replied, "You and Anthony seem very happy together."

"Yes, although sometimes I wonder what he sees in a bore like me! I'd much rather curl up with a good book than a night out! What is it that you do Mr Blacklock?"

"I work for an Insurance company, in New York" Scott answered.

"Do you enjoy it?"

"Yes, it's very interesting. And challenging."

Caroline did not really know what to ask next, and it seemed to Scott that she had really not intended for the conversation to go on this long, especially as the topic had turned to insurance. Scott avoided an embarrassing silence by saying, "Well I won't interrupt you from your book any longer. I'll see you later in the bar."

Caroline smiled and said goodbye.

Scott passed Amy and Tim but decided not to join them. He left the observation carriage and walked past the Thistlewood suites, towards his room. He decided he would quickly unpack before seeing who was in the lounge. As he entered the carriage that held his, Tim's and the Kennedy's suites, he heard raised voices from the end of the carriage.

Scott turned the corner and looked down the corridor, to where Gerry Kennedy stood red faced in his doorway, talking furiously to Rosalie.

Scott heard the words "I don't have anymore!" before Gerry slammed the door in her face. Scott walked up to her and asked, "Are you alright?"

Rosalie turned, her cheeks were slightly flushed. She regained her composure and smiled. She said in a lower voice, "I'm fine, thanks. Just a difficult customer, there wasn't enough champagne in his room."

Scott smiled and gave a nod of understanding. Rosalie said, "I'd better get back to the kitchen with his order." She turned and headed back towards the front of the train.

Scott walked back up the carriage to his suite and pulled out his keycard from his pocket. He was about to unlock his door when Clarissa Jordan walked around the corner from the observation carriage.

They were both slightly startled at the others appearance for a second, before Clarissa extended her hand and said flirtatiously, "An attractive man I haven't been introduced to yet! Clarissa Jordan."

Scott shook her hand and felt his cheeks flush slightly. "Scott Blacklock. Very nice to meet you Mrs Jordan."

She smiled; her smile was enchanting, as was her scent.

"It's nice to meet someone on this train who isn't here to surprise me. You're not going to say you followed me here too, are you?!"

Scott laughed, aware of the irony in the question. "Not at all. Although I must say, my mother is your biggest fan. She will be quite jealous!"

Clarissa's smile widened at the sound of praise. She said, "Remind me to sign something for you at some point for her. Tell me Mr Blacklock, do you play cards?"

"I have been known to play from time to time."

"I noticed there was a table in the lounge. You must join me and my husband for a game later this evening."

Scott smiled at the invitation. "It would be a pleasure."

Clarissa added, "It would be nice to have some company that doesn't have a hidden agenda, like some I could say on this train. I'm hunted down so much in my professional life; it would have been nice to have escaped that for this vacation. Just now, I've been out on the back balcony of the train. It's lovely out there. Reminds me of escaping!" She took her purse from under her arm and gestured to the direction of the lounge, "If you'll excuse me, I'm off to find my husband."

Scott watched Clarissa walk down the carriage and as he entered his room, he understood slightly more why so many men could quite easily fall for her appeal.

Cocktail hour

Scott stood in front of his mirror as he buttoned up his shirt. He looked at his reflection for a second before walking across to look out the window. The clear blue skies had given way to a red dusk, and Scott saw the lights of Pittsburgh in the distance. He watched them pass and the scenery became darker. He turned as he heard the partitioning door open. Tim appeared, looking much smarter that earlier in a shirt and trousers.

He said, "One scrubbed up secret agent reporting for duty, ready for the cocktail hour to do a little reconnaissance."

Scott pulled a face at Tim. He said, "That's not funny Tim. You know nothing about what I'm doing here, you're just on vacation. As am I, remember!"

Tim fell on Scott's bed as Scott turned to the mirror to do up his tie. Tim said,

"Come on Scott, I'm sure you could do with the extra help."

Scott spoke while still looking in the mirror. "Your extra help can be supporting my cover story. That we're on the way to L.A for a holiday and then you're going to Yosemite. Ok?" he finished while pulling his tie flat.

Tim got off the bed and handed Scott his jacket. As he opened the door he said,

"Well I don't know. I still think I can do a bit more than that. After all, I am finding out quite a lot about the delightful Amy Jordan for you."

As Tim grinned, Scott pulled his jacket on and said, "Look Tim, about Amy....."

But Tim was already out the door, he heard him saying "It's already gone eight, come on." as he headed down the carriage.

Scott sighed and picked up his keycard, before heading out after Tim.

The cocktail bar was the last carriage of the train and was situated beyond the observation carriage. The bar's decor was much more suited for the evening, with crimson walls and black leather furnishings as opposed to the green and brown hues of the lounge. The bar stood impressively down one side of the carriage, while the other side gave way to settees and tables and rounded leatherettes at the far end, by the door that led to the balcony.

The Stuarts were the only other guests that had arrived and were sat in the far corner, Anthony Stuart in a smart dinner suit and open shirt, Caroline in a dark green knee length dress. They were sipping cocktails and talking quietly. Scott and Tim headed to the bar where Bradley was waiting dutifully. He placed two silver coasters down and asked,

"What can I get you? Nobody makes a cocktail like I do!"

Before Scott and Tim could answer, he said, "But wait, let me take a guess at what you might like and come up with a concoction of my own."

He gestured to Scott. "Now you Sir, I'm guessing you like your vodka, your gin, and other light spirits, preferably mixed with something that's either dry or refreshing, but not in your typical way." He then gestured to Tim. "While you sir, also like your vodka, but like your whiskeys and rums, and like mixing it with a larger variety of things, usually something carbonated."

Scott and Tim looked at each other, impressed. Bradley grinned, "I've been serving cocktails since I can remember. It's kind of my party trick. I can always guess what kind of cocktails people like. Would one of those fit the bill for you two?"

Tim answered, "Sounds good to me." As Bradley turned to start preparing the cocktails, he said to Scott, "Damn good service on this train."

"Yes, either that or he just took a note of the drinks we ordered this afternoon."

Scott added dryly.

Bradley continued mixing the drinks, unaware of Scott's quieter comment. Tim nudged Scott's arm and said quietly, "Check out my secret agent questioning technique!"

He asked Bradley, "So, how did you end up working on the Express? Surely all the top bars in New York and L.A would kill for a barman like you."

Bradley smiled his wide grin, "I've worked in a fair few of them! But you don't get more exclusive than the Express. Plus it's a job which means I can work two of my loves!"

Tm asked rather bluntly, "Being a porter?"

Bradley replied, "Well I do have to do that also, but no, you may have noticed a piano in the dining carriage?"

Tim nodded.

"I'm also a classically trained pianist. I play during evening dinner." said Bradley. As he finished his sentence, he also finished making the cocktails, garnishing and serving them in a flamboyant style.

Tim said, "A man of many talents." As he sipped his cocktail, he said, "If you play the piano half as well as you make cocktails, then the Express is lucky to have you!"

Scott concurred with Tim's praise after a taste of his own drink. He turned to see that Harry Broadside had entered the bar and as he sat down next to Scott, he smiled briefly and ordered a beer from Bradley.

Bradley looked insulted for a second at not being asked for a cocktail, before quickly hiding it and turning to get a bottle from the fridge.

Scott turned to Harry. As he spoke, he noticed that Harry's suit was slightly too big for him, like it had been borrowed from a friend. Surprising thought Scott, as Harry already had quite a large bulky frame. Scott offered his hand and said, "Hi. Scott Blacklock. I don't believe we've been introduced yet?"

Harry paused for a second before shaking his hand. "Harry Broadside. Nice to meet you."

Scott decided to move straight in for the kill. "You're Clarissa Jordan's ex-husband, aren't you?"

Harry took a swig from his beer. "Yes. How did you know that?"

Scott lied. "My mother's a big fan of Clarissa's. She follows all the news about her. And I remember seeing you in the news."

Harry looked surprised. "You're one of the few that do. It's surprising how easy it is to fall into obscurity again."

Scott said, "So is Clarissa the reason you happen to be vacationing on this train?"

Harry stood, looking indignant. He said, "Excuse me, Mr Blacklock. But I don't believe it's any business of yours as to why I'm on this train." He picked up his beer.

"Now, if you'll excuse me, I have said that I would sit with the Stuarts."

Scott asked, "Oh sorry, are you travelling with them?"

"No. And that's none of your business either." He pushed his stool back under the bar. He said, "My advice to you Mr Blacklock. Don't concern yourself with affairs of Clarissa Jordan, when they have nothing to do with you."

As he walked away, Scott said. "They also have nothing to do with you now."

Harry stopped, and turned around. Scott continued innocently, "Well, from what I've read in the papers anyway."

Harry's face was thunderous. He almost said something, but instead thought better of it and walked away to sit with the Stuarts.

Tim leaned over. He asked, "Having a little fun?"

Scott smiled. He said, "Just getting started."

As he spied the silhouette of Jessica Rae on the balcony, he picked up his drink and said, "Anyway I think I might pop out for a cigarette before dinner."

He stood up and walked to the end of the carriage, ignoring the look that Harry gave him as he walked past. He stepped out onto the balcony, slightly startling Jessica in the process. Scott looked out at the shadowy scenery and thought how the view from the back of a train was always a satisfying one. Even more so on this particular evening, where the dying red sky made the trees look ablaze with colour. As he looked on, an old sign whizzed past, the cut out letters saying "WELCOME TO OHIO".

Scott buttoned his jacket up as he felt the coolness of the evening. He walked to the rail where Jessica stood and asked, "Good evening Jessica. Do you have a light I could borrow?"

Jessica put her hand in her ankle length evening jacket and produced a lighter. She handed it to Scott and said, "You should be careful Scott. Those things will kill you."

As Scott lit his cigarette, he nodded to the one in Jessica's hand. "Well at least I won't be going to hell."

Jessica smirked, "Heaven's far too overrated. And isn't smoking a sin anyway?"

Scott handed her the lighter back. He replied, "Probably. But only a mild one. There are other things that are far more poisonous than cigarettes."

Jessica looked at him and said, "Are you referring that to me?"

Scott took a drag. "If the shoe fits. I suppose it could refer to your work. Addictive to the general consumer, but potentially harmful to those involved."

Jessica put a hand on her hip. "What a lovely analogy! Why is it Scott, that whenever we talk, it ends up being a lecture from you about how odious my work is? And how I intrude on people's lives? You do that in your job too!"

Scott replied, "If I have to pry into someone's life, it's for truth and justice. I agree that celebrities have to accept some lack of privacy due to their work. What I find odious Jessica, is not your work, but your work ethic."

"My work ethic?! What about yours? Your work ethic is just to save your big corporation money!"

Scott said sharply, "That's not why I do it. And I'm not like you who doesn't care who gets shit on to get a story, or to get yourself promoted. People like Tim. Like your sister and James Garland. Remember them?"

Jessica snorted, "We're not back on this again!"

Scott retorted, "The bottom line is that to be honest, I don't really trust you and I don't know how far you'd go to get a story. Now Clarissa may not know who you are yet, but I do. And if I see you doing anything remotely suspicious to get a story, Clarissa will be one of the first people I tell. I hear she's got quite a temper on her."

Jessica said angrily, "Why are you so interested in Clarissa anyway?"

He replied truthfully, "What I'm interested in Jessica, is that you don't hurt anyone more than you already have."

As he flicked his stub into the designated fire bucket, he opened the door and said,

"Thanks for the light." before heading back into the bar, leaving Jessica with a dark look on her face.

Scott walked back in to see that Amy Jordan had arrived; wearing a low cut black dress. "That's going to annoy Clarissa, probably the point of the dress", thought Scott. Or perhaps for someone else's benefit, Scott corrected his thought as he noticed that Tim had been quick to join her. Scott sat down in the chair opposite them and said, "Good evening Amy. I see you've already tasted one of Bradley's concoctions?"

Amy smiled and said, "I know, he's amazing, how he can guess your type of drink!"

Scott and Tim exchanged glances at the mention of Bradley's "gift".

Amy continued, "Tim and I were just talking about Italy. And how we both had the same croissants from the same little bakery in Florence for the entire time we were there! It's such a small worl..." Amy broke off as she saw her father Mark Jordan enter, wearing a smart black tuxedo.

She called over, "Dad, come on over. I've already got you a drink."

Mark sat down next to Scott as Amy said, "Dad, these are some friends I've made. This is Tim Anderson and Scott Blacklock. My father, Mark Jordan."

Hands were shaken and polite introductions made. Tim and Amy soon went back to the conversation of Italy, leaving Mark free for Scott to talk to. Scott observed from Mark's posture that he looked like a man who found it hard to relax, the prominent features of his face always in a position of a stern frown.

Scott said, "Amy tells me you work in the Financial District. So do I."

Mark replied. "Yes, I work within the Stock Exchange. I used to be a lawyer, but realised I was more skilled with stocks and shares. What do you do Mr Blacklock?"

"I work in Insurance. Boring work but it pays well. Plenty of opportunity for bonus! It's how I can afford a trip like this! I can sometimes find it hard to switch off though. Don't you find you always want to keep an eye on the market, even when you're on vacation?" Scott asked.

Mark crossed his arms and answered, "I'm actually on a bit of a career break at the moment. I turned forty five last year, and decided to actually live a little. Plus, as you must know, I met Clarissa."

"Ah, so she's been persuading you to live the high life a little?"

Mark looked at him and his tone changed, "I hope you're not implying that I'm a scrounger."

Scott said hastily, "No, I didn't mean that for a second. I simply meant that Clarissa must be part of the reason why you decided to live a little."

Mark relaxed. "Oh, well yes. I apologise. I just find that I have to justify that fact quite a lot." He nodded over to Harry in the corner. "Maybe it's because of ex husbands in Clarissa's past."

Scott asked, "How do you find it being the husband of a star?"

Mark regarded him for a second before answering. Scott thought that Mark must often gauge people as to whether they were predatory in any way. It would seem that Scott had passed his test as he seemed quite relaxed in his response about Clarissa. He said, "It was a bit overwhelming to begin with. It still is half the time to be honest. But everyone always enter a relationship with baggage."

Clarissa's baggage was more likely an entourage, thought Scott.

"Clarissa's is that she just happens to be famous. And it can be hard at times, but it works."

Although Mark seemed quite open, Scott couldn't help but feel that Mark's answer was a little bit like a text book answer. Scott thought how he could quite easily have read that quote in a magazine.

The carriage was greeted with new arrivals as the Kennedys entered. Gerry was also dressed in a tuxedo, while Avril was wearing a long black dress, accompanied by a white fur stole and a slit in her dress that went a little too far up the leg for a woman of her age. They both took a seat close to the door and Bradley took them a selection of cocktails, expertly balanced on a silver tray.

Shortly after, Daphne Pennington arrived, adjusting her glittery jacket as she sat at the bar. No sooner had she sat down when Bradley started to put on a flairing show for her. The cocktail hour was often called "Bradley's show" by the other members of staff, especially for his tendency to show off in front of the ladies. A fact that was highlighted when Jessica returned from the balcony and took up a seat next to Daphne, both of them clearly impressed by his skill.

Clarissa Jordan entered the carriage, not hiding the fact that she must have waited in her room to again be the last to arrive. This was embellished with her outfit, which was obviously chosen to outshine all the other women on the train. As she walked over to Scott, Tim and the Jordans, her white backless dress showed off her lithe body and flawless skin perfectly.

She sat down next to Mark, and gave him a quick peck on the cheek, before smiling at Scott. She appeared to ignore Amy, and Tim too in the process.

Clarissa looked confused and said, "It's Mr Backtop. Isn't it?"

"Blacklock. But please, call me Scott."

Clarissa smiled. "I'm sorry. I can be terrible with names. But I never forget a face."

Scott indicated over to Tim. "And this is my good friend, Tim Anderson."

Clarissa turned and smiled at Tim. For a second, Tim looked slightly in awe at being sat at a table with Clarissa. Clarissa glanced over at Amy and finally acknowledged her, "Amy, that's a lovely dress. That reminds me, I must take you shopping with me in L.A. You know, get you some designer labels. Tasteful pieces, maybe not so revealing."

Before Amy could respond, Clarissa turned her back on her and snuggled closer to Mark. She said to Scott, "Scott, have you heard how Mark and I met?"

Amy scowled at Clarissa, but Tim touched her arm and said, "I think you look stunning tonight."

Amy smiled, and decided to ignore her step mother's comments, instead returning to her conversation with Tim.

Clarissa had only just started her story of how she and Mark had met in a jazz club, when her attention was diverted by Anthony Stuart heading to the bar. She stopped halfway through her sentence.

"So I said to my agent who was with me...." She started to stand up, "Sorry, can you excuse me. No one's bothered to get me a drink."

Mark went to get up. "I'll get it for you."

Clarissa placed a hand on his shoulder, "Don't worry, you finish the story."

Mark sat back down and looked awkwardly to Scott. The thought of telling a virtual stranger his recent love story was not one that Mark cherished.

Clarissa was headed to the bar when Gerry sidled up to her, "Clarissa, you look more delightful every time I see you."

Clarissa smiled thinly and meant to move around him. He side stepped and said,

"Now Clarissa, I don't mean to disturb you this evening, but I was wondering if I could steal five minutes from you tomorrow? It's just a little idea I want to run past you...."

Clarissa said, "Gerry. I've told you. Talk to my manager."

Again she tried to move past him and again he side stepped, "Clarissa, please. Just five minutes."

Clarissa rolled her eyes. Realising that it was the only way to get rid of him, she said reluctantly, "Alright. Five minutes. Tomorrow. Now get out of my way."

Gerry moved aside and went quietly to his seat, where Avril whispered something furiously in his ear.

Clarissa continued over to the bar, where Anthony was entertaining Daphne and Jessica with a rather crude joke. Clarissa pressed past Anthony and leaned over the counter to say to Bradley,

"Hello smiley, could you shake me up something sexy?"

Bradley smiled nervously. "Something sexy, coming up!"

He turned and, for the first time in his life, slightly fumbled with the shaker as he picked it up.

Clarissa turned and listened to Daphne telling Anthony about her job. As Daphne finished her story, Clarissa moved past her and extended her hand to Anthony.

"Hello, I don't believe we've been introduced. I'm ...."

Anthony smiled as he took her hand, "Clarissa Lavelle! Well I don't need to ask what you do!"

There was polite laughter from Daphne and Jessica, but as the conversation continued, it became more obvious that Clarissa had steered Anthony's attention towards her.

A fact that Scott noticed a little too obviously, as Mark turned to see what he was looking at.

Clarissa, who had been given her drink several minutes earlier, was still stood at the bar giggling with Anthony. Mark stood up and excused himself, apparently needing the bathroom. As he left, Amy said to Tim,

"You see! This is what she's like. She's either all over my father or ignoring him. In between, she's being a bitch to me!"

Scott heard Amy's point, and watched Anthony tell another joke to the ladies at the bar.

A gong sounded from further down the train and Lambert appeared in the doorway. He announced, "Ladies and Gentlemen. If you would like to make your way to the dining carriage, dinner will shortly be served."

The guests started to exit the carriage. As Scott picked up his glass he noticed another passenger's reaction to Anthony and the ladies at the bar. Still sat in the corner alone, Caroline Stuart sat with an empty glass, watching. Her lips were so thin they had disappeared.

Four courses of digestion

The passengers made their way down the train in a vague procession towards the dining carriage. As they walked through the lounge, they heard a piano playing and as they entered the dining room, they saw Bradley sat at the far end, playing soft classical music. The design of this carriage, like the rest of the train, was expensive and luxurious. A palette of soft cream offset the mahogany tables and the well placed landscape paintings by classic artists.

Scott and Tim took a table to the side, as the Jordans sat closest to the piano. Daphne sat down at a table with the Kennedys, while Harry joined the Stuarts. Jessica Rae sat at a table in the corner by herself.

No sooner had they sat down, when Rosalie appeared with a wine list and showed them the evening's menu.

- First Course -

Carpaccio of Beef served on a bed of mixed leaves with a scoop of crispy parsnip shavings

Baked Figs with Goats Cheese Broule, exposed over a lemon and rocket salad

---

Scott tasted the wine as Tim unfolded his napkin. Scott nodded and Rosalie poured, before leaving the bottle in the ice bucket. After taking their order, she moved over to the Jordans. Tim played with his cutlery and then said. "So Mr secret agent, have you found out lots of juicy info while you've been out networking this afternoon?"

Scott placed his napkin in his lap, before saying in a slightly lower voice. "I've had one or two interesting chats, yes."

Tim asked. "Any idea who might have sent those letters yet?"

Scott sipped his wine and was about to answer when Thomas delivered their first course.

As he walked away and they started on their food, Scott answered. "Let's just say there could be a few potential suspects."

"Any in particular?"

Scott took a look around the room, and watched the others eating. Instead of answering, Scott prodded his beef carpaccio with his fork, before taking a mouthful.

He left Tim hanging as he chewed the meat, then finally swallowed and answered.

"A little too early to give anything away."

Tim looked frustrated for a second. He glanced over the carriage to Jessica in the corner. She was not paying much attention to her food, instead watching the Jordans quite intently.

Tim didn't bother swallowing his food before asking. "What did you say to Jessica out on the balcony?"

Scott replied. "Just told her that I had my eye on her. And that she had better not try anything."

Tim leaned forward eagerly, "You think she's involved?"

Scott finished his last bite and hesitated, "I don't know. I have no real reason to suspect her of anything connected to my case at the moment. Apart from the coincidence that we're both following the same person."

Thomas cleared their plates and Scott added in a lower voice. "But you and I both know what she's capable of."

Tim finished, "And I'm not a great believer in coincidences."

> **-- Second Course -**
>
> *Chargrilled loin of pork simply infused with a discreet Ginger jus on a julienne of mixed vegetables*
>
> *Spicy Thai monkfish and tiger prawn curry with a flirtation of sugar snaps and steamed rice*
>
> *Roasted risotto and mozzarella cake with wilted greens on an underlying tomato and aubergine compote*

Tim poured the remains of the wine into their glasses and asked Rosalie for another bottle as she set their plates on the table. Tim said, "If all your little missions are this cushy, I think I might have to ask you to get me an application for ol' Zirconia."

Scott gave him a look. "They're not missions. And this is hardly the kind of thing I usually do."

Tim sat back and looked smug. He said, "I don't know, I think I'd be pretty good at it. I reckon one of your prime candidates is him over there." as he gestured with his wine glass. Scott turned to see who he was looking at. It was the table that the Stuarts and Harry Broadside were sat at.

Scott looked back to Tim. He asked, "You think Harry Broadside?"

Tim replied, "Well it doesn't take a genius to work it out. Her EX-Husband! A bit jealous, liked a taste for the fame and fortune. Especially the fortune part."

Scott nodded. "I agree he is a likely candidate. But this thing could pan out to involve somebody with more brains."

Tim played with his monkfish and said. "But you have to admit his motives are questionable for being here?"

"Yes" Scott said as picked up his wine glass, "his motives are definitely questionable."

Anthony held his hands wide across the table as he said, "I tell you Harry, the one I caught at Crossroads Creek was this big! You have to go further upstate if you want the big game!"

Harry made an effort to include Caroline in the conversation. He asked. "Do you like fishing Caroline?"

She smiled. "No, I don't really see the attraction. But some of the places that Anthony goes to fish are so beautiful! I'm quite happy to just sit by the river, read my book and enjoy the scenery."

Anthony added, "Plus, Caroline can make any fish I catch into the most superb meal!"

Caroline slightly blushed at the compliment. She said, "I try."

Harry said, "Maybe I'll have to pop over to yours at some point in the future and taste some of this fabulous cuisine!"

Anthony grinned and pointed with his fork at Harry's plate. "I tell you, it's better than your "world class" monkfish!"

Scott and Tim observed them as they made their way through the main course and the majority of their second bottle of wine.

As their plates were cleared, Tim asked Scott. "What about those two?"

"The Stuarts?"

"Yeah. I wouldn't put those two together. Are they suspects too Agent Blacklock?"

Scott ignored the quip. He answered, "I don't think so. I haven't really spoken to them yet. Spoke to her briefly in the observation carriage and him even more briefly at the reception."

Tim ordered more water for the table while Scott kept his eyes on the Stuarts, watching Anthony talking, remembering his flirtation with Clarissa in the Bar earlier. He said to himself, "Yes, I think I'll try and have a chat with Anthony Stuart after dinner."

> **- Third Course -**
>
> *Amaretto and Chocolate Torte bejewelled with white chocolate crystals*
>
> *Summer Cocktail Pudding: A fruity extravaganza of elegance*
>
> *Sticky Toffee Mud Tartlets: A sumptuous concoction of all that is sinful.*

While Rosalie patiently waited for Tim to decide on his dessert, Scott felt a pang for a cigarette, but restrained himself from going to have one. He looked over and was surprised to see that Jessica had not left for one yet either. Tim finally decided and Rosalie was back within minutes with their selection. Scott turned as he heard loud laughter coming from Avril Kennedy and Daphne Pennington. Gerry was sat back and looked like he was painfully enduring their conversation.

Tim said. "Poor bloke! You kind of feel sorry for him, having to listen to those two go on!"

Scott grinned. "I'd say invite him over, but he doesn't come across as an overly friendly person."

Tim asked. "Why? Were you asking too many nosy questions? You pushed a bit too hard?"

"I found I hardly had to push at all, before a front came up. And I did nothing compared to Daphne's inquisition!"

Tim said. "So that's why he looks so uncomfortable sat there!"

Scott tucked into his summer pudding as he said. "That and he's probably already heard every story his wife has told at least twenty times," Scott took another bite. "Or that they've only been talking about the best places to shop in Manhattan."

Scott was not too far from the truth as Avril had just finished telling Daphne where to get Manolo Blahniks at half the price if she mentioned her name.

Daphne almost squealed in delight. She said. "Thank you Avril. That's lovely of you. Well all I can offer you is therapy!"

Avril laughed. Her laugh was shrill and Gerry winced in his chair.

Daphne leaned forward and said, "So tell me, what happened at the last Oscars? What was the gossip?"

Avril took a sip of her drink, before she crossed her legs, as if she was getting ready for a long story. She started,

"Well, Gerry and I were on the red carpet, stood next to Bobby Foster, who was up for a nomination. And he said to me......Oh, no wait I'm thinking of the year before..."

Gerry finally decided to interject. He did so by excusing himself and headed out of the carriage.

Tim looked up from his chocolate torte and said to Scott while nodding at the departing Gerry,

"There you are! Poor bastard couldn't take it any longer! I don't blame him!"

Scott finished his dessert, and looked out of the window to see only blackness, save for two or three lights far in the distance.

Tim put his fork down and asked. "What is the story with those two? The Kennedys. They know Clarissa, don't they?"

Scott answered, "Yes, she was their leading star until she walked out on them last year. I think that's why they're taking this little vacation. In the chance of winning her back."

Tim said. "Or stealing from her?"

"Maybe. There is definitely something odd about Gerry." Scott pondered.

Tim asked. "And what about the good Dr Pennington?"

Scott looked over to see the two women still steadily whispering. He said,

"She doesn't seem to have any immediate connection to Clarissa. Just a bit of a chatty gossip. Although I did notice her profess adoration for Avril's jewellery. But a lot of women love jewellery." He turned to Tim and said, "Put it this way, I'm not definitely ruling anybody out."

Tim put a hand on his chest and said innocently, "Except me I hope!"

> **- Fourth Course -**
>
> *The Cheeseboard - A range from the young, fresh cheeses to the more mellowed and matured varieties*
>
> *Coffee – Rich, smooth and decadent. In any way, shape or form you desire, with liquor or without.*

Scott declined the coffee and cheese and instead asked for a cup of tea. This comment finally roused Tim from his gaze which had fallen on Amy Jordan in recent minutes. He pulled a face at Scott's tea as he ordered an Irish coffee.

Scott said. "What? It's the British in me!"

Scott looked in the direction of the Jordan's table. He turned back to look at Tim and said, "I can't help but notice you've become slightly enamoured with young Amy Jordan. What about Miranda?"

Tim asked, "What about Miranda?"

Scott thanked Thomas as he delivered the drinks. As he added milk, he said. "I thought you two were kind of seeing each other again."

Tim rubbed the back of his head. "We have been seeing a bit more of each other outside work again. But you know how I never know where I am with her."

Scott replied, "Or maybe half the problem is that she never knows where she is with you?"

Tim shrugged sheepishly. "Yeah, you may have a point."

Scott said as he nodded behind him at the Jordans. "Maybe you should sort out in your head what you want to do about Miranda, before letting Amy Jordan complicate things."

Over at the Jordan's table, the dinner had been a stifled affair, Amy and Clarissa were not speaking to each other while Mark was attempting to act as if everything was fine.

Clarissa stirred her coffee and said to Mark, "When do we get to L.A?"

Mark looked hurt by the question. "Tuesday. Why? Are not you enjoying yourself?"

Clarissa replied, "I'd prefer it if there were a few different passengers for a start. Why couldn't you have hired the whole thing if you wanted to take this train?"

Mark said. "Do you know how much that would have cost?!"

Clarissa looked at him like that was a stupid question "I can afford it!"

Amy let out a tut and gave a look of contempt at Clarissa's frivolous attitude towards money. The second time they had met, they had a heated discussion when Amy told Clarissa that she could give a large amount of her wealth to charity, and still not even notice the difference. Clarissa had retorted that she wouldn't be able to buy as many pretty outfits.

She reacted now to Amy's noise and leaned across the table to her.

"Remind me Amy, What is it you're doing when we get to L.A? When you leave me and your father?"

Amy said sullenly, "I'm staying with a friend."

"Well," said Clarissa as she removed her compact from her purse. "I for one can't wait until Tuesday! To be away from some of the people on this train!"

Her look fell on Amy for the last part of the sentence, and she leaned closer to Mark, putting a hand on his cheek. She said. "Maybe you and I will have to stay cuddled up in our suite for the rest of the trip! Away from everyone else."

Amy snapped and stood up, pushing her chair away and storming out of the carriage. Mark turned to see her go. He looked back at Clarissa and said,

"Clarissa, you didn't have to...."

"Oh, let her go. She'll get over it."

Clarissa was surprised to see Mark stand up and follow his daughter.

She watched him go with a bemused smile on her face. She then picked up her coffee and took a long sip, quickly winking at Bradley who was still playing the piano in front of her.

Scott finished his tea and sat back. He said to Tim on Amy's exit. "Do you think that was one little insult too many?"

Tim placed his glass back on the table before saying, "I don't know. But the more I see of Clarissa, the more I feel bad about not speaking to my mum for a week when she took all my Clarissa Lavelle posters to the junk shop!"

Poker faces

After dinner the passengers neglected to return to the bar all the way at the end of the train, and had instead settled in the lounge, next to the dining carriage. The alcohol seemed to have slightly misted any tensions for a while and as it was approaching eleven thirty, the lounge was still buzzing with lively conversation. Maybe in some cases because of their dinner companions, the guests had begun to mingle slightly.

Scott had joined Clarissa, Mark and Anthony in a game of poker at the card table.

Jessica had disappeared again, presumably for another cigarette. Daphne was sat on a settee talking to, or perhaps, talking at Caroline. Tim and Amy had taken the armchairs in the far corner while Harry was sat on a stool at the bar, with only his drink for company. The Kennedys had chosen to sit at the other end of the carriage.

Since they had moved to the lounge earlier, neither Gerry nor Avril had said much. Daphne felt she should intrude no longer and so had left to talk to other passengers.

As Avril eyed the members at the card table, she said to Gerry, "What time did you arrange to have a meeting with Clarissa tomorrow?"

Gerry took a swig of his whisky, and said gruffly, "We didn't arrange an exact time."

Avril asked pointedly. "Ok, so when are you going to go and see her then?"

"When I feel like it. It's not like she can go anywhere!" He replied, impatience in his tone.

"Look, if you're going to give her the script tomorrow, even if she agrees to look at it, you still need her to read it and give you an answer before she gets off the train!" Avril said anxiously.

Gerry snapped her a look. "I know just as well as you do that our backers won't hold past Wednesday! I think I remember! I was the one that went to the meeting!"

Avril said soothingly, "Alright! I'm just saying that you need to talk to her sooner, rather than later."

Gerry said, "And I'm just saying that I will!"

At that moment, Rosalie walked over. She looked to Avril, then Gerry and smiled rather falsely, before asking,

"Can I get you anything from the bar?"

Avril asked for a gin and tonic, while Gerry declined. As Rosalie left, Gerry said,

"Right, I 'm going to turn in."

Avril pulled a face. "But I've just ordered a drink."

Gerry stood up and retorted, "Don't let me stop you. Maybe you can go and have a chat with Daphne Pennington. You seem to get along so well. Just leave me to worry about the important things! Why don't you carry on doing exactly what you always do? Telling red carpet stories!"

As he walked away and out of the carriage, Avril picked up her drink from Rosalie and hesitated for a second. Better to let him calm down she thought, as she headed over to sit with Caroline and Daphne.

Over in the large armchairs, Tim observed to Amy, "That bloke Kennedy seems to spend his entire time walking out, probably to get away from his wife's tedious conversation!"

Amy said. "Maybe he thinks his wife should grow old gracefully, like him."

Tim grinned and added, "Yes, the slit on that dress does show more than you'd really like to see."

Amy giggled. "I am glad you're on this train. I think I'd go mad otherwise!"

Tim said. "Yes, most of them are not really what I'd call my usual crowd either! And I'm starting to see why you dislike your step-mother so much."

Amy nodded. "She's just such a bitch to me. And it makes me so mad. I've tried for her not to, but she has made me and Dad more distant. Which I know is exactly what she wants!"

Tim was about to say something but Amy continued. "And I think I could deal with it if I knew that she really cared for my father. But it won't surprise me in the least when, in six months time or a year, she'll get bored and move on to the next one. Leaving my father with a broken heart and me picking up the pieces."

Tim said gently, "Your father must have been aware of Clarissa's past?"

Amy replied, "Oh yes, and he still married her!"

Tim said, "Love can make you see things in people."

Amy folded her arms. "Well, whatever he sees, I certainly don't."

Over at the card table, Mark dealt everybody in again. The conversation had started with a tale from Anthony about his student days, and moved on to Mark's job. That then started a debate about the stock market and the current political and economical state of the country which had lasted the last six games, mainly because Mark was a fierce Republican. Clarissa had spoken the least out of the four of them, although Scott had noticed that she had fluttered her eyelashes at Anthony while Mark had been shuffling. As Scott nodded for another card, he took his chance to ask Anthony. "Anthony, what line of work are you in?"

Anthony smiled. "I'm a lecturer."

Clarissa asked. "What do you teach?"

"Technology. Mainly electronics, although I'm also into woodwork. I used to make furniture when I was younger."

"What kind of furniture?" asked Mark.

"Dressers, tables, headboards."

Clarissa said. "A man who's good with his hands. You must be handy to have around the house."

Scott looked over his cards to notice that it was a comment that wasn't missed by Mark. He avoided the awkward moment by raising Mark a hundred dollars.

Mark kept his eyes on Clarissa as he slid his chips across the table.

Clarissa placed her cards down and said, "I'm out again. I usually play so well. Anthony, what did you think of New York?"

Anthony replied. "It was only Caroline's first time there. I've been many times. Fell in love with it at first sight. If Caroline didn't love Boston so much, I'd easily try and get a transfer to the Big Apple!"

Clarissa smiled. "Really?"

Again the card game went silent until the game ended when Anthony revealed a full house. As he pulled the chips across the table, he said. "Right. Shall we get some more drinks in before the next game?"

Jessica Rae returned to the lounge, and quickly surveyed who was sat where. She made her decision and headed to the bar and sat down next to Harry Broadside.

Jessica ordered a drink from Rosalie and turned to look at Harry. He was sat, quite hunched, either intently reading the label on his beer or gazing somewhere a million miles away.

Jessica said cheerily, "Hi, I don't believe we've been introduced. My name's Jessica. We did meet briefly at that awards ceremony in Miami."

Harry slowly looked up and said bluntly. "I'm sorry, I don't remember you."

Jessica smiled. "I don't blame you. There were a lot of faces there that evening, and you must have obviously been very new to the whole celebrity thing."

Harry swung around on his stool to take a proper look at her. He asked, "You know who I am?"

Jessica picked up her drink from the bar and said, "Oh yes. I know quite a bit about you." she then added with a mischievous grin. "Bet you'd like to know what secrets I know?"

Harry looked aggressively at her before saying, "Excuse me; I need to use the bathroom. And when I get back, if you don't mind, I was rather enjoying having a quiet drink by myself."

He left the carriage as Jessica watched him before taking a large gulp from her oversized wine glass.

Over at the ladies table, once Avril had joined Daphne and Caroline, the conversation had predictably moved to fashion, a topic that Caroline felt quite obviously left out of. After sitting there politely for twenty minutes, listening to the ladies chat, she decided to head for bed and said her goodnights to Daphne and Avril.

She turned and felt her head throb slightly. She thought that was from drinking the cocktails earlier, as she was not much of a drinker usually. She made her way over to the card table to tell Anthony she was leaving. As she arrived, Clarissa was telling the three men about a horrific photo shoot she had to do in the Arctic Circle when she was twenty two.

Caroline stood behind Anthony patiently for a few moments, before tapping him on the shoulder. Anthony barely turned, and said absently, "Yes dear?"

Caroline said, "I'm heading to bed."

Anthony again hardly moved as Clarissa's story headed towards the punch line.

Caroline said, a little too snappily before walking out. "Right. Well Goodnight then."

Clarissa finished her story, just as Mark won the game with two pairs. As Scott handed his cards to Clarissa, he noticed Anthony watching Caroline leave the bar and saw a conflict on his face. After several moments, he handed his cards over and said,

"I'd better turn in also. I seem to be on a bit of a losing streak anyway."

Clarissa said, "Are you sure? You never know when your luck could change."

Anthony smiled. "No, I'd better head to bed. But thank you all for a good game."

Scott and Clarissa said goodnight, while Mark made a barely audible grunt.

Jessica who had been observing from the bar watched Anthony leave and picked up her drink. Clarissa was just about to deal the three of them in when Jessica sidled up and took the empty seat.

She smiled and said, "Hi! I thought I could make up the numbers. My name's Jessica."

Clarissa stared at her for a second, before Mark smiled and said, "I don't see why not. Mark Jordan. This is my wife Clarissa, and Scott Blacklock."

Clarissa forced a small smile before rather reluctantly dealing her in. Scott looked at Jessica and shot her a warning look. He was fairly sure that neither Clarissa nor Mark had twigged as to who she was. He doubted they would have allowed her to join them otherwise.

Jessica however was as blunt as a sledgehammer. She said to Clarissa, "I was sure it was you! I'm a big fan!"

Clarissa smiled uncomfortably. "That's nice. Are you taking a card?"

Jessica shook her head, and said, "No thanks." She then turned to Mark. "And you're the new husband. It's so nice to meet you. I must say the wedding was lovely! I especially loved all the orchids you had! How's married life treating you?"

Clarissa put down her cards and looked at Jessica. She said slowly, "We never released any photos of the wedding! How did you know that? What did you say you're name was?"

"I didn't. It's Jessica. Jessica Rae."

Clarissa stood up angrily. "I thought your face looked familiar! You're the god damn bitch who bribed that waiter for the story of our wedding! And who exposed those topless photos of me in Cuba last year!"

Jessica was about to retort but Clarissa didn't let her.

"I can't believe there's another fucking person on this train who's here to get something from me!" She pointed a threatening finger over the table at her. "You listen to me, you piece of shit. You don't come near me, or my family. Or I will make sure that you never expose anything again!"

Mark stood up with a look of disgust at Jessica. He took Clarissa's arm and led her away over to the bar. He said to her, "Come on Clarissa, let's just go to bed."

Clarissa stood there for a moment, clenching her fists, before calming herself. She shook her head and said, "In a moment. You go on. I'll be along in a minute."

"Clarissa." Mark said warningly.

"Don't worry! I'm not going to start anything with her. I'm just going to get a nightcap to bring to bed."

Jessica and Scott sat for a moment in silence, before Scott started to collect the cards up. Jessica said under her breath, "What a bitch!"

Scott observed, "I don't know. I think you quite deserved that!"

"I only asked them how married life was. And you saw that response! It gives me plenty to write about though!" retorted Jessica smugly.

She shot him a look before standing up and leaving. As she walked out, she bumped into Harry Broadside as he returned to the bar.

Mark said goodnight to Scott as he passed the card table. He ignored Harry as he smiled at Avril and Daphne, saying a quick goodnight to his daughter before leaving.

At the other end of the carriage, Rosalie had taken glasses to the kitchen leaving Bradley on the bar when Clarissa stepped up to him.

He smiled and said, "What can I get you?"

She returned the smile, "Something smooth and creamy. And with plenty of alcohol! I think I need it!"

Bradley grinned. "Poker game get a little heated?"

"You could say that." said Clarissa as she leant a little further over the bar.

As Bradley began to make a drink, Harry sat down at a stool next to Clarissa. She turned and said, "And what do you want?!"

Harry stuttered for a moment before answering, "Clarissa. Look I know why you think I'm here. But it's not for the reasons you're thinking."

Clarissa moved away slightly. "You're admitting that you're here because of me?"

Harry paused before saying, "Yes. But, like I said, not for the reasons you think!"

Clarissa stopped him. "To be honest, Harry. I don't give a shit why you're here! Just as long as you quit bugging me, because I am starting to get severely pissed off with it!"

As she snatched up her handbag, Bradley placed her drink on the bar. She picked that up with her other hand and gave Bradley a wink, before moving around Harry and walking out.

Scott stacked up the few remaining chips, while watching Harry at the bar. He moved and took the stool next to him. He said, "I couldn't help but overhear. Clarissa doesn't seem too happy?"

Harry turned around and said fiercely, "And I can't help but notice that you're an extremely nosy bastard!"

He downed the last third of his beer before heading to the sleeping carriages.

Scott sipped his drink as he watched him go, and noticed Avril leave as well. Daphne stood up and walked over to Scott. She grinned and said, "It's been an interesting evening hasn't it?"

Scott smiled. "Yes, very. Are you off to bed now?"

Daphne replied, "Yes, I'll see you in the morning. We'll have gone through Indiana by then. I must tell you the story of me at the racing in Indianapolis! Maybe at breakfast! Goodnight."

Scott smiled politely and said goodnight.

With the Lounge practically deserted, he decided bed was calling for him too. He passed Amy and Tim, the only remaining occupants of the carriage and bid them goodnight.

Scott twirled his key card as he walked through the carriages, with many thoughts from the evening on his mind, the most recent being that he hoped that Tim didn't complicate matters further by getting involved with Amy Jordan.

An invitation and a rendezvous

The sound of the phone was loud and pierced into Scott's sleep as he tried to bury his head in the pillow. The caller was persistent and after the tenth ring, Scott thrust a hand onto the nightstand, knocking the phone receiver off in the process.

As he rubbed his eyes and leant over the bed to pick up the phone, he heard a woman's voice saying hello.

He leaned back on the bed and placed the receiver against his face. "Hello" he said groggily.

"Good morning Scott. I hope I didn't wake you." It was Daphne Pennington, sounding very bright and breezy.

Before Scott could reply, Daphne continued. "I figured that you'd probably be up by now. I was just wondering if you fancied getting a bite for breakfast?"

Scott looked over to the clock, to see that it was ten thirty.

I must have had a little too much to drink last night, Scott thought, as he was someone who rarely slept past eight.

"Scott?" Daphne asked at his lack of a response.

Scott said, "Sure, Give me half an hour?"

"Sounds good. I'll see you in the dining carriage. See you in a bit." said the voice at the end of the phone, before hanging up.

Scott chucked the phone on the nightstand and let out a small groan. He had really hoped that Daphne hadn't meant the invitation last night. Daphne Pennington, just as you've woken up, was the not the perfect hangover cure.

Scott led in bed for a few minutes longer, trying to wake up his brain, before hopping out of bed and heading to the shower.

Twenty minutes later, Scott was showered and dressed, and feeling like his head was starting to clear. As he picked up his key card, he paused before leaving, and thought to check on Tim. He pulled the sliding door slowly open and looked in. Tim was sprawled out on his bed, gently snoring. Scott decided against waking him as he closed the door, glad that Tim was in his own bed, and that he was there alone.

He walked out into the passageway and headed through the train to the dining carriage. He paused to look out the window, out on to the blur of green fields. As he looked out, an announcement sounded over the speaker system. It was Lambert's voice.

"Ladies and Gentlemen, for your interest, we are just about to cross the Grand Mississippi River, the longest river in the United States. We will shortly be leaving the state of Illinois and heading into our sixth of the journey, Iowa. If you wish to take a quick look, now's the time. I think you'll agree that the view is quite splendid on this fine Sunday morning. Thank you."

Scott watched as they crossed the river, a wide expanse of blue. Lambert was certainly correct about the view, and Scott stayed for several moments watching the river fade into the distance, before remembering that he had to meet Daphne.

He walked through the lounge into the dining carriage and saw that Daphne has already arrived and was sat at a table by the window. He walked over and gave a polite smile to the Stuarts sat in the corner, the only other people dining.

Approaching Daphne, Scott noticed how well dressed she was, even for a Sunday morning. She sat in a sharp brown suit that accentuated her hair, accompanied by a flamboyant necklace. He wondered if this was always her attire, or if she was like some of the other ladies on the train, trying to out dress each other.

As he sat down, Daphne smiled and asked, "Did you just see the Mississippi?"

Scott returned the smile and said apologetically, "Yes, sorry. That's why I'm a few minutes late."

"No bother. I've only been here a moment myself. I went ahead and ordered a pot of tea. But I suppose you'd like coffee?"

"No, tea will be fine." Scott replied.

Daphne said as she poured Scott a cup. "It's not often I find anyone who drinks tea. I only became a fan from living in England."

Scott smiled as he added milk. "That's the same reason as me." He looked out the window and said, "Good choice of table."

Daphne looked out and smiled. "It is beautiful country. I love the fact that this company used a track that doesn't go through any cities. It's so lovely just seeing the real country."

She leaned forward and added with a little chuckle, "Plus the fact that Denver will be coming up and I have an awful Aunt that lives there and this is the perfect opportunity not to see her!"

After chuckling at her own comment, she continued, "I can't believe that we're almost halfway! We'll be in Los Angeles before you know it! What have you and Tim got planned when you get there?"

Scott sipped his tea. He said, "Tim's going off to Yosemite on a camping trip."

Daphne asked, "You're not going with him?"

"No, I'd like to. But it's for his work. He's a travel reporter. So, instead I plan to just see some of the sights of L.A for a few days before heading back to New York. Yourself?"

Daphne replied, "I have a few friends that have just got a new place in the Hollywood Hills, so I'll be staying with them for a week, before flying up to San Francisco to stay with my sister for another week. But I tell you, all that will seem quite dull after this journey!"

Scott smiled. "I guess it's quite easy to get used to this luxurious lifestyle."

Daphne said quickly, "No I was referring more to the antics of the passengers!"

Scott felt foolish that he hadn't guessed why she might be so excited. Scott nodded in agreement and said, "They're not your average bunch, are they?"

Daphne laughed. "No they are not! I tell you, I find that Harry Broadside the oddest one of them all. Although Gerry Kennedy seems to have a chip on his shoulder the size of Idaho!"

Scott said, "Well at least you'll have a lot to tell your friends and sister!"

"Won't I just! My sister will be so jealous to know that I've met Clarissa Lavelle!"

She picked up her tea and said, "She'll be most disappointed when I tell her what a bitch she is in real life!"

Scott didn't respond as they were joined by Tim, who walked up to them and took a seat, still looking a little too dishevelled from bed.

Tim said, "Don't mind if I join you?"

Daphne smiled. "Not at all Tim. We haven't ordered yet."

As if someone somewhere had taken a hint, Rosalie appeared with a notepad.

She took their order, and supplied them with more juice, coffee and tea. Tim quickly took a large cupful of black coffee and drank it down in one gulp.

Daphne pulled a sympathetic face. "Someone have one too many margaritas last night?"

Tim just smiled sheepishly as he took another cup of coffee.

Jessica Rae entered and, after taking a quick look around, took a table by herself in the corner. Scott watched her for a moment before returning to listen to the conversation between Tim and Daphne about Yosemite.

Several minutes later, Rosalie arrived with their breakfast. Scrambled eggs and smoked salmon for Daphne, eggs benedict for Scott, and the full works for Tim.

They ate in relative silence, enjoying the food and watching the scenery. As they were close to finishing, Amy Jordan entered and headed in the direction of their table. Again, she was wearing something that showed off a lot of one aspect of her body. That morning it was a pair of short shorts with a long cardigan over her shoulders. She indicated to the empty chair and said, "Good morning all, can I join you?"

Daphne smiled as she put her cutlery down. "Certainly honey, we've just eaten though."

Amy replied as she sat down next to Scott. "That's ok. I had a bite earlier."

Tim offered the coffee. "Would you like some?"

Amy nodded and he then poured for her. She said, "Thanks. So did everyone sleep well?"

Scott replied, "A little too well. I don't usually sleep as late as I did."

Amy said cheerily, "It's not like you have to be up for work or anything!"

Scott caught Tim's eye before Tim said, "Scott always finds it hard to unwind! Always thinking about his work!"

Amy asked, "What sort of insurance do you sell?"

Scott answered, "I don't actually sell insurance." He paused. "It's more of the Claims department. But it does get very stressful. It's a big workload with quite a small work force!"

A story had obviously come to Daphne's mind as she sat up straighter and said,

"Speaking of insurance salesman, a colleague of mine once had a patient who was having therapy because she believed insurance salesmen were actually the Devil's disciples, spreading evil over the land."

Tim said under his breath, "Doesn't sound too far from the truth!"

Daphne giggled, and then said a tad more seriously, "Well this patient actually had to be institutionalized because......"

As Daphne launched into her story about the deranged house wife's rampage through her local town's Insurance Brokers with a bread knife, Tim and Amy leaned forward, listening avidly. Scott thought once again that Daphne really didn't act like a professional psychiatrist.

While this was one of Daphne's more entertaining stories, Scott thoughts had wandered to deciding which passenger to speak to next. While the pleasantries were nice, Scott decided that he had already missed too much surveillance that morning.

At a suitable interlude in the story, Scott made his pleasant excuses and got up from the table.

He passed Thomas pouring more coffee for Jessica, and decided that he would walk the length of the train to see who else was up and about. The lounge was empty, save for Bradley polishing glasses behind the bar. Scott continued through and moved quickly across the reception so as not to get caught by Lambert. He walked through the sleeping carriages without seeing anyone, except Rosalie knocking on the Kennedy's suite and waiting patiently with a tray of food. As he arrived in the observation carriage, he saw Harry Broadside sat by himself, staring out of the window. A little further up the carriage, Avril Kennedy also sat alone, brightening up the carriage in a luminous floral dress. She was sat with her head back and had a large hat over her eyes, presumably asleep.

Scott hesitated for a moment, before taking a seat, a suitable distance away from Harry, but close enough to make him very aware that he was there. He picked up one of the information booklets from the side table and pretended to look through it. He looked up a couple of times, each time noticing that Harry, who was still looking out the window, had appeared to grow rather uncomfortable.

After several minutes, Harry swiftly stood up and made for the door, before stopping in front of Scott. He said quickly, "Look Mr Blacklock, I apologise for calling you what I did last night. It wasn't called for. I was just a little angry. But I'm going to ask you not to ask me any further questions about my ex wife. Got it? Good Day."

And as quickly as he had spoken, he had left.

Scott sat there for a moment, a little surprised at his outburst, but more so by the apology. After replacing the booklet on the table, he decided to head to the balcony for a cigarette.

As he walked past Avril, her voice came from under the large hat. "I was quite surprised too!"

Scott stopped and lowered into a chair to see her face before saying, "Mrs Kennedy. I didn't realise you were awake."

Avril pushed her hat back.

"Just resting my eyes!" She said, and then smiled mischievously. "But keeping the ears open!"

Scott asked. "Is that how you get all your juicy Hollywood gossip?! Pretending to be asleep?!"

Avril's smile widened. "Oh I've done much worse than that!"

Scott nodded his head in the direction of the door that Harry had left through and asked, "So you know him then? From when you were working with Clarissa?"

Avril nodded her head slowly. "Oh yes. Not that Clarissa ever talked to us about it. Not when she met him, not even through the whole divorce thing. I read more about it in the papers!"

Scott asked, "Divorce thing?"

Avril said, "It didn't go on for very long. From what I gather, Harry and his lawyers asked for a huge divorce settlement. This was very quickly refused by Clarissa, but then for a moment, it all looked like it was going to get very messy. There were rumours of him exposing all about her, so Clarissa paid him off. Not what he had originally asked for obviously, but more than I think most expected he would get."

Scott asked, "Had you met him before this trip?"

Avril said, "Yes, at a few parties. Whenever I met him, he was always besotted with Clarissa and pretty ignorant of everybody else around."

"You didn't like Harry when you met him?"

Avril's nose twitched, as if his name was a bad smell. She said, "I didn't particularly think much of him then, no. And from his conduct so far on this train, he hasn't endeared himself to me any further."

Scott smiled, "I think there are others on this train who would agree with you."

He took the fact that she kept settling in her chair as a hint that Avril hadn't intended for this to be a long chat. She obviously couldn't eavesdrop on the next willing victims if she wasn't "asleep" under her hat.

Scott stood up and explained that he was off out for a cigarette. He left with Avril saying a hearty comment about them being bad for you.

Scott disregarded her advice as he walked through the empty cocktail bar and pulled open the door onto the back balcony. As he walked out, he pulled a cigarette packet out of his jacket and looked up at the wide blue sky, dotted with small white clouds.

The balcony could comfortably take four or five people standing out there, and so as Scott stood there by himself, he understood what Clarissa had mentioned to him the day before, about the feeling of escape you got at the back of a train. Scott thought that the feeling of leaving all your troubles down the track would be appealing. Wouldn't do much for Clarissa, he thought, most of her troubles seemed to be on the train.

As he lit up, he thought about the letters sent to Clarissa. Was the person that wrote them on this train? Scott was fairly sure that they were. Who was the most likely candidate? On this, Scott had several answers, although there were more questions with all of them.

Scott was disturbed from his thoughts by the sound of the door opening. He turned, expecting it to be Jessica but was surprised to see

Anthony Stuart, looking casual in jeans, but with his trademark open necked shirt.

Anthony also seemed startled to see Scott, before hiding it with his big smile. He said, "Hi there. Sorry! Just gave me a jump then!"

Scott smiled and waggled his cigarette. "It's the only place you can smoke on this thing!"

Anthony moved forward and placed his hands on the rail. "I just thought I'd better come out and see it for myself. I've been told the view from the back of a train is always a nice one. Like a feeling of escape!"

The familiar comment came back to Scott. It seems he hadn't been the only one to have a conversation with Clarissa when the passengers hadn't been in a group.

As if answering Scott's question, the door opened and out on to the balcony stepped Clarissa. She too looked surprised at the presence of Scott.

Scott smiled. "Good morning Mrs Jordan. Have you come out to admire the view too?"

Clarissa cheeks flushed slightly as she looked to Anthony before answering to Scott. "Yes, I just had to get some good clean fresh air."

As Scott put out his cigarette he said, "It's good that I've just finished this then."

Scott made to leave when Clarissa spoke, "Mr Blacklock, thank you for a nice game of cards last night. Maybe we could play again this evening?"

Scott turned as he opened the door and replied, "Thank you. It would be a pleasure."

Clarissa said, "Although you will have to forgive me. I can be quite awful at it. I just can't do a good poker face, despite being an actress! I always give away what my hand is!" She laughed at herself, and the two men chuckled politely.

There was a short silence until Scott smiled and said to her,

"Yes, well maybe Anthony here can teach you a few things on discretion."

He turned and walked into the bar, letting the door close behind him.

Sunday roasting

> *Hi Miranda,*
>
> *Wish you were here! I know this is a postcard of Grand Central Station and I'll have mailed it from Los Angeles, but this damn train doesn't stop anywhere! Some amazing scenery though – have taken lots of photos! Having a very weird time so far! Clarissa Lavelle is on the train, can you believe it?! (She's a bit of a bitch in real life!) Most of the other passengers are older and quite boring, but I'm still taking advantage of the free alcohol! Scott will kill me for saying this, but there was more to this trip than he let on! I have a feeling things are going to get very interesting! Running out of space so will have to tell you all when I get back!*
>
> *Tim. X*
> *P.S. Sorry again about Saturday night!*

The Express was steaming through Iowa by the time that the passengers had eaten in spectacular fashion, finishing a large banquet of a Sunday lunch. It was approaching four in the afternoon when Gerry Kennedy, after having a brief rest in his room, arrived in the observation carriage. Despite the fact that the white fluffy clouds of the morning had given way to a darker, more overcast sky, the observation carriage was surprisingly full. At the far end of the carriage, Harry Broadside sat with Anthony and Tim, discussing a baseball game rather loudly, Anthony pausing from his story to ask Rosalie for more drinks. Mark and Amy Jordan were also sat together, playing a game of chess. Sat rather closer to him, were Daphne and Avril, deep in discussion. Before his wife could notice him, Gerry turned and headed back up through the train, quickly stopping in his suite to pick something up, before heading in the direction of the lounge.

As he arrived in the lounge, Gerry found it to be a lot quieter. Sat in the corner was Caroline, deeply immersed in a book. Further down the bar, being served a coffee by Bradley, was the person he had been looking for. Clarissa gave a warm smile to Bradley as he left, and picked up her magazine. She was about to open it when she saw Gerry walking over to her.

Her face dropped as he rather cautiously took the seat opposite her.

"Good Afternoon Clarissa, did you enjoy the lunch?"

Clarissa decided to open her magazine anyway. As she started to flick through the pages, she said shortly. "Delicious. Did you come for a chat about food?"

Gerry chuckled nervously. "You mentioned yesterday that I could quickly grab you for five minutes."

Clarissa continued to look through the magazine. "I'm busy now. Come back later."

Gerry waited patiently for a moment as she continued to flick. When it became clear, that he wasn't going to leave, Clarissa shut the magazine harshly and said shortly, "Two minutes, go."

Gerry smiled and said, "Thank you Clarissa, I won't take a second of your time. Clarissa, I know you've taken time out recently to be with your new family, but I wanted to ask you if you'd like to return to the show. It really isn't the same without you and your magnificent presence on stage."

Clarissa folded her arms, "I know. I've read the reviews."

Gerry ignored the comment and continued, "If you came back, we could organize anything you wanted, reduced shows to have more time off, anything else you might..."

Clarissa cut him off. "Gerry. Stop now. Save yourself a little bit of dignity for God's sake! I have already told you I am not returning to that show. Not now. Not ever. You could offer me whatever you want, I wouldn't take it!"

Gerry tried to retain some of his composure before giving a forced smile, "Ok Clarissa, I understand you may not want to return to that."

He pushed the manuscript he had been holding across the table between them. He said, "But I think this might interest you. It's a new film we have in the pipeline. With you as the leading lady. It's a thriller. We think it would be perfect for you."

Clarissa looked across at him. "Do you now?"

Gerry pushed it across the table a little further, "Please Clarissa, just have a read of it. No obligations. Think of it as a holiday read."

Clarissa eyed him for a minute longer before rolling her eyes and picking it up. She said, "Ok, I'll have a look over it."

Gerry smiled gratefully and when he didn't move for a moment, Clarissa said sharply,

"Well? You got what you wanted, now piss off and leave me alone! I'm not going to look at it any quicker with you watching over me!"

Gerry's face reddened as he stood up. Clarissa added, "Oh, and don't bother me every five minutes asking me if I've read it or I'll just chuck it out of one of these windows."

Gerry, now not smiling, turned and walked away, not before Clarissa finished off in a louder voice so that Gerry could still hear, "Oh, and F.Y.I Gerry, it really isn't very becoming for a grown man to beg. I'm sure Avril wouldn't like it. But then she's probably off making too many fashion mistakes to notice."

Gerry continued walking and left the lounge, resisting the urge to return and ram the manuscript down her throat.

Scott locked the door to his suite, as he headed to the lounge. He travelled down through the train and noticed that the clouds had darkened further and there was rain on the grasslands in the distance. He was stopped in the reception by Patrick Lambert, who had been hovering behind his counter. As he noticed Scott, he adjusted his pince-nez and beamed a big smile. He waddled out from behind the counter and said, "Mr Blacklock! How are you enjoying the journey? I hope everything is to your satisfaction?"

Scott smiled politely. "Everything's great thanks......"

They were interrupted by Gerry Kennedy striding past. Scott stood back to let him by, but Lambert, who hadn't seen him, almost toppled over as he passed through.

Scott put his hands in his pockets and said, "Maybe I'm not the passenger you need to be asking Mr Lambert."

He smiled again and headed into the lounge, before Lambert could engage him in any further conversation.

He entered and headed to the bar where he ordered an orange juice from Bradley. Clarissa, sat in the chair quite close to him, paid no attention to him, her head now deep in the magazine, the manuscript discarded on the coffee table.

Scott looked down the carriage at Caroline, who was still sat reading her book. Sat at either end of the carriage, the two women could not have looked more opposite. While Clarissa sat with an aura of self confidence, Caroline looked like she had no awareness of herself at all. She was sat with her legs askew and her hair falling out of an untidy bun. Scott tried to see what book she was reading, but the title was too small. Caroline looked up for a second and gave a quick smile to Scott as he was looking in her direction.

Scott took that as an opportunity to have another talk with her. He walked over and smiled as he sat down. He said, "You do like to read a lot!"

Caroline smiled. "Don't you find you never get a chance to read at home? I always read more on vacation."

Scott nodded in agreement. "I know what you mean. How are you enjoying the whole express experience so far?"

Caroline replied, "It's lovely." She stopped before adding nervously, "I'm sorry if I seemed snappy last night at the card table. I just get a bit funny with Anthony around other women."

Scott said, "That's ok. Don't worry." He suddenly felt very conscious of the balcony meeting he had unwittingly observed several hours earlier.

Caroline continued, "I know I should just try and loosen up a bit. I think it's just because Anthony and I had a few problems a while back. I mean, we're fine now. But I still find it hard sometimes."

"That's understandable."

He was actually surprised she had been that open with him. Perhaps she's fishing for clues, he thought.

They stopped talking at the arrival of Harry Broadside to the lounge, who quickly spotted Clarissa at the end and strode down towards her.

As she saw him approaching, she picked up her things and stood up. Before he could start she snapped,

"Harry, don't fucking start with me! It's enough that I have to put up with you while we're eating, but if I've said it once I'll say it a thousand fucking times, stay away from me!"

Harry said pleadingly, "But, but Clarissa, please just hear me out."

His speech was slightly slurred and Clarissa leant forward and sniffed. She said, "Good God Harry, you stink of beer! Some things don't change I see! Except that this time I'm not around to pick up the tab! But that's why you're here isn't it? Now get out of my way! The words 'restraining order' are starting to sound very tempting!"

Clarissa elbowed past him, and swiftly left the lounge. Scott and Caroline watched Harry pause for a moment, before following after her. They sat in silence for a second before Scott said, "I hope he's not about to attempt a re-match."

Caroline added, "It wouldn't surprise me. He seems like the boisterous type."

Scott turned to look at her. "You've had dinner with him, haven't you?"

Caroline replied, "Yes, we were on the same plane from Boston. He and Anthony were talking for ages about sports! I hadn't realised that he was connected to Clarissa."

She then added quietly, "It seems to be true that she attracts attention from everyone wherever she goes."

She folded her bookmark sharply before slotting it into the page and shutting the book firmly closed.

Happy Anniversary!

The overcast skies of the afternoon had made the twilight of the evening arrive early as the first specks of rain fell on the windows of the train. The clock above the dining carriage door showed it to be six thirty as Patrick Lambert pushed through the door into the kitchen.

He arrived to see Andreas Russelli glazing tartlets, while Thomas helped chop vegetables. Standing over at the other counter, Rosalie was turning napkins into different origami shapes. Lambert headed over to the chef and asked, "Andreas, is this going to be an anniversary dinner to remember?"

Andreas did not look up from his work and took his time in answering. He replied gruffly, "Of course it will be. All my dishes are remembered."

He then turned his back on Lambert to tend to something on the hob. Lambert decided not to press any further, a sulky chef was the last thing he would need tonight. He turned his attention to Thomas.

He asked, "Thomas, you know where you are and what you're doing all evening?"

Thomas looked up and said nervously, "Yes, Mr Lambert. Helping Andreas in here and then serving dinner with Rosalie. Then I'm clearing dinner away before assisting Rosalie and Bradley in the lounge and bar later."

Lambert nodded. "Good. Who's got the room service night shift tonight?"

Thomas said quietly, "Andreas has, Sir."

As Thomas answered, Andreas muttered something under his breath while he stirred one of the sauces. Lambert ignored him and walked back down the kitchen.

He gave Rosalie an appreciative nod for her napkins, before returning to the door to make his prep speech. He was about to clap his hands to get their attention when he was bumped by the kitchen door opening. Bradley peered around the door. He said, "Sorry Boss, didn't see you there!" before walking past him and leaning on the counter next to Rosalie.

Lambert clucked and pointed at his watch. Bradley responded, "Sorry I'm all of a minute and a half late, but I was just serving more room service to your most important guest!"

Rosalie muttered as she finished her last napkin, "Yes, Mrs Jordan seems very keen for room service whenever you're on duty!"

Bradley smirked at her, but turned to look at Lambert when he gave a little clap of his hands. Lambert cleared his throat and said, "Right everyone, I won't keep you a moment. Now I know I don't need to stress that this is the Express's anniversary night, so I want you to make this the slickest, most professional operation ever."

He turned to Rosalie and Bradley, "You two, I don't want to see a single guest waiting for a drink all evening. Especially Clarissa Jordan! There have already been two occasions where she hasn't been served immediately! And Rosalie, make sure you and Thomas do a good job at dinner. As you know, I will be joining the guests at dinner, so I expect you to make things run smoothly, especially with our slightly less confident, team member." Lambert said, directing a glance at Thomas, who looked up nervously and almost cut his finger instead of the leek he was chopping.

Bradley said light-heartedly, "Give him a break boss; it is his first Express trip."

Lambert said shortly, "Yes, but it's only Rosalie's third, and I don't see her having any problems. And don't interrupt me again Bradley. Right, time is pressing on, and I still need to change. Bradley, Rosalie. I shall see you in the lounge in half an hour. You know what you have to do."

Bradley made a face at Lambert's back as he left the kitchen, which was accompanied with Andreas giving him the finger. Lambert was oblivious to both as he walked through the dining carriage and headed to his room, fussing quickly with the table cloth and straightening a candle before hurrying on.

Avril Kennedy sat at her dressing table wrapped in a black fluffy dressing gown and her hair riddled with curlers. She leaned over and examined the lines around her eyes in the large mirror. As she picked up her eye liner, she made a mental note to make an appointment with Dr Hopkins, for a quick visit to his surgery and his Botox cabinet.

The door to the Kennedy's suite opened and Gerry stormed in, slamming the door behind him and sitting heavily in an armchair. Avril looked at him in the mirror for a moment before saying, "She said No?"

Gerry looked up at her and said angrily, "Do you know what she said? She said "Gerry, I didn't realise that you were so broke you went around local elementary schools looking for scriptwriters!' Can you believe it?"

Avril put her eye liner down and turned around.

"The little bitch!" Avril said venomously.

Gerry retorted sarcastically, "Just noticed that, have you?"

Avril said quickly, "What are we going to do?"

Gerry answered slowly, "I just don't know." before putting his face in his hands.

Avril stood up, and said with a slight trace of panic, "Well we have to do something! Gerry, this is our last chance. If we don't get this deal, we're going under!"

Gerry stood up and snapped, "Don't you think I know that you stupid woman!"

Almost as soon as he had said it, he winced and bent over slightly. Avril put her hand on his arm and said, "Gerry, what is it?"

He lowered himself back into the chair and replied, "I'm ok. Just a twinge of the old heart."

Avril knelt down next to him and scolded, "You were told to cut out the scotch and cigars!"

Gerry was about to retort, when he had another twinge. Avril noticed and said more soothingly, "Look, I know we're both stressed. But you have got to take it easy.

I'm sorry that I've left it all to you."

Gerry said quietly, "Not like it makes any difference now anyway."

"We're not in L.A yet. I'll try talking to her, woman to woman."

Gerry leaned back and wheezed, "I wouldn't hold your breath."

Avril smiled and squeezed his hand, "Let's not give up all hope just yet."

Mark Jordan pulled his cufflinks straight and checked himself in the mirror one last time before pulling open the partitioning door into his wife's suite. He saw that she was sat at her dressing table, her hair held up with a jewelled butterfly clip. Mark was not surprised to see that Clarissa's cocktail dress was still on the bed and not on her. He said, "Must we always be the last ones to arrive everywhere?"

Clarissa smiled in the mirror as she applied moisturizer to her neck and arms. She said, "Come now Mark, you know a girl has to have plenty of time to get ready!"

Mark looked at his watch. He said, "It's already past seven."

Clarissa dropped the smile. She replied, "What's the rush?! Anyway I was interrupted by that senile old bastard Gerry."

Mark walked further into the room and asked, "Why? Is he trying to get you to give an answer on that script?"

Clarissa answered as she began to apply her make up, "Yes he did. I told him he could forget it."

Mark seemed relieved by her answer as he asked, "Was the script terrible?"

"To tell you the truth, I only read about half a page. But that's not why I said no. I have a much better offer for a much better film. Easy Oscar contender. Jodie Foster and George Clooney are already signed on."

Mark said as he moved to stand behind her, still talking to her through the mirror,

"I thought you decided you weren't going to work again."

Clarissa dropped her make up brush and answered, "Well I wasn't. But I'm just so bored at the moment."

Mark's face fell at the comment. Clarissa turned to look up at him and placed her hand on his chest, "Oh not with you darling, just not working."

Mark removed her hand and walked away. "You're certainly acting like your bored with me, the way you practically drip off of that Stuart bloke, and always flirting with the bar tender."

Clarissa said dismissively, "That's just a bit of fun."

Mark raised his voice, "Well it happens to be a bit of fun that I don't like watching!"

Clarissa stood up and raised her voice to match his. "Don't watch it then! I have a flirtatious character! You knew that when I married you! Deal with it!"

She sat back down to her dressing table and finished, "Now if you want me to get ready any faster, you'll get my diamond choker out of the safe over there, and then get out while I finish getting ready."

Mark looked over to the safe which was part of Clarissa's bedside table. He said, "Do you really think it's a good idea to be wearing that at the moment? With the letters and everything?"

Clarissa continued to apply her make up, "I really couldn't care less what you think is or isn't a good idea. I'm not going to let a little freak with too much time on his hands scare me, nor am I going to let my husband tell me what I can or can't do. The diamond please."

Mark said through gritted teeth, "We haven't finished our conversation yet."

Clarissa turned to look at him and said, "Yes we have Mark. I'm not going to talk to you about it anymore. Now get the diamond out for me."

"Get it yourself!" Mark shouted as he walked out and slammed the door behind him.

Scott sat on his bed, waiting for Tim who was still getting ready. They had both got back to the suite at the same time, Tim a little bit tipsy and Scott with a scornful look on his face. Scott had filled Tim in about Clarissa giving Harry an ear bashing. Tim then told him that that might have been slightly his fault. He went on to explain that he had spent the afternoon sat with Anthony and Harry talking about baseball, when Anthony got the first round of drinks in.

"And then more drinks kept coming, when Harry left us, he was a bit merry!" Tim had said. Scott told him to drink two pints of water while he was getting ready and left him in his room, telling him to be ready in an hour.

Forty minutes into that hour, Scott had opened the door to find that Tim had crashed out on his bed. After a brief snap at him, he had now waited in his room, having to listen to Tim sing loudly and out of tune on his MP3 player as he was getting ready. When he decided he couldn't take the warbling any longer, he knocked on Tim's door and pulled it open. Tim was jigging around the room doing up his tie, but stopped and pulled his earphones out as he saw Scott at the door. He said, "Won't be two minutes longer!"

Scott said impatiently, "I'm going onto the lounge. Hurry up! Dinner's at seven thirty and it's already twenty past."

As he finished the knot he said, "Don't worry! I'll be there, just making myself look good for the lovely Amy!"

Scott stopped walking to the door and turned back around. He paused before saying, "Look Tim, I was trying to say it subtly last night, but I'd really prefer it if you toned things down with Amy."

Tim looked at him, "So, you're stopping me from having any fun on this train?"

Scott replied, "Tim, I'm working here. And she is the step daughter of my client. I don't want things getting complicated."

Tim shrugged, "It's only a bit of fun."

Scott snapped back, "Fun still makes things complicated. I'll see you in the lounge." as he walked back through his suite and out of the door.

Scott strode through the sleeping carriages angrily. Angry that Tim couldn't see his point, and angry at himself for snapping at him. He arrived at the lounge and was immediately accosted by Lambert at the entrance.

"Welcome Mr Blacklock to the Express's anniversary evening, we have a superb dinner about to be served." He clicked his fingers at Rosalie who walked closer and offered champagne. Scott thanked her and moved away from Lambert before he said something rude to him.

He looked around the lounge to see the Stuarts and Harry Broadside sat in the corner. Jessica Rae was sat alone at the bar, and as Scott took a seat in one of the armchairs, the Kennedys arrived with Daphne.

Scott had only just sat down when Tim arrived. He took a champagne flute from Rosalie, and walked over to Scott with a sheepish smile. As he sat down he said, "Look Scott, I'm sorry. I will do what you asked. You know, keep it friendly. I'd hate to mess your case up in any way."

Scott smiled, "Thanks. And you know what I said about Miranda last night. I do think you should think about you and her properly."

"You reckon?" Tim asked.

"You and her have flirted around the idea often enough. There must be something there for that."

"I did write her a postcard today." Tim pondered.

Anything else he was about to say was stopped by the arrival of Amy Jordan, wearing a flowing red dress. She looked as though she was intending to head over to them but had the bad luck of having Lambert intervene. Scott and Tim watched as Amy made forced conversation, until the arrival of Mark and Clarissa averted Lambert's attention and he practically ran over to Clarissa to compliment her. Clarissa in particular seemed displeased at Lambert. He had decided to greet them before they had properly entered the carriage. As it was, he had completely ruined her entrance, and was blocking the rest of the carriage from seeing her floor length black dress that had cost as much as a Trans-Oceanic ticket.

Scott and Tim observed him, and as Tim took a sip of his champagne he muttered, "He really is quite an odious ass licker, isn't he?"

Lambert turned to the rest of the carriage and said loudly, "Right, now that we're all here, may I once again welcome you all to our Trans-Oceanic anniversary. This is a very special occasion as today is the Express's twentieth anniversary. So, Ladies and Gentlemen, if you would like to take your glasses, we are now going to head into the dining carriage for the anniversary dinner. May I hope that you all have a fantastic evening and a night to remember!"

Thirteen at dinner

On entering the dining carriage, the passengers were once again greeted by soft classical music from Bradley at the piano. However they noticed immediately that the separate tables had been moved to make one long table. Clarissa muttered as she entered, "Dear God, I don't have to eat at the same table as these people!"

There were name plates at the table, so there were a few moments of place finding, and then gentlemanly chair pulling. Lambert stood at the head of the table at the far end next to the piano. Lambert had rather obviously chosen Clarissa to sit next to him, and the right side of the table sat Clarissa, Mark, Amy, Daphne and Scott. As Tim sat in his chair at the opposite end to Lambert, the other guests took their seats on the other side of the table.

To Tim's displeasure, Jessica was sat next to him. Beyond her were Harry, Gerry, Avril and Anthony, with Caroline taking the final seat on the other side of Lambert.

Lambert waited for everyone to settle and for Rosalie and Thomas to fill everyone's glasses, before clasping his hands together and saying,

"Ladies and Gentlemen, our beautiful anniversary dinner is about to be served. So, before it arrives, I just wanted to thank you all once again for travelling with us. I hope that your journey so far has been nothing short of splendid. Now, as you know the Trans-Oceanic Express is renowned the world over, and I have had many guests aboard this train, but I can honestly say that I couldn't think of a better group of people to be sharing this special night with."

There were a few quiet, polite laughs from around the table.

As he spoke, he lifted his glass, "So, without further more ado. I would like to propose a toast. To a fantastic journey, but more importantly, and I'm sure you'll all agree, new friends."

There was a rather unenthusiastic mumble of "new friends" from the rest of the table.

"Jesus Christ!" Daphne muttered to Scott as she took a large gulp from her glass.

As Lambert sat down, Rosalie and Thomas emerged from the kitchen with the first plates of the starter course. The sound of absent conversation was only masked by the noise of shuffling napkins. It seemed most of the passengers had been quite unprepared for a group dinner. Scott watched the faces of the guests around the table. It was quite obvious that most of them were either startled, disgruntled or at the very least, uncomfortable. It was Anthony who broke the short silence when he asked Lambert, "Mr Lambert, How long have you been with the Express?"

Lambert smiled at the chance to start a conversation, "I've been with Trans-Continent for fifteen years Sir."

"Always on this train?" asked Anthony.

"No I was transferred from their European headquarters twelve years ago. I've been in charge of the Express ever since. And she's never looked finer!"

"She is magnificent, I will say that." said Anthony.

Lambert looked further down the table and said, "You can ask Dr Pennington. She's travelled with us before. Don't you agree?"

Daphne looked over and said, "Oh yes, the train's looking much better than before, simply wonderful." before adding to Lambert in a deadpan voice, "And you certainly haven't lost any of your charm! And this dinner, well it's something else!"

Scott saw Avril hide a smirk by dabbing her mouth with her napkin, while resisting one himself.

The first course passed quite pleasantly. The guests had more to drink, and they were all excused with having to make conversation. Lambert was regaling them with a surprisingly entertaining story about how Trans-Continent almost didn't get planning permission with the Australian Government, and how it was all due to a mix up with the courier, involving the architectural plans and a rather lewd manuscript for a late night pay per view TV Show.

There was gentle laughter as his story came to a close. As Thomas and Rosalie began to clear the first course away, Rosalie quickly whispered something in Lambert's ear. Lambert reacted with a smile and said, "Rosalie has just informed me that we have just entered the state of Colorado. Colorado is a state of great beauty and one or two rather impressive mountains. The state actually has fifty four "fourteeners"!"

"Fourteeners?" asked Mark.

"Mountain peaks rising over fourteen thousand feet. This railroad actually takes us through Colorado at some pretty high altitudes. If you're staying up late this evening, we may even see some snow! This also means that we are now in our eighth State of the journey."

Clarissa said, "Eight? That's always been my lucky number! Maybe Colorado will be lucky for me!"

As she said it, she smiled at Lambert, although her gaze shifted to Anthony and her eyebrow rose slightly.

"Superstition's just a load of old crap!" said Harry from further down the table.

Everyone turned to look at him. Clarissa appeared unfazed as she said, "Well if you you've got a face ugly enough to crack a mirror, I'd say that's quite a few years bad luck!"

Scott felt the tension at the table rise up by several jolts, despite a chuckle from Tim at Clarissa's comment.

Daphne had evidently felt the same tension as she spoke over any comeback and said, "You know, some people take superstitions so seriously that it develops into Obsessive Compulsive Disorder. I've seen many case studies on it. It's really very fascinating. About how it makes people feel in control, or protected, or lucky by random things that have no scientific basis. And so I know I should know better given my profession, but I swear by my lucky pair of Prada boots that have gotten me through every exam or interview I've ever had!"

Tim added, "I can't walk over three drains in a row! Very bad luck!"

"Well I'm glad I've never smashed a mirror!" said Avril as she knocked on the wood of the table.

Amy had been looking around the table and said, "I've just noticed there are thirteen of us here. Isn't it bad luck to have thirteen at a dinner party?"

Lambert looked slightly embarrassed by the question. Tim at the opposite end said,

"Yes, how does it go? Once thirteen have seated to dinner, the first one to rise again is doomed to die!"

Amy giggled, but stopped quickly when Harry said gruffly, "Like I said, a load of bullshit!"

Harry's comment had created another noticeable moment of silence and several people exchanged glances across the table.

After a second, Avril coughed and said, "For god's sake Lambert, tell us another train story!"

Taking Avril's lead, Mark spoke, "I have a question. I read that this journey used to take six days, and now it takes only four. Why is that?"

Lambert was glad for the change of subject and said, "About ten years back, we noticed a decline in our popularity, only a slight dip obviously. So we took a survey of all our passengers, past and present and found out what the problem was."

"And what was the problem?" asked Caroline.

Lambert smiled. "This is America. And we have mainly American passengers. We realised it was a time issue. Most were put off by how long they would have to be away from civilisation. So we installed a faster engine and shortened the journey time. We still don't go as quickly as other services, but you have to draw the line somewhere! Americans want to get everywhere so damn fast!"

In the kitchen, Rosalie and Thomas heard the sound of laughter from the dining carriage. As they waited while Andreas was feverishly making the last preparations to each dish of the main course, Thomas nodded at the door and said, "To tell you the truth, I'm surprised Lambert is entertaining them so much."

Rosalie looked at him and said bluntly, "That's polite laughter."

As she got tired of Andreas's continual fussing, she picked up three plates closest to her.

Before heading back into the dining carriage, she finished to Thomas, "And they're only laughing because the majority of the passengers on this train are morons like Lambert."

The main course was served, and people began to eat. The conversation around the table finally broke up into smaller groups, and the claustrophobic atmosphere reduced somewhat. At the far end of the table, Lambert was talking to Caroline, and telling her yet more about the train. Clarissa, sat on his other side, was half listening, but seemed very bored by the conversation. Lambert took another sip of his wine, before saying, "So, you see, the reason this railroad was closed down in the first place, is the exact same reason that Angus Thistlewood bought it!"

"How so?" asked Caroline.

"Well" continued Lambert, "This railroad was actually one of the first built straight across America, well over a hundred years ago. It was originally built for a specific manufacturer, to get their goods from the Atlantic to the Pacific. But then, what with developing transport, more efficient railroads, and the fact that all the population centres through America weren't close enough to make it viable to stop in them either, the railroad's use was completely minimised. And then there was the problem that the track had not been maintained very well. Which eventually lead to its closure in the middle of the last century. It was left for almost forty years before Mr Thistlewood applied to buy it. He thought it was a golden idea to avoid all civilization!"

Caroline nibbled on a piece of asparagus, and listened intently, grateful that she was sat next to someone who talked so much.

Lambert paused for breath before continuing, "Obviously the track was in a terrible state of disrepair. There were whole sections of track that needed to be replaced. It was a long and arduous job, but, as you can see, it paid off in the end."

Caroline asked, "So is it still hard to maintain?"

Lambert smiled, "Not at all my dear. Don't worry; we have outposts every one hundred miles of track. If there was ever any problem with the track, we have a highly equipped maintenance team at every city nearest the location of our track. We can contact them by our remote satellite link-up. We've never had a hitch though, touch wood!" He did so on the table as he said it, "So, the outside is easy to maintain, and the inside, well....." He chuckled at her, "I'm in charge of that and I run a very tight ship!"

Caroline smiled politely, "Yes, you do seem to."

Lambert continued, "It's my job to make sure everything is just right! Everything from the speed of the train, to the requests from room service, to how well the meat is cooked for dinner!"

As the rain lashed heavier against the windows, Lambert gestured to it and said, "Alas, if only I could improve the weather!"

Caroline asked, "How do you have time to oversee all of that?"

Lambert answered, "I'm a very busy man! Not including the fact that I help out where needed, with room service also!"

Caroline looked surprised. "Really?"

Lambert smirked as he cut into his meat, "I'm the one that does the rota, so I make sure I rarely do it! I'll tell you this; I made extra sure I wasn't on tonight for the "Graveyard shift"! Not that our chef Andreas was too happy with the extra shift!"

"So one person has to stay up all night?" asked Caroline.

Lambert chuckled, "Yes, from midnight until six in the morning. Obviously one of our drivers is awake, but we couldn't really ask him to leave the controls to serve a nightcap to a guest!"

Over from Caroline, Anthony was excused from talk of the Express as he had mentioned to Avril how much he loved New York, and she had proceeded to tell him everything and anything about it. Avril had talked about the best places to eat in the Upper East Side, the best places to buy property in the Upper West Side, and was now onto the merits and downfalls of Central Park.

"So," Avril said, "Gerry and I were attending this party for a movie premiere, this has got to be going back ten, fifteen years now, and it was being held in this marquee in Central Park. It was only early October, so the organisers thought the weather would be fine. The party was a good one, not quite as good as one of our own obviously."

Avril took another sip from her glass and paused for breath.

"That was until it started to snow. Heavily. It was one of the worst snow storms on record for October. Two inches in the first twenty minutes! We were lucky to escape before being completely snowed in! I dare say that film company didn't use those party organisers again!"

Anthony said, "Wow that is quite crazy!"

Avril smiled at him, "That's New York for you! You should always expect the unexpected!"

Avril noticed across the table that Clarissa had been looking in their direction. She quietly revelled in the fact that she was engaging in conversation with the one person that Clarissa wanted to.

Further down the table, the conversation was more obviously subdued. Gerry, Harry, Jessica and Tim ate in comparative silence. Jessica was chewing quickly and obviously trying to listen to conversations further up the table. Across the table, Daphne had drawn Scott into a conversation which meant that Tim, sat at the end, was faced with a choice. Concentrate on his food, or talk to Jessica. He decided on the food.

They had lasted almost the entire main course without any words between them when Jessica put down her cutlery, bored of eating and said to Tim, "Tell me, Tim, How are things at 'Travel Today'? Any high profile stories recently? Let me guess! 'Tim Anderson's selection of greasy diners in the Mid West'?"

Tim looked at her, but didn't rise to the bait, "They're fine, thank you Jessie. Really good! There's a good chance I'll be doing a piece about Antarctica in the fall. It's somewhere I've always wanted to go!"

Jessica pulled a face, "Yeah, because that sounds like it would be fun!"

"It will be. Lots of fun."

"You really need to get a life Tim."

"Well it's more of a life than tearing a family to pieces for the sake of a headline, I imagine." said Tim as he pushed his plate away.

Jessica smiled falsely, "That's where you and I differ, isn't it?"

As she moved her food around the plate, she added, "Why aren't you doing an article on this train if you're travelling on it? A bit too high profile for you?"

Tim stayed calm. "I'm actually on my way to Yosemite. I'm doing a piece there."

Jessica said scoffing, "Camping?"

Tim said, "Yes Jessica. But as to your question about why I'm not working on this train, this is just my typical high profile vacation."

He patted her hand and said sarcastically, "It's such a shame you have to be working on an assignment to be able to get on the Express. Maybe they're not paying you enough over at your place?"

As he finished, he turned his back to her in order to indicate to Rosalie that he would like more wine.

As Thomas cleared their plates away, Daphne said to Scott, "That was fantastic!

I don't ever think I've been fed this well."

Scott nodded in agreement as he drank some water.

"Although I'm not sure how much more I can stand sitting at this table! The atmosphere is awful!" Daphne added quietly. She placed her napkin down and smiled. She said, "I'm sure they've got cameras somewhere! That this is some kind of psychological test!"

Scott smiled and said, "More likely a reality T.V show."

Sat next to Daphne, Amy had spent the majority of dinner talking to her father. Mark and Amy had talked about her next semester and which modules she would be taking. They had then moved on to plans for Thanksgiving, and finally Mark asked about Tim.

Mark set down his knife as he asked, "You seem to have gotten quite friendly with Mr Anderson?"

Amy replied, "Yes, we get on well."

Amy, who could see where this line of questioning was leading, added, "But then he and Scott are the only ones vaguely close to my age!"

Mark looked down the table at Tim. He chose the wrong moment to look as Tim was gulping the rest of his glass so that Thomas could fill him up properly.

Mark looked back to Amy, "I know that most of the people here are a bit older, and I'm sorry if it's a bit boring, but I don't want you doing anything silly."

Amy rolled her eyes at him, "I'm not going to do anything silly Dad! I'm a big girl now!"

Mark said, "I know you are. But I just want you to be careful. Ok?"

As Mark asked the question, Rosalie delivered their dessert course to them.

Amy smiled, "I will be Daddy." She then looked at the chocolate creation in front of her and said,

"Now can we consider that the fatherly pep talk over with, and get on with eating this?!"

Dessert had been cleared, the cheeseboards had been laid out, and Rosalie and Thomas had taken people's order for an after dinner drink. Once again the conversation had returned to centre on Lambert as he told them yet another story from the Express.

As Rosalie entered from the lounge carrying a tray of drinks, Lambert said, "This train has quite a long standing history of remarkable stories, dating right back to when the track was built. Several of the labourer's wives travelled with them as they slowly made their way across America, laying the track. They lived on their wagons, and by the time they made it the Pacific, most of them had a family of four or five! And then in our second year of opening, a passenger gave birth, six weeks early as we were crossing though Illinois. Both mother and baby were fine, but the beauty of it was that the baby had been conceived on the couple's first trip on the train the year before!"

Caroline said, "What a lovely story!"

As Avril was handed her drink, she said, "Ugh! Childbirth! Sounds like hell to me!"

Lambert chuckled, "There are many stories of love and romance, if you'd prefer one that didn't involve children...."

Clarissa said quietly, "Yes Please!" to which Mark responded with a look, glad to see that Amy hadn't heard it.

Lambert continued, "Well, we have had one or two high profile honeymoons on the Express, but one particular businessman was so in love with his wife, that he arranged for blimps to be flying in every state of their journey. All sending different messages of love to her."

Jessica made a noise, "Oh, how disgusting!"

Lambert shrugged and said, "I'll agree, it may be too sickly sweet for some!"

"I'll say!" That came from Daphne, who then added with a laugh, "And I can tell you that my love life was far from perfect when I last travelled on here!"

Harry spoke up, "I think it at least showed her how much he loved her."

As she spoke, Avril changed her glass with Gerry's, as hers had a mark around the rim of it, "Well the man does have a point, even though I agree, it is far too over the top."

Clarissa leaned forward and said, "I think that love should be spontaneous. The whole blimp thing is too planned. I wouldn't like it."

Harry answered back to Clarissa, "Maybe some people like to plan things? Maybe if they have security within a relationship, they can do that?"

Clarissa retorted, "Like I said, love should be spontaneous. Sometimes you can plan things, and then realise you've made a mistake. I think it's best to move on and forget it. You should never have to live with a mistake."

She finished her sentence rather obviously in Harry's direction.

Tim leaned over to Scott and said, "Is it just me, or is this starting to become a different conversation?"

Harry said, "So you think mistakes should just be quickly brushed under the carpet and forgotten about?"

Clarissa replied, "Absolutely."

"Regardless of whom it hurts?" asked Harry.

Clarissa half shrugged and half nodded.

Gerry swigged on his drink and looked up, "Is that in every aspect of life then, or just in matters of love?"

Clarissa looked at him and said bluntly, "I think it should apply to all aspects of life, but you above anyone should know that Gerry!"

Gerry's face reddened and Avril looked as though she was about to hurl abuse at her.

Lambert saw what was happening and tried feebly to intervene. He started, "Well now let me tell you about this other couple who...."

But he was cut off, not by Avril, but by Jessica who said loudly and calmly, "Can I ask you Clarissa? Is it because you have so much money and supposed 'power' that you can adopt such an attitude?"

Clarissa finally snapped at having the opposite side of the table questioning her aggressively, and pointed a finger at Jessica. She said viciously, "Look you, I told you last night not to speak to me again, or I would take action! It's enough that I have to sit at the same god damn table as you!"

Lambert said, "Look I think we should all try to calm down...."

Harry said loudly at Clarissa, "Who do you think you are, talking to people like that?!"

Mark spoke up now, "Excuse me, do not raise your voice at my wife!"

Clarissa carried on pointing at Jessica, but looking at Harry, "That little bitch at the end of the table is a nasty little tabloid reporter Harry! So I have every right to be angry! Just shut up about things that don't concern you!"

While Tim smirked at Clarissa's comment about Jessica, Scott noticed that Anthony and Caroline looked quite amazed at the proceedings. He couldn't tell whether Daphne and Amy were embarrassed or amused by it.

Harry had obviously started and wasn't going to finish. It wasn't surprising as he had probably drunk even more than Tim throughout dinner. He picked up his drink and spilled some as he brought the glass to his mouth. He said, still focusing his attention to Clarissa, "Maybe we should talk about things that do concern me! Seeing as how you've not given me a chance yet!"

It was at this point that even the most amused of spectators started to feel uncomfortable. Mark leaned over towards Harry and said sternly, "Mr Broadside. My wife has made it clear that she does not want to speak to you! Now, if you don't stop talking, I will ask Mr Lambert to remove you from the carriage."

Lambert's face had gone white, his dinner party ending in such a fiasco.

Mark's comment angered Harry and he slammed his glass down, knocking it over and surprising Gerry. As he stood up, pushing his chair back harshly, he shouted, "Oh now the devoted husband has his say! You can stay out of this too! What, just because you got a ring on her finger, you think that gives you a say! Let me tell you buddy; you're just one in a long line! She'll chew you up and then spit you out!"

Mark stood up too to look Harry in the face. He said furiously, "That's it!" He turned to Lambert, "Are you going to do something about this or do I have to?"

Lambert looked from Mark to Harry and then said weakly, "Mr Broadside..."

But Harry had seen Mark standing up as a threat and said across the table to him, "What! You want to take this outside? Is that it? Right, well come on then!"

Harry moved around the table towards Mark. Lambert looked on helplessly, as Mark took a step forward. Tim and Scott quickly looked at each other and jumped out of their seats. Tim intercepted Harry, while Scott stood in front of Mark, preventing him from moving further. Mark stopped at Scott; however the drink and anger in Harry made him less responsive to reason.

Tim grappled with Harry as he tried to pass him, shouting, "Come on then!"

Scott placed a hand on Mark's chest as he took a step forward, Anthony stood up and said loudly, "Harry, stop it!"

As the weird reality of a fist fight across the dinner table overcame the other guests, more people started to speak, and there was a blur of motion around the table.

Time seemed to slow down as the voices around the table merged.

"Mark! Just sit down and forget about the little weasel!"

"Now, come on Harry...."

"Gentlemen please!"

"I'm not going to warn him again!"

"Dad!"

"COME ON THEN! COME ON THEN!"

"I can't hold him, someone help me!"

"Please Mr Broadside..."

"Scott! I can't hold him!"

"Lambert! For god's sake, do something!"

Anthony was too late in aiding Tim as Harry pushed him off and moved quickly around the end of the table. He then lunged violently towards Mark, Scott trying to somehow keep his mass between the two of them. There was a brief moment when Scott realised he was about to take a punch for Mark as Harry pulled his fist back, but then stopped.

He stopped, as had everybody else, from the sound of a loud groan from across the table.

Gerry, still sat in his chair, groaned again and clutched his chest.

An observer looking through the train could easily have mistaken them for playing musical statues, as every one present froze in surprise or shock.

Avril grabbed his arm, and then gave a small shriek as he leant sideways, fell off of his chair and collapsed on the floor. There was silence for several seconds, as everyone stared at the empty chair, not quite believing what had just happened.

"Oh God! Gerry! Gerry!"

Avril started to scream as she knelt next to him. Daphne reacted first, and jumped out of her seat to race around the table. As she crouched next to Gerry, there were several moments of confusion as the rest of the passengers moved around the fallen body.

Avril and Daphne blocked nearly everyone's view and Scott saw Daphne feeling for a pulse. Everyone remained quiet, except Avril who now started to sob. Daphne quickly started trying to resuscitate him.

There was silence from everyone as Caroline stepped forward and comforted Avril.

Minutes passed.

Daphne kept trying.

Avril's sobs turned to a whimper.

Daphne looked up, her face as white as a sheet.

As she said the words, they shattered the silence like a gunshot.

"It's no good. He's dead."

Anyone for brandy?

Daphne's words reverberated around the carriage for several moments. The moments turned into a minute. It was only when Avril's shock started to turn into hysterical tears that anyone moved. Daphne moved around Gerry's body and put her arms around her, relieving an overwhelmed Caroline of her position. She crouched awkwardly on the floor as she comforted Avril, who remained kneeling, clutching desperately to her husband's hand.

Scott shook himself out of the shock of the last five minutes, and said soothingly,

"Daphne, maybe you should take Mrs Kennedy to her room."

Daphne nodded, and slowly helped Avril up. She stood brokenly, as if she were a puppet whose puppeteer had cut all her strings.

As Daphne and Avril left the carriage, Amy said quietly, still looking at Gerry,

"What the hell just happened there?"

Mark answered, "It looked like a heart attack."

Scott looked over to Lambert who was stood opposite him. Lambert did not look too far from death himself. He stood against the wall of the carriage, looking like he wished he could be anywhere but there in that moment. He was shaking slightly, and clearly didn't look as though he was capable of taking charge of the situation without prompting.

Scott moved over to him and said, "Mr Lambert, maybe you should move the guests to the bar?"

Lambert roused from his trance, and looked at Scott. He swallowed, and then nodded once. He said in a shaky voice, "Aah, Ladies and Gentlemen, if you would all be so kind as to move to the cocktail bar at the end of the train. Bradley will be waiting for you there to serve you drinks."

Clarissa was the first out of the door, even beating Bradley who left his position at the piano. Mark put a reassuring arm around Amy and led her out, followed by the Stuarts who left silently. As the others left, Tim noticed Jessica hesitating, obviously wanting to witness everything. He linked arms with her as he passed her, forcing her out of the room. Scott watched Harry leave and then hesitated. He turned back to Lambert, who had gone back to silently staring at Gerry's body, thinking of everything that lay ahead. A death on the Trans-Oceanic Express was not something that was going to be quickly forgotten. He was horrified at the thought of the reports, an inquest, the company's reputation, HIS reputation.

"Mr Lambert. Mr Lambert!" Scott's second attempt brought him back into the room, and Lambert turned to look at him.

"Mr Lambert, you have got to pull yourself together. You still have a train to run."

Scott said as neutrally as he could.

Lambert nodded slowly. Scott continued, "Now, do you have a place where you can keep Mr Kennedy? Preferably refrigerated?"

Lambert answered, "Yes. We have a chilled section in the storage carriage up front."

"Well then I suggest you find something to cover him with and move him there." Scott said evenly.

Lambert straightened his tie, trying to regain some sort of authority. He turned to his members of staff who had remained in the carriage, unsure what to do. Rosalie looked fairly composed, while Thomas looked as though the sight of a dead body had made him want to vomit. Lambert could see that neither would be able to help with moving the body, and he certainly wasn't going to do it. The fact that he now had to deal with moving his staff around from their duties allowed him to think of it as a simple scheduling task. This calmed him, and he said quickly, "Rosalie, go to the cocktail bar and take over from Bradley. Tell him to get back to help move the body...Mr Kennedy. Thomas, go and get Stephenson or Dunn to help also."

As Rosalie and Thomas left in opposite directions, Lambert returned to the fact that he was stood over a dead body, and his immediate problem was still to be solved. Again the thoughts of what was to come filled his head. His brief moment of calm faded, and he looked at Scott despairingly and said, "I don't know what to do next!"

Scott said calmly, "Right, do you have anyone with any medical knowledge on board? So you might find out what happened here?"

Lambert said, "Only a basic first aid officer."

"Who's that?" Scott asked.

"Um......me." Lambert answered quietly.

"And you just stood there then?!" Scott said incredulously.

"I...I panicked. And from the look of it, I wouldn't have known to do anymore than Dr Pennington did!" said Lambert quickly, hopping from one foot to the next.

"Ok. Ok." said Scott, trying to calm him again. Scott wanted to know more and realised he could take advantage of Lambert's weak state. He paused for a moment before saying, "Well, I think you should see how Avril is doing. She may have some answers. But, under the circumstances, I think I should come with you and do the talking."

Scott didn't wait for an answer of approval, and turned to leave the carriage. In doing so, he missed Lambert give an appreciative smile. Scott walked into the empty lounge, and walked behind the bar, pouring a large brandy. As Lambert followed him in, he said, "Hey, what are you doing behind there? What do you think you're doing?"

Scott walked past Lambert and thrust the glass into his hand. As he carried on through the lounge, he replied, "I think that you're going to give that to Avril. She's obviously going to need it!"

"Oh yes. Of course!" Lambert said sheepishly.

Daphne answered Avril's door several moments after Scott's knock. She opened the door wider when she saw that Lambert was also stood there. Avril had gotten into bed, but was propped up by pillows. The tears had subsided, but her breath was still ragged from crying too much. A tissue lay, practically shredded, in her hands.

The sight of Avril Kennedy, usually such a strong personality, sitting limply in bed with mascara run cheeks, took Lambert aback and words refused to come to his mouth.

Scott realised that Lambert was not offering the brandy, so took the glass from his hand and entered the room. He handed the drink to Avril, who looked up and thanked him.

Daphne took a seat, as Lambert entered and closed the door behind him. Avril swigged the contents of the tumbler in one straight gulp and placed it on the bedside table. Scott took the chair opposite the bed and said gently, "Mrs Kennedy, we're very sorry for your loss."

Avril sniffed and said, "Thank you for your kindness. But I'd prefer to be alone."

Lambert finally spoke, "Mrs Kennedy. I just wanted to let you know that we will do all we can for you. If you no longer wish to continue the journey, we completely understand. If we stop the train now, we can have someone sent out from Denver. They could be here in a couple of hours."

Avril shook her head. "No. Thank you, but that would be holding everybody else up. Besides, I have a place in Los Angeles. I'll be able to sort our affairs out better there..."

On the last words of her sentence, Avril trailed off, obviously close to tears again.

Daphne moved over on to the bed and said, "Perhaps you should leave me to it."

Scott stood up and followed Lambert to the door. He stopped to turn and ask,

"Forgive me Mrs Kennedy, but may I ask one last thing? It looked like Gerry was having some sort of seizure or attack. Did he have any health problems?"

Avril composed herself before she answered, "Yes. He had open heart surgery late last year." She paused before saying, "He hadn't been in good health recently. He was on medication, but I had to nag him to take it."

Tears welled to her eyes, but she continued.

"He was told to cut out all drinking and smoking. And to alter his diet."

And then a small sad smile came to her face, she said loudly, "But do you think the stupid bastard listened!"

"He wasn't following his doctor's orders?" asked Scott.

The smile left Avril's face as quickly as it had appeared and she shook her head.

"Thank you Mrs Kennedy, we'll leave you alone now." said Scott gently. As Lambert opened the door, Scott beckoned Daphne to follow them out.

They all walked into the corridor, Daphne pulled the door to and looked questioningly at Scott. Scott glanced at Lambert before he said to Daphne in a lowered tone, "Daphne, I know you're a psychologist, not a medical doctor. But you would still probably have the best opinion on this train. Does what Avril described fit with what happened to Gerry this evening?"

Daphne seemed puzzled by the question at first, but answered anyway, "Well, yes. It certainly looked like a heart attack or a similar seizure to me."

Daphne cast her eyes down and added, "I just wish I could have done something more."

Scott placed his hand on her arm. "Don't think that. You did everything you could, admirably."

As Scott said it, he noticed Lambert to the side of him, an uncomfortable expression on his face.

Scott nodded at the door and asked Daphne, "How do you think Avril's doing?"

Daphne said, "She's not doing well, that's for sure. I'll stay with her for tonight."

She pulled her plastic keycard out of her jacket, "That brandy helped, but I've a feeling she'll need something stronger than that to sleep tonight. Could you run along to my suite? There's a packet of sleeping pills in the cabinet above the sink."

"Sure." said Scott as he took the keycard from her hand.

Daphne smiled in way of thanks and walked back into Avril's room, shutting the door behind her.

Scott turned to see Lambert stood looking expectantly at him. As he tried to pass him, Lambert asked, "So, what next?"

Scott's patience at Lambert's ineptitude finally snapped. He replied, "I'm going to Ms Pennington's suite to get some sleeping pills like she asked. And I would suggest that you go attend to your other guests."

As Scott passed him, Lambert said, "Yes, you're right. I must make a statement to the guests."

"Good idea." Scott said as he carried on walking.

Lambert called after him, "Mr Blacklock. Thank you for your advice."

Scott grunted an acknowledgement to Lambert as he left the carriage, but his thoughts quickly went to other matters as he headed to Daphne's suite.

Of all the drama that had ensued over the dinner table, from the verbal attack on Clarissa from Harry, Jessica and the Kennedys, to Mark and Harry's prevented fist fight; nothing had prepared him for the sudden death of Gerry.

He slid the keycard down, and entered Daphne's room. He found the pills easily enough and walked back out into the corridor, closing the door behind him.

If Scott was right, and the perpetrator of Clarissa's letters was on board this train, then the events of dinner had definitely shown who the volatile suspects were.

He passed the Stuarts suite and entered the second carriage where he rounded the corner of Jessica Rae's room.

Harry Broadside made for an obvious suspect, in that he was definitely the most disgruntled of the group. But he also couldn't discount Jessica Rae from anything, knowing what lengths she would go to for a story.

Scott stared at his black shoes against the pattern of the carpet as he passed Harry Broadside and Amy Jordan's rooms, flicking the card key against the sleeping pills in his hand.

What was niggling at Scott was that, besides Harry, Gerry had been his next best option.

He had now been cleared because of his death. But had he? He could still have been the one who wrote the letters. And it was unlikely that Gerry would have acted without Avril. It was this thought that Scott dwelled on as he entered the third sleeping carriage and knocked at Avril's door. Daphne answered, but didn't open the door very far. He handed her the tub of pills. She thanked him and said a quick goodnight.

Scott could hear that Avril was crying again. The door closed and Scott made his way on up to the bar, for once actually feeling the need for a drink.

As he passed his own suite, he felt badly for Avril and the rough night ahead of her. He realised that he himself probably hadn't processed what had just happened yet, and he barely knew Gerry. He was in poor health, she must have been prepared, he thought. But it was so sudden. As he walked past the Thistlewood Suites, it was the abruptness of Gerry's death that bothered him the most.

Scott entered the bar and walked into a very quiet atmosphere. There was no mingling, nor the hum of gentle conversation. In fact, the guests had appeared to move as far away from each other as possible. Jessica Rae was sat in the far corner, writing not very discreetly, in a notepad. The Jordans were sat in the opposite corner, drinking quietly. Looking over at the bar, Tim and Harry had rather obviously taken stools at opposite ends. The Stuarts in the corner closest to Scott did at least appear to be talking, albeit in whispers to each other. Lambert who had been talking to Rosalie at the bar, saw Scott arrive and took a few steps forward into the centre of the carriage. Scott had been wondering if he had missed Lambert's statement, but it seemed Lambert had been waiting for him.

All eyes around the room fell on Lambert as he gave a small cough. He started,

"Ladies and Gentlemen. I'm sure you were all as shocked and saddened as I was following the most unfortunate...incident at dinner. I have spoken to Mrs Kennedy. She informed me that Mr Kennedy was in poor health and on medication. It would appear that he had some sort of heart failure, and sadly died from his illness. This evening's events will not be affecting our travel plans, and we will be heading straight on to Los Angeles at Mrs Kennedy's request."

"How is Mrs Kennedy?" asked Caroline.

Lambert was slightly surprised at a question. He answered, "She's resting now. Dr Pennington will be staying with her for the evening."

There was a silence as everyone was expecting Lambert to speak further. After taking a few moments to realise that, he put on a rather forced smile and said, "Now, let's make sure you all have one of our fantastic liquors in your hand!"

Lambert rather obviously hurried behind the bar to help Rosalie. The hum of chatter slowly filtered into the room and it seemed that everyone felt it more appropriate to talk at a normal level. Scott, who had been stood by the door during Lambert's speech, made his way over to the bar and sat at a stool next to Tim.

"Where have you been?" said Tim as he sipped a cocktail though a straw.

Scott absently fingered the key card in his hand before setting it down. He looked over at Lambert and Rosalie who were preparing drinks at the other end of the bar.

"Helping a certain useless manager out!" Scott said quietly.

Tim leaned back, and said, "It was never going to be a happy anniversary anyway, what with the dinner party from hell, but Gerry, well! Talk about killing a party!"

As Scott took a coffee liquor from Rosalie's passing tray, he couldn't help but feeling very disturbed with the events of the evening so far. And not just from Tim's tasteless remark.

A good hand dealt by Clarissa

As the train ploughed on high into the mountains of Colorado, the rain on the windows turned to fine snow. The end of the oppressive sound on the glass did little to lighten the spirits of the passengers in the bar. The events of the last hour had now sunk in and, while there were small pockets of conversation, voices were hushed.

The Stuarts and the Jordans were talking quietly in their respectful corners. Jessica had headed to the balcony for her seventh cigarette.

Harry sat alone, propping up the end of the bar, slowly sinking one bottle of beer after another.

Further along the bar, Scott and Tim sat, drinking in momentary silence.

Tim placed his drink down and asked, "How does this all fit into your theory Mr secret agent?"

Scott ignored the question and looked down the bar to see Harry. He didn't seem to be trying to listen to their conversation, but Scott couldn't be sure.

Caroline moved up to the bar on the other side of Scott to get a drink, stopping him from answering Tim's question. When she reached past him to get a napkin, Scott nodded to Tim, indicating the chairs in the far corner.

As they sat down, Tim realised any questioning of Scott would have to wait, as Amy had left her parents and was making her way over to join them. She sat down next to Tim, clearly still quite shaken.

Tim asked gently, "Hey, how are you doing?"

Amy replied, "It was just so sudden, wasn't it? Poor Mrs Kennedy. Clarissa's over there talking like nothing even happened!"

Clarissa often quickly becomes the topic of conversation with Amy, thought Scott.

He said quietly, "I know. It is quite a shock."

Tim said dryly, "And the dinner was going so well up until then."

Scott gave him a look, while Amy looked slightly embarrassed.

She said, "Yes, I am sorry about my father. That slimy ex of Clarissa's just wound him up the wrong way." She paused before adding, "Thank you both for stopping them."

Scott said, "Don't worry about it. I think people just had a bit too much to drink."

Lambert had been skirting around the different guests checking up on them and it was now their turn as he waddled over. He stood nervously wringing his hands and said with a false cheer, "We finally got that snow I promised! Doesn't it look beautiful? Don't you agree?"

Amy looked up and said, "Well someone just died over the dinner table, so I hadn't really noticed. But gee, yes, isn't the snow pretty!"

Lambert paled and said quickly, "Let me get you some more drinks over here. Excuse me." He headed to the bar, looking not too far off a heart attack himself.

"Idiot!" Amy said as he was out of earshot. "I'm sorry, but I just can't stand that guy."

Tim sniggered, but Scott couldn't help but feel a little sorry for Lambert. True, he was annoying, but he was only trying to do his job. And Scott couldn't quite forget the look of desperation on Lambert's face in the dining carriage after the other guests had left.

Down at the other end of the carriage, Amy was indeed correct in the fact that Gerry's death had not filled Clarissa with any remorse. As she set her martini down she remarked,

"At least the snivelling little idiot won't be pestering me about that script for the rest of the trip."

Mark looked sharply at her, "Clarissa!"

Clarissa shrugged her shoulders. "What! It's true! Him and his trumped up wife were ruining this journey for me."

Mark kept his voice low, hoping that Clarissa would do the same. "For god's sake, the man's only been dead five minutes!"

Clarissa retorted, "And that should change anything? You heard Lambert said he was sick. Why should I be expected to cry a river for an old man with a dodgy heart? Especially as I didn't even like him!"

Mark kept his voice level, so as not to anger her further. He said, "I just think a certain level of discretion wouldn't go amiss."

Clarissa picked her drink back up as she said, "Look you didn't know him. I did. He never cared about my needs, only his profits. His wife was even worse. I tell you, I for one will be enjoying this journey a whole lot more with him out of the way."

She nodded over to Harry, still drinking alone at the bar, and added. "Now if only he'd drop dead."

Mark tutted heavily and sat back in his seat, refusing to continue this conversation in the hope that Clarissa would drop it.

They sat in silence for several minutes. Clarissa uncrossed her legs and put her hands in her lap, looking like a sulky child. She said, "Well this is boring." She nodded behind her and said, "Shall we invite the Stuarts for a game of cards?"

Before Mark could answer, Clarissa had stood up and walked over to the Stuarts in the corner.

Caroline looked rather startled as Clarissa approached, while Anthony grinned widely.

Clarissa smiled, more to Anthony than Caroline, and asked, "Hello there, the atmosphere is terrible in here. I was just wondering if you fancied joining Mark and I for a game of cards?"

Anthony nodded readily and said, "Certainly. We could do with something to take our mind off things."

As he turned to Caroline, his enthusiasm was obviously not matched in her face.

Caroline said in a quiet voice, slightly intimidated by Clarissa standing before her.

"Anthony, we just said we were about to head to bed."

Anthony nudged her arm, "Oh come on, just one quick game."

Caroline stood up, "Anthony..."

Clarissa interjected, "Now Anthony, if Caroline wants her beauty sleep...."

She then made a small cough as if to highlight her need for it.

Caroline's face fell and it looked as though she was forcing back tears. Her response was to pick up her bag and hurry out of the carriage.

Anthony stood up and said, "Caroline! It was only a joke!"

But Caroline didn't turn around and just avoided colliding with Lambert as she headed for the observation carriage.

Anthony made to go after her, but Clarissa stopped him by gently touching his arm. She said, "Oh let her go. She's just a bit stressed by the events of the evening, the delicate thing. Just come along for that one game."

Anthony looked torn for a second, before smiling and picking up his glass.

Mark suddenly appeared behind Clarissa, and eyed Anthony for a second. "Your wife not joining us then Stuart?"

Clarissa replied for him, "She's having an early night. Now why don't you two head on down and I'll go and ask Mr Blacklock to join us."

Mark and Anthony looked at each other and rather uncomfortably left for the lounge.

After Scott had agreed to join the game of cards and headed out of the carriage, Clarissa turned and walked over to the bar. She stood next to the counter opposite Bradley and leant forward, emphasising her cleavage. She said sweetly, "Now Bradley, do you think you could be a honey and accompany me to the lounge? I get awfully thirsty playing cards."

Bradley smiled and his cheeks flushed. Rosalie, who was further down the bar slicing fruit, said, "I'll cover this bar for you."

Bradley nodded to her and said, "Certainly Mrs Jordan. I'll head down straight away."

Clarissa smiled and straightened to head out with Bradley, but was stopped by a rather loud "Slut!"

She turned to see Harry, who had been watching her flirtation. Amy and Tim, the only other passengers left in the carriage, looked up from their conversation. Tim noticed Amy smirk slightly.

Clarissa took a step towards him, her hand on her hip, her face venomous.

"What did you say?"

"You heard!" Harry's speech was slurred. He had obviously not slowed down on his drinking since dinner.

Clarissa pointed a manicured nail at him viciously. She spat, "That's it! First thing in the morning, I'm getting on to my lawyers to slap a restraining order on you! And I'll make damn sure your employers find out about it! That's if a lowlife like you has managed to get a job! I expect you're still living quite comfortably off what you managed to weasel out of me you little worm!"

Harry made to interject, but Clarissa wouldn't let him, pointing her finger closer to his face. She continued, "Don't even try to carry on Harry. Or I'll sue your ass for harassment! Don't think I won't do it, you little piece of shit! Now I will say this one last time. Stay away from me until we get to Los Angeles. And then fuck off out of my life for good."

Without waiting a second, she turned on her heel and stormed out of the carriage. As she entered the observation carriage, she saw Lambert heading up towards her. He looked nervous at the anger on Clarissa's face. Before he could ask if anything was wrong, she said, "You! I think it's high time someone showed Mr Broadside to his room. He's really had far too much to drink. For God's sake, don't you have policies about these kinds of things?!"

Clarissa didn't give him the option to answer by continuing to walk towards the lounge.

Tim and Amy had not been too subtle in watching Clarissa's tirade, and now they sat back and positively enjoyed Lambert's attempts to get Harry, who could now hardly stand, to his room.

Tim looked across to Amy and asked, "What did you think of all that?"

She sighed and said, "It is nice to know that others agree with my opinion, but Clarissa still won."

He set down his drink and said, "Yes, but Harry hardly seems like a worthy adversary."

As if to confirm his comment, Harry walked into the doorframe as Lambert was showing him out, causing him to stumble to the floor, taking Lambert with him.

Amy giggled rather loudly. The mood suddenly became more intimate, as the sound of Lambert and Harry crashing through the observation carriage died away.

Amy said, "I guess you're right. But Clarissa really does believe the hype about herself. It's properly gone to her head over the years."

Tim asked, "Do you think it's having the constant attention of the world on you? I mean, you must have had a bit of press attention now?"

"I have had a bit, since Dad got with her." replied Amy, and then she blushed. "Actually I have to say, I did like it a bit. But I can see how it could become intoxicating."

"Or can turn against you." added Tim.

Amy nodded, and said to Tim, "I wish it would turn against Clarissa."

She added, almost in an accusatory way, "Why do you think Scott puts up with being in her company?"

Tim finished his drink and said lightly, "Scott loves cards. He's always up for a game." before adding more quietly, "And your father puts up with a lot more of her company than Scott does."

Amy bristled at that comment. She moved away slightly and said, "Yes, well that's a rather obvious point." She placed her drink down abruptly, "It's late, I think I should head to bed."

Realising that he had offended her, Tim quickly offered to walk her to her room.

Moments after they had left the carriage, Jessica Rae opened the balcony door and looked in. The carriage was empty, save for Rosalie now tidying the bar. She turned back and flicked her stub off the end of the train, ignoring the sand bucket near her feet. She took one of the empty stools and ordered a drink from Rosalie, setting down her notepad, full of notes from the last twenty minutes eavesdropping outside in the cold.

As Tim and Amy walked through the observation carriage, Amy slowed to look at the view. They had climbed further into the mountains, and the snow had gotten thicker. The trees thinned and in the valley below, they could see the half a dozen blurry lights of a little town.

Tim didn't want the evening to end this way, so took the opportunity to say something.

He gently touched her arm to get her attention and said, "Amy. I'm sorry for what I said about your father. I know it must be hard for you."

Amy smiled. "And I'm sorry for implying Scott was an idiot for spending time with her."

The smile dropped. "I just get so angry with myself for putting so much energy into hating her. I need to stop."

She turned to him, closer than they had stood before. She said softly, "Maybe it's time I started thinking about myself for a change."

She placed her hands on Tim's chest and moved in slowly to kiss him. Tim smelt her perfume and felt himself being drawn in. Amy's eyes closed and their lips almost touched, before Tim surprised himself and pulled away. Scott's words to him were suddenly pounding in his head.

Amy pulled back, first with a look of surprise, then of embarrassment. Before she could mutter anything, Tim said, "I'm sorry. It's not you. It's kind of a difficult situation for me at the moment."

He thought quickly. "I'm sorry, I should have said something. I'm kind of seeing someone in New York. I'm just flirty by nature."

Amy's look of embarrassment turned to a mixture of anger and upset.

He continued, realising that hadn't helped the situation, "Really, it's not you. I think you're fantastic. You're smart, funny and my god, beautiful. But it's just not fair for me to take this any further."

The statement seemed to work, as Amy smiled slightly, although her cheeks had resumed blushing. She said, "Its ok. I'm sorry too. It was forward of me. I understand. I'll see you tomorrow."

She headed out of the carriage, escaping the uncomfortable situation as quickly as she could. Tim could tell she was hurrying out, but couldn't think of anything to say to stop her, and wasn't sure if he wanted to.

He watched her go and sat down, slightly stunned by what had just happened.

He sat there for several minutes, thinking about Amy's advance, and his reasons for stopping it. For what had stunned him was that, although almost immediately, he had thought of Scott's request not to do it, what had actually stopped him was almost the reason he gave. At the moment that Amy had gone to kiss him, he couldn't help but think of Miranda, and how really he wanted to be kissing her.

"Well," he said quietly to himself, "I didn't see that one coming!"

Anthony, Mark and Scott were sat waiting at the card table in the lounge when Clarissa entered. As she took a seat, Bradley served them all drinks. Mark dealt them all in, and Anthony said to Clarissa, "We were just talking about Gerry. I think I'm still in a bit of shock about it all."

Clarissa smiled, "At least it got us out of that damned dinner party!"

Mark noticed how the mention of Gerry by Anthony didn't raise Clarissa's temper at all.

Scott pondered, "I wonder what will happen with their production company?"

Mark looked up. He said gruffly, "I heard that it was in quite a lot of financial difficulty. I wouldn't be surprised if it folded now."

Clarissa said, "That makes sense. It's why the old fool was so desperate to sign me back up."

"That and for your obvious talent!" said Anthony with a grin.

Scott was sure that he heard Clarissa make a sound similar to a purr. He looked across the table and saw Mark's face, so drew his attention by folding his cards in.

"I'm out." he said rather loudly.

"Me too." said Mark, whose focus turned to Scott, and he noticed that Mark looked a little bleary eyed.

As Clarissa folded too, Anthony displayed a flush.

"Well look at that." he said, still grinning.

Scott was distracted by Jessica entering and taking a seat at the bar. There was a tense silence when the rest of the card table noticed their new arrival. The three men looked quickly at Clarissa to see if there was going to be any eruption. But there wasn't one. After quickly noting Jessica at the bar, Clarissa turned back to the table pulling a face as though she had just seen a pile of vomit.

When Anthony made no move to leave, Mark said tersely, "I thought you were only staying for one game Stuart?"

Clarissa rolled her eyes at Mark's rudeness and leaned over to Anthony saying, "You can stay for a couple more games! I need to win my money back!"

Anthony conceded and the next three games were played in a tense silence.

It was difficult to work out which had created more of an atmosphere, the arrival of Jessica, or the awkward flirtation at the table that wasn't being hidden.

After Mark folded for the third time, he stood up and rubbed his eyes. He said,

"Right. That's me done. I'm too sleepy to play anymore."

"That'll be what's affecting your card playing then!" chided Anthony and Clarissa giggled.

Mark's face darkened and he left with an obvious growl. Scott noticed that there was not even a peck on the cheek for his wife as he left. He thought how the situation seemed very different to the dossier Peterson had given him and from the reports he had read. This happy new marriage didn't seem quite so happy anymore.

Jessica, who had made no effort to pretend she wasn't listening to the conversation, practically leapt off of her stool as Mark left the carriage.

She sauntered over to the card table and said, "I couldn't help but notice that you could do with someone else joining you."

Without realising that the other had done it, both Anthony and Scott held their breath to see Clarissa's reaction.

Without bothering to look at her while she shuffled the cards, Clarissa retorted, "I think you'll find that none of us want trash like you at this table."

Jessica ignored the statement as she took the chair that Mark had just vacated. Clarissa reacted immediately. As Jessica sat down, Clarissa pushed her chair back, stood up and leaned over Jessica threateningly.

She said through gritted teeth, "How many hints does it take for you to realise that you're not wanted?! Is your life really that empty that this is the only thing you can get pleasure from?!"

Anthony and Scott remained in silence.

Jessica kept her calm and said evenly, "I could ask the same of you. Is your life really so empty that you crave the attention of any male near you to get satisfaction?"

It took a few seconds for Scott to comprehend what was about to happen, but before he could register it, there was the sound of a loud slap.

Jessica's face whipped round, feeling the back of Clarissa's hand. Anthony rather obviously jumped back, and Bradley almost dropped the glass he was cleaning.

There was silence for several seconds, and Scott prepared himself for Jessica's response. However, she took the sensible option of retreat and quickly stood up and hurried out of the lounge.

Scott and Anthony watched her leave while Bradley quickly busied himself behind the bar.

Clarissa smoothed her hair, her cheeks still flushed, and said, "I'm sorry for that. But it just gets to a point......"

She seemed to have to calm herself physically. She took a deep breath and composed herself before saying, "Really, I do apologise for my behaviour. Now if you'll excuse me, I think I'm going to head to bed. That really was the perfect end to a horrible evening."

Scott smiled politely, while Anthony jumped up and said, "Let me at least walk you to your room."

A small smile returned to Clarissa's lips. She said, "Thank you Anthony. Goodnight Mr Blacklock."

Scott said goodnight to them both, and felt particularly uneasy to see them leave together.

He was stacking up the cards when Lambert entered from the reception, still looking extremely flustered.

He approached Scott and said, "Did I just hear an argument?"

As Scott placed the cards in a pile, he turned to Lambert and said, "Yes, another one!"

He patted Lambert on the arm and said, "Let's just say I think you were a bit premature at dinner when you said you couldn't think of a better group of people to be with!"

Before Lambert could answer, he gave him a smile goodnight and headed out of the carriage.

Things that go bump in the night

Scott made his way through the sleeping carriages and allowed his mind to try and process all the information it had received that evening. He decided that he would head to the balcony for a cigarette and a chance to focus his thoughts. He stopped at his door, to pick up a packet he had left in his room. As he went to retrieve his card key from his pocket, his thought of finding cigarettes was stopped by faint whispering coming from the carriage beyond.

He stopped, and then crept slowly to the entrance of the next carriage. He opened the connecting door slightly and could now hear two distinct voices.

"I hope I made the night slightly more bearable for you."

The voice was low and quite obviously a man's.

"You could say that...." Scott easily recognised the other voice as Clarissa's.

There was silence for a second, and then Scott heard the distinct sound of kissing.

"Well that definitely has!" Again the voice was Clarissa's. "Do you want to come in for a bit?"

"I shouldn't. And he's right next door!"

"Are you letting that scare you?"

"No." There was a pause. "I should go. I'll see you later."

Scott waited for a response, and took a second too long to realise that the conversation had ended and that footsteps were now headed his way. He dashed back into his carriage, fumbled with his card key, and just got into his room to pull his door to as the man entered the carriage. As he passed, Scott peered out of his door to see Anthony Stuart returning to the front of the train to his suite.

It was approaching midnight as Lambert returned to the kitchen. Thomas was finishing mopping the floor while Andreas wiped down the surfaces. Lambert rubbed his hands together and asked, "How are things here? Almost finished?"

Thomas stowed the mop and bucket away and replied efficiently, "Yes Sir. Everything's pretty much in order here."

Lambert suddenly became uncomfortable, "And....Mr Kennedy... is stowed properly?"

Thomas nodded, still looking slightly queasy. "Yes Sir. He's in the chiller."

There was an indecipherable grumble from Andreas. Lambert caught the words, "Disgusting" and "less room for my meats to breathe."

He chose to ignore him and continued looking at Thomas.

"Are the drivers sorted for the night?" Lambert questioned.

"Yes Sir." Thomas continued, "Mr Stephenson just had some supper and has headed to bed. Mr Dunn is on until six this morning."

Lambert nodded in approval and said, "Good work Thomas. You head to bed."

Thomas took his order and retreated to the staff carriage. Lambert stood awkwardly for a moment as Andreas had completely ignored his presence in the kitchen.

Lambert dreaded having to remind Andreas that he was on room service duty and was saved from doing so by Bradley's arrival.

As Bradley pushed the swing door closed, Lambert asked, with more authority than he would use on Andreas, "The lounge is spotless, I presume?"

Bradley gave him a little mock bow and said, "Ship shape boss! Rosalie is just finishing up in the cocktail bar."

Lambert nodded, giving a quick face of dissatisfaction at Bradley's attitude.

He returned to face Andreas, but the room service phone, as if on command, began to ring.

It took five rings for Lambert to realise that Andreas was not going to move from scrubbing the invisible spot on the counter. He looked back to Bradley and said,

"Bradley, get that one before you head to bed. Give Andreas a chance to finish up properly before taking over."

Andreas made no reaction to the comment, but Lambert thought that was sufficient in giving him his orders, and headed out of the carriage as Bradley reluctantly picked up the phone.

Lambert stopped briefly on the way to his suite in the reception carriage. This was at the bar in the lounge, where he quickly helped himself to a triple shot of brandy, before pottering off to his room.

Scott had waited in the shadow of his door until he was sure that Anthony had left the carriage. He then quickly searched in the semi darkness for his cigarettes before finding them on the dresser. He took one quick look down the corridor before closing his door and heading to the back of the train.

The grandfather clock chimed midnight as Scott entered the bar, and was pleased to see that Rosalie was still there, wiping down the bar.

He sat at a stool and said, "Have I just made it in time for one last drink?"

Rosalie smiled, "We actually have a twenty four hour licence on the train. What can I get you?"

Scott asked for a single shot of Amaretto on the rocks, which she quickly placed in front of him. He thanked her and took a large sip. While Rosalie continued to tidy up, Scott observed that, at a closer look, she was very attractive. Although this seemed carefully hidden behind the uniform and pulled back hair.

"Quiet night then?" Scott asked.

Rosalie looked over and said, "Yes. I don't think anyone was in a particular party mood. After.....what happened."

Scott nodded, "Yes, I wasn't really expecting the evening to pan out this way."

As he took another sip, he commented, "It must be hard to try and concentrate on your work after an evening like tonight."

Rosalie stopped cleaning and said, smiling pleasantly, "Yes, I don't have what you'd call a typical job! I haven't been with the Express very long, but I can honestly say, I've never had a trip quite like this before."

"Not your usual bunch then, I take it?" Scott said.

Rosalie replied diplomatically, "Well, this is the Express. There's always at least one extreme personality on board."

Scott smiled, as if seeing where she was headed. "Except that there's more like half a dozen extreme personalities this time?"

Rosalie hesitated, "Yes, but I've come to realise that everyone has a story to tell, even those that don't shout it from the roof tops. I mean, everyone has a few secrets, don't you think?"

Scott nodded in agreement, and said, "Too true."

There was a cough from the balcony and Scott turned to the door and then back to Rosalie. He asked, "Is there someone out there?"

Rosalie answered, "I believe Ms Rae is still out there, smoking."

Scott said, "If you'll excuse me, I think I'll pop out for a quick one before bed myself."

As he picked up his glass, Rosalie asked hesitantly, "Will you be needing anything else from the bar tonight?"

Scott shook his head and said, "No, thank you. Please, feel free to finish. It's not been an easy evening. I'll make sure Jessica doesn't want anything else."

Rosalie smiled in gratitude, as Scott turned to the balcony.

He stepped outside and immediately felt the chill of the cold mountain air. The snow had stopped and had given way to an inky black sky. Jessica was stood in one corner, wisely having picked up a coat from her room. As she acknowledged Scott, he did up his jacket and brought the collars closer to his neck. She chose to say nothing and continued to look out at the darkness.

Scott put the cigarette to his lips, and asked dryly, "How's the cheek?"

Jessica's expression didn't change, although she dragged on her cigarette with more ferocity. She said, "Fine, thank you. I suppose you've come out here to tell me that I deserved what I got from her? That I brought this on myself? That I'm a sad pathetic bitch blah blah blah?"

Scott said quietly, "I just asked how your cheek was."

Jessica pulled a face. She said bluntly, "Fuck you Scott. You and Tim are just the same. Like two peas in a pod. Well I don't have to take crap from either of you. Or Clarissa for that matter! She's going to regret crossing me! I have a new headline now. Clarissa Jordan in vicious attack against innocent star reporter! I can even use you as an eyewitness."

Scott said calmly, "And I would say that you crossed the line."

Jessica rolled her eyes at him as if he was stupid. She said, "Scott, you really don't understand journalism! I can write what I like about what you "saw". If you bring out another story, all it will mean is that there are two versions. And two versions mean controversy and controversy means the story gets even bigger! Either way, it's dynamite for me!"

She flicked her cigarette butt viciously over the balcony, and headed for the door.

She stopped when Scott spoke. "Jessica," he said evenly, "I don't care if you take my advice or not, but you should be more careful. If you carry on with this antagonistic method of working, you could very well end up getting more than a slap."

Jessica turned quickly to give him a sharp look, but chose not to say anything and walked inside, slamming the door behind her.

Scott stood in the silence, and wondered if Jessica would listen to his advice. He knew deep down that she probably wouldn't. Some people are beyond help, thought Scott. He looked out at the ever disappearing white rock and black sky as the train carried on at speed, and became slightly mesmerised as he finished his cigarette.

As he returned to the warmth of the bar, he saw that it was empty, with nearly all of the lights out, except a couple that were heavily dimmed. Rosalie had gone from the bar and he hadn't exactly expected Jessica to be waiting for him.

With no one else in the large carriage, it lost its atmosphere and felt positively eerie. He now understood Rosalie's urge to leave. Gerry's death had created an invisible fog of uneasiness.

Scott slumped on one of the leatherettes and downed the remains of his drink. It was now that he had sat down, in silence, that he felt the energy drain from his body. He hadn't realised how the events of the evening had quietly exhausted him. Even though his face was smooth, he felt that if he looked in the mirror, he would have the skin of an eighty year old. He rubbed his tired eyes and leaned back. It was silent except for the comforting rhythm of the train.

He still tried to think about his case, but felt his eyelids start to close.

He woke with a start, unsure of what had stirred him, and slightly bewildered that he had fallen asleep in the first place. As he sat up, he noticed that the lights were still dimmed and pulled back his cuff to see his watch. It had just gone one. He had only been asleep for forty five minutes. It was then that he noticed it. There was no gentle rocking of the carriage. The train had stopped. Scott stood up, slightly alarmed at the fact. As he made towards the observation carriage, he froze as he heard a noise. The sound was a quiet whimpering. And it was coming from the balcony. Scott walked quietly to the door and slowly opened it. Sat, huddled in the corner next to the cigarette bucket, with her knees pressed against her chin, was Caroline Stuart. Her eyes were blotchy and blood shot, and her nose was red, both from the temperature and the crying. She looked cold and parts of her dress and shoes were damp.

Scott opened the door further and said, "Mrs Stuart? Are you alright?"

Caroline looked up, stunned, too busy sobbing into her knees to notice the door opening. "Oh Mr Blacklock! I didn't realise you were in the bar! I didn't want anyone to see me like this!"

Scott said, with a trace of embarrassment, " I.....fell asleep on the settee. Mrs Stuart, you shouldn't sit out here. It's freezing. Let me help you up."

As Caroline took his hand, she used her other one to wipe the tears from her eyes.

"I'm sorry." Caroline said.

Scott said gently, "Its ok. Would you like to talk about it?"

Caroline replied quietly, "Anthony and I had an argument. I was still awake when he got back from your card game and I shouted at him for taking so long."

Scott suddenly felt uncomfortable as the memories of his eavesdropping caught up with him. He managed to keep a concerned face as Caroline continued,

"It's just that I find it hard sometimes. I mean Anthony's flirtatious by nature, and it's usually fine. But when he's being flirty with Clarissa Jordan........"

"I understand." Scott said softly. "But Caroline, I'm sure that you're husband loves you. And that he wouldn't jeopardize your marriage for anybody."

He swallowed, but Caroline didn't notice it as she said, "I know you're right, and that it's just me being silly, but......"

She didn't finish her sentence and turned to look out over the balcony, her eyes brimming with tears again.

Unsure what to say, Scott also looked out at the beauty of the scene. The snow covered everything in a blanket of white, and the train had stopped next to an impressively tall tree with strong branches and roots that were sticking vertically out of the snow.

The fact that the scenery wasn't moving jolted Scott back to the more pressing matter. He looked back to Caroline and said, "Did you notice the train stop?"

Caroline came out of her sorrow filled haze and looked at him, her eyes suddenly wide. She exclaimed, "Oh my God! We have, haven't we? When did that happen?"

Scott replied, "I don't know. I was asleep."

Caroline looked ashamed. "I guess I was too busy crying to notice."

The thought of her crying seemed to bring tears back to her eyes. Scott was now anxious to find out what had happened, and didn't really want to be stuck there all night with a desperate housewife.

He took her arm gently, as she seemed quite frail, and was now starting to shiver from the cold. He said, "Let me walk you to your room. You'll feel a lot better in the morning. I think it's been quite a night for everyone."

Caroline didn't say anything, picked up her bag, and let him lead her back through the quiet bar.

They didn't see anyone as they made their way through the sleeping carriages. As they arrived at Caroline's door, she turned to Scott and said quietly, "Thank you for your concern this evening Mr Blacklock. I'd appreciate if you didn't tell anyone about my little scene out there."

"Not a problem." said Scott with a small smile.

Caroline returned the smile and silently entered her room without turning the light on.

Scott heard Anthony's snores as the door closed. He quickly turned and headed for Lambert's room in the reception carriage.

He knocked quickly three times. There was no answer. He tried again, louder this time.

When there was still no answer, he figured that if there was a problem with the train, Lambert was probably already down by the engine. Scott headed through the dimly lit lounge and dining carriage. There was still no sign of anybody.

Scott approached the kitchen door and knocked once before pushing it open, ignoring the staff only sign.

Again he was presented with a dimly lit, but empty carriage.

He decided to press on. He walked through the clean kitchen and walked into the next carriage. This carriage was much more basic than the passenger's part of the train. He walked along the corridor and was presented with four doors. Two were storage rooms. One was a walk in refrigerator, the other, a walk in freezer.

Scott shivered slightly as he passed the refrigerator, perfectly aware that the wrapped corpse of Gerry Kennedy now lay in there. He started to get anxious when he entered the staff quarters, and found there was still no sign of life. Where the passenger carriages had corridors down the side, this one had one narrow one through the middle. There were six doors, three on either side, indicating that the rooms of the staff were not much bigger than a bed. Surnames were on the doors. Up the left went Russelli, Gobetti, and Dunn. The doors on the left showed Seymour, Hawkins and Stephenson. As he hesitated, wondering which door to knock on, Bradley entered the carriage from the other end. He had a dressing gown on and looked surprised at Scott.

Scott apologised, "I'm sorry. I know I probably shouldn't be down here. But what's happened to the train?"

Bradley didn't actually look too bothered that Scott was in the staff quarters. He said,

"I was just finding out myself. Dunn..." Bradley remembered he was speaking to a passenger, "Mr Dunn told me that the power seemed to drain and that we slowly came to a stop."

That would explain why he hadn't noticed it, thought Scott.

Bradley continued, "I was just coming to wake Mr Stephenson up, to help Mr Dunn with fixing it."

Bradley looked at Scott's concerned face and said, "It's likely that it's just a small technical hitch, but two heads are better than one."

Bradley was about to knock on the door closest to him, when the centre door on the left opened and Rosalie looked out, wearing a long nightshirt.

"What's going on?" she said to Bradley, before noticing Scott behind her and retreating slightly into her doorway.

"There's something wrong with the train. Dunn's looking at it now."

"Where's Mr Lambert?" asked Scott.

Bradley shrugged, "Probably asleep. Dunn said he tried to ring him, but there was no answer."

"Don't you find that strange?" said Scott.

Bradley answered, "Not really. He is known to take one or two nightcaps before heading to bed. But don't worry Mr Blacklock, everything's under control. Our drivers are very capable. Please, don't worry yourself, and head to bed. We'll be moving when you wake up tomorrow."

Scott smiled and turned to leave, not entirely happy with the reply, but knowing there would be no more information until the morning.

As Scott left the carriage, Rosalie looked back to Bradley and said sarcastically, "You almost sounded like Lambert then!"

"Piss off! Someone had to take charge, if that short fat bastard's too lazy to get out of bed." retorted Bradley jovially.

He continued, "Speaking of fat bastards, where is Russelli? He's supposed to be on room service duty."

Rosalie indicated to the door next to hers and said, "I'll think you'll find those snores you can hear are his."

Bradley groaned. "Great. Looks like I'll have to take over. And I'm now going to get a tirade of abuse from old Stephenson for waking him up!"

Rosalie said, "Well you seem to have everything covered! I'll see you in the morning." before smiling sweetly and heading back into her room.

Scott walked back through the train and stopped again at Lambert's door. After knocking several times, he called his name. There was still no sound from the other side of the door. As Scott walked to his room, he had a troubling feeling that the events of this anniversary night were only the beginning.

The morning after

Scott awoke from his sleep with a start. He opened his eyes but still felt tired, his night filled with disturbing dreams. Had Gerry Kennedy really died at dinner last night? He still couldn't quite believe it. As he sat up in bed, he looked over to the clock. Seven forty five. It only took him a few seconds to realise that the train was still not moving. He climbed out of bed and pulled the curtains to look outside. The sky was bright and clear blue, although it appeared to have snowed again in the night. As he craned his neck to look further down the train, he could see that over an inch of snow had accumulated along the stationary wheels.

He showered and dressed quickly, starting to wonder how serious this problem could be.

Before he left his room, he quickly slid open the sliding door to check that Tim had made it to his own room. He was relieved to see him curled up in his duvet, still sleeping soundly.

He walked down to Lambert's room to again try on his door. Still getting no response, he was about to head towards the staff quarters again, when Bradley walked through from the lounge. As he approached, Scott asked, "I take it the problem is a little more serious than you first thought?"

Bradley gave his trademark grin, "Slightly. But Mr Dunn and Stephenson are quite positive that we should be going in a couple of hours."

Scott pointed to Lambert's door, "Have you still not seen Mr Lambert?"

Bradley replied, "I was just about to call on him actually. Really though Mr Blacklock, there's no worry."

Scott said, "I'd still like to speak to him, if it's ok with you. There's still no answer from his room. Do you have a key?"

Bradley, now for the first time, looked concerned about Lambert's absence. He said, "There's a master key to all the locks in Lambert's office."

He pointed to the door further up the carriage next to the reception desk. Scott walked over to it and tried the door. "This is also locked." said Scott impatiently.

Bradley said, "There's a key in the kitchen. I'll go and get it."

"I'll wait here for you then." said Scott as he sat in one of the armchairs.

Bradley left the carriage, and the troubling feeling that the train malfunction was not as innocent as it seemed grew in Scott's mind.

After several minutes, Scott heard footsteps and stood up to look down the carriage.

It wasn't Bradley however, but Rosalie, carrying a large breakfast tray.

She passed and smiled, "Mr Lambert still not up?"

"It would appear not." replied Scott.

Rosalie rolled her eyes as if this was typical of him, and carried on through to the sleeping carriages.

Bradley returned shortly afterwards with the key in his hand. As he went to open the door, he said quietly, "Mr Lambert hates anyone going in his office!"

He unlocked it and pushed the door open, or at least tried to, as there seemed to be something blocking the other side of the door. He tried to peer inside, but the room was still dark, the curtains unopened. Bradley gave the door a shove and heard something slump on the floor and the door was able to open a further six inches.

Bradley looked around the door and exclaimed, "Oh my God!" before disappearing into the room.

Scott followed him and turned on the light as he entered. Bradley was knelt over the fallen body of Patrick Lambert, his body having been the obstruction behind the door.

"Is he....?" asked Scott, holding his breath.

"No, I can feel a pulse." said Bradley as he held his wrist. "I think he's unconscious."

Scott observed the red swelling on Lambert's crown, and pointed to a paper weight on the floor near Lambert. He said, "Maybe that had something to do with it."

Bradley looked at it and then said, "There should be some whisky on the side over there....."

Bradley had gone to point at the decanter on the side by Lambert's desk, but for the first time, they both noticed the rest of the room.

Lambert's office was quite a decent size, with a large oak desk and two chairs in front of it. It was the corner of Lambert's room that had attracted their attention. Situated behind Lambert's desk was what looked like a miniature, two metre-squared version of Mission Control. Two large computers sat at a small workstation and there was an advanced satellite link up system. It would all have looked quite impressive, had it all been in working order. But Bradley and Scott had forgotten about Lambert for a second, as they stared in shock at what was someone's successful attempt at trashing the equipment. Both computer monitors were smashed and wires from extracted circuit boards dangled like small snakes crawling out of the workstation.

Scott was first to remember Lambert and collected the whisky from the side table.

He passed it to Bradley, who promptly opened it and held it under Lambert's nose.

After several moments of inhaling the vapours, Lambert's eyes fluttered and he slowly came round. As his eyes tried to focus, he felt the pain on his head for the first time, and he winced, holding his hand tenderly to his head.

"What happened?" he said weakly.

"Here, drink this." said Bradley, offering him the alcohol.

Lambert gratefully took a long swig. Colour started to return to his cheeks and he asked again, "What happened?"

Scott answered, "It looks like someone hit you with that paper weight."

Lambert looked confused, "Who? What?...Why?"

As Bradley helped him slowly up, Scott pointed to the destroyed computers. He said, "Well at a guess, that's the reason why." before adding dryly, "Unless your technology always looks this tardy."

Lambert walked over to the workstation, still in shock from the thought of someone attacking him. He stopped for a second, before realising, "The train's stopped! What the hell is going on?!"

Bradley answered, "The engine malfunctioned in the night. Dunn and Stephenson are working on it."

"Sir?"

The three of them were disturbed by Rosalie at the door to the office. Her face was white. She said quietly, "Sir I think you'd better come and see this."

Lambert snapped, "What is it?!"

Rosalie stammered, "Please Sir. Come quickly."

Before Lambert could reply, Rosalie had turned and left the doorway. Lambert looked confused for a second, before following her. Scott didn't hesitate in joining them. Bradley, now left alone in the room, walked over to the workstation to see if there was anything salvageable.

They walked through the sleeping carriages, and the pit of Scott's stomach turned as he realised which room they were headed to. Lambert, walking in front of him, was too preoccupied to question Scott as to why he was following them.

They turned into the last sleeping carriage, the Thistlewood suites, and saw that Rosalie was stood by the open door to Clarissa's room. She stood uncertainly, her tanned skin still looked pale.

Lambert and Scott approached her, and Lambert said impatiently, "What is it girl?"

Rosalie said quietly, "It's Mrs Jordan."

Lambert took a step inside the door and gasped. Scott looked in behind him and went cold at the sight.

Clarissa Jordan lay on her large bed, dressed in a half open silk dressing gown. The sheets had not been pulled down, indicating she had not slept in it. She was positioned awkwardly across the bed and one of her arms was half hanging off the end. Her head was partially propped up against a pillow, showing those entering the room a full view of her face. Her mouth was partially open and her lifeless dull eyes were frozen open, giving an expression of shock. Her skin was pallid, as though she had lain there for several hours.

There were several moments of silence as they observed her dead body. Lambert's jaw had dropped completely open, and Scott felt his heart sink.

He moved passed Lambert and looked closer at Clarissa. As he peered down, he saw that there were contusion marks around her neck. This was not a natural or accidental death. She had been strangled. He used his hand to close her eyes, losing some of the horror of her pose. It was when he looked over to the side of Clarissa's bed that he took another breath. Her safe was open.

Scott stood upright, feeling an overwhelming sense of failure. He had been watching her. And this had happened right under his nose.

Scott's inspection of Clarissa snapped Lambert out of his reverie, and he asked indignantly, "Mr Blacklock, what do you think you are doing?!"

"This woman has been murdered." said Scott quietly.

Lambert gave him a look of disbelief.

Scott suddenly became aware that to Lambert, he was just a random passenger who had barged into the room. A manager who was more together would have never let him even enter.

He turned to look at Lambert and said calmly, "Mr Lambert. I need to tell you something. Do you think we could talk in private?"

Lambert gave Scott a bizarre look, but Rosalie who had stayed by the door said,

"I'll leave you to it."

"Don't mention anything to the passengers" Lambert said quickly, as Rosalie left and closed the door behind her, looking glad to leave.

Lambert looked back round to Scott and said, "Now Mr Blacklock...."

But Scott interrupted, "Mr Lambert, if I may explain. I work for Zirconia. My company are Clarissa Jordan's insurers. She had her assets insured through us, including the Warwick diamond that she was wearing last night.

During the last month, Clarissa had been receiving threats in the post. My company were worried about a potential theft being planned. I was assigned to watch her. That's why I'm on this train."

Lambert looked as though he had received far too much information in the last five minutes and slumped into one of the armchairs. He put his hand to his head which was still throbbing. The use of the word murder was slowly sinking into Lambert's brain. At once, he began to panic. He had already been fraught at the publicity that there had been a death on the Express. And now a murder! His career would be in ruins! He managed to calm himself slightly and then looked at Scott with a mixture of suspicion and fear. He asked, "How do I know any of what you've just told me is true? For all I know, you could have done this!"

Scott replied calmly, "I have identification in my room. I also have my files on Clarissa which should prove that what I'm saying is correct."

Lambert said incredulously, "But why were you watching her?! Surely if there were threats then the police would have been involved?"

Scott maintained his calm tone, "I was assigned this case by my company, Zirconia. This was in our interest of the client. As you can imagine, her assets are worth a great deal. I know that the police were investigating, but I wasn't privy to whatever course of action they were taking."

Lambert did not seem completely satisfied with the answer, but a knock at the door stopped him from replying. He looked at the door and then back to Scott, the look of panic had returned to his face. He said unevenly, "Who is it?"

"Mr Lambert, it's Thomas Seymour."

Lambert's panic left him and he asked through the door in an annoyed tone, "What do you want?"

Thomas hesitated before saying, "Rosalie just told me what happened. I need to talk to you."

Lambert hesitated a moment longer before opening the door. Thomas Seymour stood there, still looking pale, although his face went a further shade lighter when he saw Clarissa's body.

He walked into the room and closed the door behind him. Lambert looked expectantly at him, but instead Thomas looked at Scott questioningly.

He turned to Lambert and said, "Mr Lambert, I need to speak to you in private about what's happened here."

He then looked back to Scott as if hinting for him to leave.

Instead Scott said, "I have an invested interest in what's happened here."

Thomas asked, "Really? And what's that?"

Scott replied pointedly, "I have just explained to Mr Lambert. After all, he is the manager of this train."

Lambert said shortly, "Your story still needs to be verified. Just speak, Thomas."

Thomas spoke as he removed an identification wallet from his pocket. He said, with less confidence than he should, "I also have an invested interest."

As he showed his identification he said, "Mr Lambert, my name is Detective Seymour of the N.Y.P.D. I obtained this job placement a week and a half ago in order to carry out surveillance on Clarissa Jordan. She had been receiving letters of a threatening nature. There was some concern about her being harmed."

Lambert said angrily, "WHAT! You mean your references were faked in order to get on this train! I can't believe it! And what good did it do! You haven't done a very good job!"

Scott said quietly, "Although you have helped corroborate my story."

Lambert pointed a finger at Scott, "I still want to see your identification Mr Blacklock!"

"Who are you?" asked Thomas.

Scott answered, "I work for Zirconia. Clarissa Jordan's insurers. We were concerned about the threat of a theft."

Thomas retorted, "But this has been a murder. Where's the theft?"

Scott pointed to the open safe by Clarissa's bed. There were several open boxes of jewels. He said, "I'll agree the whole room hasn't been searched yet, but I cannot see the Warwick Diamond in there."

A noise of someone moving on the bed in the adjoining room, made them all freeze.

Lambert pointed to the adjoining door and said quietly, "Mr Jordan. He was in the room right next door. It must have been him! They haven't seemed that happy on this train!"

Scott gave him a look, before Thomas moved closer to the door. He said,

"This door has been locked from this side."

"What does that prove?" asked Scott.

Thomas ignored the comment and unlocked the door. As he slowly opened the door, Lambert and Scott moved closer behind him.

Mark Jordan lay in his bed, still sleeping.

"Should we wake him?" Lambert whispered.

Thomas shut the door again and turned to them both. He swallowed, as if to muster some confidence. He said, "Mr Lambert, as an officer of the police, I am officially taking charge of this situation. Now I think we need to lock this room and go to your office to talk."

Lambert nodded, as if eager to get out of the room. As Lambert made to leave, Scott held his ground. He said, "I disagree. I think you should wake Mr Jordan now. What if he wakes up and comes to see his wife?"

Thomas replied, "We'll lock this door when we leave."

Scott explained logically, "Yes, but he could use the other door." He asked Lambert, "I presume the key to these suites opens both doors?

Lambert nodded silently.

Thomas looked annoyed at Scott questioning his authority, but saw that Scott was right. He opened the door, but then hesitated. He said to Lambert, "I think you should tell him."

Lambert looked alarmed at the idea, "You tell him! You're the police officer!"

Thomas's face again paled and Scott wondered why they had sent such a green detective to watch Clarissa. When Thomas made no move to enter Mark's room, Scott pushed past him and said, "I'll do it."

He slowly walked across the room and knelt beside Mark's bed. He placed his hand on Mark's shoulder and said his name. Mark made no movement and showed no sign of waking. When he still didn't react as Scott nudged him gently, Lambert quietly gasped. Realising what Lambert was thinking, Scott leant closer, but saw that Mark was still breathing. Discarding subtlety this time, Scott shook his shoulder. This had the desired effect as Mark jolted in the bed and opened his eyes blearily. After his eyes focused for a few seconds, they opened wider and he sat up in bed as he acknowledged the three strangers in his room.

He said gruffly, "What the hell's going on?"

He looked between all three of them, before looking back at Scott. Scott swallowed and said, "Mr Jordan. There's been an incident in the night. It's your wife...."

Scott paused, unsure how to phrase it and Mark's startled face looked to Lambert and Thomas as if they were about to finish the sentence.

"I'm afraid....." but before Scott could finish, Mark leapt out of bed and walked to the adjoining room, working out from Scott's intonation what was coming.

Lambert and Thomas awkwardly made to try and block his view, but he was taller than both of them.

"Oh.....God!"

The words came from Mark in short gasps and he clapped his hand to his mouth.

Scott said quietly, "It looks as though she's been murdered."

Mark's eyes became glassy and he made to enter the room, but Thomas stopped him. He said unsteadily, "Sir, I'm afraid you can't enter the room."

Mark looked at him fiercely, "What! Why the hell not?"

Thomas said quietly, "This is a crime scene."

Mark stared back into his wife's bedroom, and his knees sagged. He staggered back and with Scott's help managed to not miss the end of the bed.

He sat deflated, silent tears started to run down his cheeks.

Scott was surprised when Lambert spoke. He said gently, "Mr Jordan, I am very sorry for your loss. This is a tragedy," and then with an air of unease, "but I can give you some comfort to know that Thomas here happens to be a police officer. He is going to work his hardest to find out what happened here, and who committed this atrocity."

Thomas looked uncomfortable at Lambert's last statement, even more so when Mark looked up confused, and said, "But, you're a waiter! How can you be a police officer?!"

Thomas avoided the question by saying, "Sir, if you will forgive me for not explaining everything right now. We have a situation now which we must attend to. I have to use Mr Lambert's satellite uplink to get some assistance out here. I'm going to have to ask you to remain in your room for a short time."

Mark stared blankly at Thomas. He didn't seem happy with the answer, but did not seem in any state to move anywhere.

Scott asked, "Would you like me to call Amy?"

Mark said quietly, "No. No, I'll call her." He turned to Lambert and Thomas and asked nastily, "I presume my daughter is allowed to come to my room?"

"Of course." Thomas said quickly.

Lambert seemed keen for this exchange to finish quickly and headed back into Clarissa's room. Scott followed, and Thomas said, "I'm sorry for your loss Mr Jordan. I will be back shortly to tell you what's happening."

Mark nodded absently, and Thomas turned into Clarissa's room, closing the adjoining door and locking it behind him.

Lambert had already walked to the door into the corridor, eager to leave Clarissa's room. Thomas mistook Lambert's intentions and said, "Good idea. I'll take a look around here later. Let's get to your satellite uplink."

Lambert looked to Scott at the mention of the equipment. Thomas picked up on this and said, "What? What is it?"

Scott answered, "It will be easier to show you. And talking in the office would be preferable to here."

Thomas said impatiently, "I'm sorry Mr Blacklock, but I don't see why you will be joining us. Let's go Mr Lambert."

Before either Lambert or Thomas moved, Scott said firmly, "I think you will find it advantageous that I do. But before you do anything, I would suggest checking that the train still has the same number of passengers. Do you not think that someone may have stopped the train in order to get off?!"

Thomas looked to Lambert sheepishly.

Scott folded his arms. "Why don't you do that? Seeing as how you're still in costume, you can tell the passengers that you're just checking they're not alarmed by the train stopping. While you're doing that, I'll stop by my room to collect documentation proving my story and meet you in Mr Lambert's office."

Scott walked to the door and opened it. He left and Lambert quickly followed. Thomas grumbled a curse before closing the door behind him and double-locking it.

Speculation

Hi Miranda,

Me again! I know that you'll probably get this one at the same time as the first postcard, but had to tell you even more! Forgot to say in the last one that Jessica Rae is also on the train, following Clarissa! It all kicked off at dinner last night. Clarissa had a big argument with practically everyone and then there was gonna be a fist fight (which I got caught in the middle of!) but this old geezer, Gerry Kennedy the film producer, croaked it right there at the dinner table! I can't really say it's boring anymore! I've just woken up and the train seems to have stopped! Gonna go find out what's going on now!

Missing you,
Tim. X

Harry Broadside woke up on the floor of his cabin, his head groaning. He wondered for a second why he was comfortable, before noticing a pillow wedged behind his head. He pulled himself up, his large frame filling the room, and stumbled against the armchair. He wasn't quite sure how he had ended up on the floor, but his aching head reminded him that there was a lot of alcohol in his system. He needed food. He then smiled, remembering that he'd ordered breakfast in bed the day before. He opened his door and was angered to see no tray waiting.

"Good morning Mr Broadside."

Harry turned to see Daphne Pennington walking along the carriage. She stopped at his door with a sympathetic look on her face. She said, "You look like someone who had one too many last night?"

Harry winced at her, "My breakfast's not here."

Daphne said, "Normal service doesn't seem to be running this morning."

Harry looked confused. "What do you mean?"

Daphne looked at him like he was stupid. "Have you not noticed the train isn't moving?!"

Harry took a moment to think about it and then realised he hadn't noticed at all because his head was spinning so much.

"Why have we stopped?" he asked.

Daphne shrugged, "God knows why! I thought we might have been changing tracks or something, but we've been stopped for far too long. Maybe we hit an animal? There doesn't seem to be anyone about. I spent all night with Avril. I just popped back to mine for a change of clothes."

"How is she?" Harry asked, a tad insincerely.

"Not great. I left her sleeping, I should get back so I'm there when she wakes up."

Daphne smiled and turned away. As she was walking away, Harry shouted up the corridor. "If you see any of the staff, get them to send some breakfast my way."

Daphne didn't respond, quite annoyed that some people could only have food on their minds.

Lambert and Scott arrived at Lambert's office, after a brief stop at Scott's room, where he had disappeared inside for a second, before emerging with a hefty document folder.

As Lambert entered the room, he saw Bradley in the corner still looking through the carcass of the control panel.

Thomas joined them shortly afterwards, having checked on all the suites and the staff quarters. He confirmed that there were still nineteen passengers on board. Seven staff, ten guests, and two corpses. Lambert winced at the mention of the dead bodies. However Thomas didn't see it as he finally noticed what was behind Bradley in the corner of the room.

His eyes widened as he walked past Lambert.

"What happened?" he asked.

Bradley let out a sigh, and walked over to Lambert's chair and casually leant against it. "Well", he said, "It looks like someone took a crowbar to it and ripped the whole thing apart. I mean, Dunn's more of an expert than me, but I'd be surprised if he could get anything to work over there."

Thomas looked horrified. He said, "Has the wiring to the satellite been damaged?"

Bradley replied, "Pretty much everything has!"

"So there's no way to contact anybody?" Thomas asked desperately.

Bradley looked at Thomas bizarrely, not understanding his interest.

It was Scott that spoke. "I don't see what the problem is. Surely you have a cell phone?! I have one." he said as he pulled his out of his pocket.

Lambert turned to Scott and said, "Yes, but the only reason you will have had reception is because of our satellite on the roof of the train. This train runs on too isolated a track to get an unbroken signal. For our use, but also for our passengers, we require our own satellite. You wouldn't get any kind of reception up here in this part of the mountains."

As Scott looked down, he saw that Lambert was right, his handset revealed no bars on his signal gauge.

Bradley looked at each of them and said, "What's going on?"

It appeared that Rosalie had not returned to the office to tell Bradley what had happened, and Lambert did not want him in the room for any longer than was necessary. Bradley was the sort of person who asked too many questions.

"Thank you Bradley, if you would excuse us. I'm sure Andreas could use some help with breakfast preparation." said Lambert efficiently.

"That's Thomas's job." replied Bradley indignantly.

"Well go and assist Rosalie. And get Dunn up here. I want a report on the status of the train." retorted Lambert, his face getting red.

Bradley made to move to the door, eyeing Thomas warily, trying to work out why he was staying with Lambert.

As he went to close the door behind him, Lambert turned and said, "Bradley, I'm sure Rosalie will inform you of the latest news. I would ask you to remember discretion at all times."

Bradley stopped, and then nodded, closing the door with a confused look on his face.

Bradley's departure from Lambert's office created a silence for a few moments, as Thomas continued to look over the workstation. Lambert watched Thomas and didn't like the fact that the ruined equipment seemed to worry him more than Clarissa's body.

Thomas said again, "So we can't contact anybody?"

Lambert said, "Not unless Dunn can do anything. But look at it! It looks like it would be better to start from scratch."

Thomas thought for a moment and said, "But you must be able to send out some kind of distress signal?"

Lambert said quietly, "Yes we could have. But through that computer."

Scott noticed with interest that, compared to Thomas, Lambert seemed more together now. Maybe because he can shift his responsibility to Thomas, he thought.

Scott moved from where he had been quiet in the corner, and finally spoke.

He said, "Gentlemen, if I may, I'd like to give you my take on what I think has happened."

Before either of them could respond, he continued, "I think what you have here is a well orchestrated plan, perfectly executed by a rather psychotic individual. A plan that involved attacking Mr Lambert, in order to remove our communication with the outside world. That also involved sabotaging the train, stranding us here for the time being. And that then involved either stealing Clarissa's diamond, or murdering her. Or both."

Thomas said, "What do you mean?! It's quite obvious that the intent was to murder her! And we don't even know if this diamond is missing!"

Scott replied, "The intent might have been just to steal the diamond, but Clarissa startled the thief. Or you could be right. The intent could have just been murder, and the diamond may not be missing."

Lambert looked very disturbed by all that Scott had just said, but Thomas retorted,

"You seem to have a lot of theories Mr Blacklock. But as you say, the diamond may not be missing. And I still don't know why you're even here. For all I know, you could be the killer!"

Scott calmly replied, "Well then Gentlemen, shall we take a seat so I can verify my story for you?"

Bradley walked into the kitchen to see Rosalie and Andreas preparing breakfast. He placed his hands on his hips and said,

"What the hell is going on here?! Lambert's office is completely trashed! And why are Thomas and Mr Blacklock with him?"

Rosalie and Andreas looked at each other before she answered,

"Clarissa Jordan was murdered in the night!"

Bradley paled. "What! Shit!"

Andreas grunted, "And whoever did it fucked with the electricity and the timers on my ovens reset so they didn't pre-heat this morning. No one will be having my beautiful pain au chocolat for breakfast!"

Rosalie said, "Good that you're looking at the big picture Andreas. As for what Thomas and Mr Blacklock have to do with it. Beats me! When I told Thomas in the corridor, he looked like he was going to be sick, and then said he needed to speak to Lambert."

Rosalie wiped her hands with a cloth, and said, "I reckon it was either her ex-husband or her current one. Neither of them seemed happy with her. Or maybe it was that jealous little plain woman…."

She looked over to Bradley, and could see that he was still visibly shocked, an unusual look for him. She asked, "You alright there Bradley?"

He focused back in the room and stammered, "Yeah. Yeah, I'm cool."

He turned and walked back into the dining carriage.

Lambert slowly moved around the desk to sit in his chair, waiting to hear Scott's story. Although Lambert still didn't trust Scott, he realised he needed help. And Scott's calmness was more soothing than Thomas's desperation.

Scott took one of the chairs opposite and opened his file on Lambert's desk. As he began to remove some papers, Thomas finally stopped inspecting the computers and sat in the other chair opposite Lambert.

Scott began, "Now, as I have already said, I work for Zirconia, Clarissa's insurers. I was assigned this case last Thursday. I was asked to watch Clarissa discreetly. The letters that Clarissa had received caused great alarm amongst my management. As you can imagine, she has… had a considerable amount of wealth insured by us. My job was to observe from a distance and hopefully locate the perpetrator, before a theft happened, and subsequently before a large insurance claim was made to us."

Thomas interrupted, scoffing, "This is ridiculous!"

He turned to Lambert and said, "You don't really believe this?!"

He looked back to Scott, "So we're to believe that you were assigned to locate the perpetrator? And then what? You were to arrest him?! You work for an insurance company!"

Scott calmly handed him several sheets of Zirconia headed paper and said, "These are my assignment case points, given to me by my superior, Ralph Peterson. You'll see his signature at the bottom."

He pulled several other papers from the file and handed them to Lambert while Thomas pored over his case points. He pointed to what he had just given Lambert.

"This is some of the background work I did before boarding the train on Saturday."

He said, before pulling his wallet from his pocket, fishing out three cards and finishing, "And here are three pieces of photographic identification to prove I am who I say I am."

Thomas passed the case points to Lambert and examined his I.D. Scott continued,

"Within Zirconia, I work for the Department of Recovery and Investigation. I'm an investigative agent. You are right Mr Seymour,

I do work for an insurance company, but my job involves me closely liaising with the police and other agencies, to assist them in their investigations. For their benefit, and ours. Once I had deduced who was the culprit, I was to report this to my superior, who would then have contacted the police. I've worked at the company for six years now and have helped on some very big enquiries. You may remember the Glengarry murder or the Griffiths and Quaid enquiry?"

Both Lambert and Thomas looked at each other in recognition, Lambert looking quite impressed. Scott added, "Just last week, you may have heard of the arrest of Karl Stoltzkin for conspiracy and fraud."

Lambert looked up, "He'd stolen his own art collection, hadn't he?!"

Scott said, "I was a contributing factor to that arrest."

"How?" asked Thomas sceptically.

"As in I was the one that discovered his hidden treasures in his own restaurant."

There was silence for a second as Thomas returned to inspecting his I.D.

Lambert finished reading Scott's assignment and said "It says in here that you were advised not to have any direct contact with the subject."

Scott shrugged, "I hadn't planned to. But I felt it necessary to commence surveillance on her straight away. I couldn't help the fact that this train would be so intimate, and that I would have contact with her."

Thomas put the I.D on the desk and said, "This all could have been forged."

Scott replied impatiently, "Yes, I'll agree it could have. But I have one further piece of evidence to support my story."

He pulled out a newspaper that he had wedged into the back of his file. This is the paper I brought on the train with me on Saturday." He passed it to Lambert, as he felt Lambert was more accepting of his story. "You'll see on page five that there's an article on Stoltzkin. Unfortunately it doesn't mention me by name, but it does mention my department at Zirconia's assistance in the case. Again, you may say that I have forged that, but if I had committed the crime, why would I have volunteered all this information?"

Thomas gave no reply, but as Lambert handed him the paper, he said, "I think he has a point Mr Seymour. I, myself am happy with his story. And to be honest, he does seem professional."

And then Lambert surprised both of them, "Which to be honest, you don't Detective. At the moment, I think I would have more reason to suspect you. I mean, you've showed me your badge, but you do seem a little incompetent at your job."

Scott resisted saying anything, while Thomas's scrawny face gave a look of outrage.

He said, "How dare you! You're calling me incompetent! You're the most incompetent manager I've ever seen!"

Lambert stood up, "Incompetent! Tell me, did it take you long to get into character as a pathetic, unconfident waiter?!"

Thomas was about to retort when Scott put his arms up and said, "Stop it! Both of you!"

Lambert slowly sat back down, as Scott continued, "Mr Lambert, I have to say that I believe Thomas's story. I have a contact on the force who told me that Clarissa was coming on this train, but he was unable to tell me anything about their surveillance plans."

Thomas looked thankful at Scott's comment and said to Lambert bitterly, "I have files, just like Mr Blacklock in my room also."

His relaxed posture did not last long though as Scott asked him, "Although I do believe that you're a police officer, what doesn't add up is why they would send somebody so obviously inexperienced to carry out surveillance?"

Thomas looked a little scared. He said uncertainly, "I'm not inexperienced!"

"How long have you been a detective?" asked Lambert pointedly.

Thomas paused, before saying rather quietly, "Eight months."

Scott asked, "Why did you get this assignment?"

Thomas looked down at his feet, "I wasn't meant to have it. My partner, Detective Shenton was supposed to be on the train. But... he got caught in a drive by shooting in Queens two weeks ago."

Lambert asked, "And had he been with the force a little longer?"

"Eighteen years." Thomas said, now very quietly.

Much to Scott's surprise and pleasure, Lambert said in a matter of fact way, "I have little choice right now but to believe both your stories.

I think Mr Seymour that you should get over your problem with Mr Blacklock. As I think he is right. I think it would be advantageous for you to listen to him."

Anthony Stuart moved quietly out of his cabin, so as not to wake his sleeping wife. He opened the door quietly and walked out. In the corridor he found himself confronted with Jessica Rae, who had just come around the corner.

She stopped abruptly. Anthony pointed to the stationary scenery and said, "Good morning Ms Rae. I didn't realise there was a scheduled stop, did you?"

Jessica said excitedly, "There isn't. Something happened last night, I'm sure of it. That pasty waiter came to check on me and said it's just an engine fault. But we've been stopped a long time!"

She went to move past him, and then hesitated. She looked at him for a second before asking, "While I have you here Mr Stuart, what is the deal with you and Clarissa?"

Anthony replied irritably, "What do you mean? There is no deal."

"Come off it. You could have cut the sexual tension in the lounge with a knife last night. I've seen the glances she gives you."

Anthony flushed. He said in a harsh whisper, "There is nothing between me and Clarissa. I think you'll find that what happened last night was that you overstepped the mark, and got what you deserved. Excuse me Ms Rae."

He moved her physically to the side and left the carriage quickly. Once he had left, Jessica pressed her ear to the Stuart's door. She listened to see if his wife was in their suite, to explain why he had been whispering.

Back in Lambert's office, the three people in charge of the situation were interrupted by a knock at the door.

"Come in." Lambert said, and Robert Dunn entered, looking tired and red faced.

"You asked to see me Sir?"

"Yes," said Lambert, standing up. "What's the situation with the train? What happened in the night?"

Dunn answered, "It was approaching one last night. I was watching the computer monitor for the controls when the console died. The engine's power slowly drained and we came to a gradual stop. We're on a slight incline, so I manually applied the brakes to stop us rolling. Then...."

Scott interrupted, "I'm sorry, the train is run by computer?"

Dunn, like the other members of staff, gave Scott a quizzical look, wondering why a passenger was in on the consultation.

Dunn said, "Yes, like a plane's autopilot."

Scott asked Lambert, "And is that powered by your workstation over there?"

"No, it's on a separate smaller workstation in our storage compartments, beyond the kitchen."

Dunn, whose attention had been diverted by Thomas and Scott at Lambert's desk, for the first time noticed the state of the work panels. His eyes widened and he asked, "What happened in here?"

Lambert answered seriously, "I'm afraid the train engine was not the only equipment that was sabotaged."

"Sabotaged? So you think so too? It's the only thing that explains what happened." said Dunn.

"What do you mean?" asked Thomas.

"For about twenty minutes, I tried at the driver's console to restore power. Then I thought that it may be a problem at the workstation in the storage compartment. That's where I've been for most of the night. I checked the circuit boards and wiring conduits, and found a small device spliced into the wires that I'm sure hadn't been there before. I couldn't identify it, but now after what you've said, I'm wondering if it wasn't some sort of virus that imitated a small E.M.P device within the system. It would certainly fit with what happened to the train."

"E.M.P?" asked Lambert.

"Electromagnetic Pulse. It knocks out electrical equipment for a short time. Luckily the emergency lights came back on within about ten minutes. Then we got power back about two hours later, so it makes sense."

Thomas, calculating the time, said, "But if you got power back at three this morning, why are we still not moving?"

Dunn replied impatiently, slightly annoyed that he had to explain himself to Thomas.

"I was getting to that. The control systems won't let me restart the train. It's some sort of virus that I've never seen before. But it makes sense now that it was implanted by the device I found."

Lambert said, "So, what can you do about it?"

Dunn answered, "I've spent about the last five hours trying to trap the virus and wipe it." He paused and said tentatively, "I think I'm quite close now."

"Quite close?" questioned Lambert.

Dunn replied irritably, "It's a complex virus Sir. Until I can fully reset the system, the computer won't physically allow me to start the train."

Lambert said. "My passengers will be up and about soon. And they are going to start asking questions. I need a time frame."

Dunn answered. "I think I can do it in another hour."

"Good." said Lambert, "And what do you think you can do with this workstation behind me?"

Dunn walked over to the back of the room and looked over it. After a moment, he said, "Honestly Sir. Sell it as scrap metal."

Lambert didn't like the flippancy of Dunn's reply. "That's not good enough Mr Dunn. We have a serious situation on the train. I need to be able to contact the authorities."

"Well you won't be doing it from here. The wiring to the satellite's been completely ripped out. I don't have anything on board that would fix this damage." answered Dunn.

"There must be some other way!" demanded Lambert.

Dunn looked awkward for a second. He said, "That's the other thing Sir. When I realised the severity of the problem, I asked Stephenson to get our two long wave radios up and running. They were missing from their storage locker. At first, I thought they had just been misplaced. But we haven't been able to find them."

Scott and Thomas exchanged a glance.

Scott asked, "Is the door lock system connected to all this? Why weren't they deactivated as well?"

It was Lambert who replied, "No, the door locks have a separate system altogether, for reasons of security. The circuits and power supply for that are on the underside of all the train carriages."

Dunn hesitated for a second before asking,

"Sir, what kind of situation is this? Is this about Mr Kennedy?"

Lambert replied, "No it isn't Mr Dunn. You leave the situation to us. Right now, your main priority is to get the train started."

Dunn replied, "Yes Sir."

As he made his way to the door, Lambert added, "And get Stephenson to start clearing the snow from the wheels. That will take some time. I want us going as soon as possible."

Dunn nodded in way of response and left, closing the door behind him.

Scott was quietly impressed that Lambert was still able to maintain some of his authority in the situation. However, the act seemed to be more for his staff as his face filled with dread as Dunn left.

He looked at both Thomas and Scott and said quietly, "It would appear that your analysis of the situation was correct Mr Blacklock. We would appear to be completely stranded." He said more to Scott than Thomas, "Any suggestions as to what we do now?"

Scott went to speak, but it was Thomas that answered, "As the police authority at what is now a crime scene, it will be my decision as to what happens next."

Scott asked, "What are you suggesting?"

Thomas swallowed, "Weighing up all that has happened, I think it would be best if we left the crime scene as it was, get the train started, and ask the passengers to remain in their suites, until we arrive at Los Angeles where I can get proper backup and a forensics team on board."

Both Lambert and Scott seemed displeased at this idea.

Scott said, "You can't do that. For several reasons."

Thomas's anger returned, "And why not?"

Scott answered by asking Lambert, "Mr Lambert, were we not due into Los Angeles until tomorrow lunchtime? And we'll have lost ten to twelve hours stuck here, right?"

Lambert answered, "Yes. But the train hasn't been running at full speed. We could make up the lost time and still be there by midday tomorrow. Providing we can get the train started."

Scott turned back to Thomas, "That's asking these passengers to be locked up in their rooms for over twenty four hours."

He looked over at Lambert, "That's hardly fantastic customer service."

Lambert nodded in agreement.

He continued, "Also, I understand that you want to preserve the crime scene, but you're going to have to move Clarissa's body and put her in refrigeration."

Thomas argued, "But that could tamper with evidence."

Scott replied, "Mr Seymour, the temperature in these cabins is quite high because of the cold outside. If you leave her for over twenty four hours in that room, then you will hasten decomposition and possibly destroy more evidence. Also, are you still expecting to leave Mark Jordan locked up in his room, with his dead wife starting to smell next door?"

Thomas went silent. Lambert added, "The man has a good point Thomas. I have had two deaths on this train already. Both people are in the media. The repercussions of this are huge! My reputation is already in shreds. I can't imagine what will happen when we arrive in Los Angeles. But I don't want that added to by ten very angry passengers, suing us for keeping them like caged animals!"

Thomas said, "But there's a murderer amongst them?!"

He turned to Scott, "What's your perfect solution Mr Blacklock?"

Scott said calmly, "Look, Mr Lambert is right about his reputation being on the line. But so are ours. We were both assigned to watch Clarissa, and somehow a murderer has gotten past us. Now I can understand that you're feeling in over your head right now. But we all are. I can also understand you wanting to wait for back up. But we've both made mistakes. And personally I'd like to try and rectify that before our superiors find out."

Thomas scoffed, "Rectify it?! The subject of our cases has been murdered! It's a bit late for that!"

Scott answered, "We can't change what has happened. But we can try and find the culprit. This murder is going to explode across the world when we arrive in Los Angeles. Unfortunately for Mr Lambert, the connection with this train will be unavoidable. As will the fact that both the police and my company had agents watching her and failed to prevent it. Don't you think it would look better, for all of us here, if we arrived at Los Angeles with a suspect already in custody?"

"So what are you suggesting?" asked Thomas.

Scott replied, "I'm suggesting that we have Clarissa moved into refrigeration. We check her room to see if the diamond is missing, making careful not to touch anything directly of course. I'm presuming you have some prophylactic gloves for use at crime scenes?"

The question was aimed at Thomas, and he replied begrudgingly with a nod.

Scott continued, "We then ask the passengers to convene in the cocktail bar at the end of the train. There, Lambert can make an announcement and we can explain our presence here. I think then it would be advantageous to search people's rooms and the rest of the train. With Lambert's authority we can do that, and with your police authority we can question the passengers."

Lambert piped up at this, "Now hang on, I didn't say that...."

"It's not pleasant Mr Lambert, but it's better than Mr Seymour's suggestion to lock them all in their rooms. This was a calculated murder or robbery, one that was planned. And I bet our perpetrator may be surprised by the early arrival of the police. They may slip up. And they won't do that if they're locked in their room. It will mean that the culprit will have to maintain an act. Meals should still be served in the dining carriage." he added dryly to Lambert, "Although I wouldn't suggest sitting us all together again."

Lambert flushed, while Scott continued, "We can use this office to question the passengers."

Thomas remained silent for a moment before finally speaking, "You make it all sound very simple Mr Blacklock. But I think you're forgetting who the police officer is here."

Scott maintained his calm, neutral voice, "I'm not forgetting it Sir. But you have to concur that my suggestion is the most agreeable for all concerned."

"I agree." said Lambert, somewhat reluctantly.

Thomas continued to argue, "If we give the passengers the run of the train, the killer might bolt!"

"Where? This railroad is miles from anywhere!" said Scott, and then he smiled,

"And besides, don't you think they would have done that already? Stopping the train obviously wasn't for escaping. I imagine because it would make it a bit obvious who the killer was!"

"And what about the safety of the other passengers?!" Thomas continued to question.

"I'm sure we'll all feel safer, if we know that Inspector Seymour is patrolling the corridors." replied Scott.

When Thomas didn't respond, Scott looked at his watch. He was anxious that they had talked for too long and no action was being taken. He shifted in his chair and said to Lambert, "Mr Lambert, it's getting on for nine o clock. Your passengers will be up and about soon. I suggest that you go to the kitchen and organise breakfast in bed for everyone. Make an announcement, so that passengers are more likely to stay in their rooms. Then deliver breakfast yourself and tell them to meet in the cocktail bar at ten. While you do that, myself and Mr Seymour here will have a second look at Clarissa's room."

Lambert now didn't question Scott's order, nodded and got up. As Scott made for the door, Thomas remained seated. Scott looked at him and realised again how young he looked. He could have been the same age as Scott, but seemed a lot younger. Thomas said reluctantly, and even a little hopefully, "Are you really that confident that we could work out who did this before getting to Los Angeles?"

Scott smiled as he held the door open for him, "I have a knack for getting to the bottom of things under pressure."

Departure announcements

The room felt stuffy and airless as Thomas and Scott re-entered Clarissa's suite.

They had walked with Lambert to the kitchen and Scott had waited in the dining carriage while Thomas obtained a small crime scene kit from his room. Even though he had been prepared this time, walking back into the room to see Clarissa sprawled across her bed still made Scott catch his breath. Her eyes were now closed, but the position of her mouth and body still made for a horrific sight.

They stood in silence for a second and then both jumped at the sound of the train intercom as Lambert's disembodied voice filled the room.

"Good Morning Ladies and Gentlemen, your humble host Patrick Lambert here. I must sincerely apologise for the disruption to the Trans-Oceanic Express. I promise that we will be on our way again very shortly. As an apology, I will personally be delivering a champagne breakfast to each of you, so you can enjoy a decadent breakfast in bed. Thank you."

Scott was impressed at how Lambert had managed to put his performance voice back on.

As Thomas now stood hesitantly at the door of Clarissa's room, Scott nudged him and pointed to his bag. Thomas reacted by opening it and pulling out gloves and evidence bags. Scott took his and snapped them on and asked. "Do you have a finger print kit in there?"

Thomas face reddened, "Unfortunately not, no."

Thomas removed a tape recorder from the bag as Scott moved over to the window and pulled the curtains. The room filled with the bright morning sunshine. Thomas pressed record and moved over to the bed. He coughed before saying, "The time is 9.05 A.M on Monday the 22nd September. This is an inspection of a crime scene. The location: the Thistlewood suites on the Trans-Oceanic Express." He paused before saying, "The crime is that of the murder of Clarissa Jordan, actress. Those present are Detective Thomas Seymour of the N.Y.P.D and Scott Blacklock of the Zirconia Corporation."

They both moved to look at Clarissa on the bed. Thomas continued,

"The victim is lying diagonally across her bed. There are bruising and contusion marks around the neck and throat, strongly suggesting that she was strangled. The victim is wearing a loose robe. She does not appear to be wearing anything underneath. When a full autopsy is performed, the possibility of sexual assault should not be overlooked."

Thomas pressed stop on the recorder. Scott had been quietly impressed by Thomas's professional recording of the scene. That was until Thomas looked over to Scott and gave a face that asked "Was that ok?"

Thomas removed the small digital camera and began snapping pictures.

Scott turned his attention to the safe at the side of Clarissa's bed. As he started to pull the separate compartments out on to the floor, Thomas moved to the end of the bed, looking sternly at Scott as if he was about to steal something.

"What are you doing?" asked Thomas.

Scott said impatiently as he started looking through her jewellery boxes, "I'm looking to see if the diamond really is missing."

This quietened Thomas and after several minutes of Scott searching, it was evident that the diamond was not in the safe. Thomas folded his arms and said, "She was wearing it last night. She might have put it somewhere else in the room."

As Scott got up from the floor, he said, "Well I suggest we start looking then."

As the premier guest rooms on the train, the Thistlewood suites were very impressive. The two adjoining cabins took up an entire train carriage, allowing for both rooms to have a large en-suite. As well as the oversized bed, there was also a seating area, large dressing table and a bureau in the corner.

Thomas began to search her wardrobe, while Scott moved over to inspect her toiletries on her dressing table. As they were searching, Thomas asked, "Mr Blacklock, how did you get into this line of work?"

Scott hesitated for a second, not sure if Thomas was questioning him, or extending an olive branch. He decided to reply as if it was the latter. He said, "I've always been fascinated with the way people work. I took a degree in psychology at Oxford, before moving back to the U.S. My job at Zirconia wasn't planned. I kind of fell into it. And then realised how rewarding it could be."

"How so?" asked Thomas as he searched through Clarissa's clothes.

Scott replied plainly, "I love puzzles, and the claims that come through our department are usually ones that don't add up, most of the time because of fraudulence. I can't stand bad and greedy people. And if I can stop some of them from doing the bad and greedy things they do, I can feel like I've contributed something to society. The world's unfair enough as it is, don't you agree? I mean, isn't that in part why you went into the police force?"

Thomas closed the doors to the wardrobe, and looked over at Scott. He said, "Well, for me it was more of a family thing."

"Family thing?" Scott asked.

"My father was a cop, so were my two older brothers."

Scott nodded, understanding. He asked, "Was the police force not your first career choice?"

Thomas headed into the bathroom to search there. As he disappeared from Scott's sight, he replied. "Uh, ...no. I wanted to be an optician."

Scott suspected that Thomas had chosen to search the bathroom to avoid the embarrassment of the moment. But he also thought that Thomas offering this information was his way of admitting his weakness within his own job. And that he had now accepted Scott could help him out of the situation he was trapped in.

Scott had chosen not to say anything further, but was distracted anyway. As he looked up into the mirror, he noticed something protruding from the bottom of the armchair behind him, something that looked like a small silver box. He turned and knelt down to pull out the object. He got closer, and realised that it was a twenty pack of cigarettes.

He held it in his hand and looked at the silver packaging. The packet was slightly crushed, but the brand, Croughan and Matthews, could still be read clearly. He opened the pack to see that there were only three cigarettes left, no sign of the diamond or any other secrets.

Scott picked out an evidence bag from the crime scene kit and carefully placed the packet inside. As he stood up, he stopped quickly to inspect two circular marks on the table next to the chair. After pausing for a second, he looked to the bureau to continue his search there.

Twenty minutes later and Scott and Thomas stood again at the foot of Clarissa's bed, looking at her twisted position. After extensively searching the room, they had discovered that the diamond was indeed missing. Without the use of a proper forensics kit, the room had turned up little in the way of evidence. Thomas had returned from the bathroom with a manuscript for a film that he had discovered in the bin. It was entitled "The hour before dawn."

"What do you make of this?" Thomas asked.

Scott replied, "I've seen that before. It was on the coffee table next to Clarissa in the lounge yesterday."

Thomas bagged it, "So it was just something she was working on then? Why do you think it was in the bin?"

Scott thought for a moment. "It might not have been something she was working on. It might have been a film she had been offered. Just before I walked into the lounge yesterday, I saw Gerry Kennedy leaving, looking rather angry. I think he may have offered her this script."

"You think?"

"At the very least, it will be something we can ask Mrs Kennedy. I also found this."

Scott had removed the cigarette packet from his pocket. "I found these under that chair over there. I don't recall ever seeing Clarissa with a cigarette, do you?"

Thomas quietly shook his head.

Thomas tapped the bagged manuscript against his leg impatiently as he watched Scott, staring silently at the bed. After several minutes, Thomas finally asked,

"So what do you think?"

Scott answered, "I think that Clarissa let her murderer in. The door shows no forced entry and we know that the door locks were still working."

He walked over to the chair and pointed to the small table next to it. He continued, "And it looks as though she may have even entertained someone in here. These two ring marks indicate two people drinking, and forgetting to use coasters."

Thomas moved over and inspected them. Scott added, "Plus I think that's the position she died in. I can't see why anyone would place her in that position."

Thomas moved back to the end of the bed, thinking about what Scott had said.

Scott asked, "What do you think?"

He answered, "You put forward a good argument, but she could just have easily been asleep when her murderer entered. When she struggled, she moved across the bed like that."

Scott nodded, conceding his point. Thomas continued, "Plus, we also don't know that those ring marks aren't from her having a drink with her husband before dinner last night. Or even afterwards."

Scott nodded again and said, "You're right. We don't even know Mr Jordan's movements last night. He left Clarissa, Mr Stuart and I at cards last night to head to bed. But you're correct in that he could have come into speak to her when she returned back here. That's why I think it's time we go and speak to him."

Thomas folded his arms, "Wait a minute, don't you think we should wait until Lambert makes his speech?"

"Why?" asked Scott, "I don't think we can really expect Mr Jordan to attend that meeting in the bar. I'm sure he won't want to and probably won't be in any state to. We have to handle this sensitively. And just us going into have a chat with him now is the best way."

Thomas tried to reply, but had no other point.

"Let's go then" said Scott in way of ending the argument, "We don't have long."

As they made their way into the corridor, they saw Lambert puffing along with a breakfast tray. They arrived at Mark Jordan's door at the same time, and Lambert said quietly, "Ah, I'm glad you're here. I didn't know whether to knock on Mr Jordan's door again."

Scott asked, "Have you seen to the other passengers?"

Lambert paused to catch his breath, "Yes, all except young Miss Jordan. But I presumed she was here. And Mrs Kennedy was sleeping, but I spoke to Dr Pennington who had spent the night with her. They're all quite concerned about the train, but there was no mention of Clarissa. Did you find anything?"

Scott answered, "One or two clues. We were about to go and talk to Mr Jordan, so it's good that you're here. We can fully explain what's happening so that he won't have to join us in the bar."

Lambert nodded reluctantly as Scott knocked on his door. After several moments, Amy answered. Her attractive face looked lined with worry. Lambert leaned forward and said, "Miss Jordan, would you mind if we had a few words with Mr Jordan?"

Amy held the door close to her and said sharply, "This is hardly the time."

Lambert smiled gently and said, "I'd just like to inform him of what is happening now."

"Let them in." said a voice from inside the room.

Amy looked back into the room at her father before reluctantly stepping back and allowing them to enter. The three of them filed in to see Mark sat upright in his bed.

He still had the same glazed look from when they were last in the room. However he focused on Scott and said quite sharply, "Why are you here again? And for that matter, why were you here the first time?"

Instead of answering Mark, Scott turned to Amy and asked, "Amy, would you mind giving us five minutes with your father?"

Amy looked to her father for an answer. When he quietly nodded, she gave Scott one last look before walking out and closing the door behind her.

Scott asked, "Mr Jordan, would you mind if we sat down?"

Mark grunted in way of response. Scott took the answer to mean he could and took the armchair opposite him. Lambert and Thomas decided to remain standing, closer to the door.

Scott began, "Mr Jordan. To answer your question, I work for you and your wife's insurers, Zirconia. As you are aware, Clarissa had been receiving threats, indicating a theft of the Warwick diamond. I was on board this train to keep surveillance on her and possibly ascertain where this threat came from."

Thomas added, "I was here in a similar capacity for the police. I am not actually a waiter Mr Jordan. I was also here to carry out surveillance on your wife."

Mark looked between them both, slowly working through what they had just told him.

After several moments, his face became angry. He said through gritted teeth, "So, I have just lost my wife and what you're telling me is that she had not one, but two people watching her!"

Scott answered calmly, "Mr Jordan, my company had only regarded this as a possible theft threat."

Mark nodded, "Well that's understandable. Anyway it's not your job." He looked at Thomas accusingly, "It's yours. Where were you? Eh? I told Clarissa that the police weren't taking this seriously enough."

"Why did she not have any protection of her own? Did she take personal precautions of her own?" asked Scott, pulling the attack away from Thomas.

Mark saddened, "I had tried to persuade her to keep her minimum security with her. But she was as stubborn as hell. She hated vacationing with an entourage. She was quite cautious when she wanted to be though. She'd had a stalker back in the nineties, so she did take some precautions. She wouldn't answer the door to people. Not unless she was sure who it was. But then she would do stupid things like wear that choker after the threats. I told her not to… "

Mark's sentence ended with a quiet sigh, thinking of their argument the night before.

Again it was Scott that spoke. "Sir, whoever did this has been clever. This looks like it has been planned well."

Mark said, "What do you mean? Is this why the train's stopped?"

Lambert spoke for the first time, "The train has been sabotaged. My staff members are going to be able to get us started again, but all of our channels of communication have been cut."

Scott finished, "We believe the two incidents are connected. And that someone intended for us to be stranded out here."

"So what happens now?" asked Mark.

Lambert answered, "As I said, my engineers will have us up and running in a couple of hours. We will hopefully make up the lost time and arrive in Los Angeles on schedule."

Mark said incredulously, "Do you think I'm worried about keeping to a schedule?!"

Scott said, "Mr Jordan, we realise that this is a difficult time for you. Mr Lambert was just explaining that, in all likelihood, we will not be able to contact the authorities until we reach Los Angeles. Until we get there, Mr Seymour is going to conduct his own investigation. To which I will assist."

Mark looked at Scott and said, "With all due respect Mr Blacklock, I don't know you, or the work you do." He gestured over to Thomas and said scornfully, "And Mr Detective over there does not seem the most experienced of his kind. Anything must be better than his waiting skills, I suppose."

Feeling very frustrated, Mark's glare turned to Lambert.

"Mr Lambert, Is there really no way to contact anyone on this "state of the art" train?"

Lambert twitched uncomfortably, "I'm afraid that is the case Sir. There is a chance someone's cellular phone may pick up a signal in Nevada as Las Vegas is the closest city we go past. But it's not a guarantee."

Mark folded his arms, "I suggest we wait until we're in Nevada then."

Scott moved forward and spoke, "I'm afraid the decision is not yours to make Mr Jordan. As Mr Seymour is a qualified officer of the law, he will be taking command of this situation. Until he receives the appropriate backup, he will be in charge. Now Mr Lambert has arranged an announcement in the bar in a short while, but we will understand if you wish to remain here."

It looked as though the reality of Clarissa's death hit Mark again at the thought of others hearing the news, making it more real. Mark was silent for a moment before saying, "Yes, I shall remain here."

Lambert took that as their cue to leave and made for the door. As Scott stood up, he said, "Mr Jordan, before we go, I'd just like to ask you a few more questions."

"About what?" questioned Mark.

"Your actions last night." said Scott plainly.

Mark sat up in bed, the anger from before returning. "Are you asking me if I killed my wife?!"

Scott remained calm, "Sir, we are just trying to ascertain the facts. We are also trying to estimate a time of death. Did you see her when she returned from the card game in the lounge last night?"

Mark said irritably, "No. I didn't. As you know, I left you, Clarissa and that smarmy Stuart man at the card table. I came back here and fell straight to sleep. The next thing I remember is you waking me up." The memory of that moment returned to Mark and Scott thought he saw a tear forming. "That's all I know." he finished quietly.

"Thank you Mr Jordan. We will leave you for now." said Scott as he opened the door, feeling that they had asked all they could at that moment.

The three of them walked out into the corridor and moved down the carriage, out of earshot of Mark's room.

"What do you think? Could it have been him? He seems pretty distraught." asked Lambert to both of them.

Scott answered, "I'll agree, he does seem to be."

Thomas said, "Did you notice that he didn't want an investigation until later? And he has no proof that he just came back and went to sleep."

Scott replied, "He did seem tired when we were playing cards. Almost overtly so."

Lambert said, "Maybe it was an act? Part of his plan?"

Scott felt that Lambert was very keen to find the perpetrator quickly, and that this was making him pick the obvious answers. But Scott remembered how it had been hard to rouse Mark and was thinking of another alternative. He neglected to share his thoughts with the other two as he saw the antique clock further down the carriage indicate that it was almost ten. He said, pointing to the clock. "Gentlemen, we will have to continue this conversation at a later point."

As Lambert went to make his way to the bar, Scott said. "Mr Lambert, I think that your staff should be present also. Once everyone is in the bar, get Stephenson and Dunn to move Clarissa's body into refrigeration. Make sure they wear gloves."

Lambert nodded and turned back the other way to the front of the train. As he left the carriage, Thomas said, "I'll meet you there. I'm going to secure this." as he patted the evidence kit that was still clasped in his hand.

Scott nodded, and walked on alone to the end of the train.

Scott was greeted by an empty carriage as he entered the bar. Someone had arranged a tray of drinks though, so Scott took a stool and helped himself to a fruit juice. He thought back to what Mark had just told him and couldn't help but wonder if someone had wanted to make sure that Mark had slept heavily last night.

He decided to take these few moments of solitude to search the bar for anything hidden, be it the diamond or otherwise. After several minutes of cushion rummaging and a sneaky check over the bar, Scott was slightly disappointed but not surprised to find nothing suspicious.

As the large clock behind the bar chimed ten, the Stuarts walked into the bar. They passed Scott and Anthony smiled, "Good morning Mr Blacklock. It would seem the train is not quite as fantastic as Lambert keeps claiming!"

They took a seat by the window and Scott responded with a smile. They were shortly followed by Harry Broadside, who looked bleary eyed and a little hung over. He made no effort to acknowledge Scott and moved straight to where the Stuarts were sitting.

Tim arrived a moment afterward, and approached Scott with a quizzical look on his face.

As he too helped himself to a drink, he asked, "What's this all about then? What happened to the train?"

Before Scott answered, he spied Amy walk in behind Tim. She still looked pale and was wearing dark glasses. She quickly looked around the bar and took a seat in the corner. Scott watched her sit down and then said quietly,

"Something very serious. You'll find out in a moment though."

Tim turned to see where Scott had looked. When he saw Amy, he swivelled on his stool and said to Scott,

"I have news of my own, but I guess it will have to wait until after Lambert's big speech then!"

Daphne Pennington walked into the carriage, and made straight for Scott at the bar. As she sat at the stool the other side of him, she said, "I've left Avril in her room. She wasn't up for seeing people. I said I'd pass on any message."

Scott smiled and said, "Thank you. It's understandable that she doesn't want company."

Jessica Rae entered, her face positively alight with the thought of excitement and a more interesting scoop happening on the train. She took a seat on the opposite side of the carriage to Amy, and Scott noticed how she had a pen and notepad at the ready.

"So where is Lambert anyway?" asked Daphne.

Scott didn't answer as Lambert took that moment to arrive, followed by Thomas, Rosalie, Bradley and Andreas. The sudden display of the staff immediately started pockets of murmuring, from over at the Stuarts table to Daphne in Scott's ear.

Rosalie, Bradley and Andreas seemed unsure where to stand, so instead took a position behind the bar.

Everyone looked expectantly to Lambert, and it took him a second to realise everybody was present. The deaths of two passengers and the absence of their respective partners had reduced the passenger population by a third.

Lambert stepped forward into the room and began,

"Ladies and Gentlemen, the first thing that I have to do is apologise for the disruption in the train service. My engineers are working on it now, and we will be resuming our journey in a couple of hours."

Anthony Stuart leant forward and asked, "Mr Lambert, what exactly is the problem with the train?"

Lambert faltered for a second, "This leads me on to my second announcement, one of a much more serious nature. This is where I will pass you over to Mr Thomas Seymour."

"What have you got to do with anything?" asked Jessica bluntly.

Thomas moved forward past Lambert and revealed his identification badge. He said,

"My name is Detective Seymour. I work for the N.Y.P.D. I had been working incognito on this train as a waiter. I had been keeping surveillance on Mrs Clarissa Jordan."

"Yes, Where is she?" asked Daphne, looking around to see if she'd missed her coming in.

Thomas paused. He replied, "Clarissa Jordan was murdered last night in her suite."

There was an audible gasp from both Daphne and Harry, followed by a rather loud "What!" from Jessica. Scott watched from his vantage point at the bar at his fellow passenger's faces. All of them looked stunned. Harry looked extremely distraught, while Caroline's face was terrified.

With no shame, Jessica asked loudly, "How?"

Thomas said, "It would appear that she has been strangled. We suspect that the person responsible was also responsible for disabling the train and damaging our communication equipment."

"What?!" shrieked Caroline, "You mean we're stranded here! With no way to get help!"

Caroline's outburst started a chorus of other people talking anxiously, including the staff members. Amazingly, Lambert called them to order. He said loudly,

"Ladies, Gentlemen. Please. Mr Dunn and Mr Stephenson have almost fixed the train."

Thomas took over, "As far as getting help is concerned, we will continue to work on that. In the meantime, I am taking charge of this situation and will be requiring statements from all of you. Now, we believe that there is possibly a motive of theft as Mrs Jordan's valuable Warwick diamond is missing. And this is where Mr Blacklock comes in."

There were several comments of surprise as Scott stood up from the bar and moved over to stand with Thomas and Lambert. Scott turned to the group of people and said,

"You may be wondering how I fit into this. I work as an investigative agent for Zirconia, the insurance corporation. Clarissa Jordan's assets are insured through Zirconia, including the missing Warwick diamond. I, like Mr Seymour was also keeping surveillance on Clarissa."

"I'm sorry, but why was Clarissa being followed?" asked Jessica, her pen poised in her hand. Scott looked at her begrudgingly, knowing that she was licking up every juicy detail for her next column. He replied, "Clarissa had been receiving threats in the mail."

Again there was another gasp from Daphne.

Scott continued, "The threats did make a reference to her diamond, hence my involvement. I will be assisting Mr Seymour in collecting statements."

"How does he know you didn't do it?" asked Jessica bluntly.

Scott replied calmly, "I have already shown my credentials to both Mr Lambert and Detective Seymour and they are both satisfied with my background story. So should you be Jessica, as you know where I work also."

Jessica seemed annoyed at the rebuttal but didn't say anything further.

Thomas stood forward and said, "Ladies and Gentlemen, for the time being I am going to have to ask you to remain in the bar while we make a sweep of the train to search it."

Harry said loudly, "What! You're going to search our rooms!"

"Something you should be worried about?" Scott asked curtly.

Harry hesitated, "Well....No."

"Good" said Thomas, "We apologise for the inconvenience. But we will not be more than a couple of hours."

At the sound of that, several more of the passengers began to look disgruntled.

Lambert quickly added, "At which point, it will be just in time for another one of Andreas's culinary delights. Bradley and Rosalie will serve you any drinks or snacks that you require."

Thomas finished, "Now, if you'll excuse us, we will be back shortly."

Thomas and Lambert made for the door, and as Scott followed, he noticed that Amy was sat in the corner, looking disgusted at Tim. Scott got the feeling that revealing he had been watching Clarissa had not gone down too well with Amy. She was now probably questioning Tim's involvement, he thought as he passed her.

After Scott had told the other two that he had already searched the bar before the others arrived, they decided to work from the back of the train forward. They searched the observation carriage to find nothing before heading on to the Thistlewood suites. They had to disturb Mark again and asked him to wait in the observation carriage while they searched his room. He was quite angered by them, but a quick examination of his room came up with the same result as the rest.

The following carriage held Scott's, Tim's and the Kennedy's suites. To show he had nothing to hide, Scott was happy for the three of them to search his room. After going through his suite, they moved on to Tim's, finding nothing except a mess of clothes.

They knocked tentatively at Avril's door, but there was no response. They opened the door quietly, and saw her asleep in bed. Scott moved over to her and tried to wake her. He noticed the bottle of sleeping pills by her bedside and realised that nothing was waking her for a few hours.

After several moments pondering, they decided to conduct their search as best they could around the comatose Avril Kennedy. Once they had finished in her room, it was on to the next carriage. The suites occupied by Amy Jordan, Harry Broadside and Jessica Rae.

Again there were no results.

The next carriage was the suites of Mr and Mrs Stuart and Daphne Pennington.

Again, nothing.

The three of them went on to the reception area and searched Lambert's bedroom. They decided to take another look in Lambert's office as well.

As they were looking around, Scott picked up the paperweight that had been lying next to Lambert when he and Bradley had found him.

Scott turned to Lambert and asked, "If you always lock your door, how could your assailant have already been in here?"

"He wasn't." as Lambert felt the bump on his head again, "The last thing I remember was opening the door and someone hitting me from behind."

He pointed to the paperweight in Scott's hand. "That's not from my desk. It's from the reception desk. They must have waited for me to open the door before striking."

As Scott placed it down, he said, "That's one little mystery solved."

They pressed on through the lounge, dining carriage and kitchen. They checked the storage carriage, even going through the refrigeration compartment and checking the corpses of Clarissa and Gerry. It was then onto the staff quarters, and a quick search of the six cabins and bathroom in that carriage. Quick because the size of the staff's rooms meant there were not many places to hide anything.

As they arrived at the front of the train, all three of them were hot and bothered. They had looked high and low, in every pot and pan, in small service hatches and even in tubs of cosmetics. They had spent much more than the two hours they had promised to the other passengers and Lambert concluded that their search had been "fruitless". Not completely fruitless though, thought Scott as he followed the other two to the engine. Looking through the bedrooms had given Scott useful glimpses into their characters.

From Caroline Stuart's sewing kit and arts and crafts case to the empty bottles of beer under Harry Broadside's bed. Slightly more interesting were the financial statements in the Kennedy's suitcase and Amy's choice of celebrity magazine, one that had a paparazzi shot of her, Clarissa and Mark boarding a yacht on the cover. Scott was now starting to build mental profiles of all the passengers on board. There had been two things that surprised Scott though. The first was the lack of electrical equipment in Jessica's room. He had been thinking that she was one of the only people on the train likely to bring a laptop. And that it might have had a remote internet connection. But there was nothing, except copious notes on most of the people on the train. He did feel slightly suspicious about this, but realised that she couldn't have hidden it anywhere.

The second thing that had surprised and bothered him was that Jessica Rae had not been the only one keeping notes on passengers on the train. So too had Daphne Pennington.

Robert Dunn appeared out of the driver's cabin when he heard Lambert arrive.

"Mr Lambert," He said with a big smile on his face. "Good news! We're fixed! And ready to go!"

Lambert almost couldn't believe it. "We're ready to go now?"

Dunn answered, "Stephenson's just finishing clearing the last of the snow from the wheels. We should be out of here in five minutes."

"That's great news. Well done."

Thomas said, "Now, if you'll excuse us, we just need to make a quick search of this area."

Dunn shrugged and went back to his workstation. He pointed to the device he had found in the circuits. They huddled round to take a look, but none of them really knew what they were looking at. Dunn did note that it looked home made as opposed to any professional or military model. After quickly searching the locomotive and seeing that there was nothing there but machinery, the three of them made the long walk back down the train to rejoin the others in the bar.

When they arrived, the quiet conversation around the room all hushed and everyone present turned to look at the three of them.

Thomas stepped forward, "Ladies and Gentlemen, thank you for your patience. We have completed our search of the train, and after I have finished speaking, you will be free to move around again."

"Did you find the diamond?" asked Jessica.

"No, we didn't" replied Thomas.

"What does that mean?" Daphne asked, looking more to Scott than Thomas.

No one replied as a loud screech followed by an equally loud whoosh came from the front of the train. As they all turned to the direction of the sound, the carriage lurched and those standing had to steady themselves as the train slowly began to move forward.

There was a small cheer from the passengers, and several of them turned to look out the window to make sure they were actually moving. Several hours stranded on an isolated track had obviously had more of an effect on them than they realised.

The excitement of the train starting died down and Lambert took the diversion to avoid answering Daphne's question, instead saying, "Ladies and Gentlemen, as promised the train is back up and running, and we will endeavour to make up for all lost time to get to Los Angeles as quickly as possible."

Thomas continued, "As I said, you are free to move around the train now, but I will be coming to talk to you all at some point in the day. Thank you."

As soon as he had finished, nearly everyone seated stood up. Having been stuck in one carriage had clearly gotten to them.

Amy said, "I'm going to check on my father." hastily leaving the carriage.

Daphne also stood up and stated her intentions to check on Avril before departing. Scott heard Caroline saying to Anthony that she wanted to go to their room and they too left. It seemed everyone was feeling the need to justify leaving the carriage.

Jessica, obviously feeling no such need, pulled another cigarette out of her jacket pocket and headed out to the balcony.

As Lambert walked over to the bar to give out instructions to his staff, Thomas stepped over to Scott and said, "Who do you think we should talk to first?"

Scott didn't answer. Instead he walked over to one of the only passengers left.

"Mr Broadside, I'd like to start with you."

Harry looked up at him and gave a mean smile, "Now why doesn't that surprise me?"

Scott said, "Would you mind coming down with us to Mr Lambert's office?"

Harry stood up. He said, "Am I allowed to go and grab a bite to eat? Seeing as how breakfast was so pathetic?"

Scott smiled, "Certainly. Let's say we'll see you in Mr Lambert's office in fifteen minutes."

Harry muttered something inaudible, looked to Thomas, and then made his way out of the carriage. As they watched him leave, Thomas said, "Why him first? You're thinking the jealous ex-husband?"

Scott answered, "There's been one or two questions I've been meaning to ask him for a while. One of the first being how he knew Clarissa was going to be on this train."

"You think he was following her too? That he was still infatuated?"

Scott grimaced, "Infatuated may not be a strong enough word."

A tale of unrequited love

Hi Miranda,

Me again, with another postcard of Grand Central from a different angle!! Now you'll get all three of these at the same time! You'll probably hear about it before these get to you anyway but Clarissa Jordan was murdered last night!

The train was sabotaged and we were stuck in the Rockies all night. Clarissa's jewellery was stolen and Scott is working with an undercover cop to find out who did it! I just saw them talking to Clarissa's ex-husband. I told Scott he was dodgy!

Anyway, I've been thinking, and I'd really like to make Saturday night up to you properly when I get back.

Speak soon.
Tim. X

The time was approaching one thirty as Scott stared out of the window of Lambert's office. The blurring whiteness out of the window was much more comforting than the static view of the last twelve hours. Behind him, Thomas had set up a tape recorder on the desk and was now rearranging the chairs in Lambert's office to create an interrogation room.

Scott looked to the door as it opened and Lambert walked in, carrying a tray of coffee and tea.

"I brought some refreshments for you." he said as he laid the tray down on the side.

"Who are you speaking to first?"

Thomas replied, as he poured himself some coffee, "Harry Broadside should be here in a moment."

Scott folded his arms and said, "Before he arrives, I think it would be a good idea for the three of us to divulge our movements last night."

Thomas looked up from his coffee, questioning him with a look.

Scott added, "We need to work out who was where on the train last night, to try and work out a window for the time of death. Mr Lambert, could you explain your movements for us?"

Lambert hesitated for a second before asking, "From what point?"

Scott answered, "Let's go from when you spoke to everyone in the bar, after we came from Mrs Kennedy's room last night."

Lambert started, "Ok then. Let's see. Well I told everyone about how Mrs Kennedy wanted us to continue onto Los Angeles. We were all in the bar for about another hour. After you and the others left to play cards, Clarissa asked me on the way out to remove Mr Broadside as he was quite inebriated. I then spent about the next....twenty minutes helping Mr Broadside to his suite."

"Twenty minutes?!" asked Thomas incredulously.

Lambert seemed a little embarrassed, "Well Mr Broadside is quite a good deal bigger than me ...and he was finding it difficult to walk so to speak. I managed to get him lying on his bed, where he promptly passed out."

"What did you do after that?" asked Scott.

Lambert continued, "I came here. I used the satellite phone to try and ring my head office."

"Why?" asked Thomas.

"To tell them about Gerry Kennedy's death." answered Lambert. "There was no answer on my manager's phone, but I left a message saying a passenger had died of a heart attack. And that we were continuing onto Los Angeles."

Lambert now looked ashamed, "I must say that I kept the details to a minimum in the message. I was worried there may be repercussions."

He gave an ironic smile, "And that was then!"

"What did you do after that?" Scott asked.

"I did some paper work on what had happened at dinner and filed a report. Then, as I was leaving, I heard Clarissa talking loudly from the lounge, shortly followed by Ms Rae hurrying past me. I then came into the lounge as Mrs Jordan and Mr Stuart were leaving. As you will remember, I spoke to you briefly before you left. I then made my way to the kitchen."

"And who was there?" questioned Scott.

Lambert pointed to Thomas, "Detective Seymour here, and Andreas. They were both cleaning up."

Lambert gave Thomas a look at that point, a feeling of betrayal flashed across his eyes. Retelling his story had reminded him that, until several hours ago, Thomas had been one of his employees. The fact that he had been lied to still left a bitter taste in his mouth.

Lambert looked back to Scott and carried on, "I checked that all the work was completed for the evening and told Thomas to head to bed. I then reminded Andreas that he was on room service duty for the evening."

"Where were the rest of your staff at this point?" Scott asked.

"Stephenson had gone to bed. Dunn was on the night shift. Bradley arrived in the kitchen while I was still there. He told me Rosalie was finishing up in the bar. I told Bradley to get the room service phone before he turned in, as Andreas was still cleaning. I then left them both, and was going to head to bed. I stopped to get a drink in the lounge and decided to return here, to my office quickly. As I went to open the door, everything went black. The next thing I know, it was morning, and you and Bradley were stood over me."

Scott didn't say anything for a moment, taking in the story. After a minute, he said,

"Thank you Mr Lambert, that helps us. Now, if you'll excuse us, Mr Broadside will be here in a few minutes."

Thomas looked confused, while Lambert became indignant. He said, "Now hang on a second. I thought all three of us were going to explain our movements!"

Scott said calmly, "Mr Seymour and I will discuss that in a moment."

Lambert drew himself up, which didn't do much considering his height. If anything, it made him resemble a puffer fish. He said angrily, "And may I ask why I am not allowed to be privy to that?!"

Scott replied, "Mr Lambert, it will be Detective Seymour who conducts this investigation, with my assistance. Your focus now has to be the train and the remaining passengers. Detective Seymour will keep you informed with any crucial updates, but you have to understand that we won't divulge all of the information with you."

"And why not?" asked Lambert, now completely outraged.

"Mr Seymour and I have proved our intentions for being here. You have to understand that we don't completely know yours."

Lambert positively screamed, "My intentions?! What about the fact that I have been the manager of the Express for the last twelve years! The only intentions I have ever had is to make the Express a success! Are you seriously thinking that I could be a suspect?!"

Scott tried to placate him, "No Mr Lambert, if I am honest, I don't think you are a suspect. But you're not an investigator either."

"Neither are you!"

Scott stopped himself from getting angry now. "I may not work in law enforcement, but I am an investigator. And as I think I have sufficiently proven to you both now, I do have experience in this field. You Sir, do not. And, as I said before, you need to worry about the running of the train. Let us worry about the investigation."

Lambert did not reply, and Scott could see he still needed some persuasion. He tried a different approach.

He said, "Mr Lambert, by keeping the train running normally, you'll be helping us in your own way. And you'll be helping yourself as well."

"How's that then?" asked Lambert suspiciously.

"If you're keeping business as usual, it will help the passengers, those not guilty of anything, feel more at ease. As you said before, you don't want more trouble when we get to Los Angeles."

Lambert was now starting to see Scott's point. The reputation of the Express was already probably in ruins. But he might have a chance to repair some of the damage, at least with some of the passengers on the train.

Scott said, "Isn't Andreas serving lunch now? Don't you think it will look better if you're there to oversee it?"

Lambert thought for a moment before saying begrudgingly, "I suppose you're right. But I'll be back soon after. This is still my office, remember."

Lambert took this moment to retreat, slowly closing the door behind him as he went.

Scott finally moved from his position at the window and poured himself some tea. As he turned back to the desk, he saw that Thomas looked impressed.

"That was pretty sneaky work, lulling Lambert into answering your questions."

Scott smiled, "I didn't think he would take too kindly to the fact that I didn't want him to be part of the investigation."

Scott realised that he may have overstepped the mark in taking control, and added,

"You don't mind him not being involved?"

Thomas set down his coffee. He replied, "No. In fact, I agree with you."

"Well that's a good start. So, does Lambert's story fit for you?"

Thomas nodded, "Yes, Andreas and I were just finishing when he arrived in the kitchen last night."

"What time was that?" asked Scott.

"It must have been almost midnight."

Scott said hesitantly, "And if you don't mind me asking, what did you do then?"

Thomas didn't seem to take offence at the question. He replied, "I did what Lambert said. I went to bed. I'm afraid the night's events are lost to me. I fell asleep quite quickly and didn't wake until about seven this morning. I'm quite a heavy sleeper. I didn't wake when the train stopped."

"Did anything of interest happen before you went to bed?" asked Scott.

"No. After getting Stephenson to help Bradley with Gerry Kennedy's body, I spent the rest of the evening in the kitchen with Andreas. Right up until Lambert arrived. Neither of us left the whole time."

It wasn't exactly the best staff position to do surveillance." Scott noted dryly.

"It was all they could get at short notice." Thomas said defensively.

Scott sipped his tea, placing everyone in each carriage mentally. Thomas sat back in his chair. "So Mr Blacklock," he said, "Maybe you could now tell me what you saw and did. Seeing as how you were obviously more privy to Clarissa's actions that I." he finished sarcastically.

"Certainly" Scott said as he sat down opposite him. "Where would you like me to start?"

"How about from Lambert's speech in the bar?" Thomas replied.

Scott started, "Ok. After Lambert had finished, I sat with my friend Tim for a while."

"That would be Tim Anderson?"

"Yes."

"And did he know of your intentions on the train?"

"Yes."

"So you don't suspect him?"

"Of course not. Tim is beyond reproach." Scott answered, a little indignantly.

"You're close friends then?" Thomas pressed.

"Best friends. For fourteen years." Scott replied bluntly.

Thomas bridged his fingers. He said, "You do understand that while he may be your lifelong best friend, he is still on my list of suspects and I will be talking to him."

Scott was about to object, before saying, "I wouldn't expect otherwise, Detective. But I can assure you that he wasn't involved in this."

"I would appreciate you letting me get to that conclusion on my own." snapped Thomas.

Scott bit his tongue and said, "We are digressing. And Mr Broadside will be here shortly. Shall I continue with my story?"

Thomas nodded by way of reply.

"Right, where was I? Yes, I was sat at the bar with Tim. We moved to a table where Amy Jordan met us. Not long after, Clarissa invited me to play cards with her, Mr Stuart and her husband. I left the bar and walked down to the lounge to join them."

"Did anything of interest happen over cards?"

Scott paused, "We played several games together. There was some friction between Mark and Clarissa."

"How so?" asked Thomas.

"You may not have witnessed it, but there had been occasions of Clarissa flirting with other men."

Thomas nodded, "I had heard Bradley say that Clarissa seemed rather taken with him."

Scott sipped his tea, "I'm afraid her affections did not stop at Bradley. There were several comments over the card game implied at Anthony Stuart."

"In front of her husband?! That's not very discreet! Do you think maybe she was trying to get a rise out of Mark Jordan?"

Scott considered it. "It's possible. From what I could tell of Clarissa, she seemed like someone who always needed male attention, in whatever form that came."

Thomas was thinking back to the interview they had just had with Mark Jordan. He asked, "How did Mark Jordan take it? He doesn't seem like the type of man to take that lying down."

Scott explained, "It was more of an underlying atmosphere. Plus I was there trying to diffuse the conversation with more mundane topics. It was at that point that Mr Jordan seemed to be getting very tired, and retired to bed. It was after that when the argument began."

Thomas asked, "And that was between Clarissa and Jessica Rae?"

Scott nodded, "Yes. When Mark left, Jessica tried to take his place in the game. Clarissa had none of it."

"And what happened?"

"Words were exchanged between them. It ended with Clarissa slapping Jessica. They all left soon after, and that was when Lambert arrived."

Thomas leaned forward, "Tell me Mr Blacklock, what do you think Jessica Rae's involvement in all this is?"

Scott shrugged, "She's travelling on this train to get an exclusive on Clarissa. I think you could say she's got that all right!"

"Do you think she could have done this in order to get her exclusive?!"

Scott was beginning to get frustrated at Thomas's interruptions from his story to ask questions about the suspects. He was about to say as much when there was a knock at the door. He said to Thomas as he stood up, "I feel this will have to wait until later."

He moved to the door and realised that he hadn't gotten round to telling him some of his more important observations of the previous night, mainly catching Clarissa and Anthony's midnight kiss and Caroline Stuart breaking down on him on the balcony.

Scott opened the door to show Harry Broadside, waiting expectantly with his hands behind his back. He had donned a suit to smarten up, but the crumpled jacket and baggy eyes betrayed the intention.

Scott gestured for him to enter, as Thomas stood and said, "Mr Broadside, thank you for coming. Please take a seat."

As Harry sat down, Thomas resumed his seat in Lambert's chair. He had moved the other chair to his side of the table for Scott to sit down, but instead Scott chose to lean against the window.

Harry settled in his seat and looked expectantly between Scott and Thomas for them to begin. Thomas pressed record on the cassette player. He said in a clear stern voice. "The time is 1.45 P.M on Monday the 22nd September. This is an interview with Mr Henry Broadside. Detective Thomas Seymour and Mr Scott Blacklock present." Thomas interlocked his fingers and placed them on the desk. As he leaned forward, he began, "Mr Broadside, you are obviously aware that this is now a murder investigation. I take it you have no objection to this conversation being recorded."

Harry shook his head, but said nothing.

"For the record, Mr Broadside has indicated that he has no objection. Now, Mr Broadside, perhaps you could start by telling us of your actions last night."

Harry gave a smug smile, "Certainly Sir, although there isn't much to tell. After the dinner party from hell, I sat at the bar and got myself slowly drunk!"

Thomas did not return the smile. "Mr Lambert had to help you to your room, isn't that correct?"

"I vaguely remember that, yes." replied Harry.

"After Mr Lambert took you to your suite, did you leave it again that evening?" pressed Thomas.

Harry's attitude changed, "What? In order to go and kill Clarissa do you mean?"

This time it was Thomas that gave a polite smile. "Sir, we are just trying to understand the whereabouts of all the passengers at the time of the murder."

Harry sat back and folded his arms. He said defensively, "No. I didn't leave my room again. And I think you'll find that I was in no state to either! Ask Lambert if you like! The last thing I properly remember was Lambert telling us about going on to Los Angeles after that old tortoise Kennedy died. The next thing I know, it's this morning, and I wake up on the floor of my room." He chuckled to himself, "The only thing I seemed to be able to do was pull my pillow and duvet onto the floor with me!"

Scott had been observing Harry and had been uneasy with Harry's demeanour since the interview began and was sure that he was hiding something. He took a sip of tea as he looked out of the window and finally spoke. He asked, "Mr Broadside, why were you getting yourself slowly drunk last night?"

Harry's eyes flicked from Thomas to Scott, and as Scott looked back at him, he saw what he was hiding. Grief.

Harry faltered for the first time. He mumbled, "Well...I, you see..."

Scott set his cup down and interrupted him. "Forget that question for the time being. How about telling us why you happen to be on this train in the first place?"

Harry said quietly, "I think you know why already. Clarissa..."

Thomas interjected sharply, "You openly admit to being on this train because of Mrs Jordan. For what purpose? To steal her jewel? To kill her?"

"NO" cried Harry forcefully.

Thomas continued, "You must see how it looks. You are her ex husband, and your verbal differences were witnessed by everyone at the dinner table last night."

"You don't understand." said Harry, though not as strongly as before.

As he said it, Scott thought he could see moisture appearing in Harry's red rimmed eyes.

Scott moved across to the desk. "Help us understand Mr Broadside. Why don't you start from the beginning? When did you first meet Clarissa?"

Harry fidgeted with his shirt sleeve. He began, "It was just over two years ago. I was working as a barman at a charity benefit in Boston. Clarissa was the guest speaker."

Harry's eyes looked to a place back in the past. He said quietly, "I remember I was blown away when she asked me for a drink. Her smile lit up the room. And then when she started flirting with me, I was immediately taken. By the end of the night, she had left me her number on a napkin. I remember walking home from work in a daze, reading her name and number over and over, not believing that the evening had been real."

"And what happened from there?" asked Scott.

"It took me a full three days to pluck up the courage to ring her. We went out for a meal in Boston. By the following weekend, she had arranged for a flight to fly me down to New York. I was supposed to stay for three days, but I didn't end up returning to Boston. I rang my agency that had been getting me function work and told them that I wouldn't be returning. A month and a half later, Clarissa and I were married."

"She doesn't seem to waste time." Thomas said bluntly. "And how long were you married for?"

Harry looked down. "Just over six months."

"What was marriage to Clarissa like?" asked Scott, less bluntly than Thomas.

Harry smiled for the first time that day. He said, "Those eight months with Clarissa were the most exciting, adventurous times of my life. And I've been around and seen and done some things. But being with Clarissa made all of that seem insignificant in comparison."

Thomas continued with his hard line of questioning. "So was it Clarissa or her lifestyle that so attracted you? Was it when she realised you enjoyed her money more than her that she broke it off?"

Scott glanced at Thomas. He was surprised at Thomas's tone and wondered if, like Lambert, Thomas's keenness to find the culprit had made him already decide on Harry as the killer.

Harry looked up angrily. He said indignantly, "I take offence to that. I fell in love with Clarissa, the person. Not the big star that everyone else knew!"

"So all of the luxury that came with Clarissa didn't attract you at all?" continued Thomas.

"I will admit that I was able to see some wonderful parts of the world because of Clarissa, but that's not the reason that I fell in love with her, or why I married her."

"So why did it end?" questioned Thomas, "Six months isn't that long for a marriage."

Harry again looked down, saddened. "I still don't completely know why."

"So it was Clarissa that ended it?" pressed Thomas.

"Yes." Harry replied slowly.

Scott finally spoke. "I remember a certain cruel tabloid saying that Clarissa was annoyed at the lack of press attention in her marriage, and so decided divorce would get her more column inches."

Harry looked up at him. He said, "As you said, a cruel tabloid report. Clarissa wasn't like that."

"Then how was she like?" asked Scott. "From what I've seen on this train, she seemed quite a fickle person."

Again Harry's eyes started to well up. He smiled sadly. "Yes that she was. Everyone around me at the time told me that this was typical of her. That she simply got bored of people and then brushed them aside."

Scott pressed on, "Is that why the divorce turned so nasty? Because you were so angry?"

Harry sighed. "No. I mean, yes I was angry. But what happened with the divorce wasn't my fault. I hired the wrong lawyer, this guy called Gareth Lynch. He was far too greedy for his own good. He wanted to get the biggest settlement he could, so his share would be bigger. And he obviously knew what a cash cow Clarissa would be."

"But you could have stopped him?" stated Thomas.

"Yes, I could have. But I was angry at first, and then I was just really confused. By the time the settlement came through, I realised that all I really wanted was Clarissa back."

"What did you do then?" asked Scott.

Harry answered, "The press attention was still really bad in the weeks after the court hearings, so I decided to return to Boston. I've been there ever since."

"What have you been doing in Boston since then?"

"I used the money to open my own bar. I worked really hard, but I couldn't stop thinking about Clarissa."

Scott moved back across to the window. He said, "So back to my original question, how did you end up on this train?"

Harry replied, "About a month ago, I got a letter from Gareth. In it was a ticket for this train. I thought it was a bit strange as I hadn't heard from him in a while. The letter was typical of him. He had found out that Clarissa was going to be on this train. He wanted to make an opportunity for me to get some more money out of her."

"So you're admitting to coming on this train to get money out of Clarissa?" asked Thomas accusingly.

Again Harry got angry, "No! I decided to use the ticket, but not for any financial gain. I wanted to try... to try and win her back."

"And the fact that she had re-married didn't deter you?" asked Scott, a little incredulously.

"To be honest I didn't really think about it. I just wanted to see Clarissa again. I'd missed her so much."

Thomas folded his arms. He said, "It all sounds very convenient. How are we to know that you hadn't been watching her and planned this yourself? Do you still have this letter from your lawyer?"

"No, I don't. But there was nothing planned about this." Harry's expression changed and he actually smiled. "If you knew me, you'd know that I can't plan anything. I'm always late and things tend to have a habit of going wrong for me." He chuckled and continued. "I almost didn't make it to New York. My cab broke down on the way to Logan

International. It was only luck that I managed to get a later flight. Some sinister plotting murderer I'd make!"

"I think you should let us make that conclusion Mr Broadside." said Thomas as he sat back in his chair.

Harry scratched his chin with his forefinger, and his eyes showed his patience finally snapping. He said, "Look, can I go now? I've told you my whereabouts last night. I've told you why I was on the train, and I have explained my history with Clarissa."

"Yes you have." said Thomas, "And all together, they look like there's quite a motive there."

Harry raised his voice. "I've said that I only wanted to see Clarissa to tell her that I still love her. And that's the truth! I don't care if you don't believe me, but you will find no evidence that I had anything to do with this, because I didn't."

Thomas said, "Mr Broadside, there is no reason to raise your voice."

Scott spoke. "Thank you Mr Broadside for answering our questions, we'll let you know if we have anything further."

Harry looked from Thomas to Scott. He nodded and stood up to leave, not taking care to shut the door quietly as he left.

Thomas spoke into the recorder, "Interview concluded with Mr Henry Broadside."

As he switched it off, he looked over to Scott and snapped, "Mr Blacklock. If you don't mind, I will decide when an interview is over or not."

Scott stayed calm. He said, "Mr Seymour, with all due respect, I think we probably have learned all we will from him for the time being. And you were just antagonising him, when we don't have much time."

Scott was bothered by Thomas's sudden spurt of confidence, especially as it felt like he had jumped on the first suspect to coerce a confession out of him.

Thomas started to gather up his papers on the table. He said, "How about the fact that I think he is our prime suspect at the moment? And that his entire story points to solid motive?"

Scott asked, "You don't think that he was telling the truth about being in love?"

As Thomas closed his folder he said, "It's a nice story. But there was one key aspect that he "forgot" to add."

"And what was that?" asked Scott impatiently.

Thomas said smugly, "It seems that the police are a bit better on background checks than Zirconia. We had already run one on this guy after the first letter was sent to Clarissa. Harry Broadside was still residing in Boston, but he hasn't been running his own bar for over six months now. He's currently working as a barman in a small place called Fandangos after his drinking problem left his business in the toilet. His finances make an interesting read too."

"How's that?" asked Scott.

"All of the settlement money that he received a year and a half ago is gone. It seems he has a slight gambling problem. He was bankrupt. Now if you'll excuse me, I need a quick bathroom break."

As Thomas opened the door, he looked back and said, "Still think he was on the train for love?"

Scott didn't say anything and watched the door close with a mixture of embarrassment and annoyance.

Accusations and alibis

Scott paced Lambert's office while he waited for Thomas Seymour. He was angry at Thomas, angry at himself and angry with the situation. He was annoyed that Ralph Peterson had only given him this brief five days ago. How was he supposed to run extensive background checks on everyone connected to Clarissa in a day and a half and without the support of Katherine. Although no one could have predicted the course of events, he thought, stopping the personal chastisement. He also realised that he couldn't be angry at Thomas for reprimanding him on stopping the interview. He had overstepped the mark. Thomas was the law enforcement here. As he finished his tea, he came to the conclusion that what was bothering him was the lack of all the facts. And waiting for Thomas was only making him more agitated.

He quickly checked his watch before leaving the office and headed to the back of the train.

Scott's purpose for leaving was that he wanted to speak to Tim. He would have to ask him on his movements last night, and he knew that he would be able to do it with more speed and ease without Thomas. Scott knew that Thomas would want a personal history and possibly try to antagonize him into revealing a motive. He knew that while it was Thomas's duty to interview Tim properly, it would be both pointless and time wasting for him.

As he walked through the first of the sleeping carriages, he pondered where he would most likely find Tim. If I know Tim at all, at this time in the afternoon, he'll most likely be sleeping, thought Scott.

He made his way to their adjoining suites and entered through his room. He walked over to the sliding door, knocked once, and pulled the door open slightly. Scott was right about Tim's location, but was wrong on him sleeping. Tim lay on his bed, listening to music and reading a book. He saw Scott, smiled, and pulled his headphones out.

As he put his book down and sat up on his bed, he said, "You alright Detective? How's the case going?"

Scott pushed the door fully open, and leaned against the doorframe. He replied,

"We've only spoken to Harry Broadside so far."

Tim looked confused, "Why are you here then?"

As he said it, he understood why and his face turned sour. "You've come to question me? Scott, I thought you trusted me a bit better than that."

Scott said impatiently, "Of course I don't think that you did it. But I need to find out where you were last night and what you did. You may have seen something that can help me."

Tim grinned, "Hey relax! I was just joshing you! Why isn't the undercover cop with you?"

Scott answered, "I gave him the slip for a minute to talk to you in private. He'll want to know your life history and I've heard it before! So, what did you do last night after I left you in the bar?"

Tim pulled a face. He said, "Oh yeah, I didn't get round to telling you this morning. I had a bit of an awkward situation with Amy."

"How so?"

"We stayed in the bar for a while, drinking, chatting. Having a laugh at Lambert struggling to get Harry to bed! Then as I was walking Amy to her room, she tried to kiss me."

Scott asked anxiously, "What did you do?"

Tim said, "Don't worry. I didn't do anything!"

Scott now became suspicious. "Why? And what did you say to her?"

"I said I really liked her, but that I was kind of seeing someone in New York."

"Miranda?" Scott asked.

Tim grinned, "I guess you got me thinking at dinner the other night. Oh, and obviously I didn't do anything because you asked me not to of course!"

"You didn't completely forget that I mentioned that then?!" Scott said, but he smiled with it. Secretly, he was quite pleased that Tim was finally going to do something about his ridiculous on/off relationship with Miranda.

He asked, "How did Amy take that?"

Tim looked ashamed, "I think she got pretty embarrassed. She left quickly after that."

"And what did you do then?"

"I stayed in the observation carriage for a while, just watching the view. Then I came to bed. I even hung your suit that I borrowed out for pressing! Aren't I a good boy?"

Scott was hoping that Tim would have been able to add some more facts to the evening's events.

"You didn't see anyone after Amy left? Did you go straight to sleep?"

Tim replied, "I did see Bradley passing when I hung the suit out, about ten minutes after I got back. He was carrying some drinks on a tray. I went to sleep pretty much after that."

"You didn't wake up when the train stopped?"

"No, I woke up this morning, wrote a postcard to Miranda, then Detective Seymour came knocking. After that Lambert came with breakfast and told me to meet in the bar. That's all I know I'm afraid. Sorry I couldn't have been more help."

Scott smiled, and stood up straight. "That's ok. Thanks for what you did tell me. If you think of anything else, something from earlier in the night, or just something small that you might not have thought important, let me know."

"Will do."

Scott checked his watch, and said. "Right, I'd better go."

As he turned to leave, he said, "Oh, and I wasn't joking about giving your life story to Detective Seymour. I'm sure he'll track you down at some point today."

"Ooh, Fun! Can't wait!" shouted Tim sarcastically.

Scott was leaving his room when he quite literally got an elbow in the face as Amy Jordan came around the corner of the carriage quickly, tying her hair back into a pony tail. As Scott dodged and avoided getting a black eye, he consequently banged the back of his head on the door.

Amy squealed, "Oh my god! I'm so sorry! Are you alright?"

Scott rubbed the back of his head. "I'm fine. Don't worry. Where were you heading in such a hurry?"

Amy now looked embarrassed. "I was just on my way back to my room. I didn't really feel like seeing anyone today."

Scott wondered if this was out of grief for her step mother, or whether she was just hurrying past Tim's room.

Scott knew he shouldn't, but felt the urge to ask Amy a few questions. Scott had found in the past that people could be more forthcoming with information when there wasn't a police officer around.

"Would you mind if I stole a few minutes of your time?" asked Scott.

Amy looked doubtful at first and then nodded. Scott suggested the observation carriage and as he followed Amy through, he thought how many more points he was about to lose with the detective.

The sheer amount of light in the observation carriage was disarming at first as the sun shone brightly down on all the glass. They had now started their descent through the San Juan Mountains and the snow had begun to thin on the blurring rock outside the window. The carriage was empty, save for Caroline Stuart sat at the far end, reading. As they sat down, Scott noticed how Amy's whole demeanour had changed. The lively, bubbly girl seemed to have gone. Understandable, he thought, seeing as how her stepmother had just died. Yet her vocal dislike of Clarissa was still playing loudly in Scott's head.

"How's your father doing?" he asked gently.

Amy looked sad at the question. She replied, "I'd just come from his room when we met. He's bearing up, but I can tell he's devastated."

"And how are you doing?" Scott asked rather more obviously.

The tone was not lost on Amy. She said, "Do you mean am I devastated? I think it would be hypocritical of me to even pretend."

Scott raised his eyebrow. "That's quite honest."

Amy asked irritably, "So? What exactly did you want?"

Scott leaned forward in his chair. "Firstly, could you tell me of your movements last night?"

Amy folded her arms and said, "Wait a minute, shouldn't that detective waiter guy be with you?"

"He's otherwise engaged at the moment. Do you have a problem talking to me?" asked Scott. Amy sighed like a petulant child and said, "I stayed in the bar last night drinking with Tim. He walked me to my room and then I went to bed. I didn't hear anything. I didn't see anything. I didn't wake when the train stopped. There."

"That's exactly what happened?

"Yes. Satisfied?"

Scott sat back, and now it was he that folded his arms. "No" he said, "I'm not, because I know that you just lied."

Amy's eyes widened. "No I didn't. That's what happened!"

"No it's not. I know for example that Tim didn't walk you to your room. You left him in here."

Amy's lip trembled with anger. "Oh, he told you about that, did he? I'm sure you both had a nice laugh! So, I left him here. I did then walk to my room and go to bed."

Scott said, "Tim and I didn't laugh. This is a serious matter. I need you to be telling me the truth."

Amy replied loudly, "Why don't you just go ahead and accuse me of my stepmother's death! Then we can just cut the crap!"

Scott answered in a steady voice, "I'm not about to accuse you of anything, but yes, let's cut the crap. You've been very vocal about your dislike for Clarissa. It was practically one of the first things you said to me. I think that you talked so much about Clarissa, and how she is so jealous of you, because it helped you deal with the fact that you were jealous of her. Of her hold over men, namely your father. I think you have a bit of a Snow White complex, having always been the fairest one in your father's eyes. And now you've just lied to me about one part of your story, it makes me question the rest of it."

Amy stood up, tears in her eyes. She said, "You don't know the first thing about me! And you have no right to question me like that. You're not even the police! If you must know, Clarissa was always a nasty bitch to me, which is why I hated her. But I didn't kill her! And why would I steal her diamond?! You may not have noticed, but my father is loaded as well! Now, excuse me, any further questions can come from the detective."

Amy didn't give Scott the chance to respond before leaving the carriage. He breathed out slowly, taking in what had just happened. He had probably been too hard on her. But something about Amy since Clarissa's death was bugging him, and her reaction to his jealousy theory made him think he had been pretty close to the truth.

He sat there for a moment longer, knowing he should return to Lambert's office, where Thomas Seymour was no doubt impatiently waiting for him. However Caroline, sat on her own, made for too good an opportunity not to ask a few questions.

Caroline saw him approach and placed her bookmark on the page she was reading. She looked even more wooden than usual, and the knitted jumper she was wearing drowned her.

"Good afternoon Mrs Stuart. How are you doing?" asked Scott as he took the seat opposite her.

She spoke quietly, "I still can't quite believe it's all happened. It's unbelievable."

"I know. This isn't an easy time for anyone." said Scott softly.

Caroline's cheeks flushed. She said, "I just wanted to apologise for my moment last night. I wish you hadn't heard it."

As Caroline bowed her head, Scott reassured her. "Don't worry. It's not a problem. How are you feeling now?"

Caroline smiled ironically, "That point is slightly moot now, isn't it?"

She gestured to where Scott had been sat with Amy. She said surprisingly bluntly,

"I noticed you were talking to Amy. Is this my turn for an interrogation? What does the jealous wife think?"

Scott had to smile at her frankness. He said, "Well, if you could tell me your actions on the train, that is before I met you on the balcony?"

Caroline returned the smile, although hers was a forced one. "As I told you last night, Anthony and I had an argument when he returned to the room."

"About Clarissa?" asked Scott.

Caroline's face looked pained. "And other things. We've been having a few problems recently. This holiday was planned for that reason. Some escape!"

Scott pressed, "Do you mind me asking what other things?"

Caroline joked, "How much time do you have?! It was just normal marriage problems. Differences of opinion."

"On what?"

"On what we were doing with our lives." she answered. "I think Anthony wanted more excitement. He wanted to travel, to live more."

She grew quiet. "It came as a shock to me. I was perfectly happy with our life in Boston. It wasn't Hollywood, but it was all I wanted."

"So you come on this holiday, and then you end up travelling with Clarissa Jordan?"

"I know" said Caroline, amused at the irony of it. "It doesn't help that I've always been paranoid that Anthony was too good for me."

She looked up at Scott. "I guess this isn't making me sound too good in light of what happened?!"

Scott avoided the question by asking another. "How did your argument with Anthony end?"

"We argued for about twenty minutes. When the subject of Clarissa came up, he assured me that he loved me, and that he wasn't going to talk about it anymore. He then went to bed, and fell asleep pretty much straight away."

Again a look of sorrow overcame her facade. She continued, "I tried to sleep, but I couldn't. That's why I decided I needed air."

"Do you know roughly what time you left your room?" asked Scott.

Caroline's forehead creased in thought. "I'm not sure, it was probably about half twelve although I couldn't be certain."

"And did you see or hear anything on the way to the bar?"

"No, I didn't even notice you tucked away in that booth in the bar. I guess I was pretty preoccupied. After that, you walked me to my room. Anthony was asleep in bed. I took some sleeping pills and was out like a light."

"And had you gone straight to your room when we went off to play cards last night?"

"Yes, I was there, waiting up for Anthony. Getting angry..."

"I see." said Scott, looking at his watch. "Thank you Mrs Stuart. That's all I have for the moment. If you'll excuse me."

Caroline smiled as he stood up and walked away. There was more Scott would have liked to ask, but he was aware of the fact that time had been ticking on, and he had now talked to three passengers without Detective Seymour.

He walked down the train carriages quickly. He only slowed when he noticed through the window, a lone eagle gliding in the sky, flying parallel to the train. He watched it and wondered if the eagle was boasting about its superior transportation. He kept watching it as he moved through the sleeping carriages and saw it swoop away as he arrived at Lambert's office. He opened the door to be greeted with an empty room.

Expecting a red faced detective, Scott closed the door, confused. He made for the lounge and entered to see an empty carriage except for Thomas Seymour berating Lambert on his whereabouts.

As he walked in, Thomas turned and said, "Where the hell have you been? I thought we were interviewing the passengers!"

Scott said innocently, "I thought we were having a toilet break."

Thomas replied impatiently, "I was five minutes! You've been almost twenty! Anyway, you're here now. Who shall we talk to next?"

Scott didn't want to explain to Thomas just yet that he had spoken to anyone and was saved from doing so by Daphne appearing behind him.

She stopped when she saw the three of them talking. "Sorry, I'm not interrupting anything, am I? Mr Lambert, I wonder if you could fix me a drink? Avril asked for one."

Lambert nodded and was about to walk to the bar to comply, when Thomas said,

"Ms Pennington. I'm sure Mrs Kennedy won't mind waiting a few minutes for her drink. Do you think we could have a talk with you?"

Daphne smiled and replied, "Well Mr Seymour, you don't know Mrs Kennedy very well. She isn't the most patient person. But I'm sure she'll understand when I say that the police subpoenaed me!"

Several minutes later, Thomas, Scott and Daphne were sat in Lambert's office. As Daphne sat down, she straightened her skirt and flicked her polished nails against the arm rest. Thomas and Scott took their seats on the other side of the table and Thomas pressed down the record button to begin,

"The time is 2.36 P.M on Monday the 22nd of September. Interview with Dr Daphne Pennington. Detective Thomas Seymour and Mr Scott Blacklock present. Ms Pennington, do you have any objection to us recording this conversation?"

Daphne smiled, "None at all. And please, call me Daphne."

Thomas continued, "Thank you. Could you tell me what sort of a doctor you are?"

"Certainly. I am a doctor of psychiatry. I have a practice in Boston, and another one in Oxford, England."

"And how long have you been practicing?" asked Thomas.

Daphne smirked, "If I told you the exact number that may reveal my age! Let's just say, at least ten years."

Scott couldn't help smiling at Daphne's answer as Thomas asked, "And what is the nature of your relationship with Clarissa Jordan?"

Daphne looked perplexed at the question. "What relationship? I didn't know her." She corrected herself. "Well, obviously I knew of her, but I'd never met her before stepping foot on this train."

She corrected herself again, "That's not actually true. I sat behind her on the plane from Boston. I actually had more contact with her step daughter than her. Nice girl. But Clarissa treated her like crap! There was a lot of anger between those two."

Thomas crossed his arms. "Thank you for that insight. Ms Pennington, I can't help but notice that you are a person that likes jewellery. In fact, as I was waiting on you and the Kennedys at dinner on Saturday night, I happened to hear you profess adoration for Clarissa's jewellery. Do you deny it?"

"Nobody likes an eavesdropper." said Daphne, with a trace of anger in her voice, something Scott hadn't heard before. She continued, "And, no I don't deny it. I do have a love of jewels. Clarissa had fantastic jewellery, but I wouldn't have killed her to steal from her! I also like a lot of what Avril wears. Does that mean I've got her lined up next?"

Scott thought the comment was slightly amusing, but it did remind him of Daphne's interest in Avril's necklace on their first afternoon on the train.

"There's no need to get angry Ms Pennington." said Thomas.

"Well stop clutching at straws then!" replied Daphne, letting the moment of anger pass, and smiling, "And I will get properly angry in a moment if I have to say this again, please call me Daphne."

"Ok, Daphne," said Scott. "Did you leave Mrs Kennedy's room last night after I dropped off the sleeping pills to you?"

Daphne shook her head, "No. I didn't want to leave her. The sleeping pills seemed to work, but I didn't leave in case she woke in the night. I had a not too comfortable night's sleep on her rather too short chaise longue."

"Did you hear anything at all in the evening?" asked Scott.

"I heard footsteps several times outside, but I couldn't tell you at what time. I have to admit, the chaise longue was so uncomfortable that at about midnight, I took a couple of sleeping pills myself. I woke a short time after eight this morning."

"Why did you feel the need to look after Avril Kennedy so much?" asked Thomas, with a hint of suspicion in his question.

"Because I'm a compassionate human being, that's why!" said Daphne indignantly.

"I looked after my sister when her husband died, and I know how hard it can be. She's just lost her husband and was stuck on a train with people she didn't know that well. And we had bonded, so I wanted to comfort her. What's the problem with that?"

"Nothing at all." said Scott, trying to diffuse the rising atmosphere.

Scott suddenly had a thought. After a moment, he asked, "Do you mind if I ask you a personal question?"

"Not at all" said Daphne, with a smile.

Scott probed cautiously, "Do you mind telling me how your second husband died?"

Daphne looked surprised. "George? What's that got to do with anything?"

Scott shrugged, "Just out of curiosity."

Daphne shot him a look, but then replied calmly, "He died in a road accident. Why?"

Scott answered, "We're just trying to get some background on everyone on the train."

Daphne didn't seem to like Scott's answer and said, "If there's nothing else, I really should be getting back to Avril."

As she went to rise, Thomas raised a hand to stop her.

"There is just one more thing" said Thomas as he placed several sheets of paper on the desk. "As you know, we searched everyone's rooms today. And what we found in your room was quite interesting. Could you explain to us why you've been keeping notes on the passengers on the train?"

Scott observed her closely. He had found her notes interesting. Not so much for her rather obvious statements of Caroline's confidence issues, or Tim and Anthony as ladies men. But more for her assumptions that Harry was a man in love, and that Gerry had seemed fearful at times on the train.

Daphne's face looked guilty as she slowly sat back down. She fiddled with her bracelet as she said, "Oh, those. Yes, well that's..... That's what I do to calm myself."

Thomas and Scott exchanged a look of confusion.

"You do it to calm yourself?" asked Scott.

"Yes," said Daphne, blushing. "I do it all the time. It's nothing sinister, believe me. When I'm not working, I miss analyzing people. So I just make notes on people. How I think their minds work. Have you actually read that list? There's nothing about plotting or planning anything there, is there?"

Neither Scott nor Thomas said anything. In fact, when they had found it, Scott was surprised at the accuracy of some of Daphne's notes. For example, Daphne had speculated that Scott's continually smart dress code may indicate that he had problems relaxing. Something Scott was aware of in his head, but never actually acknowledged.

Daphne pulled a scrap of paper out of her pocket. She said, "See! I do it everywhere. This must have been the jacket I was wearing in the station the other day."

She passed the paper over to Thomas.

It read:

> *Couple having coffee at the counter*
> *- man - deep in newspaper.*
> *Woman - skirt too short, breasts on display - looking at men's reactions as they pass. — Under-appreciation has led to self confidence issues for her!!!*

"What's this?" asked Thomas as he passed the note to Scott.

"That's what I mean. I do it everywhere! Even if I don't know who people are! I guess I just find it hard to stop watching people, their nuances. Saying one thing, doing another. Body Language, the whole thing. It's fascinating! Do you believe me now?"

"Yes, thank you Daphne." said Scott.

Daphne leant forward, as if she was about to speak confidentially, "If you'd read my notes, that should help you work out who to look out for. My money's on Caroline Stuart. So much going on under the surface there! And I could easily see her snap."

Thomas said, "Again, thank you for your insight."

Daphne shifted in her seat, "If you're done with me, I really should check on Avril, and get her that drink."

Scott looked to Thomas who said, "Thank you Ms Pennington. If you don't mind, we will deliver Mrs Kennedy's refreshment to her, as I would like to speak to her now."

Daphne stood up, hesitated for a second, and said, "Sure. I'll go back to my room. She wanted a gin and tonic. My advice to you, don't push her. You may want to remember that her husband has just died."

"Thank you Ms Pennington. I think I know how to do my job, even if you are slightly questionable in yours. I will let you know if we need to speak to you further." said Thomas coldly as he showed her out of the room and closed the door angrily.

Scott wondered where Thomas's change of mood had come from. It was then that he noticed the note that Daphne had just passed them. On the other side of it were notes about some of the staff on the train. Scott had to stifle a chuckle when he read Daphne's scribbles. Was Thomas angry because Daphne had been accurate about him as well?

Patrick Lambert – Feels a need to please yet has Small Man complex!

Bradley the barman – Craves attention. Big smile and personality hiding a more insecure person. Cute, though!

Italian looking waitress – Deceptively smart, hiding attractiveness. – On purpose? Heart is not in her job – she wants more.

Pasty skinny waiter – No social skills - has confidence issues – haircut probably hasn't changed for ten years –- wouldn't be surprised if he still lived with his mother.

Avril Kennedy's story

After returning to the lounge, where Bradley had fixed up a gin and tonic, Scott and Thomas headed to the now half occupied Kennedy suite. On arrival, Thomas rapped sharply on the door three times.

"It's open."

Avril's voice floated through the door, sounding a lot stronger than it had the night before.

Thomas opened the door to see Avril still in bed, but dressed in her finest silk nightwear, covered by a dressing gown with ridiculously large lapels.

Avril was obviously expecting Daphne and her smile dropped slightly at Thomas and Scott.

Avril said, "Daphne told me about you two. I was wondering if I was going to be paid a visit?!'"

Scott noticed that Avril looked a lot more composed, her make up restored to its usual crafted standard. Scott was sure it must be part of the training as a perfect Hollywood wife.

Seeing the glass in Scott's hand, she asked, "Am I to presume that you intercepted Daphne and that drink is for me?"

Scott nodded and as he passed it to her, he asked, "Mrs Kennedy, may we sit down?"

Avril gestured to the armchair and smiled, "Be my guest."

Scott took the armchair and Thomas perched rather uncomfortably on the chaise longue.

"How are you feeling?" asked Scott gently.

Avril said bluntly, "Well, unsurprisingly, you feel pretty much the same the day after your husband dies, as to when it actually happens."

"I understand this is a difficult time for you Mrs Kenendy." Scott answered. He felt he had said those words too many times in the last twenty four hours.

He looked over to Thomas to take the lead. Thomas leaned forward and began,

"Mrs Kennedy, as Dr Pennington may have told you, my name is Detective Seymour of the N.Y.P.D, and Mr Blacklock here is from the Zirconia Corporation. We were both on this train keeping surveillance on Clarissa Jordan. Now, as you are aware what happened last night, we…"

Thomas was stopped by a huge smile breaking across Avril's face. She said,

"I know. It's wonderful isn't it?"

Thomas looked stunned, "It's wonderful?!"

Avril replied. "Yes. What's happened to Clarissa. Poetic Justice."

"Poetic Justice?" asked Scott.

Avril pulled a face as if what she was saying was common sense.

"Look, that woman is the reason that my husband is dead instead of being here with me."

Thomas asked, "How so? Your husband died from heart failure."

Avril retorted, "And why do you think that was? Clarissa ruined our production company. And as a result drove Gerry to an early grave."

She finished her statement by taking a large gulp of her drink.

Thomas said, "Perhaps you'd like to start from the beginning? When did you first meet Clarissa?"

Avril set her drink down. Even in mourning, she still looked pleased to tell a story. "Oh, I've known Clarissa Lavelle for years. Gerry had known her parents as well. Gerry and I first met her in the mid eighties. Our production company made the two films that allowed her to successfully jump from child actor to credible actress. Pebble Dreams and Possibility? You may remember them. As much as I despised the woman, I have to admit she was damn good in them. We then worked closely with her, both in theatre and film. That was until her famous withdrawal from public life when her parents died in close succession. She was only gone less than a year, but that's a long time in Hollywood. A lot of people cast her off. It wasn't helped by the tabloid reports of her increasingly neurotic behaviour. Gerry and I were some of the only ones to stick by her. It was our company that organised her return to Broadway that got her back on the front pages."

Thomas said, "What happened then?"

Avril took another drink. "Around the millennium, after her comeback was when Clarissa was at her biggest. She did nine films in three years. All except one were critically acclaimed. That all culminated in her Oscar win. A win that seemed even bigger because of the fact that Clarissa had been nominated six times before but had always lost out. All the headlines were about Clarissa finally getting the recognition she deserved. After her successful return to Broadway, we only worked on one film with her before she won that Oscar and decided to leave Hollywood. The irony of it was that that one film, Winter of Passion, was our biggest ever film. Seven hundred million at the box office! However, Clarissa couldn't be persuaded to continue working with us. Despite our loyalty to her in her harder times, she cast us aside when her fame and fortune reached a pinnacle."

Scott asked, "But this was all over five years ago? Had you not worked with her since?"

Avril sighed, "Yes we had, as much as we didn't like to. Not just for the way she had treated us, but also because of her never ending diva antics. But we knew that she still had box office draw. Initially we tried to get her onboard for a new film, but she was having none of it."

"Why not?" asked Thomas.

For the first time, Avril became embarrassed.

"Our last couple of films had not been very well received. She saw it as too much of a risk."

"What did you work with her on?" asked Scott.

Avril answered, "We finally got her to accept a stint on Broadway. We re-opened The Secret Diary, the play that had made her famous when she was sixteen, when she had played the daughter opposite her mother Lydia Cline. This time, she was to play the mother, opposite Sophie Stanford."

"Sophie Stanford?" asked Thomas, looking blank at the name.

Avril looked at Thomas as if he had just arrived from another planet.

She said, "You know! That little blonde girl who's getting every child part in all the films at the moment! I must say, she isn't a bad actor for a thirteen year old kid!"

"Anyway..." said Scott, feeling they were getting away from the subject.

Avril took his point. "Anyway, all went well. Press night went well. We sold out. That was until Clarissa walked out of the show after only two weeks. Little bitch!"

Scott asked, "Why did she walk out?"

Avril said bitterly, "She never even gave us a proper reason. But she was soon photographed with Mark Jordan, so I assume it was to do with him."

"Mark Jordan? As in her husband now?" questioned Thomas.

"Yes." replied Avril. "Although if you ask me, he seems to be a very boring man. But that's Clarissa all over. She never went for a man who might actually be able to pierce her hardened skin."

Scott asked carefully, "If I may ask, was Clarissa the reason you and Gerry were on the train? Were you trying to win her back?"

Avril paused before saying, "Yes. But I really don't expect you two of all people to judge me for following her onto this train."

She added, "At least I wasn't lying about it!"

Thomas and Scott looked at each other uncomfortably for a second, before Scott said,

"Mrs Kennedy. Why would two high profile executive producers feel the need to track down an actress while she was on vacation?"

"She wasn't returning our calls." said Avril defensively.

"But my point is why would you go to all that trouble? Or not work through her agent or manager? There are other actresses. It smells of desperation to me."

Thomas was surprised at Scott's comment, but Avril looked saddened by it.

She said, "I guess it was a desperate act. We... we had been having financial problems. The production company I mean. We were actually in trouble over a year ago. That had been why we'd worked so hard to get Clarissa to do The Secret Diary. Things looked promising, until she left."

"And what's happened in the last year then?" asked Scott.

"It was soon after that when Gerry had to go into hospital to have surgery on his heart. The stress of everything had really affected his health. The play carried on with a different actress, but we had to close it four months early. No one was going without Clarissa's name connected to it. Gerry had to take time off to recover from the surgery. And then, earlier this year my brother Walt died and I had to travel to Paris to deal with the legal and financial arrangements. My brother had a large estate, so I was gone for a while. I told Gerry to leave the running of our companies to our employees while I was gone. But he wouldn't listen. I came back after a month to find him in poor health from working harder than ever. Gerry was determined to fight back and prevent us from going under. That was when he decided to try and win Clarissa back again."

Scott watched as Avril drained the contents of her glass before asking,

"But if your production company was in trouble over a year ago, and you had to close your last show early, how were you keeping the company afloat?"

Avril gave a sad smile, "We were momentarily saved by the inheritance I received from my brother, but things were still hanging in the balance for us. We had to clear fifty percent of the company's debt by the middle of the year. We missed the deadline and didn't even have a project lined up to save the company. We were supposed to have a final meeting with our financial partners this week."

"And the signing up of Clarissa would have saved your bacon for a short while?" questioned Thomas.

"Yes" said Avril quietly, "Although none of that really matters anymore."

Thomas paused before speaking slowly, "Mrs Kennedy, you do realise that the story you've told gives you a strong motive for the events that have unfolded on the train. You've made no effort to hide the fact that you despised Clarissa, that you blame her for your husband's poor health and now his death. And that you were in financial trouble, which would tie in with the absence of Clarissa's diamond."

Avril was unfazed by Thomas's words. She answered calmly,

"You're quite right that I had a motive to kill her, and to be frank with you, I would have quite liked to! Not that I was in any state to last night! But you're not quite right in all of your assumptions. I would have liked to kill her, but I wouldn't have stolen from her. It was Gerry that loved the company and wanted to do everything to save it. I personally thought that we had enough to comfortably retire, but I loved my husband in the same way that he loved our company, which was why I was prepared to follow him."

As she spoke, tears formed in her eyes but she continued,

"And if I'm completely honest with you, since last night, I haven't even thought about the production company and I certainly don't care if it goes under now."

Thomas said, "I'm sorry if I've upset you Mrs Kennedy. I just think I should make it clear how it sounds from our point of view." He paused. "Did you leave your room at any point last night?"

Avril's distress turned to irritation, "Are you being serious? As I've already said, I wasn't in any state to do anything last night!"

She pointed at Scott. "He came in here. He knows! He went to get me sleeping pills. And anyway, Daphne was my alibi. She stayed in here last night. "

Thomas argued, "We've spoken to Ms Pennington. She told us that she found it hard to sleep as well, so also took a sleeping pill. You could have slipped out while she was asleep."

Avril replied tiredly, "And I've told you. After what happened at dinner, the rest of the evening was a blur. But I do remember Mr Blacklock handing Daphne sleeping pills which she then gave to me. I then woke up this morning. You can believe me or not, but you won't find a shred of evidence that connects me to Clarissa as I didn't kill her, although I'd quite like to shake the hand of the person that did."

Thomas didn't quite know how to argue that and was silent for a second.

Avril finished, "I think I've explained myself enough. Now if you wouldn't mind, I'd like to be left alone. I am grieving if you hadn't noticed."

Thomas looked to Scott and then stood up, he said, "Thank you for your time Mrs Kennedy. We'll let you know if we have any further questions."

As Scott made his way to the door, Avril stopped Thomas and offered him her empty glass. She said, "Oh, could you fetch me another gin?"

Thomas looked at the glass and said, "Mrs Kennedy, I was undercover as a waiter. I am no longer working for the Express."

Avril carried on looking at him as if he had said nothing. After a second, he conceded and took the glass from her hand.

Scott and Thomas left the carriage and exchanged a glance as they closed the door to Avril's room. They stood in the corridor and Thomas felt the recorder in his pocket and cursed himself.

"What is it?" asked Scott, walking behind him.

Thomas replied, "I forgot to record the interview. Avril threw me by jumping straight in with how pleased she was at Clarissa's murder, without any remorse. What did you think of that?"

Scott thought about it for a second. "I think she appeared quite honest with her feelings about Clarissa."

"And the rest of it?" said Thomas as he opened the door through to the next carriage.

"As for that, I think it's too early to say." replied Scott.

Thomas didn't look happy with the response and scratched the back of his head.

He said, "Thank you for that helpful response. Anyway, I'd like to head back to speak to Mark Jordan. We'll be able to get his version of why Clarissa parted ways with the Kennedys. You have any objections?"

Scott shook his head. "No." and then added dryly, "We may as well continue this cheerful afternoon of mourning spouses."

Thomas didn't appreciate the comment as he turned and walked towards the Thistlewood suites. Scott started to follow him and looked out the window. It had become a habit of his to get transfixed by the scenery as he travelled up and down the train. As he looked out now, seeing that the snow had left them, he felt a niggling at the back of his brain, telling him that he was missing something. And he had a feeling it had something to with Avril and Gerry Kennedy. Since the panic of this morning, he had become hesitant to put forward another of his theories. This hadn't stopped it swirling around in his head though. What if Gerry Kennedy's death hadn't been natural?

A matter of cigarettes

"Who is it?"

The voice was Mark Jordan's, responding to Thomas's knock at his door.

"Mr Jordan. It's Detective Seymour with Mr Blacklock. May we speak with you?"

There was silence for several moments before they heard the lock turn and the door slowly opened. Mark held the door for them as they entered. He looked more composed and had gotten dressed into a smart shirt and trousers, but still had the appearance of a broken man. He was dressed conservatively and it made Scott think of Avril's comment about him being boring.

Scott and Thomas took the settee in the corner of his room as Mark closed the door and propped himself on the end of the bed.

"So Detective," said Mark as he folded his arms, "What progress have you made? Do you have a suspect?"

Thomas replied diplomatically, "Mr Jordan, we have made some headway with our investigation, but it's too early to say anything just yet."

"Then why are you here?" asked Mark, "I've already told you what I did last night."

Thomas leaned forward. "Actually Sir, we're here to get some more background information." He pulled his recorder out and said, "You have no objection to us recording this conversation?"

Mark paused for a second, before shaking his head.

Thomas pressed record, and said, "Interview with Mr Mark Jordan. Detective Seymour and Scott Blacklock present."

Mark asked, "You want background information on what?"

"On your relationship with Clarissa." answered Scott. "You'd been married for ten months, correct?"

"Give or take a week."

"How did you meet her?"

"Is this really necessary?" asked Mark, a touch of resentment in his voice.

"I'm afraid it is." said Thomas. "We have to ascertain all of the facts."

Mark nodded gruffly, reluctantly accepting Thomas's answer. He began, "Mr Blacklock, if you remember, I had the embarrassment of having to regale the story on Saturday evening, after my wife abandoned telling it. As I said then, we met at a jazz club in New York about a year ago. She was having a drink with her agent. She got her to ask me if I'd like to join them for a drink. I was obviously flattered and I obliged. It kind of went from there."

Thomas said, "And then two months later, you were married? That's pretty quick work."

Mark took insult to the statement. He answered back, "What exactly are you implying by that? I'll have you know that it was actually Clarissa that was the aggressive one. She invited me to have a drink with her. She pursued me. And she's....she was a great woman. You're right, it didn't take me long to fall for her. But I didn't marry her for any monetary gain, if that's where you're going with this. I'm a self made millionaire in my own right. And I'm not some kind of serial romancer either. Clarissa was the first proper relationship I'd had since Amy's mother died."

Scott could see Mark getting visibly upset, and tried to calm the situation.

He said, "Mr Jordan. As Detective Seymour said, we're just trying to gain all the facts. That's all. Was Clarissa still performing on Broadway when you met?"

Mark diverted his attention to Scott. "Yes." he replied. "Although she quit a week after we met."

"Because of you?" asked Scott.

Mark thought about the answer. "I think yes, in part."

"In part?" That came from Thomas.

"She did tell me that she was quitting because she wanted to spend more time with me. But the only reason she had taken the job was because she felt obliged to. She told me that she felt she owed the Kennedys. I think she was already bored of the work."

He finished rather uncomfortably. "She told me that I had eclipsed her passion for acting."

Scott looked down at his shoes and said, "So she felt she owed the Kennedys, yet all she really did was set them up for a huge fall. Producing a huge show on the back of her name only for her to walk out? That's not really paying back a favour."

Mark's anger returned. "Look she tried. But doing a show six nights a week is hard work. And she said that if her heart wasn't in it, then it would be better for all of them if she left. I don't appreciate you attacking my wife."

Scott explained calmly, "We're just trying to understand all sides of the argument. You must have noticed the animosity between the Kennedy's and Clarissa?"

"Of course I noticed it! Clarissa was furious when she found out they were on board. The two of them, combined with that stupid bastard Broadside!"

Thomas asked, "Ah yes, let's come to Mr Broadside. Were you aware of your wife's history with him?"

Mark answered, "I knew that she'd been married before. And I knew the names of her ex-husbands, but I hadn't met any of them. That was until we boarded. Clarissa and I had never talked about them much though."

A thought occurred to Mark. He continued, "While we're on Broadside though, why aren't you questioning him? If anyone had a motive, it was him! The little words that Clarissa did speak of him were always angry ones. She was still so angry at how much money he'd wormed out of her at their divorce."

Thomas replied, "We have already interviewed Mr Broadside."

Mark questioned, "What's his story then? Why was he so conveniently on the same train as his ex-wife?"

It was Scott that spoke, "He said he wanted to try and win her back."

"And you believe that? Even if that is the real reason, Clarissa detested the fact that he was here. If he realized that, he seems off balance enough to do something like this. Surely you can see that?!"

Scott said evenly, "Unfortunately Mr Jordan, It appears that he may not have been the only one with a strong motive."

The comment seemed to quash Mark's argument. After a moment of silence, Thomas asked, "How was married life with Clarissa? How have you spent the last ten months?"

Mark looked like he wanted to continue with the Broadside thread, but he remembered who the police officer was in the room. He said, "They were great. We spent a good time travelling. After the wedding, we went to the Seychelles. We spent Christmas in Dubai, and then went on an African safari before learning to scuba dive on the Great Barrier Reef. From there, we did China, parts of India. I have a vineyard in the Loire valley. We went there for a while, and then stayed at Clarissa's house in London. We returned to New York and bought a property overlooking Central Park. We'd just come from a Mediterranean cruise when we boarded the Express."

Scott and Thomas exchanged a rather astonished look.

"Flamboyant lifestyle?" said Scott.

Mark shrugged. "We could both afford it. We'd both spent the last twenty years working very hard, and were taking some time to enjoy life. That's not a crime, is it?"

"No, not at all." said Scott, "I'm just a little jealous. But you didn't really answer the detective's question. I think he was implying how your relationship was?"

Mark said defensively, "It was fantastic. We very rarely rowed."

Scott thought of Harry's similar story of the whirlwind romance. He wondered if Mark had realised that his marriage might have very well had the same shelf life.

He asked, "But it wasn't a very realistic lifestyle for a marriage? So many new places, so much excitement."

Mark retorted, "Compared to what? Your version of reality? It was very realistic for us, let me tell you."

Scott felt that Mark was denying that truth to himself. He pressed, "Ok, but how about Clarissa's relationship with Amy?"

The question knocked Mark down a little. He said, "I'll admit that there were problems between them. But it was just a case of re-adjustment. I was confident that in time, relations would improve between them. You have to understand that this was my first serious relationship since Amy's mother died. There were bound to be initial tensions."

"But you've been married ten months." stated Thomas.

"Yes, but when we all met in Greece, it had only been the third time they had met. Clarissa and I had been away a lot and Amy was very busy at Harvard."

"Ok" said Scott, feeling Mark's heckles rising again. "How did you feel about Clarissa and the way she was with men?"

"Are you now trying to portray me as the jealous husband? I know she was flirty. It was part of her character. It's one of the things that made me fall for her. But I knew her Mr Blacklock, you didn't. If you knew her, you'd be able to tell when Clarissa means something, and when she's acting. I wasn't jealous of her flirting. I took it with a grain of salt."

Scott thought back to Mark's reactions to Clarissa throughout the journey so far, and wondered why Mark was telling such an obvious lie.

"So it didn't bother you at all the way she would look and talk to other men?" pushed Scott.

"It did a little at times. But as I said, it was part of Clarissa's character. How many more of these questions have you got for me?!"

"One more personal question I'm afraid, Mr Jordan." said Thomas. "May I ask why you and your wife had adjoining rooms?"

Mark didn't look too insulted by the question. He said, "It's not for any problems in the bedroom if that's what you're suggesting. Clarissa always liked to have her own room." He paused. "I think it made her feel regal!"

"Like the Queen of England?" said Scott, lightening the mood.

Mark even managed a small smile, "Something like that."

Scott asked, "Mr Jordan, did you have a drink with your wife in her room? Before or after the evening's events?"

Mark thought back. "No" he said, "I don't recall having a drink before we left. And as I told you earlier, I came straight back from playing cards and went to bed."

Scott ignored the impatience in Mark's voice. "Just one more question, Mr Jordan. Did Clarissa smoke? Or do you for that matter?"

Mark shook his head. "No, neither of us smoked. I've never smoked. Clarissa told me she had hypnotherapy to quit ten years ago. I'd never seen her with a cigarette."

Thomas said, "Thank you Mr Jordan. If we have anything further, we'll let you know."

He switched off the recorder, and stood up.

As Scott got up to follow Thomas out, he stopped and asked,

"Mr Jordan, when your wife did smoke, do you know if she ever used to smoke Croughan and Matthews?"

Mark looked up and chuckled, "Oh you really didn't know Clarissa! A common brand like that! She used to have her cigarettes personally made for her!"

Scott smiled, "Of course. How silly of me to presume otherwise! Thank you Mr Jordan."

Mark didn't return the smile as Scott backed out of the room and closed the door behind him.

Thomas and Scott moved a little down the carriage, before Thomas asked, "His story sounds a lot like a current version of Mr Broadside's, doesn't it?"

Scott nodded as he put his hands in his pockets. "Yes. And I think there was more of an issue with the jealousy than he let on."

Thomas agreed readily. "I know. I'd been watching his behaviour too. And Harry Broadside really bothers him. I didn't think so to begin with, but he could quite easily be capable."

Scott replied, "Yes, that's true. But then why steal her diamond? He's already rich, something he was quick to point out."

"Unless the person who stole the diamond wasn't the person who killed her?" pondered Thomas.

Scott looked at him, thinking that it was an interesting point.

Thomas continued, "Anyway I think we should talk to Amy Jordan. Yet another one with a good deal of animosity towards Clarissa."

Scott decided to avoid telling Thomas of his solo interviews and replied,

"If you don't mind, I'd quickly like to pop out for a cigarette first."

Thomas looked annoyed and replied with a grunt, "If you must."

"Thanks," said Scott, "Why don't you find Lambert and check on how things are going?"

The look of aggravation didn't leave Thomas's face, but he nodded. As Scott headed towards the end of the train, he turned and said to Thomas as he was leaving,

"Oh, and ask Lambert to pull up all of his staff files. We'll have to talk to them shortly."

"Will do." said Thomas as he left the carriage from the other end.

Scott pulled a cigarette packet out of his pocket and walked through into the observation carriage. He arrived to see the Stuarts sat at the far end, neither of them speaking, just watching the passing view. Scott thought how they looked like they were ready to go rambling with Caroline in a fleece and Anthony in a polo neck. A moment later, he noticed Amy sat in the corner. She looked up and didn't seem impressed to see him. As Scott took the seat opposite her, she put down the magazine she was reading and said,

"Look, I said before. Any more questions can come from the ACTUAL police officer."

Scott decided a different approach, "Amy, before you go on, I just wanted to apologise. I feel I was a tad insensitive when we last spoke. I know this is difficult for you. Losing someone that you weren't close to, but your father was."

A lot of the hostility left Amy's expression. She sighed and said, "I'm sorry too. I think I got angry before because you were a little too close to the mark. And it's so hard trying to empathise with my father when I detested the woman."

Amy added, "But as I said before, I may have detested her, but I had nothing to do with her death." She paused, before saying quietly, "I couldn't do it to my father."

Scott took that moment to stand up. He said, "I felt I should say that. Anyway I'll leave any more questions to the detective, if you'll excuse me."

Scott turned to walk away, pleased with his technique. By apologising and understanding her situation, he knew that the next time he questioned her; she would be more likely to let her defences down.

"Scott" said Amy, stopping him, making him return to face her. "You obviously know what happened last night? Between me and Tim?"

"Yes." said Scott, feeling uncomfortable at what the question was leading to.

Amy asked, her voice sounding vulnerable. "He told me that there was somebody else back in New York. Is that true?"

Scott paused for a second before saying, "Yes. There is."

Amy's face saddened, "Thank you."

Scott, unsure what else to say, nodded and walked away.

He approached the Stuarts and Anthony looked up over the settee, asking,

"Mr Blacklock, how is the investigation going?"

Scott decided to take another opportunity. "Well. Thank you." answered Scott. "I was actually wondering if I could have a quick word with you Mr Stuart."

Anthony gestured to the chair opposite him.

"In private. Perhaps we could go to the bar?" asked Scott.

Anthony gave a quick look to his wife, before standing up and following Scott to the end of the carriage.

The bar was empty, save for Bradley, cleaning and tidying. He quickly served them both with a drink and they moved to a table at the corner of the carriage.

As Anthony set his drink down, he gave his wide smile and said, "So Mr Blacklock, how can I assist you?"

"For a start, I was hoping you could begin with your movements last night."

"Isn't that an answer I should be giving to the Detective?" asked Anthony.

"And I'm sure he'll ask you that question himself. You have no objection telling me now though, do you?"

Anthony thought about it for a second. He shrugged, "I guess not. But I won't be able to tell you much to help you. After I walked

Clarissa to her door from leaving you at the card table, I returned to my room."

"And what did you do then?" asked Scott.

Anthony paused, "Caroline and I had a bit of an argument."

"About?"

"That's personal." said Anthony, a little defensively.

"Mr Stuart, a crime has been committed. We need to know all the circumstances of everyone in the close vicinity. Personal or not."

Anthony said nothing.

"Was the argument about Clarissa?" probed Scott.

Anthony sighed. "Yes, among other things. The thing you have to understand Mr Blacklock, is that as much as I love my wife, she can be very insecure."

"Could that have anything to do with your flirtations with other women?" Scott asked candidly.

"I don't appreciate your tone Mr Blacklock. I have a flirtatious character, I won't deny that. And I won't apologise for it either. Caroline is aware of it."

"But it obviously causes arguments between you and your wife?"

Anthony answered, frustrated, "Yes, but they're always little arguments that blow over. She knows how I feel about her."

Scott questioned, "So what did happen after your argument last night?"

"I was quite drunk, and wasn't up for a fight last night. I told her I wouldn't talk to her about it anymore. And then I went to bed."

"And Caroline?" asked Scott, interested to hear Anthony's response.

"I...I think she went out for some air. As I said, I was quite drunk, so fell asleep pretty quickly. I didn't hear her return."

Scott sat back and crossed his legs. "Ok," he said, "Now perhaps you could tell me what happened when you said goodnight to Clarissa?"

Anthony looked up at him. "What do you mean? I walked her to her room. We had a quick chat. About nothing in particular, cards I think. I then said goodnight to her and walked back to my room."

Scott asked, "What if I knew that you weren't as discreet as you would have liked to be?"

He leaned forward and said quietly, "I know that you and Clarissa shared a kiss before you said goodnight. And not a friendly peck on the cheek."

Anthony's face flushed. He leaned in closely to Scott's face and said angrily, "You damn nosy spy! Have you just been watching everybody on this train?! For your information I love my wife very much, and while I cannot deny that Clarissa did seem attracted to me, and yes, did kiss me quickly, I was not about to do anything to jeopardize my marriage!"

"Then why even let the situation arise?" questioned Scott. "Why have little liaisons on the balcony?"

Anthony's face went even redder. He said in a hushed voice, "If you're referring to yesterday morning, that was a pure coincidence."

"Really?" said Scott, raising an eyebrow.

Anthony said, even quieter still. "I don't appreciate you making it sound like Clarissa and I were having some clandestine affair…."

"Are you particularly well off Mr Stuart?" Scott cut in.

"What? What's that got to do with anything?"

"You are aware that theft seems a likely motive at the moment. And not to be rude, but you and Caroline don't seem to have jobs that would easily pay for a trip like this."

"Your point being that I'm poor so would want to steal a diamond?" asked Anthony sarcastically. "If you must know, we could afford this trip because I came into some money last year."

"How?" probed Scott.

"A friend died and left me some." Anthony answered, getting angry again.

"Ok Mr Stuart." Scott said calmly, "Let's go back to Clarissa. Is your wife privy to as much as I know?"

Anthony couldn't keep his hushed tones any longer, "No she is not, because there is nothing to tell."

Scott shrugged, "Your wife may see that differently."

Anthony stood up at this. He said, "I don't see why I should put up with this from you when you're not the authority here."

He took a deep breath and walked away. He turned and pointed his finger at Scott.

"And if my wife hears anything of this, I'll know where it's come from, and I swear to god I'll....."

"You'll what?" said Scott, folding his arms.

Anthony stood there speechless and red faced for a second, before storming out, almost knocking Jessica Rae over as she was entering.

"Pardon me!" shouted Jessica through the door, holding her arms up.

As she walked over to Scott, she leant on the arm of a chair and said,

"Well doesn't everyone seem rather angry after you've had a conversation with them?"

Scott shot her a look. "And how would you know that Jessica? Have you been doing your own form of investigation?"

Jessica smiled, "Oh of course not. Just a vibe I'm picking up on!"

"Really? Well let's see if I can break that habit. Could we have a little chat?"

"I suppose so." replied Jessica, "But we'll have to do it over a cigarette."

They stepped out onto the balcony and were treated to only a small drop in the temperature as the mid afternoon sun shone from somewhere in front of the train, lighting up the landscape as they headed on towards south east Utah. The scenery was turning more and more into desert before their eyes.

Scott took interest in Jessica's hand as she pulled out her cigarette packet, eager to see if she was the secret smoker in Clarissa's room.

Her hand moved to reveal a packet of Masons, a stronger version of the Mason Lights that he himself smoked.

"What?" said Jessica, as she noticed him eyeing her cigarettes.

"Nothing." answered Scott. "Anyway, why don't you tell me where and what you did last night?"

"Fine." said Jessica as she lit up and handed her lighter to Scott. "After I was assaulted by that bitch Clarissa in the lounge, I returned to my room to pick up my cigarettes and coat. I then came out here where I saw you. I'm still fuming that she slapped me." She jabbed her cigarette towards Scott. "I tell you. It's a shame she died, as I was seriously considering legal action!"

Scott pulled a face. "I hardly think a judge would be sympathetic to you with a case of emotional distress. Looking at the amount you've been able to create in your short career."

"Do you want me to answer your questions or not Scott? You're not giving me much incentive!"

Scott took a drag on his cigarette. "Please. Do continue. What did you do after you left me out here last night?"

"I went to my room."

"Without seeing anybody?"

"The waitress was still behind the bar. Apart from that, I didn't see a soul."

"And you went straight to your room?"

"Yes." said Jessica impatiently. "I'm getting bored of these questions."

Scott leant on the rail. "Ok, here's another one. Let's talk of your motives for harming Clarissa."

Jessica surprised him by letting out a raucous laugh. "My motives for harming Clarissa?! That's a joke! Why would I kill Clarissa? I'm supposed to be writing an exclusive on her. Do you think my editor would be pleased with that story?!"

Scott shrugged. "Well your methods on this train have been rather bizarre. I don't get why you've been so antagonistic when you could have learned more surreptitiously. And if I'm honest, I couldn't think of a better exclusive for you. I can see the headline now. Jessica Rae's first hand account of Clarissa Jordan's gruesome murder. Or perhaps you just intended to steal the diamond for an exclusive and she surprised you. Anything is possible with you Jessica."

Jessica retorted, "I forgot. I'm talking to Scott Blacklock. You're either trying to save me with your self righteous view of the world, or trying to psycho-analyze me, which is how you're attempting to justify your laughable attempt at a motive for me. But thank you for that title. I may use that for my article."

Scott said calmly, "With your questionable past, the police may see it differently."

Jessica snarled, "The only one who finds my career moves questionable are you, Tim, and that bitch partner of yours. And as for my antagonistic approach? Well that's just a new spin I'm trying on my reports, I find reading about angry or distressed celebrities sells more. Now do you have any more questions for me?"

"Just a couple" said Scott as he finished his cigarette and flicked it into the bucket.

"To clear things up, from you leaving the bar last night, you have no one to give you an alibi for your movements?"

Jessica said sullenly, "Well...No. Do you?"

Scott smiled. "I'm not one of the passengers on this train with questionable motives, or questionable morals."

Jessica huffed, "Humph, in your opinion!"

He moved to the door, and asked. "Just one more thing Jessica. Do you ever smoke Croughan and Matthews brand of cigarettes?"

Jessica choked on the final drag of her cigarette as she flicked it onto the disappearing tracks. "My god! No. They're such a cheap brand. Disgusting."

"Thank you Jessica. I'm sure we'll talk again soon."

Scott had kept the conversation short as he was aware he should be getting back to Thomas. However, he needn't have worried as on re-entering the bar, he was presented with Lambert and Thomas, the latter looking unusually red faced for his pale skin. Scott approached as Thomas started his tirade.

"What is this I've been hearing about you talking to passengers without me present?! I've just spoken to your friend Tim Anderson. And Amy Jordan! What do you think you're playing at? Who were you out on the balcony with? Another interviewee?!"

By the end of his sentence, he was almost screaming and Lambert unconsciously took a step backwards. At the bar, Bradley returned to polishing glasses, listening covertly.

Scott tried to calm Thomas. "Look. I was going to tell you. I just thought that sometimes people reveal more when they're not talking to a police officer."

"This is my investigation. Do you hear? Mine!" shouted Thomas.

"I do." said Scott placidly. "And it won't happen again. But I think that instead of getting angry, we need to concentrate on the investigation."

Thomas took a deep breath. "You're right. What have you found out?"

"For one thing, none of the passengers seem to smoke the brand of cigarettes that we found in Clarissa's room. The only known smokers were myself, Jessica and Gerry.

Gerry is obviously exonerated, and it's not a brand that Jessica or I smoke."

"That doesn't really say much though, does it?" said Thomas impatiently. "Anyone could be a secret smoker, or smoke a different brand?!"

Scott said, "What I was suggesting was that we check the staff. Lambert?"

Lambert moved away from the bar and looked enquiringly.

Scott asked, "Of your staff, does anyone smoke Croughan and Matthews?"

Lambert didn't even have to think, "Oh, yes. Bradley smokes that brand."

Lambert pointed at the man behind the bar and Thomas and Scott looked to see Bradley staring at them, having heard the conversation. The reason they had been talking about cigarettes quickly dawned on him, and as the three of them walked towards him, his face went white, and the tray of polished glasses he was carrying dropped to the floor.

Staff inquisition

Bradley Hawkins sat in the chair opposite Lambert's desk nervously chewing his nails. His face looked pallid and the happy go lucky persona that had been so evident in him before had now disappeared.

Thomas sat opposite him having set up his recorder. Scott again took his position by the window. The other chair was occupied by Lambert. Thomas had agreed for him to be present as he had demanded to know what Bradley had done.

"Look" said Bradley, ceasing the chewing and instead occupying his hands with the corner of his apron, "I know how this looks, but...."

"So those were your cigarettes then?! What the hell were you doing in her room?" shouted Lambert angrily.

"Mr Lambert, please." said Thomas. "I agreed for you to observe the interview, but I will be the one asking the questions."

Lambert sat back in his chair sulkily.

Thomas returned his gaze to Bradley and removed the cigarette packet, wrapped in an evidence bag. He placed it on the table and said, "Mr Hawkins, is it true that these are your cigarettes?"

Bradley said quickly, "Yes, but I can explain!"

"Ok." said Thomas, "Perhaps you could tell us what happened. You were working in the bar with Rosalie last night, weren't you?"

"Yes." replied Bradley, "After Mr Kennedy died, we were there with most of the passengers for the night."

"What did you do after that?"

"I went to the lounge to serve drinks for the guests who were playing cards. Mr Stuart, Mr Blacklock, and Mr and Mrs Jordan. Ms Rae joined later. When they all left, I finished tidying the lounge. It was about midnight, I think. I returned to the kitchen. Andreas and Lambert were there."

"Mr Lambert!" said Lambert indignantly.

Bradley for the first time did not seem cocky enough to ignore his boss and apologised. The apology surprised Lambert and he seemed rather taken aback.

Thomas continued, "And what happened then?"

"The room service phone rang. I was supposed to have finished for the night." answered Bradley. He then rather pointedly looked at Lambert. "And it was Andreas's shift on room service, but Mr Lambert made me take the call."

"Andreas was still cleaning the kitchen." said Lambert defensively.

"Thank you Mr Lambert." said Thomas impatiently. He looked back to Bradley,

"Who was it? On the phone?"

Bradley paused, "It was Clar..uh Mrs Jordan."

"And what did she want?"

Bradley looked down awkwardly. "Well, first she checked that it was me."

"Why would she do that?" asked Lambert, puzzled.

"She'd taken a liking to you, hadn't she?" This came from Scott, who had been looking out of the window while listening.

Bradley looked down as Thomas sat up in his chair and exclaimed,

"That's right! I remember Rosalie ribbing you for it. She kept requesting for you to serve her room service!"

"Yes." said Bradley quietly. "I found it a bit embarrassing at first."

"But you were flattered?" asked Scott.

Bradley looked at him as if he were stupid. "Well obviously! Who wouldn't be?"

Thomas said, "Let's get back to last night. What happened when Mrs Jordan knew it was you?"

"She asked for a drink, said she needed a night cap."

"And you took it to her room?" asked Thomas.

"Yes. I fixed her up a martini in the lounge. Actually she asked for two. I presumed it was for her and her husband. But then when I got to her room, she invited me in."

"And you did?" sputtered Lambert. "My God! I've a good mind to fire you!"

"Mr Lambert!" said Thomas loudly. "I am not going to warn you again. Let's just listen to his story. What happened then?"

Bradley looked at Lambert and said evenly, "If you must know, I wasn't going to go in. Whatever you think of me Mr Lambert, I am a professional. The truth is that I went in because I didn't want to piss off your most important passenger."

He looked back to Thomas. "She asked me to set the drinks down and then take a seat. I sat on her settee, she sat on her bed."

"And then?" asked Thomas.

"We talked. She asked me about my job, and told me that she thought I was a beautiful pianist."

"Was that the extent of the conversation?" questioned Scott.

"Yes. I was only there for about ten or fifteen minutes. I....I wasn't feeling very comfortable."

"Why?"

Bradley replied bluntly, "Because she was quite blatantly trying to come on to me."

"What was she wearing?" The question came from Scott. "And was she wearing her diamond choker?"

Bradley's cheeks flushed. "That was the reason I left. When I arrived, she was wearing a short negligee. When she asked me to pass her drink, I went to get it and when I turned back around she had removed it."

"She was naked?" asked Thomas, his voice sounding uncomfortably high.

"Yes, except for the choker."

"What did you do then?"

"I panicked. I said I had to go and practically ran out of the door." He lowered his head, "I guess I must have dropped my cigarettes in the rush."

"What did you do then?" asked Scott.

"I returned to my room. On the way I picked up a suit hanging on Mr Anderson's door and left it for Rosalie to press in the morning. I was still awake in bed when the train stopped. I went to see Dunn to find out what happened. He asked me to wake Stephenson, the other driver. That was when I saw you."

"Did you see anyone on your way back from Clarissa's room?"

"I saw Mr Stuart stick his head out of his bedroom door with an annoyed look on his face as I was walking through his carriage. Apart from that, I saw no one."

There was silence for a moment. Thomas eyed Bradley and said. "That's your story. Nothing happened between you and Clarissa. And then you left."

"Yes. And it's not my "story", it's the truth!" said Bradley defiantly.

"So you have a beautiful, famous naked woman in front of you, someone who's offering their body to you. And you run out?" said Thomas incredulously.

"Her husband was asleep in the next room!" retorted Bradley.

"That doesn't seem like the Bradley you've portrayed over the last week I've worked on this train." said Thomas.

Bradley got angry, "Exactly! You've known me a week! You don't know me!"

Scott moved toward Bradley and said, "That's because the Bradley you portray is just a front, isn't it? A show for the paying customers?"

Bradley looked up at him, a sad look in his eyes. "I guess if you act happy go lucky for long enough, you eventually hope you'll feel it."

Scott leaned in closer. He asked quietly, "Did you kill Clarissa Jordan?"

"NO!" cried Bradley, panic in his eyes. "I told you. She came on to me, but I didn't so much as touch her! And I certainly didn't kill her, or take her diamond."

Scott straightened and said, "Thank you Mr Hawkins. I have no further questions at the moment." He turned to Thomas. "Do you Detective Seymour?"

Thomas looked annoyed at Scott, clearly not wanting to end the interrogation. However, after several seconds, it became clear that he hadn't thought of a further question.

Scott finished. "Thank you Bradley, you can go."

Bradley stood up to leave, when Lambert said angrily, "Bradley. I may as well tell you now. I will be seriously reviewing your contract when we arrive in Los Angeles."

Bradley said quietly, "If it makes any difference Mr Lambert. I went into Mrs Jordan's room because of your orders to do everything she asked. And I left without doing anything more because of you and your reputation. And mine for that fact."

He pushed his chair back and walked out of the room.

As the door closed, Thomas stood up angrily. "Mr Blacklock! I have already warned you once about finishing interviews! I am the detective here! You will do well to remember that! We now have a suspect who has admitted to being in the room close to the time of her death. So it will be me who decides when we have finished questioning somebody."

"At least he had the guts to ask him outright if he did it." muttered Lambert.

"And you can pipe down Mr Lambert. Your interruptions weren't helpful either!"

"All I'm saying is...."

"I don't have to listen to what you're trying to say!"

Thomas and Lambert started to get into a full squabble and Scott shouted,

"Hey! Hey!"

They both stopped to look at him.

He said calmly, "The reason I asked him to go is because time is getting on. And we still have four more members of staff to interview. Mr Lambert, perhaps you could go and get your chef."

"Andreas?" Lambert questioned.

"He was on room service duty last night, wasn't he?"

Lambert saw Scott's point, nodded and left.

Lambert's exit left a pained silence as Thomas sat back down, still looking positively furious at Scott.

Scott returned to looking out of the window.

Several minutes later, Lambert returned with Andreas Russelli, who was quite obviously in a huff. They all sat down and Thomas reset the recorder. No sooner had he said his opening spiel, Andreas cut in.

"Are we on the record now?! First things first, I think it's disgusting that I now not only have one, but two corpses in my fridge! I have never been so infringed! I also find it extremely rude that you're calling me to an absurd interrogation just over two hours before you expect me to serve evening dinner for twelve passengers!"

Andreas thought for a second. "Sorry, ten passengers, but that's still not the point!"

Thomas said calmly, "Mr Russelli. If you co-operate and answer the questions we ask, this shouldn't take up too much time and you can get back to your kitchen."

Andreas crossed his arms and puffed up his chest before saying sulkily,

"Ask away then!"

The interview with Andreas was strained to say the least. Thomas began by asking him to verify what was in his work file. This made Andreas go off on a complete tangent, deciding to tell them all about his career. How he had moved to Paris as a small child and was head chef of his first restaurant by the time he was sixteen. How he had worked in most of the top restaurants around the world. From Rome to London, New York to Monte Carlo. He had then complained that they were wasting his time and that dinner would be ruined. When Thomas had tried to ask more poignant questions about Clarissa, Andreas mentioned that he had cooked for her once in Los Angeles several years ago. He then used that as a way to tell them about the reason for him being in Los Angeles, as an expert judge on a food program. America's top rated food program he had been at ends to point out.

"So finally, Mr Russelli." Thomas asked tiredly, "When you finished in the kitchen last night, what did you do then?"

"Rosalie had just come back from the bar and headed to bed. Then someone rang on the room service phone, but I..uh..I didn't get to it in time. I then diverted the room service phone to my cabin. And then I went to my room."

"What time was that?" asked Scott.

"About twenty past twelve."

Thomas suddenly thought of something. "Did it say which suite was ringing when you missed the call?"

Andreas thought for a moment. "Yes, Suite 1."

Scott asked, "Did anyone else call throughout the night?"

"No. Not a one all night."

"And you didn't leave your carriage at any point?" asked Thomas.

"No. I was working on some new recipes. My publisher wants my next book out for Christmas."

"Your publisher?!" asked Thomas.

"Yes. Did you not see my first best seller in the bookstores last year? I can tell you it contained some of the finest....."

Scott stepped forward, seeing this as the start of another story. "Thank you Mr Russelli, but that won't be necessary."

Scott looked at Thomas, but this time he looked relieved that Scott had prevented another Andreas Russelli ego trip.

"That will be all, thank you Mr Russelli." said Thomas and indicated the door to him.

"It's about time!" said Andreas as he stood up, slamming the door as he left.

In the silence that followed, Scott asked, "Remind me again who's in Suite 1."

Lambert swallowed and said, "Dr Pennington."

"The time is 5.55 pm on Monday 22nd of September. This is an interview with Ms Rosalie Gobetti. Detective Thomas Seymour, Mr Scott Blacklock and Mr Patrick Lambert present."

Thomas opened Rosalie's folder. "Rosalie," he said, "It says here you grew up in both Italy and Russia."

"Yes. My mother was Italian, my father Russian." She smiled and said, "If you hadn't guessed they were separated!"

Scott couldn't help but smile, but Thomas remained stern. "I also see that you haven't been with the Express long. And looking at your last jobs on your resume, you don't spend anywhere that long."

Rosalie remained smiling, "That's because I love to travel. I don't like getting too settled."

"I can see that. You've worked practically everywhere. The U.K, Australia, Japan, Germany, Egypt, the Czech Republic. And now here in America."

"As I said, I don't like to get too settled." answered Rosalie.

Lambert frowned at the comment. She suddenly looked worried, and turned to him. "But Mr Lambert, I'm not about to leave. You see, in all those other places, I never enjoyed those jobs very much. But here, I'm constantly travelling!"

Lambert stopped frowning, but didn't say anything.

"I just wanted to say that Mr Lambert. I didn't want you to think I wasn't grateful for this fantastic job."

"Thank you Rosalie." said Lambert, actually looking a little touched.

"Anyway," said Thomas, "Back to last night, you were serving in the bar at the end of the train for most of the night, weren't you?"

"Yes. That's right." said Rosalie, crossing her legs. "I was in the bar until just after midnight. I left Mr Blacklock and Ms Rae on the balcony."

"You left the bar while there were still guests?" said Lambert angrily.

Scott interrupted, "I told Rosalie that we didn't need any more drinks."

Lambert leaned back, looking discomfited. Thomas gave Lambert a warning look before saying, "Please continue."

"I returned to my room. I didn't see anyone on my way there. I went to sleep, but was then woken by voices in the corridor. It was Mr Blacklock and Bradley. They were talking about the problem with the train."

"What did you do after I left?" asked Scott.

Rosalie smiled, "Bradley was complaining that Stephenson was going to give him an earful for waking him in the middle of the night. And then he got more annoyed that he had to take over the room service."

"What do you mean?" questioned Thomas.

"I pointed out that the snores coming from Andreas's room meant that the room service phone was going to get ignored. Andreas is notorious for it. Whenever it's his shift, he always sleeps through it. If we ever get complaints, Andreas's denies getting the call, blaming it on the internal phone system. You probably wouldn't know that though, this was your first trip Detective."

"Did you return to your room then?" asked Thomas.

"Yes. And then I went back to sleep, until I woke at six."

Scott said, "This morning when I saw you walking to Clarissa's room, you had a breakfast tray?"

"Yes. Clarissa had an order for breakfast at a specific time every morning. Two scrambled eggs with fresh fruit and wheatgrass juice. It wasn't a room service call if that's what you were thinking."

"Thank you Rosalie. That will be all." said Thomas.

Rosalie smiled and left quietly.

Once she had gone, Thomas turned to Lambert. He said angrily, "You knew that Andreas Russelli does this?! When he's on the room service night shift?"

Lambert said weakly, "Well... Yes. But he's a top class chef. You have no idea what it costs to have him on board! And you may not have noticed, but he has quite a fiery temper, so if he's a little lax on some of his other jobs, I'll overlook it."

"As long as he cooks a fancy dinner?"

"Exactly. It's good business sense."

Scott said, "I think Detective Seymour's point is that Russelli lied to us."

Lambert pulled a face, "So he wasn't writing a new recipe. We know he was asleep now. If I were you two, I'd be more interested to see why Bradley didn't mention that!"

"Maybe because I wasn't given the chance to ask the question." muttered Thomas, shooting Scott a look.

Lambert continued, "I know he's a member of my staff, but I have to say he's highly questionable. In fact, I've a good mind to go and get him now for you."

Scott had ignored Thomas's look and said, "Mr Lambert. We will come back to Bradley. Now perhaps you could go and get Mr Dunn or Mr Stephenson."

Dunn and Stephenson were the two interviewees that seemed to have the least connection with Clarissa. Neither of them had even seen Clarissa (on the train or before) until they had been asked to move her dead body. Their files showed that they had worked impeccably in their field throughout their careers, and the interviews didn't tell them much more, except for the fact that both Dunn and Stephenson didn't really like the other one. Scott had found it amusing when they had both said that their only connection was their love of making fun of the other members of staff. He was sure that they had said "other members of staff" because Lambert was in the room.

When it came to their actions of last night, Stephenson had gone to bed at eleven thirty, and Dunn had been at the controls when the train lost power. The rest Dunn had told them that morning, and both had said that they didn't go further up the train than the storage carriage all night, although neither had anyone to back up their story.

Scott had pointed out that Mr Dunn was probably the only one with the technical ability to shut down the train. He had been quick to retort with the fact that he couldn't have left the engine workstation unattended without an alarm sounding, one of the train's safety systems. Lambert had concurred that this was correct.

Thomas switched off the recorder and sorted the files on Lambert's desk as Stephenson left the room. As he walked out, Bradley walked in, knocking on the open door as he walked past.

"Excuse me, Mr Lambert. Apparently Andreas has a problem in the kitchen."

Lambert rolled his eyes at the thought of the complaining chef.

Thomas said, "Ah Bradley, while you're here. Could you tell me why you didn't mention that you diverted the room service phone to your room?"

"You didn't ask me." said Bradley honestly.

Thomas's eyes glanced at Scott, before Bradley added, "And because I didn't receive any calls. Unlike Andreas, I did stay awake. But I didn't get a call from anyone so I didn't mention it. At six thirty, I diverted it back to the kitchen, and went to sleep."

Thomas asked, "So even though the train stopped in the night, no one rang to find out what was going on?"

"The train did stop very gently. I imagine most people slept through it. And you evidently did!" retorted Bradley. "Are there any further questions? I'm supposed to be in the bar in two minutes for the cocktail hour."

Thomas looked dissatisfied, but said, "Very well. You can go."

Bradley walked out, as Lambert stood up. "I'd better go and see to Andreas. If you'll excuse me,"

He stopped at the door and said, "But I hope you'll agree with me that all this afternoon has proved is that my staff are impeccable. Except obviously for Mr Hawkins, and believe me, he will be severely reprimanded."

Scott looked over. "Mr Lambert, if Bradley isn't telling the truth, then it won't be you reprimanding him, and if he is, then his actions were quite honourable."

Lambert didn't answer and looked very aggravated as he closed the door behind him.

Thomas looked over to Scott at the window. "Do you think Bradley is telling the truth?"

"I don't know." replied Scott honestly.

He was quiet for a moment before adding, "I'm also intrigued by that call from Daphne's room."

"I know." agreed Thomas. "She didn't mention that, did she? She said she didn't leave Mrs Kennedy's room all night."

Scott nodded. "She also said she took a sleeping pill at about midnight."

"So she lied to us." said Thomas, a trace of excitement in his voice.

Scott murmured, "Perhaps."

Thomas pushed the staff files into Lambert's desk drawer angrily. He said, "The problem is we don't know the time of death. If Bradley is telling the truth, then he was the last person to see her alive at about twelve thirty. And she wasn't discovered until eight this morning. Anyone could have gone in to her room in eight hours!"

Scott said calmly, "Yes. But we do have a tighter time frame for when the train stopped, and someone inserted that virus. Lambert went to his office shortly after midnight which was when he was attacked. Dunn said the power drained at about twelve forty five. And the murder probably happened somewhere between that time."

"You reckon?" asked Thomas.

Scott didn't reply. He was thinking. As he continued to stare out through the glass, watching the light of the day fading, he thought about how he had now spoken to everyone on the train. And somewhere, a killer had lied to him.

Quiet drinks

The interviews had taken longer than expected and it was nearly seven in the evening by the time Scott and Thomas left Lambert's office. They had decided to take a break before evening dinner, but when Scott returned to his room, he didn't get changed, instead opting to flop onto his bed.

He lay on his pillow, staring at the ceiling as the passenger's stories kept floating through his head. He knew that he was missing something. That there was a connection somewhere that he should have made, but hadn't.

His mind wandered, and his eyes closed.

He awoke with a jolt, only meaning to have closed his eyes for a second. The room was dark, save for the light of the moon coming in through the window. He lay there for a few seconds, before checking his watch. It had just gone nine thirty. He had missed dinner. The thought didn't bother him; the day had left him without an appetite. He got up off of the bed and looked out of the window. The night looked still and the pale illumination of the plateau they were travelling through gave the impression of a flat ghost land.

After several moments, Scott moved to his wardrobe and removed an evening suit. Ten minutes later, he arrived in the bar. Only six of the guests had moved to have drinks after dinner. On a settee at the far end sat Anthony and Caroline Stuart, neither of them speaking very much. Caroline sat, sucking timidly on the straw of her cocktail, while Anthony stared into space, playing with his tie.

Further up the carriage looking just as subdued was Harry Broadside, staring out of the window into the inky blackness.

Closer to Scott as he entered, were Daphne Pennington and Avril Kennedy, the only two in the whole room who seemed to be having some semblance of a normal conversation. However he neglected to join them as Tim was sat at the bar by himself, and smiled at Scott as he walked in.

"What can I get you?" asked Rosalie pleasantly as Scott took the bar stool next to Tim.

"A gin and tonic please." replied Scott as he undid his jacket to sit down.

Rosalie nodded and busied herself behind the bar.

"Sorry I didn't call on you for dinner." said Tim, leaning over. "But I knocked on your door and assumed you were still off interviewing people. Speaking of which, that Thomas Seymour doesn't half go on! Did you not tell him that I was here because of you?"

Scott smiled to Rosalie as she gave him his drink. "He's just doing his job Tim."

"Oh, now he's doing his job! Shouldn't he have been doing that before?"

Scott gave him a look. Tim took a second to realise that he had just insulted Scott in the same breath as Thomas.

He said quickly, "I'm sorry. I didn't mean that. I know you both weren't expecting this to happen."

Scott shrugged it off. "It's ok. It's the truth really. I just wish I knew something more concrete. And Los Angeles is getting closer by the minute!"

He took a long swig of his gin, and then asked, "Did I miss anything at dinner?"

"Not really. Thankfully, no big table again!" said Tim with a chuckle. "In fact, you weren't the only passenger missing. I ate with Daphne, but the only other ones there were Jessica and the Stuarts. Oh and Thomas Seymour sat at a table to eat dinner! I don't think the other members of staff were too pleased to now be waiting on him, especially Bradley who had to be serving instead of playing the piano!

I thought things might get a bit better in here, but look at it, it's like a morgue!"

Tim clapped his hand over his mouth when he realised what he just said.

"I guess no one is particularly in the party mood." said Scott dryly.

"Two deaths in twenty four hours can have that effect!" replied Tim, taking a swig of his beer.

Scott and Tim were not the only ones agreeing with that sentiment in the bar. Caroline Stuart placed her cocktail down and said quietly to her husband.

"I just can't believe this has all happened. It just doesn't seem real."

Anthony did not turn to look at her as he spoke, "I imagine it will all start to feel real enough once we get to Los Angeles."

"Why do you say that?"

"Once we get to L.A it will be all over the world. Think about it, Gerry Kennedy and Clarissa Jordan were huge names in the entertainment industry. And that they both died on the same train, one of whom was murdered. It will be huge! We'll be famous now!"

Caroline didn't look thrilled at that idea. She didn't respond and her gaze fixed on the lonely figure of Harry Broadside further down the carriage.

She nodded in his direction, "This is going to get hard for him now."

Anthony did not seem as bothered. "I'm sure it will, but he has made his bed."

"And now he has to lie in it?" asked Caroline.

Anthony responded by finishing his drink. Caroline waited for him to say something further. When he didn't, she stood up angrily and walked over to sit by Harry Broadside.

Harry barely glanced up as Caroline took the seat opposite him.

"Hello Harry." She said quietly.

He returned the greeting with a half hearted smile. As he placed his glass on the table between them, Caroline leaned forward over it.

"How are you doing?" she asked cautiously.

He finally looked at her and she could see that his eyes were glazed.

He said quietly, "I just don't know where to go from here."

Caroline misunderstood him, "You mean after Los Angeles?"

"No" he replied sadly, "With life."

And then he looked her straight in the eye and said, "I keep coming back to the same answer, that there is simply nothing more for me."

To this, Caroline could think of no way to respond.

Other conversations in the carriage were not quite as unsettling. Down at the other end, Daphne and Avril were talking quietly behind their martinis.

"I tell you, I was about to go mad if I had to spend another hour in that room." said Avril, her spirits somewhat revived. "I know it sounds awful, but I feel much better since I've heard about Clarissa."

Daphne looked sideways at her. "I don't think you should feel shameful for that. It's more honest to admit you didn't like her and that you won't miss her. And from the sound of it, she was a complete bitch to you."

"Yes, but I wasn't thinking that so much, more the fact that at least I'm not the only mourning partner on the train anymore. I don't quite get the feeling that everybody's watching me."

Daphne looked around the carriage, "Speaking of that, where is Mark Jordan?"

"You see, my point exactly. I expect he's feeling the same as I did."

"Yes, but not exactly the same as you do. After all, he had a bitch for a wife!"

Avril chuckled at Daphne's comment. She said, "Yes, I guess you're right."

She turned to Daphne, "The thing with Clarissa and her men is that I can see why there would be an obvious attraction. But I just can't see how anyone could spend longer than twenty four hours with such a shallow, over inflated ego of a woman."

"You and Gerry used to." said Daphne bluntly.

"Yes, but that was because we had to, for the work. I mean romantically speaking, maybe that's why none of her marriages worked out?" pondered Avril.

Daphne took a sip of her drink, "Maybe. Although technically her last one didn't work out because someone killed her!"

They sat there for some time in silence, the entire carriage more of a reflection pool than a bar. Avril and Daphne watched Lambert enter and pull Scott away.

"What do you think of Scott and Detective Seymour and their investigation?" asked Daphne as Scott and Lambert left the carriage.

"I don't like that Seymour man," said Avril quickly, "Almost as much as I dislike Mr Lambert! But young Mr Blacklock seems quite honourable."

"He seems to know a bit more about what he's doing." noted Daphne.

"And of course, it doesn't hurt that he's handsome!" said Avril, smirking with a twinkle in her eye.

Scott walked with Lambert into the observation carriage and asked, "What is it?"

Lambert was rubbing his hands and still looked fraught. He said as he began to pace,

"Mr Blacklock, you've now spoken to everyone on the train and you've searched the train. I was hoping that now you could tell me who the culprit is."

Scott replied, "That's not my job. Surely you should be asking this question to Detective Seymour?"

"I have." answered Lambert, "And he said that he was going to discuss things with you before talking to me."

"Then I guess I will respond in the same way." retorted Scott.

"But Mr Blacklock, we're going to be in Los Angeles by tomorrow lunch time!" said Lambert desperately.

"I'm well aware of our time frame Mr Lambert. But as I said to you before, your responsibility right now is to the passengers on this train. So I suggest you get back to doing your job. And let Detective Seymour and myself do ours."

Lambert paused for a minute. "Very well. But I expect to have a meeting with you both in the morning about this matter." He turned and toddled off towards the direction of his office. Scott was about to rejoin Tim when Thomas entered the observation carriage from the other end.

"There you are. Where have you been?" questioned Thomas.

"I've been in the bar having a drink." replied Scott honestly.

"Interrogating more suspects without me?" said Thomas, folding his arms.

"I was actually having a drink with my friend Tim. I presume that's allowed? Anyway, where have you been?"

"Typing up my report." Thomas nodded his head in the direction he'd just come.

"I just saw Lambert. Did he talk to you?"

Scott replied, "Yes he did. He asked me who the culprit was."

"What did you tell him?"

"That it wasn't my job to find out who the murderer is. That it was yours."

"What? I thought we were working together?" said Thomas.

Scott said plainly, "I am here to assist you. But don't forget that my assignment here is to recover Clarissa's lost property, not find her murderer. My objective is finding that diamond. However, I think finding one here will help us find the other. But only if we find the truth before we get to Los Angeles. After that, there may be forensic evidence that will help us trap the killer, but I think by that point, the diamond will be out of our reach."

"What are you doing now then?" asked Thomas.

"I'm going to go and finish my drink." said Scott with a smile.

"And how is that helping our situation?" retorted Thomas, a trace of anger in his voice.

"Observation, my friend. It always helps to observe." replied Scott.

Thomas unfolded his arms. "Well you go and observe then Mr Blacklock. I'm going to listen back through our interviews, see if we overlooked a reaction to a question somewhere."

"Sounds good." said Scott shortly.

"And I will expect to see you at nine tomorrow morning in Lambert's office when we shall decide on our next course of action." said Thomas trying to sound more authoritative than he was coming across. He turned on his heel and headed back to the front of the train.

Scott returned to the bar, and stopped in the door way for several seconds. Not for the first time, the lack of any hum of conversation was obvious in the room.

He felt a presence behind him and turned to see Amy Jordan.

"Oh, good evening Amy. How are you?" asked Scott politely.

"As well as can be expected I suppose." said Amy dourly.

"How's your father doing?"

Amy's face twisted, "Not as good as he was this morning if I'm honest."

"The loss of a loved one takes different amounts of time to affect people" said Scott gently.

"I know." replied Amy, "I know I still haven't fully realised what's happened. But my father did say that he appreciated what you and Detective Seymour were doing. So thank you for that."

Scott nodded by way of response.

Amy pointed to Tim at the bar. "Were you about to join Tim?"

"I was planning on it, yes."

Amy asked uncomfortably, "Do you think I could have a minute with him first?"

"Be my guest." said Scott, as he let her pass. He watched her walk over to the bar, and then decided to take a seat in the corner by himself.

Tim had just ordered another drink from Rosalie as Amy took the stool next to him.

"Hey." she said quietly.

"Hey." Tim replied, giving an awkward smile.

They sat in silence for a few seconds before Amy said,

"Tim. I'm sorry about what happened last night. It was very forward of me and I apologise."

Tim smiled, "You apologise? No, it should be me who's doing that! I should have said something sooner. I didn't mean to lead you on."

Amy returned the smile, her cheeks now flushing, "Well you didn't really. You were just being flirty. I guess I took it the wrong way."

"Is that why you've avoided me for most of the day?" said Tim grinning.

"Partly, but then when I heard about why Scott was here, I got angry that you had just flirted with me to find out information for him."

Tim put his hand on Amy's. "Amy. You can trust me when I say that that couldn't be further from the truth. Scott actually asked me to cut back on my flirting, so as not to complicate matters. And I did mean what I said last night. If I wasn't already sort of involved, I wouldn't hesitate in a second."

"Sort of involved?" asked Amy.

Tim picked up his new drink. "It's a long story."

"Care to tell it to a friend?" asked Amy smiling.

Tim smiled back, and then indicated to Rosalie that Amy was going to need a drink.

Scott sat quietly in the corner and watched the interaction of the remaining passengers. Time passed and just after eleven o clock, Avril decided to retire for the evening. Caroline, who had returned to sit with Anthony, also stood up with the intention to leave. As she wrapped her shawl around her she looked to see if Anthony was joining her. In what now seemed to be a typical exchange between them, Anthony told her he would be along to bed after a game of cards, and as he walked Caroline out of the carriage, he approached Scott.

"Mr Blacklock. There doesn't seem to be the usual crowd for poker, but perhaps you'd care to join me for a few games of Blackjack in the lounge?"

Scott smiled and said, "Sure. I'll be down in a moment. I'm just going to have a quick cigarette."

"I'll see you down there." replied Anthony, before following his wife out of the bar.

Scott sat there for a moment longer. His eyes fell to one of the only other single passengers in the room. Harry Broadside had not moved from his position, and since Caroline had left him, had returned to staring out of the window.

Scott walked over to him. Harry who sensed him approach, turned his head and said tersely,

"Mr Blacklock. Whatever you have to say to me, it can wait until tomorrow. I don't care."

Scott wondered if he had been drinking again, as he seemed to have the same demeanour.

"Mr Broadside, I...."

"Look, I said I don't care." Harry stood up quickly, and then swayed slightly, seeming a bit uneasy on his feet. "Excuse me."

He picked up his bottle of beer and pushed past him. As Scott watched him leave the bar, he muttered under his breath, "I was only going to ask if you wanted to play cards."

Daphne, who had watched their exchange called over to Scott,

"Mr Blacklock." She smiled and said, "I won't be that rude if you care to join me for a drink?"

"I was actually about to pop out for a cigarette."

"Then I'll join you. If you don't mind?" asked Daphne.

"Not at all."

The door closed with a bang as Daphne and Scott walked out into the chill of the night air. Daphne put the collars up on her jacket and put her hands under her arms as Scott lit up.

As he took the first drag, he muttered, "This could be the first time I think I've been out here and Jessica Rae hasn't been."

Daphne replied, "Yes, I haven't seen her all evening. She was at dinner, but then I don't know where she went."

"Probably doing something she shouldn't." mused Scott. "How's Mrs Kennedy?"

Daphne moved closer to the rail. "Oh you know. Her husband died yesterday. She isn't great, but she seems like a tough old cookie from what I know of her. I think she's quite glad that people have forgotten a little bit about Gerry in light of Clarissa."

"And how are you doing?" asked Scott.

Daphne thought about her answer, "I know that everyone else is either scared or shocked, but is it bad if I admit that I'm a little excited?"

"Excited?" said Scott, almost choking on his inhalation.

Daphne looked guilty for having said it. "I know what you're thinking. And I am quite ashamed to admit it. I know it's awful, but I find Clarissa's murder quite exhilarating. I mean, after the tragic death of Gerry."

"I guess that's one way to look at the situation." said Scott quietly.

"Have you made headway with your case?" asked Daphne.

"Yes, some."

"But that's all you're going to tell me, right?" asked Daphne, fishing for gossip.

"For the moment, I'm afraid." replied Scott. "I do have a question for you though"

Daphne smiled, "Anything."

Scott took a drag of his cigarette. "You said that you didn't leave Avril's room all night, after I dropped off the sleeping pills?"

Daphne nodded.

"Can you think of any reason then why a call was made from your room to the kitchen on the room service line last night?"

Daphne looked nonplussed at the question. She shook her head, "No. No idea. I didn't go back to my room until the morning. What time was the call?"

"Some time around twelve twenty." said Scott.

Daphne again shook her head. "No, that wasn't me. I told you, I took a sleeping pill at midnight and crashed out pretty much straight away."

Scott didn't say anything, wondering whether he was being told a lie.

"Not that I have anyone who can corroborate that. But then I presume a member of staff would have access to my room." Daphne suddenly thought of something.

"I have another theory for you actually." She said excitedly.

Scott raised his eyebrow.

She continued, "Lambert. Although he's all concerned about the train's reputation, I reckon it's all an act. He obviously loves this train and all the stories that go with it. The publicity for the Express will be huge, and I suspect the bookings will go up tenfold. People are morbid by nature. It's why crime novels do so well. I bet they'll be able to double the rates for the Thistlewood suites. They'll be queuing up to sleep on the bed where Clarissa Jordan died!

Scott said nothing, troubled by how accurate Daphne probably was.

She looked down at the tracks, not surprised by Scott's lack of comment on her theory. She said,

"Well I hope that you do tell me something more before we part ways! My sister will be dying to know all the details! Anyway, I hate to love you and leave you, but it is still a bit too cold out here for me. I think I'm going to head to bed."

As she turned to leave, Scott said, "I'm about to join Mr Stuart in the lounge for some cards if you'd like to join us?"

Daphne stopped at the door and replied with a smile, "Hmm, Bed or the company of two good looking young men? I know which I'll choose!"

Scott returned the smile as he flicked his cigarette into the bucket of sand, curious as to whether Daphne's charm was a façade.

Several minutes later, Daphne and Scott had joined Anthony at the card table in the lounge. They had left Tim and Amy still chatting at the bar. Scott was pleased to see that their stance seemed to be more like old friends catching up now, rather than anything more intimate.

Daphne sat down between Anthony and Scott as Bradley walked over with the chips and cards.

"Now you're going to have to take this a bit slowly." said Daphne as she took a sip of her drink. "It's been quite a while since I last played cards. Not since my first husband in fact!"

Bradley smiled politely as he dealt the first round of cards out.

Bradley looked to Anthony, his hand on the deck.

Anthony stroked the table with his cards.

Bradley was just about to deal another card when there was a faint sound of glass shattering from further down the train. This was closely followed by a quiet metallic thump against the side of the train. The four people in the lounge looked at each other in shock.

"What was that?" exclaimed Daphne as Anthony stood up.

"Shh!" said Scott and they then heard the noise of an impact on the gravel chips by the side of the tracks.

Anthony jumped from his stool and started to head up the train, followed closely by Scott, Daphne and Bradley. They moved through the reception and Anthony and Scott picked up speed as the sound got louder. As they made their way through the first sleeping carriage, Anthony and Scott's jog became a run.

They had neared the end of the corridor when the train lurched, causing Anthony to stumble and he crashed to the floor, Scott nearly falling on top of him.

Whatever had caused the sound, the drivers at the front of the train had obviously felt the need for the emergency brake.

Scott picked himself up and then helped Anthony, who was still on the floor rubbing his leg and wincing in pain. They all looked at each other; the sound had dissipated as the train was slowing.

They pressed on into the next sleeping carriage, and it was there that they saw the room to the middle suite open, Harry Broadside's room. Anthony and Scott approached the central cabin, just as Amy and Tim arrived from the other end of the carriage in search of the noise.

They all stopped at the open door. Scott pushed past and entered the empty room. Shards of the broken window still hung in the frame and something leading from the window had been tied to Harry's bed post. He looked closer and saw that it was some type of medical gauze. He moved to the window and looked out. For the second time in twenty four hours, Scott's entire body went cold. Where one end had been tied to the bedpost, the other had evidently been tied to someone's neck.

Harry Broadside's limp body hung from the train several feet down from the window, the force of the moving train having almost snapped his neck in half on impact.

The calm before

Scott splashed the cold soothing water onto his neck and face and let it drain off.

He stood up and looked at himself hard in the mirror above his wash basin. Past his reflection, he could see the clock on the wall only read quarter past eight, yet the sun was already high in the sky, glaring through his still half closed curtains.

The train had sped on through the night and passed quickly through Utah, into Arizona. The altered schedule meant that they had skirted past the edge of the Grand Canyon in the darkness, denying passengers any photo opportunity. In an hour, they would pass into Nevada and have the best chance to gain phone reception as they travelled near Boulder City, a small town on the edge of Las Vegas. Not that it would make much difference, thought Scott. In just over three hours after that, they would be in Los Angeles.

Scott returned to look at his reflection, his thoughts going back to the night before..........

In the moments after seeing Harry's body, Scott had frozen. It was only when Anthony and Daphne had started to follow him into the room that he had turned and said,

"Don't come any further!"

"Is it Harry?" said Anthony, the words coming out in a gulp.

Scott looked at him and Daphne, seeing the shocked faces of Tim, Amy and Bradley behind them.

"Yes." said Scott slowly. "Please, we should leave the room."

"Oh my God!" exclaimed Amy from the doorway. She said in a ghostly voice,

"I just remembered! He was the first to stand at dinner! When there were thirteen of us! Just like the superstition!"

Everyone fell silent at that comment.

Daphne turned to leave but noticed a piece of paper lying on Harry's bed.

"Oh God, look!" she shrieked as she moved closer.

"Don't touch it." said Scott as he pushed past Anthony.

Daphne did as Scott asked, but still leaned over to read the note.

Scott looked over Daphne's shoulder and a shudder went down his spine.

The note was composed in a similar way to ones Scott had seen recently.

Cut out letters from magazines made up the words of the note. Just like the ones that had been sent to Clarissa.

> I CANT GO ON ANY MORE.
> I CANNOT LIVE WITH THE THINGS THAT IVE DONE.
> I HAVE TAKEN MY FINAL MEMENTO.
> TELL HER FAMILY THAT IM SORRY.

The words and the weight of them sank in as Daphne gasped when she realised what she was reading.

"What's going on?!"

The loud voice came from slightly down the carriage and was that of Thomas Seymour, Lambert running along behind him. Thomas pushed past Tim and Bradley and looked into the carriage.

No one answered, so he asked again, "I said, what happened?"

Daphne blurted out, "Harry Broadside chucked himself out the window because he killed Clarissa."

"Daphne!" chastised Scott, as the jaws dropped of everyone crammed into the door frame.

"It say so right here! He left a note!" Daphne explained to Thomas.

Thomas looked confused for a second before he said, "Right. Can everybody please leave. I need to examine the room."

Daphne looked hesitant to leave, and Scott saw the excitement in her eyes that she had spoken of on the balcony.

Thomas reiterated. "Now please! I must ask everybody except Mr Blacklock and Mr Lambert to leave. Please return to your rooms."

As everybody filed out, Lambert closed the door and said,

"Is that true? Is that what happened?"

Scott pointed to the letter and said, "This would appear to be a suicide note."

And then he gestured to the window.

Thomas and Lambert looked out. From behind, Scott saw Lambert gag.

They both turned back into the room and Scott said what was bothering him,

"However this note is not in his handwriting."

Lambert looked very pale and sat in the only chair in the room.

Thomas removed an evidence bag and carefully placed the note into it. As he sealed the clear bag, he read it again. "This is the same style of letter that Clarissa was being sent, wasn't it?" asked Thomas.

Scott nodded.

Lambert asked, "What does it say?"

"I can't go on anymore. I cannot live with the things that I've done. I have taken my final memento. Tell her family that I'm sorry."

Lambert placed his hands on his knees. "There we have it then, the jealous ex-husband. The culprit has been found. I'd assumed he was one of your main suspects?"

"Yes, he was." said Thomas. "And this certainly ties things together nicely."

As Lambert went to stand up, Scott said, "If that's true, then we should take his note to mean that his final memento is the Warwick diamond. Let's take another look around his room for it. There may also be more clues as to why he did this."

Suddenly they heard an "Oh God!" from out of the window frame.

The three of them crammed around the window. Outside were Stephenson and Dunn, carrying large flashlights. They had evidently come to inspect the source of the problem.

"Another one?!" said Dunn, astounded.

"So it would appear." said Thomas as Lambert leaned back in from the window, looking queasy as the sight of Harry's body again.

Scott asked, "Have one of you got a knife so we can cut him down?"

Stephenson pulled a pen knife out of his pocket and tossed it up. Scott caught it and set about cutting through the gauze tied to the bed post. After several cuts, it broke and there was the sound of a thud outside.

As Scott returned to the window, Thomas looked down and said, "Can you search him? He may be carrying the diamond choker."

Stephenson and Dunn gave him a dirty look before conceding. They padded his body down but his pockets contained only his wallet.

"It may have fallen out of a pocket when he…you know." suggested Lambert queasily behind them.

Thomas asked the drivers, "Could you two please move Mr Broadside's body?"

"In with the others?" Dunn asked dryly.

"Yes. Please make sure you wear gloves. We'll meet you at the storage carriage to take your flashlights."

Thomas and Scott turned away from the window, only to hear the sounds of Dunn and Stephenson griping as they started to move Harry's body.

"I don't remember where it says corpse remover in my job description!"

"Man, if Andreas was pissed at the state of his refrigerator before, he's gonna go fucking mental now!"

Lambert rolled his eyes at the sound of the drivers as the three of them left Harry's room, locking it behind them with Lambert's master key.

The three of them had arrived at the storage carriage to find Stephenson and Dunn awkwardly trying to hoist Harry's corpse onto the train. Thomas and Scott took the flashlights and stepped out into the quiet desert air. With no boarding platform to hide them, the wheels were impressively large and the Express towered above them. They walked quickly back along the train to Harry's broken window and began combing the floor with their flashlights. When this provided no answers, they carried on down the track, past the end of the train until they found shards of broken glass, the point where Harry had initially gone through the window.

Once the lights of the train had left them, the flashlights were pitiful in the pitch black of the desert. The darkness enveloped them and Scott again felt a chill down his neck.

After twenty minutes of searching the surrounding area, they decided to turn back. As they were walking back down the side of the carriages, they were surprised to see Lambert approaching them with a can of spray paint.

"Did you find anything?" asked Lambert as he got closer to them.

Thomas shook his head as Scott indicated to Lambert's hand, "What's that for?"

Lambert replied, "I had an idea. I didn't think you would find anything with it being so dark. I wasn't sure what your plan of action would be, but I'm afraid we cannot wait here until daylight to search properly. The passengers will have a fit and we'll be in L.A by midday tomorrow anyway."

Scott was going to protest, but Lambert continued, "This is where the paint comes in. We can mark the spot so that the police can come back and know which area of the track to search. It's industrial paint so it won't wash away easily."

Thomas was very impressed by the idea. He said, "Good idea Mr Lambert. I agree that we should definitely press on, so that I can receive back up as soon as possible."

Before Scott said anything, Thomas had taken the spray paint and began spraying a large green X on the desert floor next to the train track.

Once he had finished, Lambert said, "We should get back on. I've told the drivers to start up as soon as we're on board."

"Fine" said Scott, "Let's finish searching Harry's room."

Harry Broadside's room, like Tim's, was the central cabin in a carriage of three. As it was, the occupants got a slightly short straw in the size of their room. However that was a good factor for Scott and Thomas as it took them little time to search the room. There was no sign of the diamond. Scott had found some interesting papers in Harry's desk when Thomas looked under the bed.

"Aha!" Thomas shouted as he pulled out a folder, "Not the diamond, but more evidence."

He opened it up to find a cut up Trans-Oceanic Express brochure, a small set of scissors, and a miniature tube of glue.

Lambert looked over it and said, "Well that settles it for me. It's clear that he murdered her and couldn't live with himself. The man was obviously obsessed. He had harassed Clarissa several times. He got drunk and lost control."

"What about the diamond?" asked Scott irritably.

Lambert replied, "It's likely that it fell from his body as he jumped. It's probably out there lying in a bush."

"Which is why we should take a look in the morning." Scott said.

Thomas intervened now. "It could have gone anywhere. It could take us just as long to find it in daylight. And as you said before, this track is miles from anywhere. No one will come looking here before we can get a proper search team out here. I agree with Lambert. I want to get to L.A as soon as possible."

Scott refused to drop it, "How come we didn't find his note making kit the first time we searched this room?"

Thomas retorted, "He was probably just very good at hiding it."

Scott scoffed, but Lambert decided the matter was resolved.

"If you'll excuse me, I'm going to bed. Here is the master key to the room. I trust you can lock it up. We can make an announcement in the morning. Shall we say nine thirty?" He said this with a grimness that made it sound like a routine duty now.

Lambert didn't wait for a response after giving Thomas the key. He opened the door and left.

Thomas moved to the door, "This settles it for me too. Come on, let's go."

Scott looked back to Harry's travel documents on the desk and nodded absently. As he went to put them back in the drawer, he noticed that Harry Broadside's name on one travel document was actually on a thin sticky label. He used his fingernail to push it off, revealing the name, Phillip McGuiness.

"Hmm." said Scott in thought, the name sounding vaguely familiar.

"Come on" said Thomas impatiently.

Scott put down the papers and followed him out. Thomas had locked the door and they were just heading their separate ways when they had both been startled again by the train returning to life……

And now Scott felt more disturbed than the night before as he put on his shirt and pulled back his curtains to fully let in the sunlight. The empty desert shimmied past and Scott couldn't help but disagree with Thomas and Lambert's assertions. Too much didn't add up and more importantly for Scott, they hadn't found the location of the diamond.

There was a knock on the adjoining door and Tim slid it open.

"Good Morning." he said cheerfully.

Scott turned and gave a small smile, continuing to button up his shirt.

"What's the matter?" asked Tim, moving into the room.

Scott shrugged it off. "It's nothing."

"I don't get it. Surely it should be a good morning. The culprit was found. You're off the hook."

Scott replied, "But I'm not, am I? The diamond still hasn't been found. And as heartless as it sounds, that's the only things my superiors are going to be interested in."

Tim patted him on the shoulder. "Well we're not in L.A until lunchtime. I have every faith that you'll work it out."

As he walked to the door he said, "You always do! Anyway I'll see you down at breakfast."

Tim closed the door behind him as Scott picked up his jacket and slipped it on.

Several seconds later, Scott emerged into the corridor and almost collided with Mark Jordan.

Mark stopped himself from walking into him and said, "Apologies Mr Blacklock."

"Not a problem." said Scott, while locking his door. Turning to look at Mark, he thought for a second before saying, "Mr Jordan, I'm not sure if you're aware but in the night...."

"Harry Broadside killed himself." Mark finished. "Yes, I heard. Amy just came to tell me."

"Oh." said Scott, surprised. As they started to walk down the carriage together, Scott asked, "Did you hear the whole story?"

"That he left a note indicating that he killed Clarissa. Yes, Amy told me that part as well. Is that the conclusion that the detective has come to?"

Scott looked uncomfortable. He answered, "I believe so."

"He was quite obviously a disturbed character."

They walked in silence then until they arrived in the lounge. At that point, Mark turned to Scott and said, "I think I should tell you. I do plan to make a formal complaint to the police force about their treatment of my wife's threats, given who she was."

Scott tried to interrupt, "Mr Jordan, I..."

"Don't worry Mr Blacklock. I will say that both you and Detective Seymour have acted admirably. But someone further up the chain of command should be made to answer for this. Excuse me; I must have breakfast with my daughter."

Mark walked away from him through the lounge. It was then that Scott noticed Avril on a settee by the bar, drinking a tall coffee. He approached her and said,

"Good morning Mrs Kennedy. How are you doing this morning?"

Avril looked up, "Bearing up. Still in a bit of shock about the whole Harry thing!"

For the second time, Scott was surprised. "How did you know?"

"Daphne told me. But when I said I was shocked, I only meant by how he did it! The whole thing doesn't surprise me in the slightest, given his obsessive behaviour.

You know, it is a shame that he killed himself. If I knew he was the one that killed Clarissa, I would have liked to congratulate him before he threw himself out a window!"

She finished with a smile before taking another sip of her coffee.

Scott was really not sure how to respond, when a red faced Lambert waddled into the lounge and beckoned him over.

Scott excused himself to Avril and followed Lambert up to his office.

As they walked in, Lambert said,

"I'm wondering if an announcement will be necessary. It seems the whole train knows already. And I have other problems at the moment!"

"You still need to make an official statement." said Scott.

"Yes, of course. I'll get Detective Seymour to let them know the case is closed."

"But it's not!" said Scott tetchily.

"What do you mean?" said Lambert indignantly, "Detective Seymour is happy with the facts. Why aren't you?"

"Because the diamond is still missing. And I'm not completely satisfied that Harry Broadside committed suicide."

Lambert folded his arms. "Or maybe you're just jealous that Detective Seymour has been successful in his side of the investigation, and you haven't."

Scott hesitated for a second before deciding not to retaliate and walked out of his office. He closed the door, refusing to engage in an argument with Lambert. It was pointless, he thought. He should have realised that Lambert would be the first to happily resolve the issue with the easiest answer.

He walked into the dining carriage to find it surprisingly empty. The Stuarts were sat in one corner, while Daphne was sat by herself in the other. He wondered why Tim and the Jordans had been so quick at breakfast, when he saw his answer in the corner.

Unusually for the Express, there was a small breakfast buffet in front of the piano displaying pastries and fruit.

Rosalie walked over to Scott at the entrance and said, "Good morning Mr Blacklock. Can I get you some coffee? Tea?"

"Tea, please." replied Scott with a smile.

As Rosalie went to head to the kitchen, Scott asked, "Rosalie. What's with the buffet?"

Rosalie turned and looked a little embarrassed. "We've had a few problems in the kitchen this morning, so unfortunately we only have a small buffet to offer you."

"What kind of problem?" asked Scott.

"It's Mr Russelli. He's refusing to work."

"What? Why?"

"He's saying that he can't work in these conditions anymore. He's locked himself in his cabin, with most of the food store keys and is refusing to come out."

"Working conditions?"

At this point, Rosalie looked at her most awkward. "Yes. It's to do with the amount of dead bodies in his refrigerator."

Scott almost felt the urge to smile. Another time, it would have been funny.

Rosalie smiled and said, "We're hoping to have talked him out before lunchtime!"

At this, Scott did smile. He thought of something quickly, and asked, "Rosalie, you were working in the bar last night. Did Mr Broadside drink much through the course of the evening?"

Rosalie thought about it for a second. "I think he had about four or five beers. It wasn't much compared to what he had been drinking the rest of the trip."

"Thank you Rosalie."

She smiled, and returned to the kitchen.

Scott walked over to the buffet table and helped himself to a croissant and some slices of mango. He looked to see where to sit and saw that Daphne was smiling at him expectantly. She had her mouth full and so patted the seat next to her.

Without much option, Scott walked over and sat down at her table.

Rosalie served Scott with tea as he asked, "So Daphne. Is there anyone on the train you haven't been able to tell about Harry Broadside?"

Daphne smiled guiltily and said, "I was just making sure people were up to date with the situation! And to answer your question, I haven't seen Jessica Rae to tell her!"

Scott muttered, "You've got the gossip you wanted for your sister now, at the very least."

"I know!" said Daphne, not picking up on the fact that Scott was slightly annoyed with her. "But what happened to the diamond? Have you found that yet?"

"No. We haven't yet." answered Scott, looking at her questioningly.

The look seemed to make Daphne uneasy. As she looked down to place her cutlery together, she said, "I'm sure a smart man like yourself will be able to find it." She picked up her bag and said, "Anyway, I should probably get back to my room and start packing. It takes me so long!"

She gave a nervous laugh as she looked through her bag. After several moments of searching, she muttered to herself,

"Where the hell is it? Don't tell me I'm going to have to ask Lambert for another one!"

"What are you looking for?" asked Scott, looking over into her lap.

"My room key. Aha!" she said as she found it and fished it out of her bag.

"You said you'd have to ask Lambert for another one?"

Daphne put her bag on her shoulder, "Yes. I'm awful at losing things. So wherever I stay, I always ask for two room keys because I'm guaranteed to lose at least one of them! You see, I'd already lost one of these the other night. Anyway, I'll see you a bit later. Enjoy your breakfast, what there is of it! This place is falling apart!"

She finished with a laugh as she stood up and left the carriage.

Scott finished eating his fruit, thinking of Daphne's slightly odd behaviour. The Stuarts in the corner got up to leave, and while Caroline walked straight out, Anthony detoured to Scott's table.

"Mr Blacklock." said Anthony, his usual grin looking a little forced.

"Mr Stuart."

"So is this the outcome you expected?" asked Anthony, putting his hands into his pockets.

Scott shrugged noncommittally.

"I can't believe it. I mean, I didn't really know him that well. But you could tell he was cut up about Clarissa. I just never thought....."

"Mr Stuart, can I ask you something?"

"Certainly."

"Yesterday, you told me that on the night of Clarissa's murder, you had an argument with your wife and then you went to bed?"

"Yes."

"Bradley mentioned seeing you looking out of your bedroom door as he passed. Why didn't you mention that?"

Anthony got a little angry at the question. "I think your question was whether I left the room or not? Which I didn't."

"Then why not mention it?"

"I probably didn't think it was important. I heard footsteps in the corridor and thought it was Caroline returning. When I saw that it wasn't, I got back into bed. Anyway, why are you asking me this? I thought the note left by Harry explained it all?"

Scott took another sip of his tea. "Yes. It would seem so."

Anthony looked confused. Instead of asking another question, he said, "Well, I'll leave you to your breakfast."

Scott nodded as Anthony left the dining carriage, leaving Scott there alone with his thoughts. And then it struck him, Daphne's mention of having two card keys and having already lost one. She hadn't lost one. She had given one to him when he had fetched sleeping pills for Avril on Sunday evening. He hadn't given it back to her. And try as he might, he couldn't remember where he had last put it.

"I wonder…" said Scott to himself, thinking about the call made from Daphne's room.

Thoughts of key cards left his head as Lambert ran into the carriage.

"Mr Blacklock! There you are!" he said, out of breath.

"What is it?"

"It's Detective Seymour! He's in my office. He's on the phone. We've picked up a phone signal from Las Vegas!"

Background backup

Lambert and Scott hurried into Lambert's office to see Thomas sat at the desk, placing his phone back on the desk.

His face did not look happy.

"What's wrong?" said Lambert as he closed the door behind them.

"I just got off the phone with my superiors. They didn't take my report too well."

"Why?" The question was from Lambert, as Scott had moved to the window, straining to hear something.

"You hear that?" said Scott, pointing to the window, and interrupting Thomas's answer.

The other two moved to the window, and the slow thupp thupp thupp sound that Scott had heard got louder.

"What is that?" asked Lambert.

Scott spotted a shadow on the desert floor and craned his neck upwards. He pointed into the sky. "It's a helicopter. Two of them I think."

Lambert looked to Thomas. "That was a pretty quick response. How did they get here so quickly?"

Thomas looked angry as he sat back down. "Because that's not the police, at least not yet. I expect those are news helicopters."

"What?" said Scott, turning to look at him, "The media knows?"

"Yes." said Thomas. "That's why my superior wasn't happy, because the media knew about it before him. The F.B.I have got involved now as well."

"Did you tell them about Harry Broadside?" asked Lambert.

"Yes. But the fact that the murder was solved didn't appease them much."

"Because the diamond is still missing?" asked Scott bluntly.

Thomas's face twisted, "Well, because I didn't mention that straight away in my report. But they already knew from the news coverage."

"But how? How could they know?" asked Lambert angrily.

"I know how." said Scott quietly, thinking about the one passenger whom he had seen very little of in the last twenty four hours. But how could she have contacted them?

He continued, "We'll deal with that in a second. Mr Seymour, do you still have reception?"

Thomas looked down at his phone. "One or two bars. The reception's not great."

"Can I borrow your phone please?" Scott asked, extending his hand.

"To ring whom?" asked Thomas suspiciously.

"My partner, Katherine Fowley."

"Why?"

"I need her to check on some things for me." replied Scott impatiently.

"Mr Blacklock, I don't want you muddying the waters here." said Thomas.

"Mr Seymour. The diamond is still missing and as an officer of the law, you still have a duty to investigate the theft element of this case." said Scott firmly.

Thomas took time in answering, "Yes, I know that, but the chances are it's somewhere in the vicinity of the track we marked. I'm confident that a proper forensics team will find something."

"In that case, what's the objection of me phoning my partner?" asked Scott, the impatience rising in his voice.

Thomas didn't answer, so Scott took the phone out of his hand and walked out of the office, pushing past Lambert as he dialled Katherine's number.

He walked into the main vestibule of the reception carriage and started pacing as he waited for Katherine to pick up.

"Come on... Answer..." muttered Scott to himself.

On the thirteenth ring, Katherine answered.

"Katherine Fowley."

"Katherine, its Scott."

Her voice went up a level.

"Scott. My God! Where are you calling from? Are you still on the train?"

"Yes, we're a couple of hours away from Los Angeles."

"You're actually just running parallel to the Providence Mountains, south of Soda Lake, California."

"What?!"

"I'm watching an aerial view of your location. Scott, the story broke half an hour ago. People all over the world have been waking up to the news. It's on every channel. It's as if the President had been assassinated! They've got a constant video feed on your train. The media's making it look like one of those high speed car chases! Can you not hear the helicopters?"

"Yes. We had noticed them." said Scott dryly. "It was Jessica, wasn't it? Is it her name on the reports?"

Katherine paused, "Yes. The first news program to air it was on her company's station. The bitch got herself another exclusive! How did she manage to contact anyone before you did?"

"I don't know, but I'm going to find out." said Scott through gritted teeth, "First I need your help."

"What do you need? I thought there was a policeman on board?"

"How much has the news report said?" asked Scott.

"That on Sunday night, Gerry Kennedy died of a heart attack, and then later that night, someone sabotaged the train and communication equipment, killed Clarissa and stole her Warwick diamond. Is that all true?" Katherine asked.

"Pretty much. But..."

"Oh, wait, there's more coming in." said Katherine, obviously having the television on in the background. Scott heard her turning the sound up, then her saying, "Listen to this."

Scott then heard the voice of a woman newsreader,

"And more news just in on the shocking story of Hollywood icon Clarissa Jordan's murder. This is unbelievable! It seems that recent developments indicate that the main suspect was her ex husband Henry Broadside, who has since taken his own life. Clarissa was married to him for only six months, before their well publicised divorce. The police have revealed today that Clarissa Jordan had been receiving threatening letters for several weeks. The main suspect for these letters is believed to be Henry Broadside. Clarissa Jordan was travelling at the time with her new husband and his daughter. We have not been able to obtain further comment from anyone on the Trans-Oceanic Express as yet. As you can see, the train is being closely monitored by several helicopters now as it makes it way into Los Angeles. Los Angeles Union station has been cordoned off and there are at least thirty television crews waiting expectantly for the "Train of Death" as the papers are now calling it. This name referring not only to the brutal murder of Clarissa Jordan, but also the death of well known Hollywood mogul Gerry Kennedy. Gerry Kennedy......."

"Is that true about her ex husband? He killed himself?!" asked Katherine, moving away from the television.

"Jessica is obviously keeping them up to date." said Scott, feeling his temperature rise.

"No wonder they're calling it the train of death!" said Katherine dryly. There was a pause.

"You don't think Henry Broadside did it." she said suddenly.

"How did you guess?" Scott asked, perplexed.

Scott could tell Katherine was smiling. "I think I know you quite well by now Scott. And you don't like the simple answers! So why don't you think he did it?"

Scott paused, "It's not that he didn't do it. He certainly had motive. But I don't think he killed himself."

"Why not?"

"Several things. The note he left was one like those sent to Clarissa."

"Cut out from magazines? That's an odd way to write a suicide note."

"Exactly." said Scott, glad that Katherine agreed with him. "Plus the fact that the diamond has yet to turn up, and I'm just not comfortable with the way Harry killed himself."

"Hanging? But why not just hang yourself in your room as opposed to jumping out of your window?"

There was a surprised silence from Scott, so Katherine explained,

"The details of each death are scrolling across the screen. Welcome to twenty first century technology!"

"I'm gonna kill her!" said Scott angrily.

"Scott. You said you needed my help?"

"Yes." said Scott, annoyed that he sidetracked himself. "I need you to gather as much information as you can on everybody on board the train."

"OK, what do you need?"

"Firstly, Mark and Amy Jordan. I want you to check his finances. Is he as rich as he claims to be? Work with the police who were carrying out surveillance on them. Find out more about their relationship. Also find out if there were any changes to Clarissa and Mark's will. I want to know if and how he was included on hers. I also want to know if Clarissa had affected any of Amy's inheritance from her father.

Next Anthony and Caroline Stuart, I still don't have much background information on them so anything you can find there would be a bonus.

Avril and Gerry Kennedy. I feel I'm missing something with those two."

He heard Katherine's frantic scribbling stop.

"But he's dead?"

"I know, but there somehow still connected to this. And I'm still not completely convinced of his natural death either. Check how financially unstable they were. I need to know how desperate they really were. Then we have Dr Pennington. Check her financial situation and find out if she's had any remote connections to any robberies. Specifically jewellery robberies. Also find out about her previous husbands. Her last one died. I'd like to know the specifics."

"Anyone else?"

"See if you can pinpoint Harry's movements before he boarded the train. And check out a Mr Gareth Lynch, his lawyer. Get his story. Who's left? Jessica Rae. See if you can find out how her career was going before this exclusive. I want to know how much rested on this for her. Believe me, it's something I'm going to ask her shortly anyway."

"Ok, Anything else?"

"I don't think you need to check anything out about Tim. Oh, and run a background check on Bradley Hawkins. I don't think the other staff are involved, but I'll give you their names, just in case. Andreas

Russelli, Rosalie Gobetti, Robert Dunn, Henry Stephenson and Patrick Lambert."

He heard her finish writing. "Scott. That's a lot to check out! You're going to be in L.A in a matter of hours!"

"I know. And I know I'm asking a lot. But this is really important. Use all resources possible. Get Dan Povey in on it. This might even be the time to call in that favour with Mathew as well."

"Oh, no! Really?" said Katherine, sounding pained.

Mathew Landau was an old flame of Katherine's who now happened to work at the F.B.I headquarters in Washington D.C. Mathew still pined for her, and she tried to avoid communication with him as much as possible.

"I really think we're going to need his help. Sorry to do this to you." said Scott apologetically.

There was a pause.

"Ok." said Katherine. "But is there anyone in particular that I should focus on? Because that would really help. Who are you leaning towards?"

"I can't say."

"Scott, we tell each other everything!"

"No, that's the problem. I really can't say at the moment, because I'm really not sure.

It's like I can see most, if not all of the pieces, but none of them make complete sense to me. I'm kind of hoping that your digging is going to unearth something and you'll know who to lean towards."

"I get it." said Katherine. "I'll try my hardest."

"Thank you." said Scott sincerely. There was a moment of silence. "So, how have you been?"

"I'm fine. The Stoltzkin case is all but wrapped up. Although you remember Golic was shot by that sniper? It was actually nothing to do with him testifying on our case. It turned out that it was a retribution killing for a previous case he had worked on."

Scott stopped in his tracks as a penny dropped. He said quickly, "Katherine, I should probably go. But I appreciate your help. Give me a call on this phone as soon as you find out anything. I don't have mine on me and the reception on it is crap at the best of times! We probably won't have much phone cover for about another hour, but keep trying. And thank you. You've already helped."

"Will do." Katherine said, giving a little laugh. "And there was you thinking it would be a nice relaxing trip of fine dining and martinis!"

Again a second thought shot through Scott's head. "Thank you again Katherine. You've just reminded me of something else. Anyway I've got to go. Speak soon."

He briefly heard Katherine say bye as he placed the phone behind the reception counter, and started to walk up the train. His target was Jessica, but speaking to Katherine had just made him think of two important points.

Firstly, what had happened to the martini glasses that were in Clarissa's room on the night of her murder? The second thought was Golic's death, and how that had been unconnected to the Stoltzkin case. What if Scott's reservations about Gerry Kennedy and his death weren't connected to Clarissa at all?

Jessica Rae's scoop

Scott marched through the sleeping carriages to Jessica's room and pounded hard on the door.

"Jessica! Jessica, let me in!"

No response. Scott banged on the door again.

He stood waiting for a few moments, before trying again. He was so preoccupied that he didn't see Caroline Stuart walk down the corridor until she was almost stood next to him. Scott felt the presence at his shoulder and swivelled to see her. If Caroline had resembled a doll before, she now looked like a fragile antique one. The events of the last couple of days seemed to be taking their toll on her.

"Oh, hello Mrs Stuart. Have you seen Jessica Rae?"

Caroline replied quietly, "She passed me when I was sat in the observation carriage."

"Thank you." replied Scott as he moved past her.

"Mr Blacklock?"

Caroline's voice was quiet, but Scott heard her and turned back around. She paused before saying, "Are those helicopters following us?"

"Yes. It would appear we have an escort to Los Angeles."

Caroline paused and asked, "Is it also true that Mr Broadside left a note?"

"Yes. It would seem so." Scott answered carefully.

Caroline looked like she was about to cry. She said, "I spoke to him last night, in the bar. He seemed so cut up about Clarissa. I mean, I tried to talk to him, but I obviously couldn't help in any way."

Scott moved back down the corridor. He said, "There is some likelihood that he may have been Clarissa's murderer. If that is the case, then you have no need to feel guilty or responsible, as...."

"Harry brought this on himself?" finished Caroline.

"That wasn't what I was going to say, but you can't be responsible for someone else's obsession."

"I guess you're right. You are right about him being obsessed. We were on the same plane into New York and she was all he talked about, even then."

A bell rang in Scott's head and he replied absently, "As I said then, you can't be responsible for someone else's obsession."

"I know. I just can't believe all this has happened. It's like some horrible nightmare."

Scott was anxious to find Jessica and felt that he could be there for some time with Caroline, so said a little dismissively,

"Well, in a couple of hours, the nightmare should be over."

Caroline gave a small smile at this. Scott said, "Now, if you'll excuse me Mrs Stuart, I have some pressing business."

He smiled and walked on up the train, bumping into Bradley as he passed by the Thistlewood suites.

Bradley gave a nervous smile as he approached him. Scott stopped him as he went to pass him.

"Bradley, could you tell me if you've seen Jessica Rae?"

"Yes. She was just in the observation carriage."

"Thank you."

Bradley passed him when Scott called him back.

"A couple of other things, who was on room service duty last night?"

"I was, Sir. I took over once everybody had gone to bed after the Mr Broadside.....incident."

"Did you have any calls during the night?"

"No Sir. Not one." replied Bradley, looking a little worried that Scott might not believe him.

"Thank you Bradley." said Scott. "Just one more thing. You know how you went into Clarissa's room on the night of her murder?"

"Yes." said Bradley, looking uncomfortable.

"You said you took two martinis with you? And then Clarissa invited you in. I presume you set them down?"

"Yes," answered Bradley, thinking.

"When Clarissa……made her intentions clear, and you hurried out of the room. Did you pick up the drinks?"

Bradley thought about it for all of a second. "No. I didn't. I just completely panicked and left straight away."

"Thank you Bradley. That's all." replied Scott, turning on his heel and heading to the observation carriage.

"Mr Blacklock?" This time it was Bradley who stopped Scott.

"Yes?" He said, as he returned.

Bradley said uncomfortably, "It's something else I remembered about the night of Clarissa's murder."

"Yes?"

"On returning from Clarissa's room, I passed Harry Broadside's door. It wasn't closed properly and I heard a thump as I was passing. I checked to see if he was ok, but he must have rolled out of bed in his drunken state."

"What did you do?" asked Scott.

"I tried to help him back onto the bed, but he was out for the count. In the end, I stuck a pillow behind his head and put his duvet over him."

He nodded as if to indicate the end of the story, "I just remembered it and thought you should know."

"Thank you Bradley." replied Scott as he carried on his way.

Scott thought how Bradley may have just confirmed his suspicion that Harry wasn't capable of killing Clarissa on the night she died.

He arrived in the observation carriage to find not Jessica, but Amy as the sole occupant. She sat in the large armchair in the middle of the carriage, a magazine on her lap, sipping from a large mug of coffee. He walked over to her and said,

"Good morning Amy, how are you?"

She looked up at him, an apprehensive look on her face.

"Not great to be honest."

"Why?"

"The helicopters. It just hit me how big this is going to be when we get to Los Angeles."

Scott folded his arms. "In what way?"

"The media. They'll be all over me and my father."

"And yet here you are sat in the one carriage where those helicopters can see you. And you know they'll work out who you are. I'm sure they're probably using their cameras with telescopic lenses right now to work out what magazine article you're reading."

Amy asked irately, "What are you implying?"

"I'm implying that you can act apprehensive for the stress that your father is about to have, but don't do it while making a show for the cameras. It's hypocritical."

"Do you really think I'm that calculated?" Amy spat.

"To be honest, I don't know you well enough to make that conclusion."

Amy stood up and made for the sleeping carriages. She turned and said to him,

"Was there something you actually wanted?"

"Yes," said Scott, putting his hands in his pockets. "Were you with Tim the whole time between me leaving the bar and when you got to Harry Broadside's room last night?"

"Yes I was." retorted Amy indignantly.

"And what are your thoughts on what happened to Harry?"

"On what? Him killing himself? I think he was a stupid dick for being so obsessed with that witch. How could anyone possibly be that madly in love with her?!"

"Your father was, and I imagine still is." said Scott quietly.

The words brought tears to Amy's eyes. She walked towards him and said angrily,

"Are you comparing my father to that pathetic excuse for a man?! My father would never have killed anybody, or taken his own life!"

"I didn't mean it like that." said Scott, seeing he had upset her. "I apologise if it came across that way."

"Well you should be." said Amy, walking away, "I tell you, as an investigator, you really need to work on your interviewing technique."

She had almost left the carriage, when a random unconnected thought entered Scott's head.

"Amy?"

She turned and looked around the door frame.

"That murder at your campus you were talking about the other day. The janitor who was obsessed with the girl, Emma Jones? Do you remember his name?"

Amy looked slightly bewildered by the question. She thought about it for a moment.

"Um.....No."

Scott nodded disappointedly, "Thank you anyway."

The look of confusion didn't leave her as she closed the door behind her.

Scott's quest for Jessica was still fruitless when he arrived in the bar. He then saw a silhouette of someone on the balcony, and realised that he needn't have asked people if they'd seen her.

He walked out into the heat of the desert. The sound of the helicopters, which had now totalled seven in number, became a lot louder.

Jessica looked around, and gave a smug smile as Scott closed the door.

"I was getting lonely out here without my smoking partner!" said Jessica, lighting up a fresh cigarette.

Scott moved over to the railings to face her.

"I imagine you've got all the company you need with four film crews just above your head." he replied.

Jessica's smile widened. "I was wondering when you were going to come and find me, to talk about my story. Curious as to how I did it?"

Scott didn't rise to the bait.

Instead Jessica dug into the large side pocket of her long jacket and removed a cross between a large cellular phone and a miniature laptop.

"Satellite phone." She said, "State of the art, latest model. The only other people using these at the moment are scientists in Antarctica and Alaska. One of my many perks. In my job, you can never depend on a regular phone. I mean, look what happened here! I'd never have gotten all the awards I'm going to get from this if it hadn't been instant news!"

Scott took a step forward. He said angrily, "Jessica. Do you realise what you may have compromised by doing this?"

"Compromised?! Scott, the story is over. Harry Broadside, ex husband of Clarissa Jordan murders her in a jealous rage. And let me tell you Scott, it's a good story. An excellent story! Especially because the only ones that are compromised in this are you and Detective Seymour, allowing all this to happen right under your nose! I will enjoy writing that follow up report! "Incompetent Scott Blacklock in Zirconia scandal!" "

"Jessica, I swear to god I...."

Scott was stopped from finishing his sentence by the balcony door opening. They both turned to see Tim walk out, obviously a little surprised by their angry stances.

He said, "Scott. Lambert's looking for you."

"What now?" said Scott impatiently.

"I think he's got Katherine on the phone for you."

Scott was angry at having to leave Jessica, but realised that his phone call was more important.

"Thank you." he said to Tim, before pushing away from the railing and leaving the two of them.

Tim slowly walked over to where Scott had been standing.

Jessica offered her cigarette packet. "Smoke?" she asked.

Tim shook his head and looked up as another two helicopters had joined the others following them.

"I take it this is your doing?" said Tim, not looking at her.

"Of course." said Jessica with a smile.

"Happy with yourself?"

Jessica replied by widening her grin.

Tim looked down at the moving tracks. "How did you become such a bitch?"

"Years of experience." replied Jessica unremorsefully.

Tim finally turned to look at her. "Do you ever stop to think about how your actions affect others?"

Jessica took a final drag of her cigarette and flicked it over the side.

"Never." she said as she blew smoke indirectly in Tim's face.

"And anyway," she said, "I don't even see how that applies to this situation. I was only telling the facts as they happened."

"You don't think Mark and Amy Jordan might have appreciated more discretion?"

"Oh please!" said Jessica, putting her hands on her hips. "Amy Jordan seems the perfect type of person to crave instant celebrity! I left her sunning herself in that glass box with all those photographers above her! You're only saying that because you don't like me and you've probably slept with her!"

Tim replied, "You're right that I don't like you, but for your information, I'm saying this because I'm a moral human being."

"So we're back to this again!"

Tim had had enough and walked to the door. He stopped as he opened it and looked at her.

"Why did you just say that I'd probably slept with Amy?" he asked.

"Well you've been fawning all over her this entire journey!" Jessica spat.

She hadn't meant it to, but the words came out tinged with jealousy.

They both realised this at the same time, and Jessica quickly looked away.

"Does that bother you?" asked Tim, looking closely for her reaction.

"Of course not!" replied Jessica, pushing her hair behind her ear.

Tim stared at her. She rolled her eyes. "Don't be ridiculous! I got over you a long time ago Tim."

"Yeah, I kind of got that when you stabbed me in the back." Tim muttered.

"Come on. We were young. We both would have done anything to get that job. It was nothing personal." Jessica scoffed.

"Nothing personal? I was falling in love with you!" said Tim angrily.

"You what?" said Jessica, startled.

Tim was embarrassed for a second, before shrugging it off. "I was falling in love with you. But you were so focused on your career, you didn't even notice. From what I've heard, no one else has bothered getting close to you since, probably because they couldn't trust you."

Jessica looked down at her feet.

He said after a moment, "You know Jessica. I've just realised why you live the life you do. You've pushed everyone away so much, you have this belief that the public want and need you, because you have no one else in your life that does."

"That's not true!" snapped Jessica. The statement obviously weakened her.

Tim shrugged, "Whatever helps you sleep at night."

As he turned to leave, Jessica said desperately, "That's not true! Your friend Scott needs me!"

Tim stopped and said scornfully, "And why would Scott need you?"

"Maybe I know a few things that would be of interest to him."

"Like what?"

The next words that came out of Jessica's mouth stunned Tim. She clearly didn't mean to say them.

"Maybe it paid off to have the room next to Harry Broadside. Maybe I know that he didn't kill himself."

The pieces of the puzzle

Scott arrived in the reception to find Lambert behind the counter, his face furiously creased in concentration.

Scott leaned over the counter to see what he was working on. It appeared he was doing some mathematics.

"Tim said you had Katherine on the phone." Scott said, a little impatiently.

Lambert looked up from his paper work. "We did." he answered. "But we lost reception again."

He nodded to the phone on the side. "I'm sure she'll try again."

Scott silently cursed and looked at his watch. It had just gone eleven.

"How long until we get there?" he asked.

Lambert checked his watch, and answered. "I spoke to Dunn a little while ago. We should be there in just over an hour."

Time's running out, thought Scott. He needed to speak to Katherine. He had started to form clearer suspicions now, but motive was only one part. He was still going to need more definite proof.

As Lambert went back to his work, Scott asked absently, "What are you working on?"

He started tapping numbers into the computer and said, "I'm just working out everyone's bills. Under the circumstances, I'm obviously not charging the Jordans or the Kennedys. Do you think I should charge others for their room service?"

Scott replied, "I think under the circumstances, this might be one trip where room service is on the house."

Lambert now looked slightly embarrassed for asking.

"Yes." he said, "You're probably right."

Scott looked over Lambert's shoulder and noticed something that he hadn't paid attention to before. Behind the reception counter, mounted on the wall was a map of North America.

Scott moved round the counter to look at it more closely. As he got closer, he saw small red light bulbs mounted in the map, in a rough line across the United States, the lit ones stopping in Colorado.

"What are these?" asked Scott, pointing to the map.

Lambert turned around and said, "Oh, those lights represent our company's outhouses along the route of the track. There's an electrical marker on the track that makes each light turn red as the train passes it. It's a nice way to see our progress. Unfortunately, it doesn't appear to have come back online since the train got back up and running."

Scott looked at the last lit bulb and a thought occurred to him.

It was then that the phone on the counter next to Lambert started ringing, making them both jump. They both looked at it for a second before Scott ran forward and picked it up.

"Hello."

"Scott? It's Katherine."

"Thank God, the line's still not very good."

Scott moved to try and improve the crackling and started to head to his room. This was a conversation where he would need privacy.

"Katherine, please tell me you've got something."

"Oh, believe me I have." she said, her voice sounding urgent. "I have plenty, but I hope you might be able to make more sense of it than I do."

"Hit me."

"Firstly, I had a hunch of my own on how someone could know how to sabotage the train. Did you know that the architectural plans for the Trans-Oceanic Express are at the West Virginia Railroad museum? They're not on general display, so you have to sign a register to see them. Not many people know they're there. There was only one entry in the last month. A Phillip McGuiness."

When Katherine said the name of the person, Scott had a flash of recognition.

"Does that name mean something to you?" Katherine asked.

"Yes. I think it does." said Scott, getting to the door to his suite and letting himself in.

"What else do you have?"

"I was able to check Clarissa and Mark's will. Neither had changed them since they married. They also had a pre-nuptial agreement. I don't think there would have been any financial gain from her death from Mark or Amy. I also spoke to a Gareth Lynch, Harry's Broadside's lawyer. He told me that he hasn't had any correspondence with Harry for over a year. And he said he certainly didn't send him a ticket for the Trans-Oceanic Express. That's not all though. You have a lot to thank me for Scott. I had to agree to a drink with Mathew for this! But I think you'll be glad I did. Without his level of clearance on this...."

"What is it Katherine?"

"Are you aware there is someone on that train going by an alias?"

"What!"

"I'll get to that. First, you were right about thinking you were missing something about the Kennedys......"

Ten minutes later, Scott was sat on his bed, the information Katherine had just given him numbing him slightly. Now he knew everything, he remembered an observation he had completely overlooked.

"That conversation when I saw her at his door. Of course!" Scott murmured to himself, forgetting Katherine was still on the phone.

"What are you going to do?" her voice sounding tense, breaking his thought.

Scott took his time answering, "I'm going to settle this before we get to Los Angeles."

"Are you sure that's wise?" asked Katherine nervously.

"I have to. I want to be able to sort this before anyone else gets involved. Detective Seymour is here. He has the authority to arrest, and if what you say is true, I don't want the chance of escape, that will be harder on board a moving train."

"Ok. Do you need me to do anything else?"

"Yes." Scott replied, after a moment, "I need you to find one more thing out for me. There was a murder at the Harvard campus a couple of years back of a girl called Emma Jones. Find out who was convicted."

"Will do."

"Katherine?"

"Yes?"

"Be quick."

Thousands of miles away, Katherine put down the phone and looked at her scribbled notes. Where to start? It was then that Colette, one of the receptionists for D.R.I, knocked on her door and walked in. She was holding a manila envelope.

"Katherine." She said, "The courier just dropped this off."

Katherine thanked her and ripped open the envelope. She pulled out a folder and saw that it was the file on Daphne Pennington's second husband. Katherine's eyes widened when she saw the title of the report.

Daphne Pennington's husband had been murdered very gruesomely.

Scott walked out of his room in a daze, still slightly overwhelmed at the picture slowly falling into place for him. He was in such a mind of his own that he walked straight into Tim.

"Hey." said Tim, stopping quickly.

Scott apologised, "Sorry. I was thinking."

He then looked at Tim properly and saw that he looked shaken.

"What is it?" Scott asked.

"I think you need to go talk to Jessica. She's been withholding evidence, so to speak."

"What do you mean?"

"An eyewitness account. Hers."

"Of what?"

"Of who she's saying killed Harry Broadside."

"What! Who?" asked Scott in disbelief.

"She didn't tell me." Tim answered. "But we had a talk. And she said she would talk to you."

Scott looked stunned. He nodded and said, "Ok. Where is she?"

"She's waiting for you on the balcony."

Scott went to pass Tim when he heard Thomas's voice travelling up the corridor.

"Mr Blacklock. I don't appreciate you walking off with my phone!"

Thomas walked up to them, holding a file under his arm.

He held his hand out expectantly. Scott replied firmly, "I just have to wait for one more phone call. What's that?"

Thomas pulled the folder out from under his arm. "This is my report I've been writing up. I thought you might want to counter sign it."

"No."

"No?" asked Thomas surprised.

"No, because your report does not reflect what happened here. I need you and Lambert to gather everybody in the bar in ten minutes."

Thomas's jaw dropped. "What! Why?"

Scott answered calmly, "I'm going to explain what happened."

"You're....you're what?!"

Thomas's words of shock were matched in Tim's face.

Scott continued, "Yes. Detective Seymour, are you carrying a firearm?"

Thomas answered nervously, "Yes. Why?"

"Good. Make sure you have it on you in the bar. And do you have handcuffs?"

"I have one pair."

"Not enough. Get Bradley to bring some rope, or tape, whatever he can."

As Scott went to turn away, Thomas said angrily, "This is ridiculous! I don't know what you're playing at, but I don't like it! The case is solved."

"No it isn't!" said Scott angrily. "Your report hasn't been able to explain the exact location of the diamond! And your belief that Harry Broadside was responsible for everything is ill advised. Shall I tell you the other important elements that are crucial? How about the nature of the letters to Clarissa? Or the actual reason Harry Broadside happened to be on this train? Or the timing of the sabotage? There are also the other factors of the missing martini glasses, the importance of room service duty and the connection of two men to this whole story. Phillip McGuiness and Walteau Lenoir. Believe me, you'll want to listen to what I have to say. Ten minutes, everyone in the bar."

Thomas was baffled but looked like he was going to be sick, the naive young detective showing through again. He wanted to argue further, but secretly had been grateful for Scott's presence throughout the last two days. He felt that he at least owed listening to him. He finally nodded his head and said, "Everybody?"

"Well you'd better leave the drivers driving the train." replied Scott with a smile.

Thomas nodded again, turned and walked back the way he had come.

Scott watched him go, and then looked at Tim.

Tim was leant against the wall, looking pale and shocked at the conversation.

Scott's eyes met Tim's and he said, "See you in ten minutes." before he walked off to meet Jessica.

Scott encountered nobody on the way to the balcony, except the view of the helicopters as he walked through the glaring observation carriage. He walked through the bar and stopped at the booth where he had fallen asleep two nights before. Examining the booth confirmed his suspicions. He nodded, and moved on.

He walked out onto the balcony to see Jessica stood where he had left her.

She turned and smiled. She looked like she'd been crying and Scott had never seen her look so vulnerable.

She offered him a cigarette. "One last cigarette with your smoking partner before the end of the journey?"

Scott leaned forward and took one from her packet. She lit it for him and he leaned against the railing as he took a drag.

Scott inhaled and then coughed. "You see, this is why I stick to Mason lights. These are so much stronger."

"You're just a pussy." said Jessica as she lit her own cigarette.

"You know, these ones will kill you, the amount you smoke!"

Jessica looked out. "I'm sure I'll die of something more exciting than cancer sticks!"

The sound of the helicopters suddenly lessened as five of the nine veered off to the right and flew out of sight.

Scott and Jessica both looked up.

"Those are the television crews leaving. The police must have been able to get an order to restrict the airspace around the train."

"It's more likely that they're just getting ahead to have a good spot on the ground." replied Jessica sardonically.

"Spoken like a pro." said Scott, turning to look at her. "So, Tim tells me you have information for me."

"Yes. I know that Harry Broadside didn't kill himself. I know who did."

"But you used your little satellite phone there to report that Harry Broadside killed himself after killing Clarissa?!"

Jessica took a drag on her cigarette. "No, I reported that that was the policeman's conclusion of what had happened."

"Why, so you could blackmail the person you saw last night?" asked Scott.

Jessica looked guilty. "I did think that for a moment, but then I realised that it would be much better for my career to blow open a whole police incompetence story."

"But you haven't yet. And you won't be able to, because all it will do is entangle you in a murder enquiry that's supposedly closed. It will only be your word against theirs. And that might not be quite so good for your career."

Jessica looked like Scott had just stated the obvious. She said, "Well, I soon realized that they'd question why I hadn't mentioned it earlier, which is why I'm talking to you."

Scott asked, "I don't mean to sound rude, but this is you we're talking about, which brings me back to the question. Why haven't you blackmailed this person?"

Jessica said sadly, "To be honest with you, it was what I had decided to do. But Tim said some things to me today. I don't know, I guess they just made me think. I guess I just felt it was due time for me to do a good deed."

"Why didn't you tell Tim this information?" asked Scott.

Jessica looked at him, "You piss me off less than Tim! Do you want to know what I know or not?"

"Go on."

Jessica pulled her satellite phone out and flipped it open to show a small screen.

She said smugly, "Perhaps it will be easier if you watch this. Not exactly my word against theirs!"

Jessica tapped a button and the screen lit up. The picture showed a wonky view of Jessica's room before the view straightened and Jessica entered the picture to sit on her bed. Scott noticed how she had altered the light in her room to make it more flattering. Jessica composed herself on the bed before beginning,

"Good evening viewers, this is Jessica Rae on Jessica's secret diaries. I'm currently sat in my suite on the Trans-Oceanic Express, or what is now being called the Train of Death after the shocking deaths of Gerry Kennedy and Clarissa Jordan. Now, I can tell you my eyewitness accounts of everything that has...."

Jessica stopped speaking at the sound of smashing glass. Scott watched Jessica's shocked face and noticed how much louder the sound was on the recording.

At the sound of Harry's body banging against the side of the train, Scott saw Jessica quickly leaping into action, before the screen went jerky again and the view dipped down to the carpet.

After several seconds, Scott heard a door opening and the camera darted around giving a view of the corridor. Jessica had evidently led on the floor to peer out of the door as the camera lens was at ground level. After a second, a figure pulled out of Harry's room and ran in the other direction.

Scott didn't need to watch it again to recognise who the person was. He took a deep breath.

Jessica pressed stop and the screen went dark.

She looked up at Scott and asked, "Are you surprised?"

Scott didn't say anything. Even though he couldn't quite believe it, the video had confirmed his suspicions.

"I think I get what happened. It makes sense to me!" asked Jessica.

The phone in Scott's hand started to ring.

"Thank you Jessica, if you'd like to go and take a seat in the bar. Everyone else will be joining shortly."

"Why? What's happening?"

"Just wait in the bar, and keep that phone close to hand."

Jessica hesitated, then flicked her cigarette butt and walked in, as Scott answered the phone.

"Katherine?"

"Scott. I found it."

"What?" asked Scott bewildered.

"Emma Jones. The girl who was murdered at Harvard? I got it for you, the name of the campus murderer."

"Is it the name I think it is?"

"Yes! Phillip McGuiness! How did you know?! Is this making any sense to you? I don't get how this person is connected to your situation at all!"

"I'll tell you all about it really soon, thank you Katherine. You're an angel. And I never would have even started to make sense of this if you hadn't told me about Golic."

"Golic?" Katherine asked.

"Yes. How his death was completely unconnected to the Stoltzkin case. The same thing with Gerry Kennedy's death has happened here. It made me start looking at things more clearly. So thank you."

"My pleasure Scott. It's not the only thing that's been unconnected. I found out the details about Daphne Pennington's husband. It was road rage that turned nasty and he ended up getting stabbed. But I don't think she was connected to it. She wasn't even in the country when it happened. Ah, Shit!"

"What?!" said Scott, suddenly alarmed.

"Oh, it's nothing." replied Katherine. "I just broke another nail on this damn desk drawer!"

Scott smiled, "I've been saying you should get someone in to fix that for ages!"

Scott thought about the information he'd just heard, then noticed his watch and said, "Thanks again Katherine. I'd better get going. I'll speak to you at the station."

"You take care."

Scott hung up, and let the phone drop to his side.

He stood in the sunshine for several more minutes, preparing his thoughts. He felt confident in his theories, but there was still little evidence to back them up.

And then it hit him. Katherine's broken nail. Why hadn't he thought of it earlier?

He turned quickly and left the balcony. He paced through the bar and headed down the train. His destination: the refrigerator.

As he made his way through the corridors, he started to pass passengers on their way to the bar.

Most of them gave him an odd look but he avoided all of them.

That was until he arrived at the reception where Thomas and Lambert were standing.

Thomas looked at him, "What are you doing here? I thought you wanted everyone in the bar?"

"I do." said Scott quickly, turning to Lambert. "Lambert, I need to borrow your master key."

Lambert didn't question him and handed it over.

Thomas however, didn't look happy. He asked, "What are you doing?"

"I'll explain all shortly. Just make sure everyone's in the bar. I'll be along in a few minutes."

Scott didn't give them a chance to respond as he walked away into the lounge.

He passed Rosalie, Bradley and Andreas as he was going through the dining carriage. As Bradley passed him, Scott said, "One moment Bradley. Could I ask you one last question?"

Bradley stopped and nodded cautiously.

Scott waited for Andreas and Rosalie to leave before asking, "On the night of Clarissa's murder, when you were returning from her room. You said that you spotted Anthony Stuart looking out into the corridor?"

"Yes." said Bradley nervously.

"Do you know if he was alone in the room?"

Bradley tilted his head in thought. "He had pretty much closed the door by the time I walked past, but I think I remember voices."

Scott nodded. "Thank you Bradley. That's all."

Bradley nodded as he watched Scott head on to the kitchen.

Aware of the time, Scott hurried to Andreas's room to pick up the refrigerator key, a room that could not be unlocked by Lambert's master key. He also stopped by Thomas's room and picked up some gloves, a pen knife and an evidence bag. This is a long shot, he thought as he made his way to the refrigerator.

Katherine's broken nail had made him think of Clarissa. Even if she had let someone into her room, there should have been some signs of a struggle on Clarissa's body. And although they had inspected the bruising around her neck, they had not checked her fingernails.

Standing there alone, between the sheeted bodies, Scott tried to ignore his discomfort. Even covered in sheets, Clarissa's body was easy to determine, being so much smaller than the others.

Scott snapped on the gloves and removed the sheet next to her hand. He crouched down and inspected the fingers closely. He felt a pang of disappointment as the first hand showed clean nails. He moved over to the other side and inspected the other. What he found there exhilarated and repulsed him in the same instant. Beneath three of her fingernails were distinct pieces of torn human skin.

Scott stood up, vindicated by yet more physical evidence.

Scott looked at what was in front of him and smiled, thinking of a certain passenger's change in attire over the journey. He had just found the final piece of the puzzle. On the way back to the bar, he would use Lambert's master key one last time and felt sure that he would then have all the evidence he needed.

Unlocked

"The Trans-Oceanic Express now has just half an hour before it pulls into Los Angeles' Union Station, where the L.A.P.D, the F.B.I and over a hundred journalists have gathered, waiting to hear the full unbelievable story from the occupants of the train. The cordon for the public, a crowd well into the thousands has been pushed back to one block in every direction of Union Station.

For those of you just joining us, Clarissa Jordan, international star and actress has been murdered aboard the Trans-Oceanic Express by her estranged ex-husband Henry Broadside who has since taken his own life. Earlier in the journey, media mogul, Gerry Kennedy died from heart problems. Gerry Kennedy and Clarissa Jordan had worked together for many years. This is now a double tragedy for Hollywood; however the details are still uncertain. And we won't know the full story until the train arrives in L.A. I'm just hearing news of a special report coming through, so please stay with us. This is Eleanor Lane for S.C.N, bringing you news twenty four hours a day. We'll see you after this commercial break........"

Scott walked into the bar from the observation carriage with his heart beating much faster than usual. He was greeted by thirteen pairs of eyes looking at him expectantly.

Lambert had moved some chairs to create a slight semi-circle. For some strange reason, everyone seemed to have slightly dressed up for the occasion. All of the men were wearing ties, with Anthony wearing a rather odd cravat.

Mark and Amy Jordan sat on a settee on one side, Anthony and Caroline on the opposite one. Tim, Daphne, Avril and Jessica sat on individual chairs in between them.

Lambert stood with Bradley, Rosalie and Andreas by the bar. Thomas was stood next to one of the far booths. Scott slowly walked over to Thomas and motioned for him to start the recorder he had brought with him.

As Thomas pressed record, Scott began,

"Thank you all for arriving so quickly. I appreciate your time. I've asked you to join me as I feel it's time things were explained. Mr Jordan, some of what is about to be said may not be pleasant, but I think you should listen to it. I would like to start from the beginning if I may. Now as you all know, I work for Zirconia Insurance and I was on this train to watch Clarissa Jordan, the reason being that she had received threats in the last month. Letters that indicated something would be taken from her. We assumed this to be her diamond. Sadly, we did not realise this would mean her life. These letters...."

"But we already know about these letters!" interrupted Daphne. "I thought Harry Broadside sent them!"

Scott didn't appreciate the interruption but didn't show it. "Yes, but did he? There have been several clever mis-directions on board this train. And the reason I have gathered you all here is because Harry Broadside did not kill Clarissa. His death was not a suicide, just one of the mis-directions. He was also murdered."

Caroline gasped, and several of the other passengers looked shocked.

Scott began to move slowly around the group. He said, "Now as I was looking at a motive for all this, several names evidently came to the forefront."

He turned to Caroline, "Mrs Stuart. You had a motive in that you were evidently threatened by Clarissa's advances on your husband."

"Yes, but I..."

Scott didn't wait to listen to her as he continued. "Avril. You and Gerry were obviously on this train to win Clarissa back into your company, and were both evidently bitter at the trouble she had caused you and that your futures depended on her. Amy. You and your step mother had a very acrimonious relationship and you were also a good candidate. Mr Jordan, you were not ruled out as a suspect. You and your wife clearly had issues over her loyalty to you. Jessica Rae, you could have concocted this whole scenario to further your career."

Scott waved his hand, "And as for the rest of you, well, the absence of the diamond strongly indicated that the likely motive for this murder was theft. Ms Pennington, Mr Stuart, you both could have been guilty of greed as a motive. So, you see, it wasn't an easy job. But then there was Harry Broadside, the obvious choice. A man so obsessed with Clarissa that he would follow her to try and win her back, even though she had re-married. And we all know that murders of passion are common. On top of that he was bankrupt and probably desperate for money. But this was the problem. It was all too convenient for me, especially after his 'suicide'."

He moved back to the centre of the room and continued, "So, let's go back to the night in question. The night Clarissa was murdered and the train was sabotaged and let's look at people's alibis and motives. Gerry Kennedy's death had obviously exonerated him. Avril was practically comatose all night, so I found it very unlikely that she would have been able to commit the murder."

He paused, "I had been trying to pick off suspects in that logical order until I realised that the clues in Clarissa's room were enough to shortlist the number of suspects.

Clarissa was found dead on her bed, with her nightgown on, and had evidently been entertaining somebody. I didn't imagine Clarissa had been having late night drinks with any of the women on the train, so this reduced my list of likely suspects to four.

Mark Jordan. You were an obvious suspect. As much as you may try to deny it, you did have a problem with your wife's flirting and suspected infidelity. And it made sense that you would have done it. You were right next door after all. But then I remembered your demeanour at cards before you went to bed, and how heavily you were asleep the following morning. I have a good inclination that you may have been drugged that evening because you were right next door and the murderer could not take the chance of you waking. If this was true, it took you out of the equation, and in doing so also removed Harry Broadside. I had thought Harry was the culprit at first, but if Mark Jordan was drugged, that would mean that this crime was premeditated. And if Harry had been capable of the deed, I could only have seen him doing it out of a jealous rage. This brings us back to the sabotaging of the train, something I never believed Harry Broadside had anything to do with. I don't mean to belittle him, but he did not seem like the kind of man who would have had the forethought to commit such a clever crime."

Scott walked over to the bar. "This left me with only two people. One of whom actually left evidence in the room."

He turned to Bradley, "Bradley, you visited Clarissa's room that night. She rang for room service and asked for two martinis. You took them to her and she invited you in to drink with her. Isn't that right?"

Bradley had gone white, and nodded quickly, aware of Mark Jordan's eyes boring into him.

"You told us that she flirted with you and you panicked. You ran out of the room, dropping your cigarettes in the process. But more importantly, you said that you forgot to pick up the empty martini glasses?"

"They weren't empty." Bradley replied. "Neither of us had touched them before I left."

"Which is interesting" said Scott, "As when myself and Mr Lambert arrived there in the morning, they were gone, with nothing left but ring marks. This made me think that Clarissa had had another visitor after you left. And who would she share a drink with at that time in the morning? Her husband? He was asleep. Harry Broadside? Unlikely."

He turned to face the rest of the passengers and said, "No. I believe that person was Anthony Stuart."

There were mixed reactions around the room. Thomas, to Scott's left, had looked like his knees buckled. Mark's face was full of fury, while Daphne and Avril's eyes were wide open. Caroline looked mortified.

However, Anthony stared up at Scott and gave his usual wide grin, revealing too many of his teeth.

"You believe that person to be me, Mr Blacklock?" he asked casually.

Scott moved closer. "Yes I do Mr Stuart. I believe that the events on this train were carefully orchestrated by you, for the purpose of stealing Clarissa's Warwick diamond. I believe that you made to seduce Clarissa, you then sabotaged the train, murdered her, and stole her diamond. All the while, setting up Harry Broadside to be your patsy as it were."

Anthony laughed. A hollow laugh. "So, you think I did all this, and then what? Last night, I sneaked into Harry's room and chucked him out of the window! If you remember correctly, I was playing cards with you at the time Mr Broadside exited the train!"

Several of the other passengers looked uncertainly at Scott. He folded his arms and said,

"Yes, I'm well aware of that fact Mr Stuart. I think that you may have made a good point to be in my company at the time of Mr Broadside's murder. I had inadvertently been witness to two of your attempts at seducing Clarissa and you knew that I was suspicious of you. But this has been a double act all along, hasn't it? You had your accomplice do it, so you could have the perfect alibi for Harry's murder. You even slowed us down on the way to Harry's room to give them time to escape. Your stumble was not bad enough for the amount of pain you seemed to be in."

"His accomplice?" said Thomas unbelievably.

"Yes," replied Scott. "His wife, Caroline."

"What!" shouted Anthony. "This is ridiculous!"

He looked around at the rest of the room. "Are the rest of you believing this?"

The faces of the others looked at him questioningly, not sure if Scott could be right or not.

"Let me explain myself fully." said Scott. "This story actually starts a year and a half ago in Boston. With the murder of Emma Jones."

"Emma Jones? Who the hell is Emma Jones?" said Daphne loudly, although Amy was looking at Scott in surprise.

"Emma Jones was a student at the Harvard campus who was murdered the November before last. She was found dead in her dorm room, the day after she emptied her savings account of almost a million dollars, a million dollars that was never found. Now I vaguely remembered the story when it happened. But it was only when Amy told me about it on Saturday afternoon, and told me that there were rumours of Emma Jones possibly having a secret affair with a lecturer, that I began to make connections. An affair with a lecturer. Who was a lecturer from Harvard on this train? Anthony Stuart. And who was a woman with a lot of money? Clarissa Jordan. I knew that a janitor on the campus had been convicted for the murder of this Emma Jones, but I couldn't for the life of me remember the name.

So I got my partner to find it out for me. And it's a name that is now twice linked to this train."

"What was the name?" asked Amy.

"The man arrested for Emma Jones's murder was a Mr Phillip McGuiness. When my partner told me the name, the story came back to me. He was reportedly a simple fellow who had been madly in love with Emma Jones. His fingerprints were found in her room and it was deemed that he killed her out of a jealous rage."

He paused for a second, before saying, "Is anyone else seeing a pattern here?"

"What is this?" said Anthony angrily, putting an arm around his wife.

"This was your first murder Mr Stuart. You were the lecturer that Emma Jones had an affair with. I believe that you seduced her, knowing that she was wealthy and then persuaded her to withdraw her savings. For what? Maybe you promised her to run away together. From what I understand, she wasn't a very popular girl and the attention of a handsome man probably made it very hard for her to say no. I believe that you then set the janitor Phillip McGuiness up to take the fall for you."

"This is preposterous!" cried Anthony.

Scott continued. "I had my partner do extensive background checks of everybody on board. Caroline, you told me that you used to work in a bar? And that was how you two met?"

"Yes." said Caroline quietly.

"What you didn't tell me though is that you worked in a bar part-time until just over a year ago, isn't that right?"

"Yes."

"You worked at Fandangos, didn't you? And when Harry Broadside started working there, you told your husband and you started to plan this, didn't you?"

"What!" said Caroline.

"My guess is that after Anthony got away with the first murder, his greed took over, and he wanted a bigger challenge. You saw Harry

Broadside's connection with Clarissa Jordan and immediately put your plan into action. Caroline, you left your job so that Harry wouldn't know who you were and then you started to ensnare him. I expect you've spent this last year tracking Clarissa, looking for an opportunity. And when this one came up, you sent Harry Broadside a bogus letter from his lawyer to get him on board the train. You knew that he was still obsessed with Clarissa and would jump at the chance.

You then started sending the letters to Clarissa, to build the case up against Harry. Extra evidence that you knew would be found in his room, which you yourself put there Caroline."

"Where are you getting this all from?" asked Anthony.

"I'm getting this from evidence. I asked my partner to check Harry Broadside's actions before he got on the Express. It made for interesting reading. Harry Broadside flew into New York last Friday from Boston. However, he missed the flight he was supposed to get, and caught the next one. I thought it was unusual that he was able to get a ticket on the next flight at short notice, when I remembered Caroline saying to me they had been on the same flight on the way down."

"Yes, so?" replied Caroline petulantly.

"You slipped up Caroline. On Sunday afternoon you said you were unaware of Harry's connection to Clarissa, and yet this morning you told me that she was all he talked about on the flight to New York. I believe you were on the same plane, because you were making sure that he would get to New York. Last night, when I was in Harry's room, I found his plane ticket.

He had had to change the name on his ticket at the last moment. The original name on the ticket was one Phillip McGuiness. Harry Broadside was apparently notorious for never being on time. I myself was witness to the fact that he almost missed this train from Grand Central. I believe that you booked yourselves on the flight after Harry to ensure that he made it to New York. You even went so far as to have a spare ticket on you, in case he missed his flight. It was vital for you that he was on board, which is why you purchased a third ticket under the name Phillip McGuiness."

Daphne gasped in recognition.

Scott carried on, "I'll admit it was a nice little in joke for you, using your previous scapegoat's name. But it was a stupid one, as it's led to you being revealed."

"There must be thousands of people called Phillip McGuiness! It means nothing!" said Anthony, looking a little shaken now.

"Yes, but you were stupid enough to use it twice." said Scott coolly.

"What do you mean?" asked Lambert.

"The architectural plans for this train are on display at the West Virginia Railroad museum. They're not on general display so you have to sign in to look at them. Only one person has looked at them in the last month, a Mr Phillip McGuiness."

"What does that mean?" asked Avril, looking a bit confused.

"It means that Anthony Stuart used that name again to sign in and study the architectural plans for the train, which is how he knew where and how to sabotage the train. You shouldn't have revealed that you studied electronics Mr Stuart."

Anthony's face went red.

"I must say," said Scott. "It was an admirable ploy. You started your act from the very beginning. Clarissa generally went for confident cocky men, and you knew this."

"If all this is true then Mr Blacklock," said Anthony snidely, "What did we do with the diamond?"

Everyone in the bar turned to look at Scott.

"I'm getting to that." Scott answered calmly. "Back to the night of Clarissa's murder, Gerry's death had taken everybody by surprise, and I'm sure you questioned whether you should go through with your plan. However, I think that you probably felt too many pieces were in place, so I suspect that during our card game, Anthony drugged Mark Jordan's drink. Now let's move ahead to later in the evening. After Mark had left for bed, Anthony, you walked Clarissa to her room. You then set up the seduction scene with Clarissa, to which I overheard. However, when she invited you in, you knew that it was still too early and that there were still too many people awake."

"This is ridiculous!" said Anthony.

"You can keep saying that Mr Stuart, but the more I explain it, the less ridiculous it becomes. It was roughly midnight when you left

Clarissa. From her room, you then went to the reception carriage, where you accosted Mr Lambert, pulled him into his office, and set about destroying the computers and workstation. At this time, rebuffed by you, Clarissa had ordered room service and Bradley had made his way to her room. And then there was an event that stumped me. About twenty minutes after that there was a room service call made to the kitchen from Daphne Pennington's suite. Mr Lambert and I had left Daphne in Avril's room and she had told me that she didn't leave all night. Now Daphne could very well have been lying, something I wasn't sure about."

As Scott glanced over at Daphne, he noticed that she looked quite pleased at inadvertently being part of the plot.

"But then this morning at breakfast, Daphne mentioned to me that she had lost one of her key cards. It took me a while to realise that she hadn't lost one, she'd given one to me in order to get sleeping pills from her room for Mrs Kennedy. The last place I remember having it was at the bar, shortly after Lambert's speech about Gerry. And who sat down next to me just as I left the bar? Caroline Stuart. It made sense that whoever sabotaged the Express would have had to make a bogus room service call, to get the one member of staff awake away from the front of the train. A fact Caroline had found out from Lambert earlier at dinner that evening."

He turned to Caroline, "I imagine you were probably going to make a call from your own room, but when you saw the key on the bar, just after Lambert had said Ms Pennington was spending the night with Mrs Kennedy, you saw an opportunity to further remove yourself from any unusual behaviour. So you took the key, to place the call from Daphne's room. Whether you had time to tell Anthony that no one had answered and that someone may still be in the kitchen, he took the risk anyway. It didn't matter though as Andreas Russelli, the staff member on duty was asleep anyway."

A few people looked over at Andreas, who shrugged unashamedly.

Scott followed on, "What is relevant is that you planted the virus in the circuit boards of the train, having studied the wiring and design from the plans. I imagine that examination of the device will show some kind of timer. How long did you give yourself? Ten Minutes?"

Anthony looked at the others. "Do you all seriously buy this bullshit?"

"Are you denying that you are probably the only one on this train with the knowledge and skills to use such a device?" asked Scott calmly.

Anthony went silent.

"So after setting the device, you then returned to your room where Caroline was waiting, having returned from Daphne's room. When Bradley saw you look out of your door as he returned from Clarissa's room, you weren't looking for Caroline. She was waiting behind you and you were seeing if the coast was clear, Bradley hearing your voices as you closed the door. You then both went to Clarissa's room. Caroline lurked in the shadows, while you waited for Clarissa to invite you in.

She did, and you spent a few minutes seducing her. Unfortunately Bradley had left the martinis and I assume Clarissa offered you a drink. This was presumably before you had put gloves on which is why you removed the evidence. After seducing her, you strangled and killed her."

The words were harsh and left a silence in the room.

Scott continued, "Now on to what they did with the diamond. Let me ask you all, why sabotage the train if not to escape?"

Lambert answered, "To prevent us from reaching or contacting anybody."

"But they could have destroyed all the communication equipment without stopping the train. It would have been a lot less conspicuous. There was a reason.

And this is where Caroline's part came in." said Scott. "Anthony located the diamond choker and passed it out to Caroline, along with the empty martini glasses I imagine.

While Anthony covered his tracks in Clarissa's room, Caroline ran to the end of the train."

He looked at her and said, "And this is where I imagine you were quite surprised to come across me."

Tim and Daphne looked at each other in confusion, and Avril said, "What?"

Scott pointed to the booth behind him. He said, "I fell asleep in that booth shortly after midnight on the night of the murder. When I awoke, the train had stopped and I found Caroline out on the balcony, crying. She told me that she and Anthony had had an argument and that she had come out for some fresh air. What I had yet to realise, was that while Anthony had finished in Clarissa's room and returned to his suite, Caroline had waited for the train to stop, jumped off, buried the diamond in the snow, and then got back on board. Why she didn't return to her room is probably because she heard me stirring and so concocted the poor desperate wife story for me, part of the act that she had been playing all along."

Avril asked in disbelief, "Wait a second; you're saying that she just left a multi million diamond in some snow on a Colorado mountain! What kind of a plan is that?!"

"A very good one." said Scott seriously. "They knew they couldn't hide it on the train. There's a map on the wall in the reception that showed them pretty much exactly which stretch of track they would be on. They could have waited for this whole affair to die down and collect it months later, in a place where it would be impossible to find, unless you knew where to look. When Detective Seymour and I looked for the diamond after Harry's death, Lambert had the idea to mark the track with paint, so we would know where we had stopped. It made me think that it would be an excellent way to mark where the diamond was hidden."

Lambert beamed proudly.

Scott ignored this and continued, "So I thought about when the train had stopped before, on the night of Clarissa's murder. And when I thought back to standing out on the balcony with Caroline, I remembered a large tree that had roots coming out of the ground. I think it was only the darkness that had prevented me from seeing that they weren't roots, but sticks, to pinpoint the location. So they could come and collect the diamond at a later date."

"My God!" said Daphne slowly.

"They knew the train would be searched, and that if someone did come to the conclusion it had been thrown from the train, there would be thousands of miles of track to comb. There were three factors that cinched it for me. One, that Caroline told me she didn't notice the train stop which I found hard to believe, standing outside. And second, that she didn't notice me on the way out. I accepted this at the time and then I realised....."

He moved past Thomas to the booth. He then proceeded to lie down on it. All the passengers looked over at him oddly, until they understood his point. Even led down in the booth, his lower legs were still clearly visible. Especially for someone having to walk past the booth to the balcony door.

Scott sat back up, and smiled. "Do you see my point? So why lie about it?"

As he walked back into the centre of the room, he said, "You saw me there Mrs Stuart. But given the weight of your circumstances, you had to risk it. The last thing, which I didn't pick up on at the time, was that your shoes and the bottom of your dress were damp. It wasn't just from being sat on the floor. It was because you had been out walking over the snow."

Caroline looked at him sourly, but said nothing.

Scott continued, "And now we move on to Harry. I don't know if you planned to kill Harry or just trap him, but I have a feeling the presence of myself and a police officer on board rattled you both slightly. Maybe you thought that Harry alive might leave too many questions open? Anyway, last night, Caroline sat with Harry for a short while. At that time I imagine that you used some of the sleeping pills you'd used on Mark. Rosalie told me that Harry had hardly drunk anything compared to his standards, yet when I spoke to him, his motor responses seemed off. Anthony then distracted me with cards, while Caroline went to his room and did the deed, leaving the note and the other "evidence"."

There was silence for several seconds before Anthony said, "Do you seriously think Caroline is capable of that?!"

"Yes I do. Even though he was a big man, effects from a drug could have incapacitated him. And when I had the unpleasant duty of cutting Harry down, it didn't catch with me where I had seen that medical gauze before. Then I realised that it had been in Caroline Stuart's first aid kit when we searched the train. The one she told me she never travelled without on our first afternoon."

"My God!" Daphne said again, louder this time.

Scott added, "And moving onto Harry's suicide note. The letters had been cut from one of the Express brochures, but I couldn't recall scissors and glue in his room when we had searched it the first time. And then I remembered where I had seen those items before, in Caroline's arts and crafts case. I stopped by your room on the way here to check that case. They weren't in there because they're in one of Detective Seymour's evidence bags, after he found them under Harry's bed."

Thomas moved forward. He spoke to Anthony and Caroline, "Is this true? Did you do all this?"

Anthony pulled his smile again, "Mr Seymour. It's a nice story. But the evidence is all circumstantial. You can't prove any of it."

Scott smiled back, "While you may have been careful, you haven't been careful enough. My partner is currently working with the Boston police force in your connection to the murder of Emma Jones. The money you had to afford the Express, from your "friend" who left you money last year when they died. I have a strong feeling that that money will be tied to Emma Jones. Then there is the evidence of the use of the name Phillip McGuiness and the medical gauze which is also now missing from Caroline's first aid kit……I could go on. Plus if the diamond is where I say it is, it's not going to look too good."

"That's still not enough and you know it!" snarled Anthony.

Scott's smile became bigger, as he finished, "Did I not mention that I have damning evidence on both of you?"

Anthony and Caroline looked at each other, uncertainty in their eyes for the first time.

Thomas looked at Scott. "What?"

Scott said, "Well the first being that I have video footage of Caroline Stuart leaving Harry Broadside's room at the time of his death."

He looked across the room and Jessica smiled smugly and stood up. She pulled out her satellite phone from her jacket pocket. She fiddled with a few buttons, before snapping it open, showing the screen to the majority of the room. She pressed play.

Everyone craned their necks to try and get a better look. The video began again with Jessica starting her report. There was a gasp from Daphne as everyone in the room heard the window smash again. There was a sound of annoyance from someone as the image went blurry. Thomas leaned right into Jessica's hand to see the final image of Caroline running away. His mouth opened as he looked over at Caroline. She couldn't see the screen clearly, but could tell that it was obviously her.

Jessica smiled, "Too bad I'm such an excellent reporter!"

She pointed at Caroline. "You're going down!"

"Thank you Jessica." said Scott in an annoyed tone. "Please sit down."

Jessica complied. Scott returned to look at Anthony and Caroline. They both looked beaten. But while Anthony's façade now showed one of fear and shock, Caroline looked angry.

She finally spoke.

"Mr Blacklock. I'm not going to lie to you anymore. You are correct in your assumptions."

"Caroline!" Anthony shouted at her desperately.

"No Anthony! For once I'm going to have my say!" she said, surprisingly fiercely.

She looked back to Scott and said, "You are right. But this has not been an act for me. You have no idea how I've felt about all of this."

"So tell us." said Scott.

Caroline was aware of Anthony watching her, but carried on with a surprising strength.

"I didn't know about the Emma Jones murder until the night after it happened."

"Caroline!" cried Anthony urgently, but she continued.

"Anthony suddenly told me what he had done. How he had seduced her and persuaded her to run away with him. Then he told me how he killed her and set up that janitor. He told me he had been planning it for months. I was sick. I couldn't believe he would do such a thing. I couldn't sleep, couldn't eat. I knew I should leave but I just couldn't. When he told me that it was because he was so bored with his life, and that this was the first time he had felt truly alive, I knew I would have to forgive him."

She started to cry, pulling a tissue from her pocket, unaware of the looks of astonishment from some of the others.

"I couldn't bear the thought of life without him. And I knew that he would leave me behind if I didn't share in his dreams. And then he came up with the Clarissa idea....."

Thomas stepped forward and said, "So you conspired with him, murdered an innocent human being, just because you loved you husband?"

"Yes..." Caroline said through the tears. "There were times when I wished I hadn't mentioned Harry to Anthony. But he became so obsessed with the idea. It was the only way to stay a part of his life. I love him so much."

Scott said, "I'm afraid love doesn't exclude you from your responsibility in this."

"I don't exclude myself." said Caroline.

Scott looked at her without remorse. He said, "You always have choices Caroline. I told you earlier that you can't be responsible for someone else's obsession. But you can if you join in with that obsession, like you did with your husband. You chose to live the life you were leading. Apart from giving Anthony an alibi at the card game, did you kill Harry Broadside to prove something to your husband? That you could do it? That you could be like him?"

The whole room waited in silence until Caroline answered.

"Yes. The plan hadn't been to kill Harry. I think Anthony guessed what I had done and stalled you. Since this whole thing started, I found myself trying to prove myself to Anthony. When we were doing surveillance on Harry, it was my idea to involve Gareth Lynch. But I never seemed to impress him. I found myself doing more daring things. It was my idea to use Daphne's keycard. When I saw you with it at the bar, you weren't even paying attention. It was so easy. I had thought that Anthony would have appreciated my cunning, but he barely acknowledged it. Instead he came back from the card game buzzing that he had managed to drug Mark Jordan's drink in front of you. After Clarissa's death, Anthony became worried about you two being on board, and that Harry had gotten so drunk that it made him a less likely suspect. For the first time, I saw that he was scared. Which is when I saw that I could fix it for him, what greater gift could a wife give? I didn't tell him what I was planning. Instead I made the note. I then slipped a sleeping pill in Harry's drink when I went to talk to him in the bar. I left shortly afterwards and waited in my room for five minutes. I just walked up to his door and knocked. He let me in after a few moments. I just said I needed to ask him something. I could tell that the pill was working. He was really out of it. And then I.... " She stopped herself, looking sick at the thought running through her head again.

Scott folded his arms. "You've looked like hell since Harry died. I get the feeling that's why you wanted to talk to me this morning, asking questions about Harry. Your husband evidently deals with guilt a lot better than you do Mrs Stuart."

Anthony chided, "I haven't confessed to anything! I don't know what Caroline's going on about!"

No one in the room seemed uncertain about whether he was telling the truth now.

"Really?" said Scott. "Then let's move on to my final piece of evidence."

As he said this, he pulled what appeared to be an empty evidence bag out of his pocket.

Several people leaned forward to try and get a look. Scott flattened the bag and held it up to the light for them.

He continued, "What this bag contains is torn skin removed from Clarissa Jordan's fingernails. I believe that this belongs to the killer, and that DNA testing will reveal that person to be Anthony Stuart."

"How's that?" retorted Anthony, his voice shaking.

Scott continued, "This skin evidently came from Clarissa putting up a struggle, which would mean that the killer should have a corresponding wound pattern."

He turned to Anthony. "Mr Stuart, you are a man who is obviously proud of his physique, particularly your chest. Your casual open shirts on this journey highlighted this. Yet since Clarissa's death, you have seemed conscious to cover up, right to your neck. Now why would that be? Could you be hiding scratch marks, I wonder?"

"You're reaching!" snarled Anthony.

Scott folded his arms and replied, "In that case, you'll have no objection to removing that cravat you're wearing?"

Anthony's face reddened, but he didn't move.

Caroline sighed and said, "Just let it go Anthony. It's over."

Anthony shot her a look of disgust.

"Why have you told us so much today Caroline?" asked Scott.

She looked up at him through bloodshot eyes, "I told you because I don't care anymore."

She added quietly. "I just wanted this life I was leading to be over. Now it will be."

Scott turned his head. "Detective, have you heard enough?"

Thomas said, a little uncertainly. "Yes. Anthony and Caroline Stuart, I am arresting you for the murders of Clarissa Jordan and Henry Broadside......"

As Thomas read them their rights, and handcuffed them together, Scott looked around the room and saw the stunned faces of the remaining passengers. All of them watched as Anthony and Caroline were arrested. Anthony didn't react when Scott leaned over and pulled his cravat down. It revealed three small scratch marks just above his collar bone.

Scott stood back up and rejoined Thomas, who asked Lambert, "Do you have a place where we can keep them?"

Scott put his hand up and said,

"Not quite just yet Thomas. I still need to tell you one more thing. How and why Gerry Kennedy was killed."

End of the line

"What!" said Avril Kennedy, half rising from her seat.

Scott looked over, not intending for his voice to carry further than Thomas and Lambert.

"Did you just say what I think you did?" said Avril, her voice in an odd high tone.

"That somebody killed Gerry!"

The rest of the passengers looked towards Scott in a mixture of awe and horror.

Scott looked at his feet for a second, before saying,

"Yes Mrs Kennedy. Please, sit back down. I have to warn you that what I am about to say will not be pleasant. But I'm sure you are someone who would like to know the whole truth."

Avril's shocked face nodded as she sat back down. She answered, "Yes. I would."

Scott looked around him and began, "If I'm completely honest with you all, Gerry's death never sat very comfortably with me. I was bothered by his sudden attack, and even more so after Clarissa's murder. Mrs Kennedy, knowing you and your husband's connection to Clarissa, I couldn't help but think that the two deaths were connected somehow. And this was the path I was taking, until I realised that not everything has to be connected. I was sure that I had missed something with you, and with Gerry's death, so I had my partner do some digging on you both.

My partner has an associate at the F.B.I and when she asked him to find out information about the people on the train, some very interesting facts came out."

Scott moved over to Thomas and whispered, "Did you bring your firearm with you?"

"Yes." Thomas stuttered, his face going white.

"Good." said Scott. He walked closer to the bar and said in a louder voice, pointing to one person in particular.

"Then I would like you to arrest Rosalie Gobetti."

Almost the whole carriage gasped in unison.

"What!" said Avril.

Thomas asked uncertainly over Scott's shoulder. "What do you mean?"

Rosalie, who had been standing unassumingly between Andreas and Bradley, looked at Scott, her face bewildered.

"Rosalie Gobetti is not who she claims to be. And like so many on this train, she also had an ulterior motive for being here."

Rosalie rolled her eyes at Scott.

He continued, "Rosalie. Or should I call you Rosa Cozzubo? How about Helena Dovsky? Or Tara Cavill? Or maybe Alice Hopkins? I could go on." said Scott, looking Rosalie straight in the eye.

"What is going on?" asked Lambert, flabbergasted.

"My partner's contact at the F.B.I told her that Rosalie Gobetti is very likely an alias for who the F.B.I knew until recently as Rosa Cozzubo. They had been working with their European counterparts as it was thought Rosa Cozzubo had entered the United States last month."

"Who the hell is Rosa Cozzubo?!" said Daphne.

"To put it simply, Rosa Cozzubo, if that is her real name, is a trained killer for hire. She was born in Italy, raised mainly in Russia. Her father was a KGB spy and is believed to have taught her all she knows. During the fall of the Soviet Union, she disappeared. After a particularly brutal murder in England five years ago involving an important Member of Parliament, M.I.5 have been trying to keep track of this woman, working collaboratively with agencies from nine different countries. It's been very hard. She covers her tracks well, changing name and country as often as we change clothes."

"What has all this got to do with Gerry?" asked Avril.

Scott turned to look at her. "Mrs Kennedy, you would not have known this, but your husband had become involved in their investigation."

"What? How?" she said, the words barely coming out of her mouth.

"Payments had been made from your husband's private account into a temporary one of a Ms Rosa Cozzubo. One for $500,000 in February this year. Then two more of the same in April and June."

"What for?" asked Avril.

Scott replied with a question. "Does the name Walteau Lenoir mean anything to you?"

Avril slumped in her seat. "Walt...."

"Who's Walteau Lenoir?" Amy blurted the question out.

"My brother." Avril said, her voice a whisper.

Scott continued, "Your brother who died earlier this year?"

"Yes."

"Your brother, Walteau Lenoir died suddenly and there was an inconclusive post-mortem report. Where did he die Mrs Kennedy?"

"Prague." She said.

"In what month?"

"February." Tears started to form in her eyes, seeing where Scott was heading.

Scott looked back at Rosalie, who was now looking very stony faced.

He said, "Which is where Rosa Cozzubo was based at the time. Right in the area of Prague that Walteau Lenoir used to frequent so much. When my partner told me all this, I immediately thought back to your personnel file. All the places you'd "worked" across the world. And then it all made sense to me, what wasn't adding up with Gerry Kennedy and why he was so agitated on the train. Even Ms Pennington had observed that he seemed fearful of something. I think it was always when he was around you. When I was told all this, I suddenly thought of how Gerry had reacted when you first offered him a drink at the champagne reception."

He looked back to Avril. "Mrs Kennedy, I'm sorry to say this to you. But I believe Gerry hired Rosalie Gobetti to kill your brother. Your inheritance saved you and your company financially in the short term and I believe Gerry was desperate enough to commit such a horrible act. But he hadn't counted on his assassin starting to blackmail him."

Turning to stare Rosalie in the face, he said, "You killed Walteau Lenoir. But you obviously wanted something more from Gerry. Was it to start blackmailing him? I think you got the job on this train to hunt him down and get more money from him. Holding down a job while you were staking out your victim was second nature to you. You're always clever. You plan ahead, holding down a job several weeks or months in advance to reduce suspicion. That was why I saw you so many times at the door to his room, so that you could threaten him in private. That's why I saw him shouting at you in his doorway on that first afternoon. You told me that it was because he didn't have enough champagne in his room. I think he was telling you he didn't have any more money for you. Your mere presence or verbal threats were clearly not working. This is why I believe, that when we were all sat at the dinner table on Sunday night, you brought the drinks in after dinner and poisoned him."

Rosalie said nothing for a moment, before smiling and saying, "That's a ridiculous story. Even compared to the one you've just told about the Stuarts over there."

Scott remained cool. He replied, "It may seem ridiculous to some of the people in this room, but then so did the Stuart story five minutes ago. And there are a whole bunch of law enforcement agencies waiting just a few miles down the track who will be convinced, just by seeing your face."

"And it's enough for me to be convinced." said Thomas, from behind Scott's shoulder, reaching for his holster.

Rosalie's reflexes were quick and feline. Before Thomas's hand had even gotten to his hip, Rosalie had lunged at Lambert stood near her. She grabbed him by the neck with one hand, the other disappearing into her apron for a second, before whipping out a small pistol and pointing it at Lambert's head.

Amy screamed as Scott and Thomas froze in front of Rosalie and Lambert.

"NOBODY MOVE!" screamed Rosalie.

As she moved into the centre of the room, she yelled, "Everybody! Hands on heads!"

Everyone complied. Scott thought quickly, he looked around for a solution.

He was stood slightly in front of Thomas, obscuring his line of shot. Trying to wrestle the gun from her was also out of the question as he was still several feet from Rosalie, and she had already shown extremely quick reflexes. He looked around for help from someone else. Lambert was clearly not in a position to do anything, and the only others close to her, Bradley and Andreas, had cowered behind the bar at the sight of the gun. As Scott finally placed his hands on his head, he moved slightly to the right, clearing himself from Thomas. Rosalie saw in a second what he was doing.

She looked at Thomas, who was still frozen in the same position, his hand on his gun.

"DROP THAT WEAPON RIGHT NOW! Put it down on the ground, or I will shoot. Don't think I won't kill this fat piece of shit!"

Lambert's face had gone red as Rosalie's arm choked him.

Thomas slowly removed the gun from his holster and placed it on the floor.

"Kick it down to the end of the carriage." shouted Rosalie tersely.

Thomas did as he was told and the gun skidded all the way to the door out to the balcony.

Keeping a tight hold on Lambert's neck, Rosalie slowly edged her way through the room to the door of the observation carriage.

Everyone turned to look at her, fear in all their eyes. All except Anthony Stuart, who seemed utterly bemused by the whole experience.

Rosalie looked at Scott. Her face was not the one that Scott had become accustomed to. She smiled, not in a nice way. "I congratulate you Mr Blacklock. You were almost correct. But you were wrong on two counts. I wasn't blackmailing Gerry Kennedy. He did hire me to kill Walteau Lenoir, which I did effortlessly by the way, but it was him that went back on the deal."

Scott could see pride in her eyes as she continued, "I'm very expensive. The contract was for 2.5 million. He still owed me two more payments, the tight fisted bastard! That was why I was on the train, to get the money I was duly owed. He was being very evasive."

"So you killed him?" said Scott, knowing that he probably shouldn't be speaking.

"That was point number two Mr Blacklock. I don't kill people I'm not hired to. It's unprofessional. If you must know, it was Mrs Kennedy here that killed him!"

"What!" cried Avril, mortified.

"My threats obviously weren't working. I had to do something to scare him. I planned to poison you." Rosalie said to Avril viciously, "That way it would shake him up, and he would know I was serious. The dose wouldn't have killed a healthy human being. But it was you who swapped your glass with him at the dinner table. His weak heart obviously couldn't handle the small dose."

Again the evil smile came back to her face. She added. "Sleep tight with that thought. Anyway, I'm going to be leaving now."

She started to back into the doorway, when she stopped and looked over at Caroline.

"Just have to say! Medical gauze around the neck! Nice work there missy!"

She made to move back, when a loud beep emitted through the room.

"What was that?" shouted Rosalie.

Everyone in the carriage, with their hands on their heads, tried to look around for the sound without moving too much. It would have looked comical if not for the seriousness of the situation. Then the sound came again. This time, it came more clearly from a specific individual.

Rosalie looked over at her, and Jessica Rae went red.

"What is that?" Rosalie asked.

Jessica slowly moved her hand, and Rosalie indicated for her to pull the object out of her pocket.

"Slowly" she said, as Jessica reached into her pocket and revealed the satellite phone.

Scott groaned as Rosalie asked, "Why is it beeping?"

Jessica said quietly, "The battery's running low as it's feeding a transmission. I have it on loudspeaker. Before Scott started, I got my office to run this whole conversation as a live report."

"What!" Thomas and Scott shouted simultaneously.

Jessica continued, "Every network picked it up. Practically the whole world is listening right now."

This time it was Jessica who smiled, her role in all the events giving her an invincible elated feeling. She said, "You won't be getting anywhere Ms Gobetti. And your career is over."

Rosalie took all this in and did nothing for a moment. Scott couldn't read her face at all, and was very troubled. Rosalie had positioned herself so that no one could easily get to her. She looked like she was weighing things up.

She leaned her head to one side and said, "Oh well. It won't be unprofessional to do this then."

Before anyone could react, Rosalie moved the gun away from Lambert's temple and fired across the room.

The shot caught Jessica in the chest and she flew backwards, dropping the satellite phone. There was a chorus of screams and everybody dived to the floor.

Scott looked up first, and looked in the direction of Jessica. She lay on the floor, barely moving. He saw blood in her mouth.

He looked to the door. In the panic, Rosalie had gone, having left Lambert lying slumped against the doorframe, struggling to breathe.

Scott leapt up, "Thomas! Come on!" he shouted as he ran for the door. Thomas collected his gun and followed Scott as they ran into the already empty observation carriage.

Tim and Daphne were the first to reach Jessica. They scrambled across the floor to her, and as Tim tried to prop her onto his lap, Daphne undid her jacket. Her breath caught, when opening the jacket revealed a large bloody smear across Jessica's chest.

"Where's she heading?" asked Thomas nervously as he hurried behind Scott, both of them half crouching as they ran past the Thistlewood Suites.

"To the engine." replied Scott.

They ran through the sleeping carriages and Scott realised that they had reached the outer suburbs of Los Angeles. If Rosalie managed to stop the train, she could easily escape into the city. Or she could be prepared to do worse, thought Scott as they arrived in the reception carriage.

As they entered the lounge, they were both startled to see Rosalie, stood in the doorframe to the dining carriage. She pointed the gun at them, and both were only seconds away from the two shots she fired, as they dived in either direction behind the furniture.

They waited for only a few moments before they heard her footsteps running away. Then Scott, followed reluctantly by Thomas jumped up and continued the chase.

Rosalie had run fast, and they didn't see any sign of her through the dining carriage, kitchen or the storage compartment. When they arrived at the staff carriage, they were confronted by the body of Stephenson, lying on his back in the middle of the corridor, a red bump on his forehead.

They jumped over his body to get to the door to the engine.

Scott arrived first and Thomas a second later to see Rosalie in the connector between the carriages, with a gun to Robert Dunn's head.

"Back away and shut the connecting door!" screamed Rosalie, a crazy look in her eye.

Scott said slowly and calmly, "Rosalie. We can end this the right way. Right now. There's no need for anyone else to get hurt."

Rosalie spoke now as if unhinged, "Are you talking about that bitch Jessica Rae? She deserved it. She may have blown my cover to most of the known world, but I will never be caught. I've been a trained assassin since I was thirteen. I know how to be evasive. I got out of the Soviet Union during the collapse so I can certainly escape a few lame ass American cops. Stop and turn back now. I will not be caught. You hear me! I never have and I never will!"

Her grip tightened on Dunn and she moved her finger onto the trigger.

Lambert lay crumpled where Rosalie had left him, now in a state of shock.

Avril too had not moved, slumped in her chair, drowning in her own tears.

Bradley and Andreas had both taken knives from the bar and watched over the Stuarts numbly. Mark Jordan placed a comforting arm around his daughter as she looked on at the trio on the floor.

Tim was comforting Jessica. A quick shake of the head from Daphne had told Tim what he had dreaded. She may not have been a doctor, but she knew a fatal gun shot when she saw one.

Jessica briefly opened her eyes, a thin trickle of blood falling down her cheek. Her voice was barely there, so Tim leaned closer as she spoke.

"I do one good thing and see what happens!"

As Tim looked at her, she managed a smile, and he smiled back.

"Hope I still make it into hell!"

Her eyelids fluttered and she lay still in his arms. Tim's tears fell onto her silent face as he hugged her tighter still.

The situation at the front of the train was no less tense as Scott and Thomas remained poised in the narrow vestibule between the train carriages. Rosalie grew tired of Scott's resistance and cocked the trigger against Dunn's forehead.

"Rosalie… Please…" Scott pleaded.

"Enough! Now, get on the other side of that door now. Or it will be your fault this man dies!"

Scott waited for a second longer before conceding. He and Thomas moved out of the connecting partition and stepped back into the staff carriage, the door sliding back closed behind them.

There was a square window in the door and Scott and Thomas peered through to see Rosalie asking Dunn something in his ear. The doors were airtight, so they couldn't hear what they were saying, but Dunn was indicating to a control panel on the door to the locomotive.

"What's she doing?" asked Scott.

"I think she's going to disconnect the engine from the train." replied Thomas.

Sure enough, Rosalie had positioned herself in the doorframe, the gun still pointing at Dunn's head as he knelt down to activate the control panel. He was there for several moments as a warning siren went off.

"What's that?" asked Scott.

"There shouldn't be any disconnections when the train is in motion."

Scott and Thomas whirled, as the voice had been Stephenson's. He was leaning against the corridor wall, holding his hand to his head.

"Can it be overridden?" asked Scott desperately.

His question was answered by the alarm turning off and the sound of a large whoosh in the connecting compartment, as the two carriages began to disconnect.

He looked through the window to see Dunn still on his knees looking up at Rosalie, the gun still pointed at his face.

She looked over to Scott and stared him straight in the eyes as she pulled the trigger.

Dunn's body fell through the widening gap between the carriages as Scott screamed through the window.

As Rosalie began to close the door to enter the departing locomotive, she blew Scott a kiss and waved goodbye.

Scott stared in disbelief as the locomotive pulled away from the rest of the train and he had the weird sensation of suddenly being at the front of the train, seeing the tracks below and in front of him.

The carriages started to slow down. "It's the automatic brakes on the carriages. They activate automatically if the locomotive disengages while in motion." Stephenson explained.

Scott pulled the door open to get a full view of the escaping engine. His heart fell at the view of the receding locomotive as it was about to vanish behind some trees. Suddenly he was almost knocked backward when it unmistakably erupted in a devastating explosion, followed by a wave of yellow flame. The sound was horrific and the ball of fire spewed fifty feet into the air. Thomas looked on incomprehensibly as Scott's feet gave way beneath him and he slipped to the floor, astounded by what had just happened. He watched the inferno in the distance, as if some meaning would come out of the fire.

Grand Terminal

"For those of you just joining us, I'm Eleanor Lane of S.C.N, and the main story of the moment is the incredible tale of the now branded "Train of Death.". The world renowned Trans-Oceanic Express travelling from New York to Los Angeles finished its journey in explosive devastation just an hour ago. As the train was making its way through East Los Angeles, the locomotive engine of the train disconnected, before exploding on the tracks several seconds later. No explanation for this has yet been given, and the area has been sealed off. In an exclusive live report from Jessica Rae, celebrity journalist, it was revealed that Harry Broadside was not the culprit of international star Clarissa Jordan's murder. Instead it seems a couple from Boston, Mr Anthony and Caroline Stuart, had planned a daring jewellery heist, implicating Mr Broadside in the process. And in the second shocking revelation, Hollywood producer Gerry Kennedy, who had also died during the journey, was actually murdered. The culprit was a killer he himself had hired, to assassinate his brother-in-law, in order to prevent his financial downfall.

It would seem that the person who revealed all of this was a Mr Scott Blacklock, an agent for Clarissa Jordan's insurance company Zirconia. At this time neither Zirconia nor Trans-Continent Inc. have released a statement. Oh....I'm just getting reports in......Oh my....It seems that there have been several more deaths.....Yes. I can now confirm that.... the reason Jessica Rae's report abruptly ended was....was because she was fatally shot, along with the Express's chief maintenance engineer, Mr Robert Dunn. This is shocking! While we wait for an update on that, we're going live to our reporter outside Union Station, Adele Buczek. Adele, can you tell us what's happening down there now?"

Scott stood in the striking vaulted atrium of Union Station, holding a cup of rapidly cooling coffee, in desperate need of a cigarette. He had been unable to escape outside as hundreds of journalists and onlookers had camped all around the station. The fact that the station resembled a Spanish church had made it look like a crazed religious mass in the streets outside. His stomach grumbled and he realised that he had hardly eaten all day. Traxx, the restaurant opposite from where he stood would have looked inviting, had it not been evacuated by the police. He looked around at the bustle of police and F.B.I agents as they ran through the room. The media had not been able to get inside and for that Scott was grateful.

The train had been stopped for less than two minutes before the police had arrived. Most of the last six hours had been a blur, the F.B.I coming on board, travelling down the remaining mile of the track to the station in separate F.B.I sedans. Then they had all immediately been questioned, away from the prying eyes of the media.

He looked across the vestibule to see Anthony and Caroline Stuart emerging from an office with several policemen around them. As they were escorted through the waiting room, Scott locked eyes with them both. Anthony met his glare with a defiant stare, while Caroline, who now practically looked like a ghost, caught him looking for a second before returning to look at the floor.

They left through a side door and Scott kept his eyes on the door long after it closed.

"I have to say. That was very impressive work!"

Scott jumped as Tim appeared right next to him. Tim smiled and said,

"Sorry! Didn't mean to scare you!"

Scott returned the smile and said, "I think I've had my quota of scares for this trip."

"Tell me about it."

Scott looked to the floor. He finally said what had been building up all afternoon.

"God Tim, I screwed up big time. I shouldn't have said what I thought. Two people are dead because of me."

Tim put his hand on Scott's shoulder. He said, "But what you thought was right. And because of you, the bad guys got caught. You weren't to know how psycho Rosalie would get."

"Yes, but I knew that she was a hired killer. They can hardly be the most complacent type of people." said Scott miserably.

Tim said gently, "Look, you ran this whole investigation because you were doing your job. Detective Seymour was doing it for the same reason. You could have left it until we arrived here. But anything could have happened. And either one of them might have gotten away or someone would have gotten to the diamond. It was Detective Seymour's job to handle Rosalie, not yours. And besides, I doubt anybody could handle Rosalie. She was a pretty nasty piece of work."

"She fooled me right up until the end." Scott said honestly.

"That's because she was very good at her job." Tim said. He finished with a smile, "But you're better at yours."

Scott leaned against the wall. He said thoughtfully, "I wonder what will become of Detective Seymour. I haven't seen him all afternoon. He was whisked away pretty quickly."

"In all honesty, I don't think he really deserved a badge." said Tim.

Scott replied, "I don't think it was ever what he really wanted to do." He smiled and said, "I hope he becomes an optician."

Tim looked at him oddly for a second, before they were both distracted by another office door opening. Out stepped Bradley Hawkins, Henry Stephenson and Andreas Russelli. They all looked tired, and the bump on Stephenson's head had turned into a colourful bruise. They were led through the atrium and Tim said with a grin, "Wonder if they'll be going back to work on the Express anytime soon?"

Scott gave him a look and he dropped the grin.

Out of the office where the remnants of the staff had emerged now came Mark and Amy Jordan with Daphne Pennington.

The three of them walked over to them, and there were the awkward smiles of people who had just been through a horrific ordeal. A collective group distraught by the events, yet glad to have made it through alive.

"Where's Avril?" asked Scott.

It was Daphne that answered.

"She got taken to the hospital. She was in severe shock. Lambert also went there. It appears he had a small heart attack. He's going to be fine though."

Suddenly there was a moment that hit all of them. Out of the thirteen at dinner two nights ago, these five were all that were left.

Mark broke the silence first.

"Well, we've been allowed to leave now. They're taking us to a secluded safe house."

It was then that Amy pulled Tim away from the others.

Mark looked back to Scott and said,

"I just wanted to thank you, for what you did. I'm glad I know the truth. A Detective just told me that the F.B.I found the diamond. It was on the section of track you said it would be. In their search they also found some pliers, gloves, a small shovel and a pair of martini glasses, along with the key to Ms Pennington's room and the Express's two long wave radios. The sticks from the trees you saw were apparently positioned into a cross."

Scott said dryly, "X marks the spot. Just like Lambert's idea."

Mark replied. "Exactly. Anyway, Thank you again. If anyone asks me to comment on your conduct, I shall say it was admirable."

They shook hands and Scott said, "Thank you. And Mr Jordan, I am sorry for your loss."

Mark nodded appreciatively.

"Well we're going to be heading off soon" said Amy as she sat Tim down on a bench.

"I just wanted to have a proper goodbye and to say no hard feelings. I'm really glad I met you, and I really had a nice time with you. I mean before....."

"Everyone started dying?!" said Tim, a small grin trying to emerge.

"I was going to say the awkward kiss thing, but yeah, that too obviously!" replied Amy, seeing Tim's grin and smirking herself.

She said, "So...keep in touch."

Tim wasn't sure if it was a question or a statement. So he went with the answer,

"Well, next time I'm in Boston I will definitely look you up. We can reminisce about the Express!"

At this Amy did giggle. "Stop it Tim. You're terrible!"

"I know. I'm sorry. I didn't mean to be insensitive about Clarissa." said Tim.

"I was thinking it was more insensitive to Jessica."

Tim looked at her and said, "Maybe that's just my way of dealing with things."

Amy looked back at him and said, "By making it a joke? Essentially running away from things?"

This point did strike a chord in Tim.

"Amy? Are you ready?"

The voice was Mark's as he waited a discreet distance away.

Amy looked back to Tim.

"I've got to go. But hey, I'll see you soon."

She kissed him quickly on the cheek and said, "Don't be a stranger."

She jumped off the bench and walked over to her father. Mark nodded to Tim as he put his arm around his daughter and walked away through the foyer. Tim watched them go and then pulled the three postcards he had written to Miranda out of his pocket. He flipped them over several times in his hands before standing up.

"I don't think I'll ever be able to take another vacation! How will anything top this?!" said Daphne to Scott as Tim rejoined them.

Scott replied, "You'll certainly have a lot to tell your sister."

Daphne said, almost with an annoyed tone, "That's the thing! She'll already know! She watches television twenty four hours a day! She'll have known most of all this before me!"

"Are you off to a safe house as well?" asked Scott.

Daphne shook her head, "No. I've asked to be taken to the hospital. I'd like to check on Avril."

"How do you think she's doing?" asked Tim.

Daphne replied, "On the way here to the station, she told me that her brother Walt had been dying, that he only had six months at best. Walteau hadn't told her, but she found out after he died that he had confided in Gerry, which might have in part explained Gerry's actions.

She said that she can never forgive Gerry now. But she still loved him and has the guilt of knowing that she unintentionally killed him by swapping her glass with his. Such a conflict of emotions, I have no idea how I'd be feeling!"

She added, "But one thing about Avril Kennedy is she seems like a tough old cookie. I'm sure she'll get through this. And I'm going to be there for her if I can."

"You've really became quite close, haven't you?" Scott observed.

"I know what it's like to suddenly be alone. And she's a good lady." said Daphne.

"So are you." said Scott honestly.

Daphne suddenly blushed, and said quickly, "Well, I must be going. My ride's waiting."

She quickly kissed both of them on the cheek and then dug into her pockets.

She handed them both a card.

"Here's my card. Just in case you ever feel the need! Both my U.S and U.K address is on there. Hope to see you again some time."

Scott and Tim watched her walk out, quite obviously flirting with the policeman as he held the door open for her.

They looked at each other and grinned.

"So, what now for you?" Tim asked.

Scott set his coffee down and said, "I'm going to get a flight back to New York. I'm sure Peterson is going to want to see me ASAP. And I'll have a lot of work on this when I get back. Are they letting you go to Yosemite?"

Tim nodded, smiling. "Yep. I told them that where I was going was more secluded than any safe house they'd put me in! Although I am going to use this as an excuse to get out of that conference tomorrow! Are you heading back tonight?"

"If I can."

"Right I'm going to go find a payphone. Do you know what I'm going to do?"

"What?" asked Scott.

"I'm ringing Miranda. I'm going to see if she can get some time off work. Join me out here to come to Yosemite."

"Really?" said Scott, impressed.

Tim nodded. "It's time I stopped running away from things."

He smiled and walked off to look for a phone.

Scott smiled as he watched his friend walk away from him, only to see an F.B.I agent walking towards him with a phone.

As he walked over to him, he extended the phone.

"Scott Blacklock?"

Scott nodded.

"I have a Katherine Fowley on the line for you."

Scott took the phone from him. He said, "Thank you. Do they know why the engine exploded yet?"

The agent responded, "Forensics are still working on it, but it looks like gunshots into the fuel tank."

Scott nodded and was about to move away when the F.B.I agent hesitated for a second, and Scott looked at him questioningly.

He finally spoke. "Sir, are you sure you saw Rosalie Gobetti on board the locomotive as it disconnected?"

"Yes. Why?"

"Well we've searched the whole area around the train extensively. And we haven't found a body. Or even any remains."

Scott went numb. When he gave the agent no response, he shrugged and walked away.

It took a full minute for Scott to remember that Katherine was on the phone. He put it to his ear and said,

"She's not dead."

"Scott? What? Who's not dead?"

"Rosalie Gobetti. They haven't found a body."

"But the television is saying there were six deaths on the train?"

"Well this is one thing they haven't found out yet." said Scott sourly.

"But how did she get away?" asked Katherine.

"I don't know. But I have a feeling that won't be the last of her."

"It will be by that name at least." said Katherine.

Hearing Scott pause, Katherine asked gently,

"How are you doing Scott?"

"Oh, I'm holding in there. In desperate need of a cigarette!"

"When are you coming back?"

"I'm going to try and get a flight this evening. Have you seen Peterson yet?"

"Yes. I'm here at the office now. Nearly everybody's snuck into the presentation room to watch the news on the big screen!"

"How was Peterson?" asked Scott, a little nervously.

Katherine replied, "Oh, he was his usual terse self. But I have a feeling, despite Clarissa's murder; he's secretly chuffed about the diamond being found, and obviously the massive coverage for Zirconia."

Scott rolled his eyes. "Why am I not surprised!"

Katherine said, "Do you want me to pick you up from the airport when you get back?"

"Yeah, that would be great."

Scott paused, and then said, "Something bugged me the other day though. I've only just thought of it again."

"What? Something about a motive?"

"No. You remember when you met me and Tim at Grand Central on Saturday?"

"Yes, to give you the tickets."

"Yes. And you got our tickets off of honeymooners?"

"Yes...."

"So, I asked you if we had to share a room, and you said we didn't."

"Yes...."

"What you actually said was 'Don't worry. You won't have to put up with Tim's incessant snoring'."

"So?"

"Well, how is that you know Tim snores?!"

"................"

"Katherine?"

The Blacklock
Mysteries

will continue in

Backpacker Trail

THANKS

Firstly, thanks to you reading this, as hopefully this means you've read the book. I hope you enjoyed it! Thank you to Ross and everyone at Authorhouse for making this possible for me. Special thanks need to go to Rae, Daniel and Sophie, for their hours of frank, honest advice on every aspect of the book. I'm so glad I could bounce all my ideas off you! Another special nod to Colette, who has the proud title of being the first person to have read the complete story.

Thank you to Josephine for taking a month out to trek across the United States with me, you were a perfect travelling companion.

Thank you to my good friend James for his advice and support, and to my other distant friends, Guy, Daniel, Patrick and Steven, who I do not see nearly enough of.

Thanks to all my close friends at the office who have kept me sane over the last few years.

Thank you to Terri for your support and excitement, to Rachel for allowing me to use your beautiful picture, and to Matthew for capturing it.

Thank you to Rebecca for giving up her time and being an excellent photographer.

Thank you to Mat for all the insults.

To Jen, love you, Jack.

And to all my fantastic friends that I've missed, if you read the book closely, you'll see your thank you!

Finally thank you to all of my wonderful family, who I am so proud to be a part of, and thank you to EB,AK,LX,ST,BP,CC and J for the music!

About the Author

Steven Clifford has been writing since he was seven, the initial version of his first novel was written when he was in the final year of primary school, much to the surprise of his teachers!

Throughout school and college, Steven turned to writing scripts for theatre, many of which he also performed in. Several of these were entered into the "In your own write" competition at the Ustinov Studios in Bath.

Steven's play, "The Question to your Answer" was performed in the New Vic studio at the Bristol Old Vic in April 2001.

In his late teens, Steven caught the travel bug and has travelled extensively across America, Europe and Australia.

This is Steven's first novel, and he has at least five books planned for the THE BLACKLOCK MYSTERIES. He is currently writing the second installment, Backpacker Trail.

Steven currently resides in Bristol.

Printed in the United Kingdom
by Lightning Source UK Ltd.
136019UK00002B/127-216/P